THE E

HENRY LAWSON
THE BUSH UNDERTAKER

AND

OTHER STORIES

Selected by
COLIN RODERICK

ANGUS
& ROBERTSON

AN ANGUS & ROBERTSON BOOK

First published in Australia
by Angus & Robertson Publishers in 1970
Revised edition 1974
Reprinted 1975 (twice), 1977, 1979
Arkon paperback edition 1982
Reprinted 1983, 1986, 1987 (twice)
Eden paperback edition 1988
Reprinted in 1989
This edition published by Collins/Angus & Robertson
Publishers Australia in 1990

Collins/Angus & Robertson Publishers Australia
Unit 4, Eden Park, 31 Waterloo Road, North Ryde
NSW 2113, Australia

William Collins Publishers Ltd
31 View Road, Glenfield, Auckland 10, New Zealand

Angus & Robertson (UK)
16 Golden Square, London W1R 4BN, United Kingdom

ISBN 0 207 16184 4.

Cover illustration: " Settler's Camp" by Arthur Streeton,
courtesy of the Robert Holmes à Court Collection

Printed in Australia

19   18   17   16   15   14
95   94   93   92   91   90

CONTENTS

Page

PREFACE, by Colin Roderick   6

1

The Bush Undertaker   11
The Drover's Wife   18
The Union Buries Its Dead   25
"Rats"   29

2

Stiffner and Jim (Thirdly, Bill)   32
Steelman   38
Steelman's Pupil   40
The Geological Spieler   44
How Steelman Told His Story   51

3

Going Blind   55
Our Pipes   59
Bill, the Ventriloquial Rooster   62
The Blindness of One-eyed Bogan   66
The Hero of Redclay   74
The Boozers' Home   89

4

The Iron-bark Chip   94
The Loaded Dog   98
Gettin' Back on Dave Regan   105

5

No Place for a Woman   113
Joe Wilson's Courtship   121
Brighten's Sister-in-law   147
"Water Them Geraniums"   165
A Double Buggy at Lahey's Creek   189

6

Send Round the Hat   208
A Fragment of Autobiography: I-III   223

COMMENTARY, by Colin Roderick   248

PREFACE

For each of his books Lawson wanted to arrange as many of the component stories as he could in sequences. When his first prose book, *While the Billy Boils*, appeared in August 1896, A. G. Stephens, then editor of the Red Page of the Sydney *Bulletin*, criticized the order of the stories: the result, he wrote, was "like a bad cook's ragoût". Stephens recognized that many of Lawson's compositions did fall into series: "there is a 'Mitchell' sequence, a 'Steelman' sequence, a bush sequence, a city sequence, and so on". He believed that these should have been brought together "so that continuity might be unbroken and the characters might gain force and distinctness from the massing of impressions".

Commenting bitterly on Stephens's review in a letter to his publisher, George Robertson, a few weeks later, Lawson pointed out that he had tried to do this, but that the practice of J. F. Archibald, editor of the *Bulletin*, of holding stories for long periods after buying them, to strengthen any possible future weak issues, prevented his doing so.

This lag in periodical publication hindered a forceful arrangement of Lawson's stories in all of his publications before 1901. Only with *Joe Wilson and His Mates* did he achieve something of his aim to bring a series of stories together; but even in that book the result is not entirely satisfactory, since a number of aspects of Joe Wilson's life raised in the stories included are left unresolved.

Once the books appeared the die was cast. The contents could not be reorganized into different books without creating both sales resistance and bibliographical confusion. Short of a complete rejection of the collections of Lawson's stories that formed the various books published under his name in his lifetime, any collected edition of his prose work is bound by them. As things are, an editor is faced with the dilemma posed by the republication of the stories in *Children of the Bush* (1902) as two separate volumes entitled *Send Round the Hat* (1907) and *The Romance of the Swag* (1907).

Fortunately, no such problem faces the editor of a selection of the stories. It is obviously not possible to include in a selection all the stories comprising any particular sequence. What is desirable is that Lawson's development of the sequence be illustrated in stories of high literary quality, and that the unity of the sequence be demonstrated and preserved. It is on these principles that the present selection has been made.

This selection is the first to carry into effect the belief—in which I share—that Lawson did aim at harmonious sequences of stories, however separated in time the composition of the individual stories may have been. He put the germ of an idea away in the back of his mind to be developed and expanded subsequently into a related story.

What was it that governed his approach to the stories intended for a particular sequence? My view is that the central character in each sequence developed as an artistic projection of an aspect of Lawson's own personality—recognized as such by him and expressed in a time-honoured and distinctive way. And this identification of himself with the central character extended to that character's inevitable foil: they became dual aspects of Lawson's personality. Steelman represents Lawson's staircase wit, while Smith represents, as Lawson himself wrote, "the weaker side of my nature". Lawson identified himself with Mitchell, the homespun philosopher—not without the assistance of Mark Twain. Lawson the practical joker found identity in Dave Regan and party. As for Joe Wilson, one has only to read Lawson's epilogue to the sequence to see that although he began with an idealization of himself—in "Brighten's Sister-in-law"—the character developed into a human being who also displayed shortcomings Lawson recognized in himself.

This is not to say that these sequences, or the stories comprising them, are autobiographical. Far from it. Lawson has warned us against reading them as such. They are parts of a created world. They rise out of the artist's ability to stand off and analyse the composition of his own personality and to make use of its parts in the creation of distinctive characters to inhabit that world. This artists have done in all ages, and Lawson is clearly no exception. To compare the world of Lawson the artist with the world occupied by Lawson the social personality, the selection closes with the first three chapters of his fragment of autobiography.

Such unity as this selection aims at, then, rests in the presentation of sequences of stories that reveal an artist's development towards self-realization through the activity of created characters in the world of his mind. Since this development began under the powerful influence of a bush upbringing, the selection begins with four stories in which the bush attains the nature of a character—much as Egdon Heath does in *The Return of the Native*. Anyone who reads on into the later stories will, on looking back, discern the germ of their themes in a phrase or a sentence uttered by a character or in an authorial aside or comment in an earlier story. This early work, so heavily charged with bitterness, is painfully affecting; but at the end Lawson wins through to a clear and fully developed expression of the charity that gradually supplants the 'bitterness.

During his lifetime the following collections of Lawson's stories appeared: *Short Stories in Prose and Verse* (1894); *While the Billy Boils* (1896), containing most of the stories in the preceding book; *On the Track* and *Over the Sliprails* (1900); *The Country I Come From* (1901), a selection from previous publications; *Joe Wilson and His Mates* (1901); *Children of the Bush* (1902); *Send Round the Hat* and *The Romance of the Swag* (1907), reprinting the prose work in *Children of the Bush*; *The Rising of the Court* (1910); *Mateship* (1911); *Triangles of Life* (1913).

Of posthumous editions, the most extensive is *Henry Lawson: Collected Prose*, ed. Colin Roderick, 2 vols. (1972). Volume One, *Short Stories and Sketches*, contains Lawson's imaginative work; Volume Two, *Autobiographical and Other Writings*, contains the full text of his fragment of autobiography, of which the extract given in the present book is a significant sample.

Among periodical articles on Lawson and his work not referred to in the Commentary herein are the following:

Mutch, T. D., "The Early Life of Henry Lawson", Royal Australian Historical Society, *Journal*, Vol. 18, Pt 6, 1932

Hope, A. D., "Steele Rudd and Henry Lawson", *Meanjin*, No. 1, 1956

Roderick, Colin, "Henry Lawson's Formative Years", R.A.H.S., *Journal*, Vol. 45, Pt 3, 1959

Ibid., "Henry Lawson's Norwegian Forbears", *Southerly*, Vol. 24, No. 3, 1964

Phillips, A. A., "Henry Lawson Revisited", *Meanjin*, No. 1, 1965

Douglas, Dennis, "The Text of Lawson's Prose", *Australian Literary Studies*, Vol. 2, No. 4, 1966

Roderick, Colin, "Henry Lawson: The Middle Years, 1893-1896", R.A.H.S., *Journal*, Vol. 53, Pt 2, 1967

Ibid., "Henry Lawson and Hannah Thornburn", *Meanjin*, No. 1, 1968

Barnes, John, "Henry Lawson and the Short Story in Australia", *Westerly*, No. 2, 1968

Roderick, Colin, "Henry Lawson: The Middle Years (Part II) 1896-1900", R.A.H.S., *Journal*, Vol. 55, Pt 4, 1969

COLIN RODERICK

HENRY LAWSON

The Bush Undertaker
And Other Stories

1

THE BUSH UNDERTAKER

"Five Bob!"

The old man shaded his eyes and peered through the dazzling glow of that broiling Christmas Day. He stood just within the door of a slab-and-bark hut situated upon the bank of a barren creek; sheep-yards lay to the right, and a low line of bare brown ridges formed a suitable background to the scene.

"Five Bob!" shouted he again; and a dusty sheep-dog rose wearily from the shaded side of the hut and looked inquiringly at his master, who pointed towards some sheep which were straggling from the flock.

"Fetch 'em back," he said confidently.

The dog went off, and his master returned to the interior of the hut.

"We'll yard 'em early," he said to himself; "the super won't know. We'll yard 'em early, and have the arternoon to ourselves."

"We'll get dinner," he added, glancing at some pots on the fire; "I cud do a bit of doughboy, an' that theer boggabri'll eat like tater-marrer along of the salt meat." He moved one of the black buckets from the blaze. "I likes to keep it jist on the sizzle," he said in explanation to himself; "hard bilin' makes it tough—I'll keep it jist a-simmerin'."

Here his soliloquy was interrupted by the return of the dog.

"All right, Five Bob," said the hatter, "dinner'll be ready dreckly. Jist keep yer eye on the sheep till I calls yer; keep 'em well rounded up, an' we'll yard 'em arterwards and have a holiday."

This speech was accompanied by a gesture evidently intelligible, for the dog retired as though he understood English, and the cooking proceeded.

"I'll take a pick an' shovel with me an' root up that old black-fellow," mused the shepherd, evidently following up a recent train of thought; "I reckon it'll do now. I'll put in the spuds."

The last sentence referred to the cooking, the first to a supposed blackfellow's grave about which he was curious.

"The sheep's a-campin'," said the soliloquizer, glancing through the door. "So me an' Five Bob'll be able to get our dinner in peace. I wish I had just enough fat to make the pan siss; I'd treat myself to a leather-jacket; but it took three weeks' skimmin' to get enough for them theer doughboys."

In due time the dinner was dished up; and the old man seated himself on a block, with the lid of a gin-case across his knees for a table. Five Bob squatted opposite with the liveliest interest and appreciation depicted on his intelligent countenance.

Dinner proceeded very quietly, except when the carver paused to ask the dog how some tasty morsel went with him, and Five Bob's tail declared that it went very well indeed.

"Here y'are, try this," cried the old man, tossing him a large piece of doughboy. A click of Five Bob's jaws and the dough was gone.

"Clean into his liver!" said the old man with a faint smile.

He washed up the tinware in the water the duff had been boiled in, and then, with the assistance of the dog, yarded the sheep.

This accomplished, he took a pick and shovel and an old sack, and started out over the ridge, followed, of course, by his four-legged mate. After tramping some three miles, he reached a spur running out from the main ridge. At the extreme end of this, under some gum trees, was a little mound of earth, barely defined in the grass, and indented in the centre as all blackfellows' graves were.

He set to work to dig it up, and sure enough, in about half-an-hour he bottomed on payable dirt.

When he had raked up all the bones, he amused himself by putting them together on the grass and by speculating as to whether they had belonged to black or white, male or female. Failing, however, to arrive at any satisfactory conclusion, he dusted them with great care, put them in the bag, and started for home.

He took a short cut this time over the ridge and down a gully which was full of ring-barked trees and long white grass. He had nearly reached its mouth when a great greasy black goanna clambered up a sapling from under his feet and looked fightable.

"Dang the jumpt-up thing!" cried the old man. "It gin me a start!"

At the foot of the sapling he espied an object which he at first thought was the blackened carcass of a sheep, but on closer examination discovered to be the body of a man; it lay with its forehead resting on its hands, dried to a mummy by the intense heat of the western summer.

"Me luck's in for the day and no mistake!" said the shepherd, scratching the back of his head, while he took stock of the remains. He picked up a stick and tapped the body on the shoulder; the flesh sounded like leather. He turned it over on its side; it fell flat on its back like a board, and the shrivelled eyes seemed to peer up at him from under the blackened wrists.

He stepped back involuntarily, but, recovering himself, leant on his stick and took in all the ghastly details.

There was nothing in the blackened features to tell aught of name or race, but the dress proclaimed the remains to be those of a European. The old man caught sight of a black bottle in the grass, close beside the corpse. This set him thinking. Presently he knelt down and examined the soles of the dead man's Blucher boots, and then, rising with an air of conviction, exclaimed: "Brummy! by gosh!—busted up at last!"

"I tole yer so, Brummy," he said impressively, addressing the corpse. "I allers told yer as how it 'ud be—an' here y'are, you thundering jumpt-up cuss-o'-God fool. Yer cud earn mor'n any man in the colony, but yer'd lush it all away. I allers sed as how it 'ud end, an' now yer kin see fur y'self.

"I spect yer was a-comin' t' me t' get fixt up an' set straight agin; then yer was a-goin' to swear off, same as yer allers did; an' here y'are, an' now I expect I'll have t' fix yer up for the last time an' make yer decent, for 'twon't do t' leave yer a-lyin' out here like a dead sheep."

He picked up the corked bottle and examined it. To his great surprise it was nearly full of rum.

"Well, this gits me," exclaimed the old man; "me luck's in this Christmas, an' no mistake. He must a' got the jams early in his spree, or he wouldn't be a-making for me with near a bottleful left. Howsomenever, here goes."

Looking round, his eyes lit up with satisfaction as he saw some waste bits of bark which had been left by a party of strippers who had been getting bark there for the stations. He picked up two pieces, one about four and the other six feet long, and each about two feet wide, and brought them over to the body. He laid the longest strip by the side of the corpse, which he proceeded to lift on to it.

"Come on, Brummy," he said, in a softer tone than usual, "yer ain't as bad as yer might be, considerin' as it must be three good months since yer slipped yer wind. I spect it was the rum as preserved yer. It was the death of yer when yer was alive, an' now yer dead, it preserves yer like—like a mummy."

Then he placed the other strip on top, with the hollow side downwards—thus sandwiching the defunct between the two pieces —removed the saddle strap which he wore for a belt, and buckled it round one end, while he tried to think of something with which to tie up the other.

"I can't take any more strips off my shirt," he said, critically examining the skirts of the old blue overshirt he wore. "I might get a strip or two more off, but it's short enough already. Let's see; how long have I been a-wearin' of that shirt? Oh, I remember, I bought it jist two days afore Five Bob was pupped. I can't afford a new shirt jist yet; howsomenever, seein's it's Brummy, I'll jist borrow a couple more strips and sew 'em on agen when I git home."

He up-ended Brummy, and, placing his shoulder against the middle of the lower sheet of bark, lifted the corpse to a horizontal position; then, taking the bag of bones in his hand, he started for home.

"I ain't a-spendin' sech a dull Christmas arter all," he reflectéd, as he plodded on; but he had not walked above a hundred yards when he saw a black goanna sidling into the grass by the side of the path.

"That's another of them theer dang things!" he exclaimed. "That's two I've seed this mornin'."

Presently he remarked: "Yer don't smell none too sweet, Brummy. It must 'a' been jist about the middle of shearin' when yer pegged out. I wonder who got yer last cheque? Shoo! theer's another black gohanner—theer must be a flock on 'em."

He rested Brummy on the ground while he had another pull at the bottle, and, before going on, packed the bag of bones on his shoulder under the body, but he soon stopped again.

"The thunderin' jumpt-up bones is all skew-whift," he said. "'Ole on, Brummy, an' I'll fix 'em;" and he leaned the dead man against a tree while he settled the bones on his shoulder, and took another pull at the bottle.

About a mile further on he heard a rustling in the grass to the right, and, looking round, saw another goanna gliding off sideways, with its long snaky neck turned towards him.

This puzzled the shepherd considerably, the strangest part of it being that Five Bob wouldn't touch the reptile, but slunk off with his tail down when ordered to "sick 'em".

"Theer's sothin' comic about them theer gohanners," said the old man at last. "I've seed swarms of grasshoppers an' big mobs of kangaroos, but dang me if ever I seed a flock of black gohanners afore!"

On reaching the hut the old man dumped the corpse against the wall, wrong end up, and stood scratching his head while he endeavoured to collect his muddled thoughts; but he had not placed Brummy at the correct angle, and, consequently, that individual fell forward and struck him a violent blow on the shoulder with the iron toes of his Blucher boots.

The shock sobered him. He sprang a good yard, instinctively hitching up his moleskins in preparation for flight; but a backward glance revealed to him the true cause of this supposed attack from the rear. Then he lifted the body, stood it on its feet against the chimney, and ruminated as to where he should lodge his mate for the night, not noticing that the shorter sheet of bark had slipped down on the boots and left the face exposed.

"I spect I'll have ter put yer into the chimney trough for the night, Brummy," said he, turning round to confront the corpse. "Yer can't expect me to take yer into the hut, though I did it when yer was in a worse state than————Lord!"

The shepherd was not prepared for the awful scrutiny that gleamed on him from those empty sockets; his nerves received a shock, and it was some time before he recovered himself sufficiently to speak.

"Now look a-here, Brummy," said he, shaking his finger severely at the delinquent, "I don't want to pick a row with yer; I'd do as much for yer an' more than any other man, an' well yer knows it; but if yer starts playin' any of yer jumpt-up pranktical jokes on me, and a-scarin' of me after a-humpin' of yer 'ome, by the 'oly frost I'll kick yer to jimrags, so I will."

This admonition delivered, he hoisted Brummy into the chimney trough, and with a last glance towards the sheep-yards, he retired to his bunk to have, as he said, a snooze.

He had more than a "snooze", however, for when he woke it was dark, and the bushman's instinct told him it must be nearly nine o'clock.

He lit a slush lamp and poured the remainder of the rum into a pannikin; but, just as he was about to lift the draught to his lips, he heard a peculiar rustling sound overhead, and put the pot down on the table with a slam that spilled some of the precious liquor.

Five Bob whimpered, and the old shepherd, though used to the weird and dismal, as one living alone in the bush must necessarily be, felt the icy breath of fear at his heart.

He reached hastily for his old shot-gun, and went out to investigate. He walked round the hut several times and examined the roof on all sides, but saw nothing. Brummy appeared to be in the same position.

At last, persuading himself that the noise was caused by 'possums or the wind, the old man went inside, boiled his billy, and, after composing his nerves somewhat with a light supper and a meditative smoke, retired for the night. He was aroused several times before midnight by the same mysterious sound overhead, but, though he rose and examined the roof on each occasion by the light of the rising moon, he discovered nothing.

At last he determined to sit up and watch until daybreak, and for this purpose took up a position on a log a short distance from the hut, with his gun laid in readiness across his knee.

After watching for about an hour, he saw a black object coming over the ridge-pole. He grabbed his gun and fired. The thing disappeared. He ran round to the other side of the hut, and there was a great black goanna in violent convulsions on the ground.

Then the old man saw it all. "The thunderin' jumpt-up thing has been a-havin' o' me," he exclaimed. "The same cuss-o'-God wretch has a-follered me 'ome, an' has been a-havin' its Christmas dinner off of Brummy, an' a-hauntin' o' me into the bargain, the jumpt-up tinker!"

As there was no one by whom he could send a message to the station, and the old man dared not leave the sheep and go himself, he determined to bury the body the next afternoon, reflecting that the authorities could disinter it for inquest if they pleased.

So he brought the sheep home early, and made arrangements for the burial by measuring the outer casing of Brummy and digging a hole according to those dimensions.

"That 'minds me," he said, "I never rightly knowed Brummy's religion, blest if ever I did. Howsomenever, there's one thing sartin—none o' them theer pianer-fingered parsons is a-goin' ter take the trouble ter travel out inter this God-forgotten part to hold sarvice over him, seein' as how his last cheque's blued. But as I've got the fun'ral arrangements all in me own hands, I'll do jestice to it, and see that Brummy has a good comfortable buryin' —and more's unpossible."

"It's time yer turned in, Brum," he said, lifting the body down. He carried it to the grave and dropped it into one corner like a post. He arranged the bark so as to cover the face, and, by means of a piece of clothes-line, lowered the body to a horizontal position. Then he threw in an armful of gum leaves, and then, very reluctantly, took the shovel and dropped in a few shovelfuls of earth.

"An' this is the last of Brummy," he said, leaning on his spade and looking away over the tops of the ragged gums on the distant range.

This reflection seemed to engender a flood of memories, in which the old man became absorbed. He leaned heavily upon his spade and thought.

"Arter all," he murmured sadly, "arter all—it were Brummy."

"Brummy," he said at last, "it's all over now; nothin' matters now—nothin' didn't ever matter, nor—nor don't. You uster say as how it 'ud be all right termorrer" (pause); "termorrer's come, Brummy—come fur you—it ain't come fur me yet, but—it's a-comin'."

He threw in some more earth.

"Yer don't remember, Brummy, an' mebbe yer don't want to remember—*I* don't want to remember—but—well, but, yer see, that's where yer got the pull on me."

He shovelled in some more earth and paused again.

The dog rose, with ears erect, and looked anxiously first at his master, and then into the grave.

"Theer oughter be somethin' sed," muttered the old man; "'tain't right to put 'im under like a dog. There oughter be some sort o' sarmin." He sighed heavily in the listening silence that followed this remark, and proceeded with his work. He filled the grave to the brim this time, and fashioned the mound carefully with his spade. Once or twice he muttered the words: "I am the rassaraction." As he laid the tools quietly aside, and stood at the head of the grave, he was evidently trying to remember the something that ought to be said. He removed his hat, placed it carefully on the grass, held his hands out from his sides and a little to the front, drew a long deep breath, and said with a solemnity that greatly disturbed Five Bob: "Hashes ter hashes, dus ter dus, Brummy—an'—an' in hopes of a great an' gerlorious rassaraction!"

He sat down on a log near by, rested his elbows on his knees and passed his hand wearily over his forehead—but only as one who was tired and felt the heat; and presently he rose, took up the tools, and walked back to the hut.

And the sun sank again on the grand Australian bush—the nurse and tutor of eccentric minds, the home of the weird, and of much that is different from things in other lands.

[*1892   revised 1894, 1895, 1900*]

THE DROVER'S WIFE

THE two-roomed house is built of round timber, slabs, and stringy-bark, and floored with split slabs. A big bark kitchen standing at one end is larger than the house itself, verandah included.

Bush all round—bush with no horizon, for the country is flat. No ranges in the distance. The bush consists of stunted, rotten native apple-trees. No undergrowth. Nothing to relieve the eye save the darker green of a few she-oaks which are sighing above the narrow, almost waterless creek. Nineteen miles to the nearest sign of civilization—a shanty on the main road.

The drover, an ex-squatter, is away with sheep. His wife and children are left here alone.

Four ragged, dried-up-looking children are playing about the house. Suddenly one of them yells: "Snake! Mother, here's a snake!"

The gaunt, sun-browned bushwoman dashes from the kitchen, snatches her baby from the ground, holds it on her left hip, and reaches for a stick.

"Where is it?"

"Here! gone into the wood-heap!" yells the eldest boy—a sharp-faced, excited urchin of eleven. "Stop there, mother! I'll have him. Stand back! I'll have the beggar!"

"Tommy, come here, or you'll be bit. Come here at once when I tell you, you little wretch!"

The youngster comes reluctantly, carrying a stick bigger than himself. Then he yells, triumphantly:

"There it goes—under the house!" and darts away with club uplifted. At the same time the big, black, yellow-eyed dog-of-all-breeds, who has shown the wildest interest in the proceedings, breaks his chain and rushes after that snake. He is a moment late, however, and his nose reaches the crack in the slabs just as the end of its tail disappears. Almost at the same moment the boy's club comes down and skins the aforesaid nose. Alligator takes small notice of this and proceeds to undermine the building; but he is subdued after a struggle and chained up. They cannot afford to lose him.

The drover's wife makes the children stand together near the dog-house while she watches for the snake. She gets two small dishes of milk and sets them down near the wall to tempt it to come out; but an hour goes by and it does not show itself.

It is near sunset, and a thunderstorm is coming. The children must be brought inside. She will not take them into the house, for she knows the snake is there, and may at any moment come up through the cracks in the rough slab floor; so she carries several armfuls of firewood into the kitchen and then takes the children there. The kitchen has no floor—or, rather, an earthen one, called a "ground floor" in this part of the bush. There is a large, roughly made table in the centre of the place. She brings the children in and makes them get on this table. They are two boys and two girls—mere babies. She gives them some supper, and then, before it gets dark, she goes into the house and snatches up some pillows and bedclothes—expecting to see or lay her hand on the snake any minute. She makes a bed on the kitchen table for the children and sits down beside it to watch all night.

She has an eye on the corner, and a green sapling club laid in readiness on the dresser by her side, together with her sewing basket and a copy of the *Young Ladies' Journal*. She has brought the dog into the room.

Tommy turns in, under protest, but says he'll lie awake all night and smash that blinded snake.

His mother asks him how many times she has told him not to swear.

He has his club with him under the bedclothes, and Jacky protests:

"Mummy! Tommy's skinnin' me alive wif his club. Make him take it out."

Tommy: "Shet up, you little ————! D'yer want to be bit with the snake?"

Jacky shuts up.

"If yer bit," says Tommy, after a pause, "you'll swell up, an' smell, an' turn red an' green an' blue all over till yer bust. Won't he, mother?"

"Now then, don't frighten the child. Go to sleep," she says.

The two younger children go to sleep, and now and then Jacky complains of being "skeezed". More room is made for him. Presently Tommy says: "Mother! listen to them (adjective) little 'possums. I'd like to screw their blanky necks."

And Jacky protests drowsily:

"But they don't hurt us, the little blanks!"

Mother: "There, I told you you'd teach Jacky to swear." But the remark makes her smile. Jacky goes to sleep.

Presently Tommy asks:

"Mother! Do you think they'll ever extricate the (adjective) kangaroo?"

"Lord! How am I to know, child? Go to sleep."

"Will you wake me if the snake comes out?"

"Yes. Go to sleep."

Near midnight. The children are all asleep and she sits there still, sewing and reading by turns. From time to time she glances round the floor and wall-plate, and whenever she hears a noise she reaches for the stick. The thunderstorm comes on, and the wind, rushing through the cracks in the slab wall, threatens to blow out her candle. She places it on a sheltered part of the dresser and fixes up a newspaper to protect it. At every flash of lightning, the cracks between the slabs gleam like polished silver. The thunder rolls, and the rain comes down in torrents.

Alligator lies at full length on the floor, with his eyes turned towards the partition. She knows by this that the snake is there. There are large cracks in that wall opening under the floor of the dwelling-house.

She is not a coward, but recent events have shaken her nerves. A little son of her brother-in-law was lately bitten by a snake, and died. Besides, she has not heard from her husband for six months, and is anxious about him.

He was a drover, and started squatting here when they were married. The drought of 18—— ruined him. He had to sacrifice the remnant of his flock and go droving again. He intends to move his family into the nearest town when he comes back, and, in the meantime, his brother, who keeps a shanty on the main road, comes over about once a month with provisions. The wife has still a couple of cows, one horse, and a few sheep. The brother-in-law kills one of the sheep occasionally, gives her what she needs of it, and takes the rest in return for other provisions.

She is used to being left alone. She once lived like this for eighteen months. As a girl she built the usual castles in the air; but all her girlish hopes and aspirations have long been dead. She finds all the excitement and recreation she needs in the *Young Ladies' Journal*, and, Heaven help her! takes a pleasure in the fashion-plates.

Her husband is an Australian, and so is she. He is careless, but a good enough husband. If he had the means he would take her to the city and keep her there like a princess. They are used to being apart, or at least she is. "No use fretting," she says. He may forget sometimes that he is married; but if he has a good cheque when he comes back he will give most of it to her. When he had money he took her to the city several times—hired a railway sleeping compartment, and put up at the best hotels. He also bought her a buggy, but they had to sacrifice that along with the rest.

The last two children were born in the bush—one while her husband was bringing a drunken doctor, by force, to attend to her. She was alone on this occasion, and very weak. She had been ill with a fever. She prayed to God to send her assistance. God sent Black Mary—the "whitest" gin in all the land. Or, at least, God sent "King Jimmy" first, and he sent Black Mary. He put his black face round the door-post, took in the situation at a glance, and said cheerfully: "All right, Missis—I bring my old woman, she down alonga creek."

One of her children died while she was here alone. She rode nineteen miles for assistance, carrying the dead child.

.   .   .

It must be near one or two o'clock. The fire is burning low. Alligator lies with his head resting on his paws, and watches the wall. He is not a very beautiful dog to look at, and the light shows numerous old wounds where the hair will not grow. He is afraid of nothing on the face of the earth or under it. He will tackle a bullock as readily as he will tackle a flea. He hates all other dogs —except kangaroo-dogs—and has a marked dislike to friends or relations of the family. They seldom call, however. He sometimes makes friends with strangers. He hates snakes and has killed many, but he will be bitten some day and die; most snake-dogs end that way.

Now and then the bushwoman lays down her work and watches, and listens, and thinks. She thinks of things in her own life, for there is little else to think about.

The rain will make the grass grow, and this reminds her how she fought a bushfire once while her husband was away. The grass was long, and very dry, and the fire threatened to burn her out. She put on an old pair of her husband's trousers and beat out the flames with a green bough, till great drops of sooty perspiration stood out on her forehead and ran in streaks down her blackened arms. The sight of his mother in trousers greatly amused Tommy, who worked like a little hero by her side, but the terrified baby howled lustily for his "mummy". The fire would have mastered her but for four excited bushmen who arrived in the nick of time. It was a mixed-up affair all round: when she went to take up the baby he screamed and struggled convulsively, thinking it was a "black man"; and Alligator, trusting more to the child's sense than his own instinct, charged furiously, and (being old and slightly deaf) did not in his excitement at first recognize his

mistress's voice, but continued to hang on to the moleskins until
choked off by Tommy with a saddle-strap. The dog's sorrow for
his blunder, and his anxiety to let it be known that it was all a
mistake, was as evident as his ragged tail and a twelve-inch grin
could make it. It was a glorious time for the boys; a day to look
back to, and talk about, and laugh over for many years.

She thinks how she fought a flood during her husband's absence.
She stood for hours in the drenching downpour, and dug an
overflow gutter to save the dam across the creek. But she could
not save it. There are things that a bushwoman cannot do. Next
morning the dam was broken, and her heart was nearly broken too,
for she thought how her husband would feel when he came home
and saw the result of years of labour swept away. She cried then.

She also fought the pleuro-pneumonia—dosed and bled the few
remaining cattle, and wept again when her two best cows died.

Again, she fought a mad bullock that besieged the house for a
day. She made bullets and fired at him through cracks in the
slabs with an old shot-gun. He was dead in the morning. She
skinned him and got seventeen-and-six for the hide.

She also fights the crows and eagles that have designs on her
chickens. Her plan of campaign is very original. The children cry
"Crows, Mother!" and she rushes out and aims a broomstick at
the birds as though it were a gun, and says "Bung!" The crows
leave in a hurry; they are cunning, but a woman's cunning is
greater.

Occasionally a bushman in the horrors, or a villainous-looking
sundowner, comes and nearly scares the life out of her. She
generally tells the suspicious-looking stranger that her husband and
two sons are at work below the dam, or over at the yard, for he
always cunningly inquires for the boss.

Only last week a gallows-faced swagman—having satisfied himself that there were no men on the place—threw his swag down
on the verandah and demanded tucker. She gave him something to
eat; then he expressed his intention of staying for the night. It was
sundown then. She got a batten from the sofa, loosened the dog,
and confronted the stranger, holding the batten in one hand and
the dog's collar with the other. "Now you go!" she said. He looked
at her and at the dog, said "All right, mum," in a cringing tone,
and left. She was a determined-looking woman, and Alligator's
yellow eyes glared unpleasantly—besides, the dog's chawing-up
apparatus greatly resembled that of the reptile he was named after.

She has few pleasures to think of as she sits here alone by the
fire, on guard against a snake. All days are much the same to
her; but on Sunday afternoon she dresses herself, tidies the

children, smartens up baby, and goes for a lonely walk along the bush-track, pushing an old perambulator in front of her. She does this every Sunday. She takes as much care to make herself and the children look smart as she would if she were going to do the block in the city. There is nothing to see, however, and not a soul to meet. You might walk for twenty miles along this track without being able to fix a point in your mind, unless you are a bushman. This is because of the everlasting, maddening sameness of the stunted trees—that monotony which makes a man long to break away and travel as far as trains can go, and sail as far as ships can sail—and further.

But this bushwoman is used to the loneliness of it. As a girl-wife she hated it, but now she would feel strange away from it.

She is glad when her husband returns, but she does not gush or make a fuss about it. She gets him something good to eat, and tidies up the children.

She seems contented with her lot. She loves her children, but has no time to show it. She seems harsh to them. Her surroundings are not favourable to the development of the "womanly" or sentimental side of nature.

.   .   .

It must be near morning now; but the clock is in the dwelling-house. Her candle is nearly done; she forgot that she was out of candles. Some more wood must be got to keep the fire up, and so she shuts the dog inside and hurries round to the wood-heap. The rain has cleared off. She seizes a stick, pulls it out, and—crash! the whole pile collapses.

Yesterday she bargained with a stray blackfellow to bring her some wood, and while he was at work she went in search of a missing cow. She was absent an hour or so, and the native made good use of his time. On her return she was so astonished to see a good heap of wood by the chimney that she gave him an extra fig of tobacco, and praised him for not being lazy. He thanked her, and left with head erect and chest well out. He was the last of his tribe and a King; but he had built that wood-heap hollow.

She is hurt now, and tears spring to her eyes as she sits down again by the table. She takes up a handkerchief to wipe the tears away, but pokes her eyes with her bare fingers instead. The handkerchief is full of holes, and she finds that she has put her thumb through one and her forefinger through another.

This makes her laugh, to the surprise of the dog. She has a keen, very keen, sense of the ridiculous; and some time or other she will amuse bushmen with the story.

She has been amused before like that. One day she sat down "to have a good cry", as she said—and the old cat rubbed against her dress and "cried too". Then she had to laugh.

.   .   .

It must be near daylight. The room is very close and hot because of the fire. Alligator still watches the wall from time to time. Suddenly he becomes greatly interested; he draws himself a few inches nearer the partition, and a thrill runs through his body. The hair on the back of his neck begins to bristle, and the battle-light is in his yellow eyes. She knows what this means, and lays her hand on the stick. The lower end of one of the partition slabs has a large crack on both sides. An evil pair of small, bright, bead-like eyes glisten at one of these holes. The snake—a black one—comes slowly out, about a foot, and moves its head up and down. The dog lies still, and the woman sits as one fascinated. The snake comes out a foot further. She lifts her stick, and the reptile, as though suddenly aware of danger, sticks his head in through the crack on the other side of the slab and hurries to get his tail round after him. Alligator springs, and his jaws come together with a snap. He misses, for his nose is large and the snake's body close down in the angle formed by the slabs and the floor. He snaps again as the tail comes round. He has the snake now, and tugs it out eighteen inches. Thud, thud comes the woman's club on the ground. Alligator pulls again. Thud, thud. Alligator gives another pull and he has the snake out—a black brute, five feet long. The head rises to dart about, but the dog has the enemy close to the neck. He is a big, heavy dog, but quick as a terrier. He shakes the snake as though he felt the original curse in common with mankind. The eldest boy wakes up, seizes his stick, and tries to get out of bed, but his mother forces him back with a grip of iron. Thud, thud—the snake's back is broken in several places. Thud, thud—its head is crushed, and Alligator's nose skinned again.

She lifts the mangled reptile on the point of her stick, carries it to the fire, and throws it in; then piles on the wood, and watches the snake burn. The boy and dog watch, too. She lays her hand on the dog's head, and all the fierce, angry light dies out of his yellow eyes. The younger children are quieted, and presently go to sleep. The dirty-legged boy stands for a moment in his shirt, watching the fire. Presently he looks up at her, sees the tears in her eyes, and, throwing his arms round her neck, exclaims:

"Mother, I won't never go drovin'; blast me if I do!"

And she hugs him to her worn-out breast and kisses him; and they sit thus together while the sickly daylight breaks over the bush.

[*1892   revised 1894, 1895, 1900*]

THE UNION BURIES ITS DEAD

WHILE out boating one Sunday afternoon on a billabong across the river, we saw a young man on horseback driving some horses along the bank. He said it was a fine day, and asked if the water was deep there. The joker of our party said it was deep enough to drown him, and he laughed and rode farther up. We didn't take much notice of him.

Next day a funeral gathered at a corner pub and asked each other in to have a drink while waiting for the hearse. They passed away some of the time dancing jigs to a piano in the bar parlour. They passed away the rest of the time sky-larking and fighting.

The defunct was a young union labourer, about twenty-five, who had been drowned the previous day while trying to swim some horses across a billabong of the Darling.

He was almost a stranger in town, and the fact of his having been a union man accounted for the funeral. The police found some union papers in his swag, and called at the General Labourers' Union Office for information about him. That's how we knew. The secretary had very little information to give. The departed was a "Roman", and the majority of the town were otherwise— but unionism is stronger than creed. Drink, however, is stronger than unionism; and, when the hearse presently arrived, more than two-thirds of the funeral were unable to follow. They were too drunk.

The procession numbered fifteen, fourteen souls following the broken shell of a soul. Perhaps not one of the fourteen possessed a soul any more than the corpse did—but that doesn't matter.

Four or five of the funeral, who were boarders at the pub, borrowed a trap which the landlord used to carry passengers to and from the railway station. They were strangers to us who were on foot, and we to them. We were all strangers to the corpse.

A horseman, who looked like a drover just returned from a big
trip, dropped into our dusty wake and followed us a few hundred
yards, dragging his pack-horse behind him, but a friend made
wild and demonstrative signals from a hotel verandah—hooking
at the air in front with his right hand and jobbing his left thumb
over his shoulder in the direction of the bar—so the drover hauled
off and didn't catch up to us any more. He was a stranger to the
entire show.

We walked in twos. There were three twos. It was very hot
and dusty; the heat rushed in fierce dazzling rays across every
iron roof and light-coloured wall that was turned to the sun. One
or two pubs closed respectfully until we got past. They closed
their bar doors and the patrons went in and out through some
side or back entrance for a few minutes. Bushmen seldom grumble
at an inconvenience of this sort when it is caused by a funeral.
They have too much respect for the dead.

On the way to the cemetery we passed three shearers sitting
on the shady side of a fence. One was drunk—very drunk. The
other two covered their right ears with their hats, out of respect
for the departed—whoever he might have been—and one of them
kicked the drunk and muttered something to him.

He straightened himself up, stared, and reached helplessly for
his hat, which he shoved half off and then on again. Then he
made a great effort to pull himself together—and succeeded. He
stood up, braced his back against the fence, knocked off his hat,
and remorsefully placed his foot on it—to keep it off his head
till the funeral passed.

A tall, sentimental drover, who walked by my side, cynically
quoted Byronic verses suitable to the occasion—to death—and
asked with pathetic humour whether we thought the dead man's
ticket would be recognized "over yonder". It was a G.L.U. ticket,
and the general opinion was that it would be recognized.

Presently my friend said:

"You remember when we were in the boat yesterday, we saw
a man driving some horses along the bank?"

"Yes."

He nodded at the hearse and said:

"Well, that's him."

I thought awhile.

"I didn't take any particular notice of him," I said. "He said
something, didn't he?"

"Yes; said it was a fine day. You'd have taken more notice if
you'd known that he was doomed to die in the hour, and that
those were the last words he would say to any man in this world."

"To be sure," said a full voice from the rear. "If ye'd known that, ye'd have prolonged the conversation."

We plodded on across the railway line and along the hot, dusty road which ran to the cemetery, some of us talking about the accident, and lying about the narrow escapes we had had ourselves. Presently someone said:

"There's the Devil."

I looked up and saw a priest standing in the shade of the tree by the cemetery gate.

The hearse was drawn up and the tail-boards were opened. The funeral extinguished its right ear with its hat as four men lifted the coffin out and laid it over the grave. The priest—a pale, quiet young fellow—stood under the shade of a sapling which grew at the head of the grave. He took off his hat, dropped it carelessly on the ground, and proceeded to business. I noticed that one or two heathens winced slightly when the holy water was sprinkled on the coffin. The drops quickly evaporated, and the little round black spots they left were soon dusted over; but the spots showed, by contrast, the cheapness and shabbiness of the cloth with which the coffin was covered. It seemed black before; now it looked a dusky grey.

Just here man's ignorance and vanity made a farce of the funeral. A big, bull-necked publican, with heavy, blotchy features and a supremely ignorant expression, picked up the priest's straw hat and held it about two inches over the head of his reverence during the whole of the service. The father, be it remembered, was standing in the shade. A few shoved their hats on and off uneasily, struggling between their disgust for the living and their respect for the dead. The hat had a conical crown and a brim sloping down all round like a sunshade, and the publican held it with his great red claw spread over the crown. To do the priest justice, perhaps he didn't notice the incident. A stage priest or parson in the same position might have said: "Put the hat down, my friend; is not the memory of our departed brother worth more than my complexion?" A wattlebark layman might have expressed himself in stronger language, none the less to the point. But my priest seemed unconscious of what was going on. Besides, the publican was a great and important pillar of the Church. He couldn't, as an ignorant and conceited ass, lose such a good opportunity of asserting his faithfulness and importance to his Church.

The grave looked very narrow under the coffin, and I drew a breath of relief when the box slid easily down. I saw a coffin get stuck once, at Rookwood, and it had to be yanked out with difficulty, and laid on the sods at the feet of the heart-broken relations, who howled dismally while the grave-diggers widened the hole. But they don't cut contracts so fine in the West. Our grave-digger was not altogether bowelless, and, out of respect for that human quality described as "feelin's", he scraped up some light and dusty soil and threw it down to deaden the fall of the clay lumps on the coffin. He also tried to steer the first few shovelfuls gently down against the end of the grave with the back of the shovel turned outwards, but the hard, dry Darling River clods rebounded and knocked all the same. It didn't matter much —nothing does. The fall of lumps of clay on a stranger's coffin doesn't sound any different from the fall of the same things on an ordinary wooden box—at least I didn't notice anything awesome or unusual in the sound; but, perhaps, one of us—the most sensitive—might have been impressed by being reminded of a burial of long ago, when the thump of every sod jolted his heart.

I have left out the wattle—because it wasn't there. I have also neglected to mention the heart-broken old mate, with his grizzled head bowed and great pearly drops streaming down his rugged cheeks. He was absent—he was probably "Out Back". For similar reasons I have omitted reference to the suspicious moisture in the eyes of a bearded bush ruffian named Bill. Bill failed to turn up, and the only moisture was that which was induced by the heat. I have left out the "sad Australian sunset" because the sun was not going down at the time. The burial took place exactly at mid-day.

The dead bushman's name was Jim, apparently; but they found no portraits, nor locks of hair, nor any love letters, nor anything of that kind in his swag—not even a reference to his mother; only some papers relating to union matters. Most of us didn't know the name till we saw it on the coffin; we knew him as "that poor chap that got drowned yesterday".

"So his name's James Tyson," said my drover acquaintance, looking at the plate.

"Why! Didn't you know that before?" I asked.

"No; but I knew he was a union man."

It turned out, afterwards, that J.T. wasn't his real name—only "the name he went by".

Anyhow he was buried by it, and most of the "Great Australian Dailies" have mentioned in their brevity columns that a young man named James John Tyson was drowned in a billabong of the Darling last Sunday.

We did hear, later on, what his real name was; but if we ever chance to read it in the "Missing Friends Column", we shall not be able to give any information to heart-broken Mother or Sister or Wife, nor to anyone who could let him hear something to his advantage—for we have already forgotten the name.

[*March 1893   revised 1894, 1895, 1900*]

"RATS"

"WHY, there's two of them, and they're having a fight! Come on."

It seemed a strange place for a fight—that hot, lonely, cotton-bush plain. And yet not more than half-a-mile ahead there were apparently two men struggling together on the track.

The three travellers postponed their smoke-oh and hurried on. They were shearers—a little man and a big man, known respectively as "Sunlight" and "Macquarie", and a tall, thin, young jackeroo whom they called "Milky".

"I wonder where the other man sprang from? I didn't see him before," said Sunlight.

"He muster bin layin' down in the bushes," said Macquarie. "They're goin' at it proper, too. Come on! Hurry up and see the fun!"

They hurried on.

"It's a funny-lookin' feller, the other feller," panted Milky. "He don't seem to have no head. Look! he's down—they're both down! They must ha' clinched on the ground. No! they're up an' at it again. . . . Why, good Lord! I think the other's a woman!"

"My oath! so it is!" yelled Sunlight. "Look! the brute's got her down again! He's kickin' her! Come on, chaps; come on, or he'll do for her!"

They dropped swags, water-bags and all, and raced forward; but presently Sunlight, who had the best eyes, slackened his pace and dropped behind. His mates glanced back at his face, saw a peculiar expression there, looked ahead again, and then dropped into a walk.

They reached the scene of the trouble, and there stood a little withered old man by the track, with his arms folded close up under his chin; he was dressed mostly in calico patches; and half-a-dozen corks, suspended on bits of string from the brim of his hat, dangled before his bleared optics to scare away the flies.

He was scowling malignantly at a stout, dumpy swag which lay in the middle of the track.

"Well, old Rats, what's the trouble?" asked Sunlight.

"Oh, nothing, nothing," answered the old man, without looking round. "I fell out with my swag, that's all. He knocked me down, but I've settled him."

"But look here," said Sunlight, winking at his mates, "we saw you jump on him when he was down. That ain't fair, you know."

"But you didn't see it all," cried Rats, getting excited. "He hit *me* down first! And, look here, I'll fight him again for nothing, and you can see fair play."

They talked awhile; then Sunlight proposed to second the swag, while his mate supported the old man, and after some persuasion Milky agreed, for the sake of the lark, to act as time-keeper and referee.

Rats entered into the spirit of the thing; he stripped to the waist, and while he was getting ready the travellers pretended to bet on the result.

Macquarie took his place behind the old man, and Sunlight up-ended the swag. Rats shaped and danced round; then he rushed, feinted, ducked, retreated, darted in once more, and suddenly went down like a shot on the broad of his back. No actor could have done it better; he went down from that imaginary blow as if a cannon-ball had struck him in the forehead.

Milky called ʼme, and the old man came up, looking shaky. However, he got in a tremendous blow which knocked the swag into the bushes.

Several rounds followed with varying success.

The men pretended to get more and more excited, and betted freely; and Rats did his best. At last they got tired of the fun, Sunlight let the swag lie after Milky called time, and the jackeroo awarded the fight to Rats. They pretended to hand over the stakes, and then went back for their swags, while the old man put on his shirt.

Then he calmed down, carried his swag to the side of the track, sat down on it and talked rationally about bush matters for a while; but presently he grew silent and began to feel his muscles and smile idiotically.

"Can you len' us a bit o' meat?" said he suddenly.

They spared him half-a-pound; but he said he didn't want it all, and cut off about an ounce, which he laid on the end of his swag. Then he took the lid off his billy and produced a fishing-line. He baited the hook, threw the line across the track, and waited for a bite. Soon he got deeply interested in the line, jerked it once or twice, and drew it in rapidly. The bait had been rubbed off in the grass. The old man regarded the hook disgustedly.

"Look at that!" he cried. "I had him, only I was in such a hurry. I should ha' played him a little more."

Next time he was more careful; he drew the line in warily, grabbed an imaginary fish, and laid it down on the grass. Sunlight and Co. were greatly interested by this time.

"Wot yer think o' that?" asked Rats. "It weighs thirty pound if it weighs an ounce! Wot yer think o' that for a cod? The hook's half-way down his blessed gullet."

He caught several cod and a bream while they were there, and invited them to camp and have tea with him. But they wished to reach a certain shed next day, so—after the ancient had borrowed about a pound of meat for bait—they went on, and left him fishing contentedly.

But first Sunlight went down into his pocket and came up with half-a-crown, which he gave to the old man, along with some tucker. "You'd best push on to the water before dark, old chap," he said, kindly.

When they turned their heads again, Rats was still fishing: but when they looked back for the last time before entering the timber, he was having another row with his swag; and Sunlight reckoned that the trouble arose out of some lies which the swag had been telling about the bigger fish it caught.

.   .   .

And late that evening a little withered old man with no corks round his hat and with a humorous twinkle instead of a wild glare in his eyes called at a wayside shanty, had several drinks, and entertained the chaps with a yarn about the way in which he had "had" three "blanky fellers" for some tucker and "half a caser" by pretending to be "barmy".

[1893   revised 1894, 1895]

2

STIFFNER AND JIM

(THIRDLY, BILL)

WE were tramping down in Canterbury, Maoriland, at the time, swagging it—me and Bill—looking for work on the new railway line. Well, one afternoon, after a long, hot tramp, we comes to Stiffner's Hotel—between Christchurch and that other place—I forget the name of it—with throats on us like sun-struck bones, and not the price of a stick of tobacco.

We had to have a drink, anyway, so we chanced it. We walked right into the bar, handed over our swags, put up four drinks, and tried to look as if we'd just drawn our cheques and didn't care a curse for any man. We looked solvent enough, as far as swagmen go. We were dirty and haggard and ragged and tired-looking, and that was all the more reason why we might have our cheques all right.

This Stiffner was a hard customer. He'd been a spieler, fighting man, bush parson, temperance preacher, and a policeman, and a commercial traveller, and everything else that was damnable; he'd been a journalist, and an editor; he'd been a lawyer, too. He was an ugly brute to look at, and uglier to have a row with—about six-foot-six, wide in proportion, and stronger than Donald Dinnie.

He was meaner than a gold-field Chinaman, and sharper than a sewer rat: he wouldn't give his own father a feed, nor lend him a sprat—unless some safe person backed the old man's I O U.

We knew that we needn't expect any mercy from Stiffner; but something had to be done, so I said to Bill:

"Something's got to be done, Bill! What do you think of it?"

Bill was mostly a quiet young chap, from Sydney, except when he got drunk—which was seldom—and then he was a lively customer from all round. He was cracked on the subject of spielers. He held that the population of the world was divided into two classes—one was spielers and the other was mugs. He reckoned that he wasn't a mug. At first I thought that he was a spieler, and afterwards I thought that he was a mug. He used to say that a man had to do it these times; that he was honest once and a fool, and was robbed and starved in consequence by his friends and relations; but now he intended to take all that he could get. He said that you either had to have or be had; that men were driven to be sharps, and there was no help for it.

Bill said:

"We'll have to sharpen our teeth, that's all, and chew somebody's lug."

"How?" I asked.

There was a lot of navvies at the pub, and I knew one or two by sight, so Bill says:

"You know one or two of these mugs. Bite one of their ears."

So I took aside a chap that I knowed and bit his ear for ten bob, and gave it to Bill to mind, for I thought it would be safer with him than with me.

"Hang on to that," I says, "and don't lose it for your natural life's sake, or Stiffner'll stiffen us."

We put up about nine bob's worth of drinks that night—me and Bill—and Stiffner didn't squeal: he was too sharp. He shouted once or twice.

By-and-by I left Bill and turned in, and in the morning when I woke up there was Bill sitting alongside of me, and looking about as lively as the fighting kangaroo in London in fog time. He had a black eye and eighteen-pence. He'd been taking down some of the mugs.

"Well, what's to be done now?" I asked. "Stiffner can smash us both with one hand, and if we don't pay up he'll pound our swags and cripple us. He's just the man to do it. He loves a fight even more than he hates being had."

"There's only one thing to be done, Jim," says Bill, in a tired, disinterested tone that made me mad.

"Well, what's that?" I said.

"Smoke!"

"Smoke be damned," I snarled, losing my temper. "You know dashed well that our swags are in the bar, and we can't smoke without them."

"Well, then," says Bill, "I'll toss you to see who's to face the landlord."

"Well, I'll be blessed!" I says. "I'll see you further first. You have got a front. You mugged that stuff away, and you'll have to get us out of the mess."

It made him wild to be called a mug, and we swore and growled at each other for a while; but we daren't speak loud enough to have a fight, so at last I agreed to toss up for it, and I lost.

Bill started to give me some of his points, but I shut him up quick.

"You've had your turn, and made a mess of it," I said. "For God's sake give me a show. Now, I'll go into the bar and ask for the swags, and carry them out on to the verandah, and then go back to settle up. You keep him talking all the time. You dump the two swags together, and smoke like sheol. That's all you've got to do."

I went into the bar, got the swags from the missus, carried them out on to the verandah, and then went back.

Stiffner came in.

"Good morning!"

"Good morning, sir," says Stiffner.

"It'll be a nice day, I think."

"Yes, I think so. I suppose you are going on?"

"Yes, we'll have to make a move to-day." Then I hooked carelessly on to the counter with one elbow, and looked dreamy-like out across the clearing, and presently I gave a sort of sigh and said: "Ah, well! I think I'll have a beer."

"Right you are! Where's your mate?"

"Oh, he's round at the back. He'll be round directly; but he ain't drinking this morning."

Stiffner laughed that nasty empty laugh of his. He thought Bill was whipping the cat.

"What's yours, boss?" I said.

"Thankee! . . . Here's luck!"

"Here's luck!"

The country was pretty open round there—the nearest timber was better than a mile away, and I wanted to give Bill a good start across the flat before the go-as-you-can commenced; so I talked for a while, and while we were talking I thought I might as well go the whole hog—I might as well die for a pound as a penny, if I had to die; and if I hadn't I'd have the pound to the good, anyway, so to speak. Anyhow, the risk would be about the same, or less, for I might have the spirit to run harder the more I had to run for—the more spirits I had to run for, in fact, as it turned out—so I says:

"I think I'll take one of them there flasks of whisky to last us on the road."

"Right y'are," says Stiffner. "What'll yer have—a small one or a big one?"

"Oh, a big one, I think—if I can get it into my pocket."

"It'll be a tight squeeze," he said, and he laughed.

"I'll try," I said. "Bet you two drinks I'll get it in."

"Done!" he says. "The top inside coat pocket, and no tearing."

It was a big bottle, and all my pockets were small; but I got it into the pocket he'd betted against. It was a tight squeeze, but I got it in.

Then we both laughed, but his laugh was nastier than usual, because it was meant to be pleasant, and he'd lost two drinks; and my laugh wasn't easy—I was anxious as to which of us would laugh next.

Just then I noticed something, and an idea struck me—about the most up-to-date idea that ever struck me in my life. I noticed that Stiffner was limping on his right foot this morning, so I said to him:

"What's up with your foot?" putting my hand in my pocket.

"Oh, it's a crimson nail in my boot," he said. "I thought I got the blanky thing out this morning; but I didn't."

There just happened to be an old bag of shoemaker's tools in the bar, belonging to an old cobbler who was lying dead drunk on the verandah. So I said, taking my hand out of my pocket again:

"Lend us the boot, and I'll fix it in a minute. That's my old trade."

"Oh, so you're a shoemaker," he said. "I'd never have thought it."

He laughs one of his useless laughs that wasn't wanted, and slips off the boot—he hadn't laced it up—and hands it across the bar to me. It was an ugly brute—a great thick, iron-bound, boiler-plated navvy's boot. It made me feel sore when I looked at it.

I got the bag and pretended to fix the nail; but I didn't.

"There's a couple of nails gone from the sole," I said. "I'll put 'em in if I can find any hobnails, and it'll save the sole," and I rooted in the bag and found a good long nail, and shoved it right through the sole on the sly. He'd been a bit of a sprinter in his time, and I thought it might be better for me in the near future if the spikes of his running-shoes were inside.

"There, you'll find that better, I fancy," I said, standing the boot on the bar counter, but keeping my hand on it in an absent-minded kind of way. Presently I yawned and stretched myself, and said in a careless way:

"Ah, well! How's the slate?"

He scratched the back of his head and pretended to think.

"Oh, well, we'll call it thirty bob."

Perhaps he thought I'd slap down two quid.

"Well," I says, "and what will you do supposing we don't pay you?"

He looked blank for a moment. Then he fired up and gasped

and choked once or twice; and then he cooled down suddenly and
laughed his nastiest laugh—he was one of those men who always
laugh when they're wild—and said in a nasty, quiet tone:

"You thundering, jumped-up crawlers! If you don't (something) well part up I'll take your swags and (something) well
kick your gory pants so you won't be able to sit down for a month
—or stand up either!"

"Well, the sooner you begin the better," I said; and I chucked
the boot into a corner and bolted.

He jumped the bar counter, got his boot, and came after me.
He paused to slip the boot on—but he only made one step, and
then gave a howl and slung the boot off and rushed back. When
I looked round again he'd got a slipper on, and was coming—and
gaining on me, too. I shifted scenery pretty quick the next five
minutes. But I was soon pumped. My heart began to beat against
the ceiling of my head, and my lungs all choked up in my throat.
When I guessed he was getting within kicking distance I glanced
round so's to dodge the kick. He let out; but I shied just in time.
He missed fire, and the slipper went about twenty feet up in the
air and fell in a waterhole.

He was done then, for the ground was stubbly and stony. I
seen Bill on ahead pegging out for the horizon, and I took after
him and reached for the timber for all I was worth, for I'd seen
Stiffner's missus coming with a shovel—to bury the remains, I
suppose; and those two were a good match—Stiffner and his
missus, I mean.

Bill looked round once, and melted into the bush pretty soon
after that. When I caught up he was about done; but I grabbed
my swag and we pushed on, for I told Bill that I'd seen Stiffner
making for the stables when I'd last looked round; and Bill thought
that we'd better get lost in the bush as soon as ever we could,
and stay lost, too, for Stiffner was a man that couldn't stand
being had.

The first thing that Bill said when we got safe into camp was:
"I told you that we'd pull through all right. You need never be
frightened when you're travelling with me. Just take my advice
and leave things to me, and we'll hang out all right. Now——"

But I shut him up. He made me mad.

"Why, you——! What the sheol did *you* do?"

"Do?" he says. "I got away with the swags, didn't I? Where'd
they be now if it wasn't for me?"

Then I sat on him pretty hard for his pretensions, and paid
him out for all the patronage he'd worked off on me, and called
him a mug straight, and walked round him, so to speak, and

blowed, and told him never to pretend to me again that he was a battler.

Then, when I thought I'd licked him into form, I cooled down and soaped him up a bit; but I never thought that he had three climaxes and a crisis in store for me.

He took it all pretty cool; he let me have my fling, and gave me time to get breath; then he leaned languidly over on his right side, shoved his left hand down into his left trouser pocket, and brought up a boot-lace, a box of matches, and nine-and-six.

As soon as I got the focus of it I gasped:

"Where the deuce did you get that?"

"I had it all along," he said, "but I seen at the pub that you had the show to chew a lug, so I thought we'd save it—nine-and-sixpences ain't picked up every day."

Then he leaned over on his left, went down into the other pocket, and came up with a piece of tobacco and half-a-sovereign. My eyes bulged out.

"Where the blazes did you get that from?" I yelled.

"That," he said, "was the half-quid you give me last night. Half-quids ain't to be thrown away these times; and, besides, I had a down on Stiffner, and meant to pay him out; I reckoned that if we wasn't sharp enough to take him down we hadn't any business to be supposed to be alive. Anyway I guessed we'd do it; and so we did—and got a bottle of whisky into the bargain."

Then he leaned back, tired-like, against the log, and dredged his upper left-hand waistcoat pocket, and brought up a sovereign wrapped in a pound-note. Then he waited for me to speak; but I couldn't. I got my mouth open, but couldn't get it shut again.

"I got that out of the mugs last night, but I thought that we'd want it, and might as well keep it. Quids ain't so easily picked up nowadays; and, besides, we need stuff more 'n Stiffner does, and so——"

"And did he know you had the stuff?" I gasped.

"Oh yes, that's the fun of it. That's what made him so excited. He was in the parlour all the time I was playing. But we might as well have a drink!"

We did. I wanted it.

     .   .   .

Bill turned in by-and-by, and looked like a sleeping innocent in the moonlight. I sat up late, and smoked, and thought hard, and watched Bill, and turned in, and thought till near daylight, and then went to sleep, and had a nightmare about it. I dreamed I

chased Stiffner forty miles to buy his pub, and that Bill turned
out to be his nephew.

Bill divvied up all right, and gave me half-a-crown over, but
I didn't travel with him long after that. He was a decent young
fellow as far as chaps go, and a good mate as far as mates go;
but he was too far ahead for a peaceful, easy-going chap like me.
It would have worn me out in a year to keep up to him.

[*1894   revised 1895, 1900*]

STEELMAN

STEELMAN was a hard case. If you were married, and settled
down, and were so unfortunate as to have known Steelman in
other days, he would, if in your neighbourhood and dead-beat,
be sure to look you up. He would find you anywhere, no matter
what precautions you might take. If he came to your house, he
would stay to tea without invitation; and, if he stayed to tea, he'd
ask you to "fix up a shakedown on the floor, old man", and put
him up for the night; and, if he stopped all night, he'd remain—
well, until something better turned up.

There was no shaking off Steelman. He had a way about him
which would often make it appear as if you had invited him to
stay and pressed him against his roving inclination, and were glad
to have him round for company, while he remained only out of
pure goodwill to you. He didn't like to offend an old friend by
refusing his invitation.

Steelman knew his men.

The married victim generally had neither the courage nor the
ability to turn him out. He was cheerfully blind and deaf to all
hints, and if the exasperated missus said anything to him straight,
he would look shocked and reply, as likely as not:

"Why, my good woman, you must be mad! I'm your husband's
guest!"

And if she wouldn't cook for him, he'd cook for himself.

There was no choking him off. Few people care to call the
police in a case like this; and, besides, as before remarked, Steel-

man knew his men. The only way to escape from him was to shift —but then, as likely as not, he'd help pack up and come along with his portmanteau right on top of the last load of furniture, and drive you and your wife to the verge of madness by the calm style in which he proceeded to superintend the hanging of your pictures.

Once he quartered himself like this on an old schoolmate of his, named Brown, who had got married and steady and settled down. Brown tried all ways to get rid of Steelman, but he couldn't do it. One day Brown said to Steelman:

"Look here, Steely, old man, I'm very sorry, but I'm afraid we won't be able to accommodate you any longer—to make you comfortable, I mean. You see, a sister of the missus is coming down on a visit for a month or two, and we ain't got anywhere to put her except in your room. I wish the missus's relations to blazes! I didn't marry the whole blessed family; but it seems I've got to keep them."

Pause—very awkward and painful for poor Brown. Discouraging silence from Steelman. Brown rested his elbows on his knees, and, with a pathetic and appealing movement of his hand across his forehead, he continued desperately:

"I'm very sorry, you see, old man—you know I'd like you to stay—I *want* you to stay. . . . It isn't *my* fault—it's the missus's doings. I've done my best with her, but I can't help it. I've been more like a master in my own house—more comfortable—and I've been better treated since I've had you to back me up. . . . I'll feel mighty lonely, anyway, when you're gone. . . . But . . . you know . . . as soon as her sister goes . . . you know . . ."

Here poor Brown broke down—very sorry he had spoken at all; but Steely came to the rescue with a ray of light.

"What's the matter with the little room at the back?" he asked.

"Oh, we couldn't think of putting you there," said Brown with a last effort; "it's not fixed up; you wouldn't be comfortable, and, besides, it's damp, and you'd catch your death of cold. It was never meant for anything but a wash-house. I'm sorry I didn't get another room built on to the house."

"Bosh!" interrupted Steelman, cheerfully. "Catch a cold! Here I've been knocking about the country for the last five years—sleeping out in all weathers—and do you think a little damp is going to hurt me? Pooh! What do you take me for? Don't you bother your head about it any more, old man; I'll fix up the lumber-room for myself, all right; and all you've got to do is to let me know when the sister-in-law business is coming on, and I'll shift out of my room in time for the missus to get it ready for her. Here, have you got a bob on you? I'll go out and get some beer. A drop'll do you good."

"Well, if you can make yourself comfortable, I'll be only too glad for you to stay," said the utterly defeated Brown.

"You'd better invite some woman you know to come on a visit, and pass her off as your sister," said Brown to his wife while Steelman was gone for the beer. "I've made a mess of it."

Mrs Brown said: "I knew you would."

Steelman knew his men.

.   .   .

But at last Brown reckoned that he could stand it no longer. The thought of it made him so wild that he couldn't work. He took a day off to get thoroughly worked up in, came home that night full to the chin of indignation and Dunedin beer, and tried to kick Steelman out. And Steelman gave him a hiding.

Next morning Steelman was sitting beside Brown's bed with a saucer of vinegar, some brown paper, a raw beef-steak, and a bottle of soda.

"Well, what have you got to say for yourself now, Brown?" he said, sternly. "Ain't you jolly well ashamed of yourself to come home in the beastly state you did last night, and insult a guest in your house, to say nothing of an old friend—and perhaps the best friend you ever had, if you only knew it? Anybody else would have given you in charge and got you three months for the assault. You ought to have some consideration for your wife and children, and your own character—even if you haven't any for your old mate's feelings. Here, drink this, and let me fix you up a bit; the missus has got the breakfast waiting."

[*1894   revised 1895*]

STEELMAN'S PUPIL

STEELMAN was a hard case, but some said that Smith was harder. Steelman was big and good-looking, and good-natured in his way; he was a "spieler", pure and simple, but did things in humorous style. Smith was small and weedy, of the sneak variety; he had

a whining tone and a cringing manner. He seemed to be always
so afraid you were going to hit him that he would make you *want*
to hit him on that account alone.

Steelman "had" you in a fashion that would make your friends
laugh. Smith would "have" you in a way which made you feel
mad at the bare recollection of having been taken in by so contemptible a little sneak.

They battled round together in the North Island of Maoriland
for a couple of years.

One day Steelman said to Smith:

"Look here, Smithy, you don't know you're born yet. I'm
going to take you in hand and teach you."

And he did. If Smith wouldn't do as Steelman told him, or
wasn't successful in cadging, or "mugged" any game they had in
hand, Steelman would threaten to "stoush" him; and, if the warning proved ineffectual after the second or third time, he *would*
stoush him.

One day, on the track, they came to a place where an old
Scottish couple kept a general store and shanty. They camped
alongside the road, and Smith was just starting up to the house to
beg supplies when Steelman cried:

"Here!—hold on. Now where do you think you're going to?"

"Why, I'm going to try and chew the old party's lug, of course.
We'll be out of tucker in a couple of days," said Smith.

Steelman sat down on a stump in a hopeless, discouraged sort
of way.

"It's no use," he said, regarding Smith with mingled reproach
and disgust. "It's no use. I might as well give it best. I can see
that it's only waste of time trying to learn you anything. Will I
ever be able to knock some gumption into your thick skull? After
all the time and trouble and pains I've took with your education,
you hain't got any more sense than to go and mug a business
like that! When will you learn sense? Hey? After all, I———
Smith, you're a born mug!"

He always called Smith a "mug" when he was particularly wild
at him, for it hurt Smith more than anything else.

"There's only two classes in the world, spielers and mugs—
and you're a mug, Smith."

"What have I done, anyway?" asked Smith helplessly. "That's
all I want to know."

Steelman wearily rested his brow on his hand.

"That will do, Smith," he said listlessly; "don't say another
word, old man; it'll only make my head worse; don't talk. You
might, at the very least, have a little consideration for my feelings

—even if you haven't for your own interests." He paused and regarded Smith sadly. "Well, I'll give you another show. I'll stage the business for you."

He made Smith doff his coat and get into his worst pair of trousers—and they were bad enough; they were hopelessly "gone", beyond the extreme limit of bush decency. He made Smith put on a rag of a felt hat and a pair of "'lastic sides" which had fallen off a tramp and lain baking and rotting by turns on a rubbish-heap; they had to be tied on Smith with bits of rag and string. He drew dark shadows round Smith's eyes, and burning spots on his cheek-bones with some grease-paints he used when they travelled as "The Great Steelman and Smith Combination Star Shakesperian Dramatic Co.". He damped Smith's hair to make it dark and lank, and his face more corpse-like by comparison—in short, he "made him up" to look like a man who had long passed the very last stage of consumption and had been artificially kept alive in the interests of science.

"Now you're ready," said Steelman to Smith. "You left your whare the day before yesterday and started to walk to the hospital at Palmerston. An old mate picked you up dying on the road, brought you round, and carried you on his back most of the way here. You firmly believe that Providence had something to do with the sending of that old mate along at that time and place above all others. Your mate also was hard-up; he was going to a job—the first show for work he'd had in nine months—but he gave it up to see you through; he'd give up his life rather than desert a mate in trouble. You only want a couple of shillings or a bit of tucker to help you on to Palmerston. You know you've got to die, and you only want to live long enough to get word to your poor old mother, and die on a bed.

"Remember, they're Scotch up at that house. You understand the Scotch barrack pretty well by now—if you don't it ain't my fault. You were born in Aberdeen, but came out too young to remember much about the town. Your father's dead. You ran away to sea and came out in the *Bobbie Burns* to Sydney. Your poor old mother's in Aberdeen now—Bruce or Wallace Wynd will do. Your mother might be dead now—poor old soul!— anyway, you'll never see her again. You wish you'd never run away from home. You wish you'd been a better son to your poor old mother; you wish you'd written to her and answered her last letter. You only want to live long enough to write home and ask for forgiveness and a blessing before you die. If you had a drop of spirits of some sort to brace you up you might get along the road better. (Put this delicately.) Get the whine out of your voice and breathe with a wheeze—like this; get up the nearest approach to a death-rattle that you can. Move as if you were badly hurt in your wind—like this. (If you don't do it better'n that, I'll stoush you.) Make your face a bit longer and keep your lips dry—don't lick them, you damned fool!—*breathe* on them; make 'em dry as chips. That's the only decent pair of breeks you've got, and the only 'shoon'. You're a Presbyterian—not a U.P., the Auld Kirk. Your mate would have come up to the house, only—well, you'll have to use the stuffing in your head a bit; you can't expect me to do all the brain-work. Remember it's consumption you've got—galloping consumption; you know all the symptoms—pain on top of your right lung, bad cough, and night sweats. Something tells you that you won't see the new year —it's a week off Christmas now. And, if you come back without anything, I'll blessed soon put you out of your misery."

.   .   .

Smith came back with about four pounds of shortbread and as much various tucker as they could conveniently carry; a pretty good suit of cast-off tweeds; a new pair of 'lastic sides from the store stock; two bottles of patent medicine and a black bottle half-full of home-made consumption-cure; also a letter to a hospital committee man, and three shillings to help him on his way to Palmerston. He also got about half a mile of sympathy, religious consolation, and medical advice which he didn't remember.

"*Now*," he said triumphantly, "am I a mug or not?"

Steelman kindly ignored the question. "I *did* have a better opinion of the Scotch," he said contemptuously.

.   .   .

Steelman got on at a hotel as billiard-marker and decoy, and in six months he managed that pub. Smith, who'd been away on his own account, turned up in the town one day clean-broke, and in a deplorable state. He heard of Steelman's luck, and thought he was "all right", so went to his old friend.

Cold type—or any other kind of type—couldn't do justice to Steelman's disgust. To think that this was the reward of all the time and trouble he'd spent on Smith's education! However, when he cooled down, he said:

"Smith, you're a young man yet, and it's never too late to mend. There is still time for reformation. I can't help you now; it would only demoralize you altogether. To think, after the way I trained you, you can't battle round any better'n this! I always thought you were an irreclaimable mug, but I expected better things of you towards the end. I thought I'd make *something* of you. It's enough to dishearten any man and disgust him with the

world. Why! you ought to be a rich man now with the chances
and training you had! To think—but I won't talk of that; it has
made me ill. I suppose I'll have to give you something, if it's
only to get rid of the sight of you. Here's a quid, and I'm a mug
for giving it to you. It'll do you more harm than good; and it ain't
a friendly thing nor the right thing for me—who always had your
welfare at heart—to give it to you under the circumstances. Now,
get away out of my sight, and don't come near me till you've
reformed. If you do, I'll have to stoush you out of regard for my
own health and feelings."

But Steelman came down in the world again and picked up
Smith on the road, and they "battled round" together for another
year or so; and at last they were in Wellington—Steelman "flush"
and stopping at a hotel, and Smith stumped, as usual, and staying
with a friend. One night they were drinking together at the hotel,
at the expense of some mugs whom Steelman was "educating".
It was raining hard. When Smith was going home, he said:

"Look here, Steely, old man. Listen to the rain! I'll get wringing
wet going home. You might as well lend me your overcoat to-night.
You won't want it, and I won't hurt it."

And, Steelman's heart being warmed by his successes, he lent
the overcoat.

Smith went and pawned it, got glorious on the proceeds, and
took the pawn-ticket to Steelman next day.

Smith had reformed.

"And *I* taught him!" Steelman would say proudly in after years.
"Poor old Smith. *He* could battle round all right. I taught him."

[*1894   revised 1895, 1900*]

THE GEOLOGICAL SPIELER

There's nothing so interesting as geology, even to common and ignorant
people, especially when you have a bank or the side of a cutting, studded
with fossil fish and things and oysters that were stale when Adam was
fresh to illustrate by. (*Remark made by Steelman, professional wanderer,
to his pal and pupil Smith.*)

THE first man that Steelman and Smith came up to on the last
embankment, where they struck the new railway line, was a heavy,

gloomy, labouring man with bowyangs on and straps round his wrists. Steelman bade him the time of day and had a few words with him over the weather. The man of mullock gave it as his opinion that the fine weather wouldn't last, and seemed to take a gloomy kind of pleasure in that reflection; he said there was more rain down yonder, pointing to the south-east, than the moon could swallow up—the moon was in its first quarter, during which time it is popularly believed in some parts of Maoriland that the south-easter is most likely to be out on the wallaby and the weather bad. Steelman regarded that quarter of the sky with an expression of gentle remonstrance mingled as it were with a sort of fatherly indulgence, agreed mildly with the labouring man, and seemed lost for a moment in a reverie from which he roused himself to inquire cautiously after the boss. There was no boss; it was a co-operative party. That chap standing over there by the dray in the end of the cutting was their spokesman—their representative: they called him Boss, but that was only his nickname in camp. Steelman expressed his thanks and moved on towards the cutting, followed respectfully by Smith.

Steelman wore a snuff-coloured sac suit, a wide-awake hat, a pair of professional-looking spectacles, and a scientific expression; there was a clerical atmosphere about him, strengthened however by an air as of unconscious dignity and superiority, born of intellect and knowledge. He carried a black bag, which was an indispensable article in his profession in more senses than one. Smith was decently dressed in sober tweed and looked like a man of no account who was mechanically devoted to his employer's interests, pleasures, or whims, whatever they may have been.

The Boss was a decent-looking young fellow with a good face —rather solemn—and a quiet manner.

"Good day, sir," said Steelman.

"Good day, sir," said the Boss.

"Nice weather this."

"Yes, it is, but I'm afraid it won't last."

"I am afraid it will not by the look of the sky down there," ventured Steelman.

"No, I go mostly by the look of our weather prophet," said the Boss with a quiet smile, indicating the gloomy man.

"I suppose bad weather would put you back in your work?"

"Yes, it will; we didn't want any bad weather just now."

Steelman got the weather question satisfactorily settled; then he said:

"You seem to be getting on with the railway."

"Oh, yes, we are about over the worst of it."

"The worst of it?" echoed Steelman, with mild surprise: "I should have thought you were just coming into it;" and he pointed to the ridge ahead.

"Oh, our section doesn't go any further than that pole you see sticking up yonder. We had the worst of it back there across the swamps—working up to our waists in water most of the time, in mid-winter too—and at eighteenpence a yard."

"That was bad."

"Yes, rather rough. Did you come from the terminus?"

"Yes, I sent my baggage on in the brake."

"Commercial traveller, I suppose?" asked the Boss, glancing at Smith, who stood a little to the rear of Steelman, seeming interested in the work.

"Oh no," said Steelman, smiling; "I am—well—I'm a geologist; this is my man here," indicating Smith. "(You may put down the bag, James, and have a smoke.) My name is Stoneleigh—you might have heard of it."

The Boss said "Oh", and then presently he added "indeed", in an undecided tone.

There was a pause—embarrassed on the part of the Boss— he was silent, not knowing what to say. Meanwhile Steelman studied his man and concluded that he would do.

"Having a look at the country, I suppose?" asked the Boss presently.

"Yes," said Steelman; then after a moment's reflection: "I am travelling for my own amusement and improvement, and also in the interest of science, which amounts to the same thing. I am a member of the Royal Geological Society—vice-president in fact of a leading Australian branch;" and then, as if conscious that he had appeared guilty of egotism, he shifted the subject a bit. "Yes. Very interesting country this—very interesting indeed. I should like to make a stay here for a day or so. Your work opens right into my hands. I cannot remember seeing a geological formation which interested me so much. Look at the face of that cutting, for instance. Why! you can almost read the history of the geological world from yesterday—this morning as it were—beginning with the super-surface on top and going right down through the different layers and stratas—through the vanished ages—right down and back to the prehistorical—to the very primeval or fundamental geological formations!" And Steelman studied the face of the cutting as if he could read it like a book, with every layer or stratum a chapter, and every streak a note of explanation. The Boss seemed to be getting interested, and Steelman gained confidence and proceeded to identify and classify the different "stratas and layers", and fix their ages, and describe the conditions and politics of Man in their different times, for the Boss's benefit.

"Now," continued Steelman, turning slowly from the cutting, removing his glasses, and letting his thoughtful eyes wander casually over the general scenery—"now the first impression that this country would leave on an ordinary intelligent mind—though maybe unconsciously—would be as of a new country, new in a geological sense; with patches of an older geological and vegetable formation cropping out here and there; as for instance that clump of dead trees on that clear alluvial slope there, that outcrop of limestone, or that timber yonder," and he indicated a dead forest which seemed alive and green because of the parasites. "But the country is old—old; perhaps the oldest geological formation in the world is to be seen here, as is the oldest vegetable formation in Australia. I am not using the words old and new in an ordinary sense, you understand, but in a geological sense."

The Boss said, "I understand," and that geology must be a very interesting study.

Steelman ran his eye meditatively over the cutting again, and turning to Smith said:

"Go up there, James, and fetch me a specimen of that slaty outcrop you see there—just above the coeval strata."

It was a stiff climb and slippery, but Smith had to do it, and he did it.

"This," said Steelman, breaking the rotten piece between his fingers, "belongs probably to an older geological period than its position would indicate—a primitive sandstone level perhaps. Its position on that layer is no doubt due to volcanic upheavals. Such disturbances, or rather the results of such disturbances, have been and are the cause of the greatest trouble to geologists—endless errors and controversy. You see we must study the country, not as it appears now, but as it would appear had the natural geological growth been left to mature undisturbed; we must restore and reconstruct such disorganized portions of the mineral kingdom, if you understand me."

The Boss said he understood.

Steelman found an opportunity to wink sharply and severely at Smith, who had been careless enough to allow his features to relapse into a vacant grin.

"It is generally known even amongst the ignorant that rock grows—grows from the outside—but the rock here, a specimen of which I hold in my hand, is now in the process of decomposition; to be plain, it is rotting—in an advanced stage of decomposition—so much so that you are not able to identify it with any geological period or formation, even as you may not be able to identify any other extremely decomposed body."

The Boss blinked and knitted his brow, but had the presence of mind to say: "Just so."

"Had the rock on that cutting been healthy—been alive, as it were—you would have had your work cut out; but it is dead and has been dead for ages perhaps. You find less trouble in working it than you would ordinary clay or sand, or even gravel, which formations together are really rock in embryo—before birth as it were."

The Boss's brow cleared.

"The country round here is simply rotting down—simply rotting down."

He removed his spectacles, wiped them, and wiped his face; then his attention seemed to be attracted by some stones at his feet. He picked one up and examined it.

"I shouldn't wonder," he mused, absently, "I shouldn't wonder if there is alluvial gold in some of these creeks and gullies, perhaps tin or even silver, quite probably antimony."

The Boss seemed interested.

"Can you tell me if there is any place in this neighbourhood where I could get accommodation for myself and my servant for a day or two?" asked Steelman presently. "I should very much like to break my journey here."

"Well, no," said the Boss. "I can't say I do—I don't know of any place nearer than Pahiatua, and that's seven miles from here."

"I know that," said Steelman reflectively, "but I fully expected to have found a house or accommodation of some sort on the way, else I would have gone on in the van."

"Well," said the Boss. "If you like to camp with us for to-night, at least, and don't mind roughing it, you'll be welcome, I'm sure."

"If I was sure that I would not be putting you to any trouble, or interfering in any way with your domestic economy——"

"No trouble at all," interrupted the Boss. "The boys will be only too glad, and there's an empty whare where you can sleep. Better stay. It's going to be a rough night."

After tea Steelman entertained the Boss and a few of the more thoughtful members of the party with short chatty lectures on geology and other subjects.

In the meantime Smith, in another part of the camp, gave selections on a tin whistle, sang a song or two, contributed, in his turn, to the sailor yarns, and ensured his popularity for several nights at least. After several draughts of something that was poured out of a demijohn into a pint pot, his tongue became loosened, and he expressed an opinion that geology was all bosh, and said if he had half his employer's money he'd be dashed if he would go rooting round in the mud like a blessed old anteater; he also irreverently referred to his learned boss as "Old Rocks" over there. He had a pretty easy billet of it though, he said, taking it all round, when the weather was fine; he got a couple of notes a week and all expenses paid, and the money was sure; he was only required to look after the luggage and arrange for accommodation, grub out a chunk of rock now and then, and (what perhaps was the most irksome of his duties) he had to appear interested in old rocks and clay.

Towards midnight Steelman and Smith retired to the unoccupied whare which had been shown them, Smith carrying a bundle of bags, blankets, and rugs which had been placed at their disposal by their good-natured hosts. Smith lit a candle and proceeded to make the beds. Steelman sat down, removed his specs and scientific expression, placed the glasses carefully on a ledge close at hand, took a book from his bag, and commenced to read. The volume was a cheap copy of Jules Verne's *Journey to the Centre of the Earth*. A little later there was a knock at the door. Steelman hastily resumed the spectacles, together with the scientific expression, took a note-book from his pocket, opened it on the table, and said: "Come in." One of the chaps appeared with a billy of hot coffee, two pint pots, and some cake. He said he thought you chaps might like a drop of coffee before you turned in, and the boys had forgot to ask you to wait for it down in the camp. He also wanted to know whether Mr Stoneleigh and his man would be all right and quite comfortable for the night, and whether they had blankets enough. There was some wood at the back of the whare and they could light a fire if they liked.

Mr Stoneleigh expressed his thanks and his appreciation of the kindness shown him and his servant. He was extremely sorry to give them any trouble.

The navvy, a serious man, who respected genius or intellect in any shape or form, said that it was no trouble at all, the camp was very dull, and the boys were always glad to have someone come round. Then, after a brief comparison of opinions concerning the probable duration of the weather which had arrived, they bade each other good night, and the darkness swallowed the serious man.

Steelman turned into the top bunk on one side and Smith took the lower on the other. Steelman had the candle by his bunk, as usual; he lit his pipe for a final puff before going to sleep, and held the light up for a moment so as to give Smith the full benefit of a solemn, uncompromising wink. The wink was silently applauded and dutifully returned by Smith. Then Steelman blew out the light, lay back, and puffed at his pipe for a while. Presently he chuckled, and the chuckle was echoed by Smith; by-and-by Steelman chuckled once more, and then Smith chuckled again. There was silence in the darkness, and after a bit Smith chuckled twice. Then Steelman said:

"For God's sake give her a rest, Smith, and give a man a show to get some sleep."

Then the silence in the darkness remained unbroken.

The invitation was extended next day, and Steelman sent Smith on to see that his baggage was safe. Smith stayed out of sight for two or three hours, and then returned and reported all well.

They stayed on for several days. After breakfast and when the men were going to work Steelman and Smith would go out along the line with the black bag and poke round amongst the "layers and stratas" in sight of the works for a while, as an evidence of good faith: then they'd drift off casually into the bush, camp in a retired and sheltered spot, and light a fire when the weather was cold, and Steelman would lie on the grass and read and smoke and lay plans for the future and improve Smith's mind until they reckoned it was about dinner time. And in the evening they would come home with the black bag full of stones and bits of rock, and Steelman would lecture on those minerals after tea.

On about the fourth morning Steelman had a yarn with one of the men going to work. He was a lanky young fellow with a sandy complexion, and seemingly harmless grin. In Australia he might have been regarded as a "cove" rather than a "chap", but there was nothing of the "bloke" about him. Presently the cove said:

"What do you think of the Boss, Mr Stoneleigh? He seems to have taken a great fancy for you, and he's fair gone on geology."

"I think he is a very decent fellow indeed, a very intelligent young man. He seems very well read and well informed."

"You wouldn't think he was a University man," said the cove.

"No, indeed. Is he?"

"Yes. I thought you knew!"

Steelman knitted his brows. He seemed slightly disturbed for the moment. He walked on a few paces in silence and thought hard.

"What might have been his special line?" he asked the cove.

"Why, something the same as yours. I thought you knew. He was reckoned the best—what do you call it?—the best minrologist in the country. He had a first-class billet in the Mines Department, but he lost it—you know—the booze."

"I think we will be making a move, Smith," said Steelman,

later on, when they were private. "There's a little too much intellect in this camp to suit me. But we haven't done so bad anyway. We've got three days' good board and lodging with entertainments and refreshment thrown in." Then he said to himself: "We'll stay for another day anyway. If those beggars are having a lark with us, we're getting the worth of it anyway, and I'm not thin-skinned. They're the mugs and not us, anyhow it goes, and I can take them down before I leave."

But on the way home he had a talk with another man whom we might set down as a "chap".

"I wouldn't have thought the Boss was a college man," said Steelman to the chap.

"A what?"

"A University man—University education."

"Why! Who's been telling you that?"

"One of your mates."

"Oh, he's been getting at you. Why, it's all the Boss can do to write his own name. Now that lanky sandy cove with the birth-mark grin—it's him that's had the college education."

"I think we'll make a start to-morrow," said Steelman to Smith in the privacy of their whare. "There's too much humour and levity in this camp to suit a serious scientific gentleman like myself."

[*1895*]

HOW STEELMAN TOLD HIS STORY

IT was Steelman's humour, in some of his moods, to take Smith into his confidence, as some old bushmen do their dogs.

"You're nearly as good as an intelligent sheep-dog to talk to, Smith—when a man gets tired of thinking to himself and wants a relief. You're a bit of a mug and a good deal of an idiot, and the chances are that you don't know what I'm driving at half the time—that's the main reason why I don't mind talking to you. You ought to consider yourself honoured; it ain't every man I take into my confidence, even that far."

Smith rubbed his head.

"I'd sooner talk to you—or a stump—any day than to one of

those silent, suspicious, self-contained, worldly-wise chaps that
listen to everything you say—sense and rubbish alike—as if you
were trying to get them to take shares in a mine. I drop the man
who listens to me all the time and doesn't seem to get bored.
He isn't safe. He isn't to be trusted. He mostly wants to grind his
axe against yours, and there's too little profit for me where there
are two axes to grind, and no stone—though I'd manage it once,
anyhow."

"How'd you do it?" asked Smith.

"There are several ways. Either you join forces, for instance,
and find a grindstone—or make one of the other man's axe. But
the last way is too slow, and, as I said, takes too much brain-work
—besides, it doesn't pay. It might satisfy your vanity or pride,
but I've got none. I had once, when I was younger, but it—well,
it nearly killed me, so I dropped it.

"You can mostly trust the man who wants to talk more than
you do; he'll make a safe mate—or a good grindstone."

Smith scratched the nape of his neck and sat blinking at the
fire, with the puzzled expression of a woman pondering over a
life-question or the trimming of a hat. Steelman took his chin in
his hand and watched Smith thoughtfully.

"I—I say, Steely," exclaimed Smith suddenly, sitting up and
scratching his head and blinking harder than ever; "wha—what
am I?"

"How do you mean?"

"Am I the axe or the grindstone?"

"Oh! your brain seems in extra good working order to-night,
Smith. Well, you turn the grindstone and I grind." Smith settled.
"If you could grind better than I, I'd turn the stone and let *you*
grind—I'd never go against the interests of the firm—that's fair
enough, isn't it?"

"Ye-es," admitted Smith; "I suppose so."

"So do I. Now, Smith, we've got along all right together for
years, off and on, but you never know what might happen. I
might stop breathing, for instance—and so might you."

Smith began to look alarmed.

"Poetical justice might overtake one or both of us—such things
have happened before, though not often. Or, say, misfortune or
death might mistake us for honest, hard-working mugs with big
families to keep, and cut us off in the bloom of all our wisdom.
You might get into trouble, and, in that case, I'd be bound to
leave you there, on principle; or I might get into trouble, and you
wouldn't have the brains to get me out—though I know you'd be
mug enough to try. I might make a rise and cut you, or you might

be misled into showing some spirit, and clear out after I'd stoushed you for it. You might get tired of me calling you a mug, and bossing you and making a tool or convenience of you, you know. You might go in for honest graft (you were always a bit weak-minded) and then I'd have to wash my hands of you (unless you agreed to keep me) for an irreclaimable mug. Or it might suit me to become a respected and worthy fellow-townsman, and then, if you came within ten miles of me, or hinted that you ever knew me, I'd have you up for vagrancy, or soliciting alms, or attempting to levy blackmail. I'd have to fix you—so I give you fair warning. Or we might get into some desperate fix (and it needn't be very desperate, either) when I'd be obliged to sacrifice you for my own personal safety, comfort, and convenience. Hundreds of things might happen.

"Well, as I said, we've been at large together for some years, and I've found you sober, trustworthy, and honest; so, in case we do part—as we will sooner or later—and you survive, I'll give you some advice from my own experience.

"In the first place: if you ever happen to get born again—and it wouldn''t do you much harm—get born with the strength of a bullock and the hide of one as well, and a swelled head, and no brains—at least, no more brains than you've got now. I was born with a skin like tissue-paper, and brains; also a heart.

"Get born without relatives, if you can; if you can't help it, clear out on your own just as soon after you're born as you possibly can. I hung on.

"If you have relations, and feel inclined to help them any time when you're flush (and there's no telling what a weak-minded man like you might take it into his head to do)—don't do it. They'll get a down on you if you do. It only causes family troubles and bitterness. There's no dislike like that of a dependant. You'll get neither gratitude nor civility in the end, and be lucky if you escape with a character. (You've got *no* character, Smith; I'm only just supposing you have.) If you help relations more than once they'll begin to regard it as a right; and when you're forced to leave off helping them, they'll hate you worse than they'd hate a stranger. No one likes to be deprived of his rights—especially by a relation. There's no hatred too bitter for, and nothing too bad to be said of, the mug who turns. The worst yarns about a man are generally started by his own tribe, and the world believes them at once on that very account. Well, the first thing to do in life is to escape from your friends.

"If you ever go to work—and miracles have happened before—no matter what your wages are, or how you are treated, you can take it for granted that you're sweated; act on that to the best of your ability, or you'll never rise in the world. If you go to see a show on the nod you'll be found a comfortable seat in a good place; but if you pay, the chances are the ticket clerk will tell you a lie, and you'll have to hustle for standing room. The man that doesn't ante gets the best of this world; anything he'll stand is good enough for the man that pays. If you try to be too sharp you'll get into gaol sooner or later; if you try to be too honest, the chances are that the bailiff will get into your house—if you have one—and make a holy show of you before the neighbours. The honest softy is more often mistaken for a swindler, and accused of being one, than the out-and-out scamp; and the man that tells the truth too much is set down as an irreclaimable liar. But most of the time crow low and roost high, for it's a funny world, and you never know what might happen.

"And if you get married (and there's no accounting for a woman's taste), be as bad as you like, and then moderately good, and your wife will love you. If you're bad all the time she can't stand it for ever, and if you're good all the time she'll naturally treat you with contempt. Never explain what you're going to do, and don't explain afterwards, if you can help it. If you find yourself between two stools, strike hard for your own self, Smith— strike hard, and you'll be respected more than if you fought for all the world. Generosity isn't understood nowadays, and what the people don't understand is either 'mad' or 'cronk'. Failure has no case, and you can't build one for it. . . . I started out in life very young—and very soft."

.   .   .

"I thought you were going to tell me your story, Steely," remarked Smith.

Steelman smiled sadly.

[1895?   revised 1899, 1900]

3

GOING BLIND

I MET him in the Full-and-Plenty Dining Rooms. It was a cheap place in the city, with good beds upstairs let at one shilling per night—"Board and residence for respectable single men, fifteen shillings per week." I was a respectable single man then. I boarded and resided there. I boarded at a greasy little table in the greasy little corner under the fluffy little staircase in the hot and greasy little dining-room or restaurant downstairs. They called it dining-rooms, but it was only one room, and there wasn't half enough room in it to work your elbows when the seven little tables and forty-nine chairs were occupied. There was not room for an ordinary-sized steward to pass up and down between the tables; but our waiter was not an ordinary-sized man—he was a living skeleton in miniature. We handed the soup, and the "roast beef one", and "roast lamb one", "corn beef and cabbage one", "veal and stuffing one", and the "veal and pickled pork one"—or two, or three, as the case might be—and the tea and coffee, and the various kinds of pudding—we handed them over each other, and dodged the drops as well as we could. The very hot and very greasy little kitchen was adjacent, and it contained the bath-room and other conveniences, behind screens of whitewashed boards.

I resided upstairs in a room where there were five beds and one wash-stand; one candle-stick, with a very short bit of soft yellow candle in it; the back of a hair-brush, with about a dozen bristles in it; and half a comb—the big-tooth end—with nine and a half teeth at irregular distances apart.

He was a typical bushman, not one of those tall, straight, wiry, brown men of the West, but from the old Selection Districts, where many drovers came from, and of the old bush school; one of those slight, active little fellows whom we used to see in cabbage-tree hats, Crimean shirts, strapped trousers, and elastic-side boots—"larstins", they called them. They could dance well; sing indifferently, and mostly through their noses, the old bush songs; play the concertina horribly; and ride like—like—well, they *could* ride.

He seemed as if he had forgotten to grow old and die out with this old colonial school to which he belonged. They *had* careless and forgetful ways about them. His name was Jack Gunther, he said, and he'd come to Sydney to try to get something done to his eyes. He had a portmanteau, a carpet bag, some things in a three-bushel bag, and a tin box. I sat beside him on his bed, and struck up an acquaintance, and he told me all about it. First he asked me would I mind shifting round to the other side, as he was rather deaf in that ear. He'd been kicked on the side of the head by a horse, he said, and had been a little dull o' hearing on that side ever since.

He was as good as blind. "I can see the people near me," he said, "but I can't make out their faces. I can just make out the pavement and the houses close at hand, and all the rest is a sort of white blur." He looked up: "That ceiling is a kind of white, ain't it? And this," tapping the wall and putting his nose close to it, "is a sort of green, ain't it?" The ceiling might have been whiter. The prevalent tints of the wall-paper had originally been blue and red, but it was mostly green enough now—a damp, rotten green; but I was ready to swear that the ceiling was snow and that the walls were as green as grass if it would have made him feel more comfortable. His sight began to get bad about six years before, he said; he didn't take much notice of it at first, and then he saw a quack, who made his eyes worse. He had already the manner of the blind—the touch in every finger, and even the gentleness in his speech. He had a boy down with him—a "sorter cousin of his"—and the boy saw him round. "I'll have to be sending that youngster back," he said. "I think I'll send him home next week. He'll be picking up and learning too much down here."

I happened to know the district he came from, and we would sit by the hour and talk about the country, and chaps by the name of this and chaps by the name of that—drovers mostly, whom we had met or had heard of. He asked me if I'd ever heard of a chap by the name of Joe Scott—a big, sandy-complexioned chap, who might be droving; he was his brother, or, at least, his half-brother, but he hadn't heard of him for years; he'd last heard of him at Blackall, in Queensland; he might have gone overland to Western Australia with Tyson's cattle to the new country.

We talked about grubbing and fencing and digging and droving and shearing—all about the bush—and it all came back to me as we talked. "I can see it all now," he said once, in an abstracted tone, seeming to fix his helpless eyes on the wall opposite. But he didn't see the dirty blind wall, nor the dingy window, nor the skimpy little bed, nor the greasy wash-stand: he saw the dark blue ridges in the sunlight, the grassy sidings and flats, the creek with clumps of she-oak here and there, the course of the willow-fringed river below, the distant peaks and ranges fading away into a lighter azure, the granite ridge in the middle distance, and the rocky rises, the stringy-bark and the apple-tree flats, the scrubs, and the sunlit plains—and all. I could see it, too—plainer than ever I did.

He had done a bit of fencing in his time, and we got talking about timber. He didn't believe in having fencing-posts with big butts; he reckoned it was a mistake. "You see," he said, "the top of the butt catches the rain water and makes the post rot quicker. I'd back posts without any butt at all to last as long or longer than posts with 'em—that's if the fence is well put up and well rammed." He had supplied fencing stuff, and fenced by contract, and—well, you can get more posts without butts out of a tree than posts with them. He also objected to charring the butts. He said it only made more work, and wasted time—the butts lasted longer without being charred.

I asked him if he'd ever got stringy-bark palings or shingles out of mountain ash, and he smiled a smile that did my heart good to see, and said he had. He had also got them out of various other kinds of trees.

We talked about soil and grass, and gold-digging, and many other things which came back to one like a revelation as we yarned.

He had been to the hospital several times. "The doctors don't say they can cure me," he said; "they say they might be able to improve my sight and hearing, but it would take a long time—anyway, the treatment would improve my general health. They know what's the matter with my eyes," and he explained it as well as he could. "I wish I'd seen a good doctor when my eyes first began to get weak; but young chaps are always careless over things. It's harder to get cured of anything when you're done growing."

He was always hopeful and cheerful. "If the worst comes to the worst," he said, "there's things I can do where I come from. I might do a bit o' wool-sorting, for instance. I'm a pretty fair expert. Or else when they're weeding out I could help. I'd just have to sit down and they'd bring the sheep to me, and I'd feel the wool and tell them what it was—being blind improves the feeling, you know."

He had a packet of portraits, but he couldn't make them out very well now. They were sort of blurred to him, but I described them and he told me who they were. "That's a girl o' mine," he said, with reference to one—a jolly, good-looking bush girl. "I got a letter from her yesterday. I managed to scribble something, but I'll get you, if you don't mind, to write something more I want to put in on another piece of paper, and address an envelope for me."

Darkness fell quickly upon him now—or, rather, the "sort of white blur" increased and closed in. But his hearing was better, he said, and he was glad of that and still cheerful. I thought it natural that his hearing should improve as he went blind.

One day he said that he did not think he would bother going to the hospital any more. He reckoned he'd get back to where he was known. He'd stayed down too long already, and the "stuff" wouldn't stand it. He was expecting a letter that didn't come. I was away for a couple of days, and when I came back he had been shifted out of the room and had a bed in an angle of the landing on top of the staircase, with the people brushing against him and stumbling over his things all day on their way up and down. I felt indignant, thinking that—the house being full—the boss had taken advantage of the bushman's helplessness and good nature to put him there. But he said that he was quite comfortable. "I can get a whiff of air here," he said.

Going in next day I thought for a moment that I had dropped suddenly back into the past and into a bush dance, for there was a concertina going upstairs. He was sitting on the bed, with his legs crossed, and a new cheap concertina on his knee, and his eyes turned to the patch of ceiling as if it were a piece of music and he could read it. "I'm trying to knock a few tunes into my head," he said, with a brave smile, "in case the worst comes to the worst." He tried to be cheerful, but seemed worried and anxious. The letter hadn't come. I thought of the many blind musicians in Sydney, and I thought of the bushman's chance, standing at a corner swanking a cheap concertina, and I felt very sorry for him.

I went out with a vague idea of seeing someone about the matter, and getting something done for the bushman—of bringing a little influence to his assistance; but I suddenly remembered that my clothes were worn out, my hat in a shocking state, my boots burst, and that I owed for a week's board and lodging, and was likely to be thrown out at any moment myself; and so I was not in a position to go where there was influence.

When I went back to the restaurant there was a long, gaunt, sandy-complexioned bushman sitting by Jack's side. Jack introduced him as his brother, who had returned unexpectedly to his native district, and had followed him to Sydney. The brother was rather short with me at first, and seemed to regard the restaurant people—all of us, in fact—in the light of spielers, who wouldn't hesitate to take advantage of Jack's blindness if he left him a moment; and he looked ready to knock down the first man who stumbled against Jack, or over his luggage—but that soon wore off. Jack was going to stay with Joe at the Coffee Palace for a few weeks, and then go back up country, he told me. He was excited and happy. His brother's manner towards him was as if Jack had just lost his wife, or boy, or someone very dear to him. He would not allow him to do anything for himself, nor try to—not even lace up his boots. He seemed to think that he was thoroughly helpless, and when I saw him pack up Jack's things, and help him at the table, and fix his tie and collar with his great brown hands, which trembled all the time with grief and gentleness, and make Jack sit down on the bed whilst he got a cab and carried the traps down to it, and take him downstairs as if he were made of thin glass, and settle with the landlord—then I knew that Jack was all right.

We had a drink together—Joe, Jack, the cabman, and I. Joe was very careful to hand Jack the glass, and Jack made a joke about it for Joe's benefit. He swore he could see a glass yet, and Joe laughed, but looked extra troubled the next moment.

I felt their grips on my hand for five minutes after we parted.

[1895   revised 1895]

OUR PIPES

THE moon rose away out on the edge of a smoky plain, seen through a sort of tunnel or arch in the fringe of mulga behind which we were camped—Jack Mitchell and I. The "timber" proper was just behind us, very thick and very dark. The moon looked like a big new copper boiler set on edge on the horizon of the plain, with the top turned towards us and a lot of old rags and straw burning inside.

We had tramped twenty-five miles on a dry stretch on a hot day—swagmen know what that means. We reached the water about two hours "after dark"—swagmen know what that means. We didn't sit down at once and rest—we hadn't rested for the last

ten miles. We knew that if we sat down we wouldn't want to get
up again in a hurry—that, if we did, our leg-sinews, especially
those of our calves, would "draw" like red-hot wires. You see,
we hadn't been long on the track this time—it was only our third
day out. Swagmen will understand.

We got the billy boiled first, and some leaves laid down for our
beds and the swags rolled out. We thanked the Lord that we had
some cooked meat and a few johnny-cakes left, for we didn't feel
equal to cooking. We put the billy of tea and our tucker-bags
between the heads of our beds, and the pipes and tobacco in the
crown of an old hat, where we could reach them without having
to get up. Then we lay down on our stomachs and had a feed.
We didn't eat much—we were too tired for that—but we drank
a lot of tea. We gave our calves time to tone down a bit; then we
lit up and began to answer each other. It got to be pretty comfortable, so long as we kept those unfortunate legs of ours straight,
and didn't move round much.

We cursed society because we weren't rich men, and then we
felt better and conversation drifted lazily round various subjects
and ended in that of smoking.

"How I came to start smoking?" said Mitchell. "Let's see."
He reflected. "I started smoking first when I was about fourteen
or fifteen. I smoked some sort of weed—I forget the name of it—
but it wasn't tobacco; and then I smoked cigarettes—not the ones
we get now, for those cost a penny each. Then I reckoned that, if
I could smoke those, I could smoke a pipe."

He reflected.

"We lived in Sydney then—Surry Hills. Those were different
times; the place was nearly all sand. The old folks were alive
then, and we were all at home, except Tom."

He reflected.

"Ah, well! . . . Well, one evening I was playing marbles out in
front of our house when a chap we knew gave me his pipe to
mind while he went into a church-meeting. The little church was
opposite—a 'chapel' they called it."

He reflected.

"The pipe was alight. It was a clay pipe and nigger-head
tobacco. Mother was at work out in the kitchen at the back,
washing up the tea-things, and, when I went in, she said: 'You've
been smoking!'

"Well, I couldn't deny it—I was too sick to do so, or care much,
anyway.

" 'Give me that pipe!' she said.

"I said I hadn't got it.

" '*Give—me—that—pipe!*' she said.

"I said I hadn't got it.

" 'Where is it?' she said.

" 'Jim Brown's got it,' I said, 'it's his.'

" 'Then I'll give it to Jim Brown,' she said; and she did; though it wasn't Jim's fault, for he only gave it to me to mind. I didn't smoke the pipe so much because I wanted to smoke a pipe just then, as because I had such a great admiration for Jim."

Mitchell reflected, and took a look at the moon. It had risen clear and had got small and cold and pure-looking, and had floated away back out amongst the stars.

"I felt better towards morning, but it didn't cure me—being sick and nearly dead all night, I mean. I got a clay pipe and tobacco, and the old lady found it and put it in the stove. Then I got another pipe and tobacco, and she laid for it, and found it out at last; but she didn't put the tobacco in the stove this time— she'd got experience. I don't know what she did with it. I tried to find it, but couldn't. I fancy the old man got hold of it, for I saw him with a plug that looked very much like mine."

He reflected.

"But I wouldn't be done. I got a cherry pipe. I thought it wouldn't be so easy to break if she found it. I used to plant the bowl in one place and the stem in another because I reckoned that if she found one she mightn't find the other. It doesn't look much of an idea now, but it seemed like an inspiration then. Kids get rum ideas."

He reflected.

"Well, one day I was having a smoke out at the back when I heard her coming, and I pulled out the stem in a hurry and put the bowl behind the water-butt and the stem under the house. Mother was coming round for a dipper of water. I got out of her way quick, for I hadn't time to look innocent; but the bowl of the pipe was hot and she got a whiff of it. She went sniffing round, first on one side of the cask and then on the other, until she got on the scent and followed it up and found the bowl. Then I had only the stem left. She looked for that, but she couldn't scent it. But I couldn't get much comfort out of that. Have you got the matches?

"Then I gave it best for a time and smoked cigars. They were the safest and most satisfactory under the circumstances, but they cost me two shillings a week, and I couldn't stand it, so I started a pipe again and then Mother gave in at last. God bless her, and God forgive me, and us all—we deserve it. She's been at rest these seventeen long years."

Mitchell reflected.

"And what did your old man do when he found out that you were smoking?" I asked.

"The old man?"

He reflected.

"Well, he seemed to brighten up at first. You see, he was sort of pensioned off by Mother and she kept him pretty well inside his income. . . . Well, he seemed to sort of brighten up—liven up —when he found out that I was smoking."

"Did he? So did my old man, and he livened me up, too. But what did your old man do—what did he say?"

"Well," said Mitchell, very slowly, "about the first thing he did was to ask me for a fill."

He reflected.

"Ah! many a solemn, thoughtful old smoke we had together on the quiet—the old man and me."

He reflected.

"Is your old man dead, Mitchell?" I asked softly.

"Long ago—these twelve years," said Mitchell.

[*1895?*]

BILL, THE VENTRILOQUIAL ROOSTER

"WHEN we were up country on the selection, we had a rooster at our place, named Bill," said Mitchell; "a big mongrel of no particular breed, though the old lady said he was a 'brammer'— and many an argument she had with the old man about it too; she was just as stubborn and obstinate in her opinion as the governor was in his. But, anyway, we called him Bill, and didn't take any particular notice of him till a cousin of some of us came from Sydney on a visit to the country, and stayed at our place because it was cheaper than stopping at a pub. Well, somehow this chap got interested in Bill, and studied him for two or three days, and at last he says:

" 'Why, that rooster's a ventriloquist!'

" 'A what?'

" 'A ventriloquist!'

" 'Go along with yer!'

" 'But he is. I've heard of cases like this before; but this is the first I've come across. Bill's a ventriloquist right enough.'

"Then we remembered that there wasn't another rooster within five miles—our only neighbour, an Irishman named Page, didn't have one at the time—and we'd often heard another cock crow, but didn't think to take any notice of it. We watched Bill, and sure enough he *was* a ventriloquist. The 'ka-cocka' would come all right, but the 'co-ka-koo-oi-oo' seemed to come from a distance. And sometimes the whole crow would go wrong, and come back like an echo that had been lost for a year. Bill would stand on tiptoe, and hold his elbows out, and curve his neck, and go two or three times as if he was swallowing nest-eggs, and nearly break his neck and burst his gizzard; and then there'd be no sound at all where he was—only a cock crowing in the distance.

"And pretty soon we could see that Bill was in great trouble about it himself. You see, he didn't know it was himself—thought it was another rooster challenging him, and he wanted badly to find that other bird. He would get up on the wood-heap, and crow and listen—crow and listen again—crow and listen, and then he'd go up to the top of the paddock, and get up on the stack, and crow and listen there. Then down to the other end of the paddock, and get up on a mullock-heap, and crow and listen there. Then across to the other side and up on a log among the saplings, and crow 'n' listen some more. He searched all over the place for that other rooster, but, of course, couldn't find him. Sometimes he'd be out all day crowing and listening all over the country, and then come home dead tired, and rest and cool off in a hole that the hens had scratched for him in a damp place under the water-cask sledge.

"Well, one day Page brought home a big white rooster, and when he let it go it climbed up on Page's stack and crowed, to see if there was any more roosters round there. Bill had come home tired; it was a hot day, and he'd rooted out the hens, and was having a spell-oh under the cask when the white rooster crowed. Bill didn't lose any time getting out and on to the wood-heap, and then he waited till he heard the crow again; then he crowed, and the other rooster crowed again, and they crowed at each other for three days, and called each other all the wretches they could lay their tongues to, and after that they implored each other to come out and be made into chicken soup and feather pillows. But neither'd come. You see, there were *three* crows— there was Bill's crow, and the ventriloquist crow, and the white rooster's crow—and each rooster thought that there was *two* roosters in the opposition camp, and that he mightn't get fair play, and, consequently, both were afraid to put up their hands.

"But at last Bill couldn't stand it any longer. He made up his mind to go and have it out, even if there was a whole agricultural show of prize and honourable-mention fighting-cocks in Page's yard. He got down from the wood-heap and started off across the ploughed field, his head down, his elbows out, and his thick awkward legs prodding away at the furrows behind for all they were worth.

"I wanted to go down badly and see the fight, and barrack for Bill. But I daren't, because I'd been coming up the road late the night before with my brother Joe, and there was about three panels of turkeys roosting along on the top rail of Page's front fence; and we brushed 'em with a bough, and they got up such a blessed gobbling fuss about it that Page came out in his shirt and saw us running away; and I knew he was laying for us with a bullock whip. Besides, there was friction between the two families on account of a thoroughbred bull that Page borrowed and wouldn't lend to us, and that got into our paddock on account of me mending a panel in the party fence and carelessly leaving the top rail down after sundown while our cows was moving round there in the saplings.

"So there was too much friction for me to go down, but I climbed a tree as near the fence as I could and watched. Bill reckoned he'd found that rooster at last. The white rooster wouldn't come down from the stack, so Bill went up to him, and they fought there till they tumbled down the other side, and I couldn't see any more. Wasn't I wild? I'd have given my dog to have seen the rest of the fight. I went down to the far side of Page's fence and climbed a tree there, but, of course, I couldn't see anything, so I came home the back way. Just as I got home Page came round to the front and sung out, 'Insoid there!' And me and Jim went under the house like snakes and looked out round a pile. But Page was all right—he had a broad grin on his face, and Bill safe under his arm. He put Bill down on the ground very carefully, and says he to the old folks:

" 'Yer rooster knocked the stuffin' out of my rooster, but I bear no malice. 'Twas a grand foight.'

"And then the old man and Page had a yarn, and got pretty friendly after that. And Bill didn't seem to bother about any more ventriloquism; but the white rooster spent a lot of time looking for that other rooster. Perhaps he thought he'd have better luck with him. But Page was on the look-out all the time to get a rooster that would lick ours. He did nothing else for a month but ride round and inquire about roosters; and at last he borrowed a game-bird in town, left five pounds deposit on him, and brought him home. And Page and the old man agreed to have a match—about the only thing they'd agreed about for five years. And they fixed it up for a Sunday when the old lady and the girls and kids were going on a visit to some relations, about fifteen miles away—to stop all night. The guv'nor made me go with them on horseback; but I knew what was up, and so my pony went lame about a mile along the road, and I had to come back and turn him out in the top paddock, and hide the saddle and bridle in a hollow log, and sneak home and climb up on the roof of the shed. It was an awful hot day, and I had to keep climbing backward and forward over the ridge-pole all the morning to keep out of sight of the old man, for he was moving about a good deal.

"Well, after dinner, the fellows from round about began to ride in and hang up their horses round the place till it looked as if there was going to be a funeral. Some of the chaps saw me, of course, but I tipped them the wink, and they gave me the office whenever the old man happened around.

"Well, Page came along with his game-rooster. Its name was Jim. It wasn't much to look at, and it seemed a good deal smaller and weaker than Bill. Some of the chaps were disgusted, and said it wasn't a game-rooster at all; Bill'd settle it in one lick, and they wouldn't have any fun.

"Well, they brought the game one out and put him down near the wood-heap, and rousted Bill out from under his cask. He got interested at once. He looked at Jim, and got up on the wood-heap and crowed and looked at Jim again. He reckoned *this* at last was the fowl that had been humbugging him all along. Presently his trouble caught him, and then he'd crow and take a squint at the game 'un, and crow again, and have another squint at gamey, and try to crow and keep his eye on the game-rooster at the same time. But Jim never committed himself, until at last he happened to gape just after Bill's whole crow went wrong, and Bill spotted him. He reckoned he'd caught him this time, and he got down off that wood-heap and went for the foe. But Jim ran away—and Bill ran after him.

"Round and round the wood-heap they went, and round the shed, and round the house and under it, and back again, and round the wood-heap and over it and round the other way, and kept it up for close on an hour. Bill's bill was just within an inch or so of the game-rooster's tail feathers most of the time, but he couldn't get any nearer, do how he liked. And all the time the fellers kept chyackin' Page and singing out, 'What price yer game

'un, Page! Go it, Bill! Go it, old cock!' and all that sort of thing
Well, the game-rooster went as if it was a go-as-you-please, an
he didn't care if it lasted a year. He didn't seem to take an
interest in the business, but Bill got excited, and by-and-by h
got mad. He held his head lower and lower and his wings furthe
and further out from his sides, and prodded away harder an
harder at the ground behind, but it wasn't any use. Jim seeme
to keep ahead without trying. They stuck to the wood-heap toward
the last. They went round first one way for a while, and then th
other for a change, and now and then they'd go over the top t
break the monotony; and the chaps got more interested in th
race than they would have been in the fight—and bet on it, too
But Bill was handicapped with his weight. He was done up a
last; he slowed down till he couldn't waddle, and then, when h
was thoroughly knocked up, that game-rooster turned on him an
gave him the father of a hiding.

"And my father caught me when I'd got down in the excitement
and wasn't thinking, and *he* gave *me* the step-father of a hiding
But he had a lively time with the old lady afterwards, over th
cock-fight.

"Bill was so disgusted with himself that he went under th
cask and died."

[*1893? revised 1899*

THE BLINDNESS OF ONE-EYED BOGAN

"They judge not and they are not judged—'tis their philosophy—
(There's something wrong with every ship that sails upon the sea)."

The Ballad of the Rouseabout

"AND what became of One-eyed Bogan?" I asked Tom Hall whe
I met him and Jack Mitchell down in Sydney with their shearin
cheques the Christmas before last.

"You'd better ask Mitchell, Harry," said Tom. "He can tel
you about Bogan better than I can. But first, what about the drink
we're going to have?"

We turned out of Pitt Street into Hunter Street and across
George Street, where a double line of fast electric tramway wa

running, into Margaret Street and had a drink at Pfahlert's Hotel, where a counter lunch—as good as many dinners you get for a shilling—was included with a sixpenny drink. "Get a quiet corner," said Mitchell, "I like to hear myself cackle." So we took our beer out in the fernery and got a cool place at a little table in a quiet corner amongst the fern boxes.

"Well, One-eyed Bogan was a hard case, Mitchell," I said. "Wasn't he?"

"Yes," said Mitchell, putting down his "long-beer" glass, "he was."

"Rather a bad egg?"

"Yes, a regular bad egg," said Mitchell, decidedly.

"I heard he got caught cheating at cards," I said.

"Did you?" said Mitchell. "Well, I believe he did. Ah, well," he added reflectively, after another long pull, "One-eyed Bogan won't cheat at cards any more."

"Why?" I said. "Is he dead then?"

"No," said Mitchell, "he's blind."

"Good God!" I said, "how did that happen?"

"He lost the other eye," said Mitchell, and he took another drink; "ah, well, he won't cheat at cards any more—unless there's cards invented for the blind."

"How did it happen?" I asked.

"Well," said Mitchell, "you see, Harry, it was this way. Bogan went pretty free in Bourke after the shearing before last, and in the end he got mixed up in a very ugly-looking business: he was accused of doing two new-chum jackeroos out of their stuff by some sort of confidence trick."

"Confidence trick," I said. "I'd never have thought that One-eyed Bogan had the brains to go in for that sort of thing."

"Well, it seems he had, or else he used somebody else's brains; there's plenty of broken-down English gentlemen sharpers knocking about out back, you know, and Bogan might have been taking lessons from one. I don't know the rights of the case: it was hushed up, as you'll see presently; but anyway, the jackeroos swore that Bogan had done 'em out of ten quid. They were both Cockneys and I suppose they reckoned themselves smart, but Bushmen have more time to think. Besides, Bogan's one eye was in his favour. You see, he always kept his one eye fixed strictly on whatever business he had in hand; if he'd had another eye to rove round and distract his attention and look at things on the outside, the chances are he would never have got into trouble."

"Never mind that, Jack," said Tom Hall. "Harry wants to hear the yarn."

"Well, to make it short, one of the jackeroos went to the police and Bogan cleared out. His character was pretty bad just then, so there was a piece of blue paper out for him. Bogan didn't seem to think the thing was so serious as it was, for he only went a few miles down the river and camped with his horses on a sort of island inside an anabranch, till the thing should blow over or the new-chums leave Bourke.

"Bogan's old enemy, Constable Campbell, got wind of Bogan's camp, and started out after him. He rode round the outside track and came in onto the river just below where the anabranch joins it, at the lower end of the island and right opposite Bogan's camp. You know what those billabongs are: dry gullies till the river rises from the Queensland rains and backs them up till the water runs round into the river again and makes anabranches of 'em—places that you thought were hollows you'll find above water, and you can row over places you thought were hills. There's no water so treacherous and deceitful as you'll find in some of those billabongs. A man starts to ride across a place where he thinks the water is just over the grass, and blunders into a deep channel—that wasn't there before—with a steady undercurrent with the whole weight of the Darling River funnelled into it; and if he can't swim and his horse isn't used to it—or sometimes if he can swim—it's a case with him, and the Darling River cod hold an inquest on him, if they have time, before he's buried deep in Darling River mud for ever. And somebody advertises in the missing column for Jack Somebody who was last heard of in Australia."

"Never mind that, Mitchell, go on," I said.

"Well, Campbell knew the river and saw that there was a stiff current there, so he hailed Bogan.

" 'Good day, Campbell,' shouted Bogan.

" 'I want you, Bogan,' said Campbell. 'Come across and bring your horses.'

" 'I'm damned if I will,' says Bogan. 'I'm not going to catch me death o' cold to save your skin. If you want me you'll have to bloody well come and git me.' Bogan was a good strong swimmer, and he had good horses, but he didn't try to get away—I suppose he reckoned he'd have to face the music one time or another—and one time is as good as another out back.

"Campbell was no swimmer; he had no temptation to risk his life—you see it wasn't as in war with a lot of comrades watching ready to advertise a man as a coward for staying alive—so he argued with Bogan and tried to get him to listen to reason, and

swore at him. 'I'll make it damned hot for you, Bogan,' he said,
'if I have to come over for you.'

" 'Two can play at that game,' says Bogan.

" 'Look here, Bogan,' said Campbell, 'I'll tell you what I'll do.
If you give me your word that you'll come up to the police-station
tomorrow I'll go back and say nothing about it. You can say you
didn't know a warrant was out after you. It will be all the better
for you in the end. Better give me your word, man.'

"Perhaps Campbell knew Bogan better than any of us.

" 'Now then, Bogan,' he said, 'don't be a fool. Give your word
like a sensible man, and I'll go back. I'll give you five minutes to
make up your mind.' And he took out his watch.

"But Bogan was nasty and wouldn't give his word, so there was
nothing for it but for Campbell to make a try for him.

"Campbell had plenty of pluck, or obstinacy, which amounts
to the same thing. He put his carbine and revolver under a log,
out of the rain that was coming on, saw to his handcuffs, and then
spurred his horse into the water. Bogan lit his pipe with a stick
from his camp fire—so Campbell said afterwards—and sat down
on his heels and puffed away and waited for him.

"Just as Campbell's horse floundered into the current Bogan
shouted to go back, but Campbell thought it was a threat and
kept on. But Bogan had caught sight of a log coming down the
stream, end on, with a sharp, splintered end, and before Campbell
knew where he was, the sharp end of the log caught the horse in
the flank. The horse started to plunge and struggle sideways, with
all his legs, and Campbell got free of him as quick as he could.
Now, you know, in some of those Darling River reaches the
current will seem to run steadily for a while, and then come with
a rush. (I was caught in one of those rushes once, when I was
in swimming, and would have been drowned if I hadn't been
born to be hanged.) Well, a rush came along just as Campbell got
free from his horse, and he went down stream one side of a snag
and his horse the other. Campbell's pretty stout, you know, and
his uniform was tight, and it handicapped him.

"Just as he was being washed past the lower end of the snag
he caught hold of a branch that stuck out of the water and held on.
He swung round and saw Bogan running down to the point opposite him. Now, you know there was always a lot of low cunning
about Bogan, and I suppose he reckoned that if he pulled Campbell out he'd stand a good show of getting clear of his trouble;
anyway, if he didn't save Campbell it might be said that he killed
him—besides, Bogan was a good swimmer, so there wasn't any
heroism about it anyhow. Campbell was only a few feet from the

bank, but Bogan started to strip—to make the job look as big as
possible, I suppose. He shouted to Campbell to say he was coming,
and to hold on. Campbell said afterwards that Bogan seemed an
hour undressing. The weight of the current was forcing down the
bough that Campbell was hanging on to, and suddenly, he said,
he felt a great feeling of helplessness take him by the shoulders.
He yelled to Bogan and let go.

"Now, it happened that Jake Boreham and I were passing away
the time between shearings, and we were having a sort of fishing
and shooting loaf down the river in a boat arrangement that Jake
had made out of boards and tarred canvas. We called her the
Jolly Coffin. We were just poking up the bank in the slack water,
a few hundred yards below the billabong, when Jake said: 'Why,
there's a horse or something in the river;' then he shouted: 'No,
by God, it's a man,' and we poked the *Coffin* out into the stream
for all she was worth. 'Looks like two men fighting in the water,'
Jake shouts presently. 'Hurry up, or they'll drown each other.'

'We hailed 'em, and Bogan shouted for help. He was treading
water and holding Campbell up in front of him now in real professional style. As soon as he heard us he threw up his arms and
splashed a bit—I reckoned he was trying to put as much style as
he could into that rescue. But I caught a crab, and, before we
could get to them, they were washed past into the top of a tree
that stood well below flood-mark. I pulled the boat's head round
and let her stern down between the branches. Bogan had one arm
over a limb and was holding Campbell with the other, and trying
to lift him higher out of the water. I noticed Bogan's face was
bleeding—there was a dead limb stuck in the tree with nasty
sharp points on it, and I reckoned he'd run his face against one
of them. Campbell was gasping like a codfish out of water, and
he was the whitest man I ever saw (except one, and *he'd* been
drowned for a week). Campbell had the sense to keep still. We
asked Bogan if he could hold on, and he said he could, but he
couldn't hold Campbell any longer. So Jake took the oars and
I leaned over the stern and caught hold of Campbell, and Jake
ran the boat into the bank, and we got him ashore; then we went
back for Bogan and landed him.

"We had some whisky and soon brought Campbell round; but
Bogan was bleeding like a pig from a nasty cut over his good
eye, so we bound wet handkerchiefs round his eyes and led him
to a log and he sat down for a while, holding his hand to his
eye and groaning. He kept saying: 'I'm blind, mates, I'm blind!
I've lost me other eye!' But we didn't dream it was so bad as that:
we kept giving him whisky. We got some dry boughs and made a

big fire. Then Bogan stood up and held his arms stiff down to his sides, opening and shutting his hands as if he was in great pain. And I've often thought since what a different man Bogan seemed without his clothes and with the broken bridge of his nose and his eyes covered by the handkerchiefs. He was clean shaven, and his mouth and chin are his best features, and he's clean limbed and well hung. I often thought afterwards that there was something of a blind god about him as he stood there naked by the fire on the day he saved Campbell's life—something that reminded me of a statue I saw once in the Art Gallery. (Pity the world isn't blinder to a man's worst points.)

"Presently Jake listened and said: 'By God, that's lucky!' and we heard a steamer coming up river and presently we saw her coming round the point with a couple of wool-barges in tow. We got Bogan aboard and got some clothes on him, and took him ashore at Bourke to the new hospital. The doctors did all they knew, but Bogan was blind for life. He never saw anything again —except 'a sort of dull white blur', as he called it—or his past life sometimes, I suppose. Perhaps he saw that for the first time. Ah, well!

"Bogan's old enemy, Barcoo-Rot, went to see him in the hospital, and Bogan said: 'Well, Barcoo, I reckon we've had our last fight. I owe you a hiding, but I don't see how I'm going to pay you.' 'Never mind that, Bogan, old man,' says Barcoo. 'I'll take it from anyone yer likes to appoint, if that worries yer; and, look here, Bogan, if I can't fight you I can fight for you—and don't you forget it!' And Barcoo used to lead Bogan round about town in his spare time and tell him all that was going on; and I believe he always had an ear cocked in case someone said a word against Bogan—as if any of the chaps would say a word against a blind man.

"Bogan's case was hushed up. The police told us to fix it up the best way we could. One of the jackeroos, who reckoned that Bogan had swindled him, was a gentleman, and he was the first to throw a quid in the Giraffe's hat when it went round for Bogan, but the other jackeroo was a cur: he said he wanted the money that Bogan had robbed him of. There were two witnesses, but we sent 'em away, and Tom Hall, there, scared the jackeroo. You know Tom was always the best hand we had at persuading witnesses in union cases to go home to see their mothers."

"How did you scare that jackeroo, Tom?" I asked.

"Tell you about it some other time," said Tom.

"Well," said Mitchell, "Bogan was always a good wool-sorter, so, next shearing, old Baldy Thompson—you know Baldy Thomp-

son, Harry, of West-o'-Sunday Station—Baldy had a talk with
some of the chaps, and took Bogan out in his buggy with him
to West-o'-Sunday. Bogan would sit at the end of the rolling tables,
in the shearing shed, with a boy to hand him the fleeces, and he'd
feel a fleece and tell the boy what bin to throw it into; and
by-and-by he began to learn to throw the fleeces into the bins
himself. And sometimes Baldy would have a sheep brought to him
and get him to feel the fleece and tell him the quality of it. And
then again Baldy would talk, just loud enough for Bogan to
overhear, and swear that he'd sooner have Bogan, blind as he
was, than half-a-dozen scientific jackeroo experts with all their
eyes about them.

"Of course Bogan wasn't worth anything much to Baldy, but
Baldy gave him two pounds a week out of his own pocket, and
another quid that we made up between us; so he made enough
to pull him through the rest of the year.

"It was curious to see how soon he learned to find his way
about the hut and manage his tea and tucker. It was a rough
shed, but everybody was eager to steer Bogan about—and, in
fact, two of them had a fight about it one day. Baldy and all of us
—and especially visitors when they came—were mighty interested
in Bogan; and I reckon we were rather proud of having a blind
wool-sorter. I reckon Bogan had thirty or forty pairs of eyes
watching out for him in case he'd run against something or fall.
It irritated him to be messed round too much—he said a baby
would never learn to walk if it was held all the time. He reckoned
he'd learn more in a year than a man who'd served a lifetime to
blindness; but we didn't let him wander much—for fear he'd fall
into the big rocky water-hole there, by accident.

"And after the shearing season Bogan's wife turned up in
Bourke—"

"Bogan's wife!" I exclaimed. "Why, I never knew Bogan was
married."

"Neither did anyone else," said Mitchell. "But he was. Perhaps
that was what accounted for Bogan. Sometimes, in his sober
moods, I used to have an idea that there must have been something behind the Bogan to account for him. Perhaps he got trapped
—or got married and found out that he'd made a mistake—
which is about the worst thing a man can find out—"

"Except that his wife made the mistake, Mitchell," said Tom
Hall.

"Or that both did," reflected Mitchell. "Ah, well!—never mind—
Bogan had been married two or three years. Maybe he got married
when he was on the spree—I knew that he used to send money

to someone in Sydney and I suppose it was her. Anyway, she turned up after he was blind. She was a hard-looking woman— just the sort that might have kept a third-rate pub or a sly-grog shop. But you can't judge between husband and wife, unless you've lived in the same house with them—and under the same roofs with their parents right back to Adam for that matter. Anyway, she stuck to Bogan all right; she took a little two-roomed cottage and made him comfortable—she's got a sewing-machine and a mangle and takes in washing and sewing. She brought a carroty-headed youngster with her, and the first time I saw Bogan sitting on the verandah with that youngster on his knee I thought it was a good thing that he was blind."

"Why?" I asked.

"Because the youngster isn't his," said Mitchell.

"How do you know that?"

"By the look of it—and by the look on her face, once, when she caught me squinting from the kid's face to Bogan's."

"And whose was it?" I asked, without thinking.

"How am I to know?" said Mitchell. "It might be yours for all I know—it's ugly enough, and you never had any taste in women. But you mustn't speak of that in Bourke. But there's another youngster coming, and I'll swear that'll be Bogan's all right.

"A curious thing about Bogan is that he's begun to be fidgety about his personal appearance—and you know he wasn't a dood. He wears a collar now, and polishes his boots; he wears elastic sides, and polishes 'em himself—the only thing is that he blackens over the elastic. He can do many things for himself, and he's proud of it. He says he can see many things that he couldn't see when he had his eyes. You seldom hear him swear, save in a friendly way; he seems much gentler, but he reckons he would stand a show with Barcoo-Rot even now, if Barcoo would stand up in front of him and keep yelling—"

"By the way," I asked, "how did Bogan lose the sight of his other eye?"

"Sleeping out in the rain when he was drunk," said Mitchell. "He got a cold in his eye." Then he asked, suddenly:

"Did you ever see a blind man cry?"

"No," I said.

"Well, I have," said Mitchell. "You know Bogan wears goggles to hide his eyes—his wife made him do that. The chaps often used to drop round and have a yarn with Bogan and cheer him up, and one evening I was sitting smoking with him, and yarning about old times, when he got very quiet all of a sudden, and I saw a tear drop from under one of his shutters and roll down his cheek. It wasn't the eye he lost saving Campbell—it was the old wall-eye he used to use in the days before he was called 'One-eyed Bogan'. I suppose he thought it was dark and that I couldn't see his face. (There's a good many people in this world who think you can't see because they can't.) It made me feel like I used to feel sometimes in the days when I felt things—"

"Come on, Mitchell," said Tom Hall, "you've had enough beer."

"I think I have," said Mitchell. "Besides, I promised to send a wire to Jake Boreham to tell him that his mother's dead. Jake's shearing at West-o'-Sunday; shearing won't be over for three or four weeks, and Jake wants an excuse to get away without offending old Baldy and come down and have a fly round with us before the holidays are over."

Down at the telegraph-office Mitchell took a form and filled it in very carefully: "Jacob Boreham. West-o'-Sunday Station. Bourke. Come home at once. Mother is dead. In terrible trouble. Father dying.—MARY BOREHAM."

"I think that will do," said Mitchell. "It ought to satisfy Baldy, and it won't give Jake too much of a shock, because he hasn't got a sister or sister-in-law, and his father and mother's been dead over ten years."

"Now, if I was running a theatre," said Mitchell, as we left the office, "I'd give five pounds a night for the face Jake'll have on him when he takes that telegram to Baldy Thompson."

[*1897?   revised 1901, 1907*]

THE HERO OF REDCLAY

THE "boss-over-the-board" was leaning with his back to the wall between two shoots, reading a reference handed to him by a green-hand applying for work as picker-up or wool-roller—a shed rouseabout. It was terribly hot. I was slipping past to the rolling-tables, carrying three fleeces to save a journey; we were only supposed to carry two. The boss stopped me:

"You've got three fleeces there, young man?"

"Yes."

Notwithstanding the fact that I had just slipped a light ragged fleece into the belly-wool and bits basket, I felt deeply injured, and righteously and fiercely indignant at being pulled up. It was a fearfully hot day.

"If I catch you carrying three fleeces again," said the boss quietly, "I'll give you the sack."

"I'll take it now if you like," I said.

He nodded. "You can go on picking-up in this man's place," he said to the jackeroo, whose reference showed him to be a non-union man—a "free-labourer", as the pastoralists had it, or, in plain shed terms, "a blanky scab". He was now in the comfortable position of a non-unionist in a union shed who had jumped into a sacked man's place.

Somehow the lurid sympathy of the men irritated me worse than the boss-over-the-board had done. It must have been on account of the heat, as Mitchell says. I was sick of the shed and the life. It was within a couple of days of cut-out, so I told Mitchell—who was shearing—that I'd camp up the billabong and wait for him; got my cheque, rolled up my swag, got three days' tucker from the cook, said so-long to him, and tramped while the men were in the shed.

I camped at the head of the billabong, where the track branched, one branch running to Bourke, up the river, and the other out towards the Paroo—and Hell.

About ten o'clock the third morning Mitchell came along with his cheque, and his swag, and a new sheep-pup, and his quiet grin; and I wasn't too pleased to see that he had a shearer called "the Lachlan" with him.

The Lachlan wasn't popular at the shed. He was a brooding, unsociable sort of man, and it didn't make any difference to the chaps whether he had a union ticket or not. It was pretty well known in the shed—there were three or four chaps from the district he was reared in—that he'd done five years' hard for burglary. What surprised me was that Jack Mitchell seemed thick with him: often, when the Lachlan was sitting brooding and smoking by himself outside the hut after sunset, Mitchell would perch on his heels alongside him and yarn. But no one else took notice of anything Mitchell did out of the common.

"Better camp with us till the cool of the evening," said Mitchell to the Lachlan, as they slipped their swags. "Plenty time for you to start after sundown, if you're going to travel to-night."

So the Lachlan was going to travel all night and on a different track. I felt more comfortable, and put the billy on. I did not care so much what he'd been or had done, but I was green and soft yet, and his presence embarrassed me.

They talked shearing, sheds, tracks, and a little unionism—the Lachlan speaking in a quiet voice and with a lot of sound, common sense, it seemed to me. He was tall and gaunt, and might have been thirty, or even well on in the forties. His eyes were dark brown and deep set, and had something of the dead-earnest sad expression you saw in the eyes of union leaders and secretaries—the straight men of the strikes of '90 and '91. I fancied once or twice I saw in his eyes the sudden furtive look of the "bad egg" when a mounted trooper is spotted near the shed; but perhaps this was prejudice. And with it all there was about the Lachlan something of the man who has lost all he had and the chances of all he was ever likely to have, and is past feeling or caring, or flaring up—past getting mad about anything—something, all the same, that warned men not to make free with him.

He and Mitchell fished along the billabong all the afternoon; I fished a little, and lay about the camp and read. I had an instinct that the Lachlan saw I didn't cotton on to his camping with us, though he wasn't the sort of man to show what he saw or felt. After tea, and a smoke at sunset, he shouldered his swag, nodded to me as if I was an accidental but respectful stranger at a funeral that belonged to him, and took the outside track. Mitchell walked along the track with him for a mile or so, while I poked round and got some boughs down for a bed, and fed and studied the collie pup that Jack had bought from the shearers' cook.

I saw them stop and shake hands out on the dusty clearing, and they seemed to take a long time about it; then Mitchell started back, and the other began to dwindle down to a black peg and then to a dot on the sandy plain that had just a hint of dusk and dreamy far-away gloaming on it between the change from glaring day to hard, bare, broad moonlight.

I thought Mitchell was sulky, or had got the blues, when he came back; he lay on his elbow smoking, with his face turned from the camp towards the plain. After a bit I got wild—if Mitchell was going to go on like that he might as well have taken his swag and gone with the Lachlan. I don't know exactly what was the matter with me that day, but at last I made up my mind to bring the thing to a head.

"You seem mighty thick with the Lachlan," I said.

"Well, what's the matter with that?" asked Mitchell. "It ain't the first felon I've been on speaking terms with. I borrowed half-a-caser off a murderer once, when I was in a hole and had no one else to go to; and the murderer hadn't served his time, neither. I've got nothing against the Lachlan, except that he's a white man and bears a faint family resemblance to a certain branch of my tribe."

I rolled out my swag on the boughs, got my pipe, tobacco, and matches handy in the crown of a spare hat, and lay down.

Mitchell got up, relit his pipe at the fire, and mooned round for a while, with his hands behind him, kicking sticks out of the road, looking out over the plain, down along the billabong, and up through the mulga branches at the stars; then he comforted the pup a bit, shoved the fire together with his toe, stood the tea-billy on the coals, and came and squatted on the sand by my head.

"Joe! I'll tell you a yarn."

"All right; fire away! Has it got anything to do with the Lachlan?"

"No. It's got nothing to do with the Lachlan now; but it's about a chap he knew. Don't you ever breathe a word of this to the Lachlan or anyone, or he'll get on to me."

"All right. Go ahead."

"You know I've been a good many things in my time. I did a deal of house-painting at one time; I was a pretty smart brush hand and made money at it. Well, I had a run of work at a place called Redclay, on the Lachlan side. You know the sort of town—two pubs, a general store, a post-office, a blacksmith's shop, a police-station, a branch bank, and a dozen private weatherboard boxes on piles, with galvanized-iron tops, besides the humpies. There was a paper there, too, called the *Redclay Advertiser* (with which was incorporated the *Geebung Chronicle*), and a Roman Catholic Church, a Church of England, and a Wesleyan chapel. Now, you see more of private life in the house-painting line than in any other—bar plumbing and gasfitting; but I'll tell you about my house-painting experiences some other time.

"There was a young chap named Jack Drew editing the *Advertiser* then. He belonged to the district, but had been sent to Sydney to a grammar-school when he was a boy. He was between twenty-five and thirty; had knocked round a good deal, and gone the pace in Sydney. He got on as a boy reporter on one of the big dailies; he had brains, and could write rings round a good many, but he got in with a crowd that called themselves 'Bohemians', and the drink got a hold on him. The paper stuck to him as long as it could, for the sake of his brains, but they had to sack him at last.

"He went out back, as most of them do, to try and work out

their salvation, and knocked round amongst the sheds. He 'picked-up' in one shed where I was shearing, and we carried swags together for a couple of months. Then he went back to the Lachlan side and prospected amongst the old fields round there with his elder brother Tom, who was all there was left of his family. Tom, by the way, broke his heart digging Jack out of a cave in a drive they were working, and died a few minutes after the rescue. But that's another yarn. Jack Drew had a bad spree after that; then he went to Sydney again, got on his old paper, went to the dogs, and a Parliamentary push that owned some city fly-blisters and country papers sent him up to edit the *Advertiser* at two quid a week. He drank again, and no wonder—you don't know what it is to run a *Geebung Advocate* or *Mudgee Budgee Chronicle*, and live there. He was about the same build as the Lachlan, but stouter, and had something the same kind of eyes; but he was ordinarily as careless and devil-may-care as the Lachlan is grumpy and quiet.

"There was a doctor there, called Dr Lebinski. They said he was a Polish exile. He was fifty or sixty, a tall man, with the set of an old soldier when he stood straight; but he mostly walked with his hands behind him, studying the ground. Jack Drew caught that trick off him towards the end. They were chums in a gloomy way, and kept to themselves—they were the only two men with brains in that town. They drank and fought the drink together. The Doctor was too gloomy and impatient over little things to be popular. Jack Drew talked too straight in the paper, and in spite of his proprietors, about pub spieling and such things—and was too sarcastic in his progress committee, town council, and toady reception reports. The Doctor had a hawk's nose, pointed grizzled beard and moustache, and steely-grey eyes with a haunted look in them sometimes (especially when he glanced at you sideways), as if he loathed his fellow-men, and couldn't always hide it; or as if you were the spirit of morphia or opium, or a dead girl he'd wronged in his youth—or whatever his devil was, beside drink. He was clever, and drink had brought him down to Redclay.

"The bank manager was a heavy snob named Browne. He complained of being a bit dull of hearing in one ear—after you'd yelled at him three or four times; sometimes I've thought he was as deaf as a book-keeper in both. He had a wife and youngsters, but they were away on a visit while I was working at Redclay. His niece—or, rather, his wife's niece—a girl named Ruth Wilson, did the housekeeping. She was an orphan, adopted by her aunt, and was general slavey and scapegoat to the family—especially to the brats, as is often the case. She was rather pretty, and lady-like, and kept to herself. The women and girls called her Miss

Wilson, and didn't like her. Most of the single men—and some of the married ones, perhaps—were gone on her, but hadn't the brains or the pluck to bear up and try their luck. I was gone worse than any, I think, but had too much experience or common sense. She was very good to me—used to hand me out cups of tea and plates of sandwiches, or bread and butter, or cake, mornings and afternoons the whole time I was painting the bank. The Doctor had known her people, and was very kind to her. She was about the only woman—for she was more woman than girl—that he'd brighten up and talk for. Neither he nor Jack Drew were particularly friendly with Browne or his push.

"The banker, the storekeeper, one of the publicans, the butcher (a popular man with his hands in his pockets, his hat on the back of his head, and nothing in it), the postmaster, and his toady, the lightning squirter, were the scrub-aristocracy. The rest were crawlers mostly, pub spielers and bush larrikins, and the women were hags and larrikinesses. The town lived on cheque-men from the surrounding bush. It was a nice little place, taking it all round.

"I remember a ball at the local town hall, where the scrub-aristocrats took one end of the room to dance in and the ordinary scum the other. It was a saving in music. Some day an Australian writer will come along who'll remind the critics and readers of Dickens, Carlyle, and Thackeray mixed, and he'll do justice to these little customs of ours in the little settled-district towns of Democratic Australia. This sort of thing came to a head one New Year's Night at Redclay, when there was a 'public' ball and peace on earth and goodwill towards all men—mostly on account of a railway to Redclay being surveyed. We were all there. They'd got the Doc. out of his shell to act as M.C.

"One of the aristocrats was the daughter of the local store-keeper; she belonged to the lawn-tennis clique, and they *were* select. For some reason or other—because she looked upon Miss Wilson as a slavey, or on account of a fancied slight, or the heat working on ignorance, or on account of something that comes over girls and women that no son of sin can account for—this Miss Tea-'n'-sugar tossed her head and refused Miss Wilson's hand in the first set, and so broke the ladies' chain and the dance. Then there was a to-do. The Doctor held up his hand to stop the music, and said, very quietly, that he must call upon Miss So-and-so to apologize to Miss Wilson—or resign the chair. After a lot of fuss the girl did apologize in a snappy way that was another insult. Jack Drew gave Miss Wilson his arm and marched her off without a word—I saw she was almost crying. Someone said: 'Oh, let's go on with the dance.' The Doctor flashed round on them, but they were too paltry for him, so he turned on his heel and went out without a word. But I was beneath them again in social standing, so there was nothing to prevent me from making a few well-chosen remarks on things in general—which I did; and broke up that ball, and broke some heads afterwards, and got myself a good deal of hatred and respect, and two sweethearts; and lost all the jobs I was likely to get, except at the bank, the Doctor's, and the Royal.

"One day it was raining—general rain for a week. Rain, rain, rain, over ridge and scrub and galvanized iron, and into the dismal creeks. I'd done all my inside work, except a bit under the Doctor's verandah, where he'd been having some patching and altering done round the glass doors of his surgery, where he consulted his patients. I didn't want to lose time. It was a Monday and no day for the Royal, and there was no dust, so it was a good day for varnishing. I took a pot and brush and went along to give the Doctor's doors a coat of varnish. The Doctor and Drew were inside with a fire, drinking whisky and smoking, but I didn't know that when I started work. The rain roared on the iron roof like the sea. All of a sudden it held up for a minute, and I heard their voices. The Doctor had been shouting on account of the rain, and forgot to lower his voice. 'Look here, Jack Drew,' he said, 'there are only two things for you to do if you have any regard for that girl; one is to stop this' (the liquor I suppose he meant) 'and pull yourself together; and I don't think you'll do that—I know men. The other is to throw up the *Advertiser*—it's doing you no good—and clear out.' 'I won't do that,' says Drew. 'Then shoot yourself,' said the Doctor. '(There's another flask in the cupboard.) You know what this hole is like. . . . She's a good true girl—a girl as God made her. I knew her father and mother, and I tell you, Jack, I'd sooner see her dead than . . .' The roof roared again. I felt a bit delicate about the business and didn't like to disturb them, so I knocked off for the day.

"About a week before that I was down in the bed of the Redclay Creek fishing for 'tailers'. I'd been getting on all right with the housemaid at the Royal—she used to have plates of pudding and hot pie for me on the big gridiron arrangement over the kitchen range; and after the third tuck-out I thought it was good enough to do a bit of a bear-up in that direction. She mentioned one day, yarning, that she liked a stroll by the creek sometimes in the cool of the evening. I thought she'd be off that day, so I said I'd go for a fish after I'd knocked off. I thought I might get a bite. Anyway, I didn't catch Lizzie—tell you about that some other time.

"It was Sunday. I'd been fishing for Lizzie about an hour, when I saw a skirt on the bank out of the tail of my eye—and thought I'd got a bite, sure. But I was had. It was Miss Wilson, strolling along the bank in the sunset all by her pretty self. She was a slight girl, not very tall, with reddish frizzled hair, grey eyes, and small pretty features. She spoke as if she had more brains than the average, and had been better educated. Jack Drew was the only young man in Redclay she could talk to, or who could talk to a girl like her; and that was the whole trouble in a nutshell. The newspaper office was next to the bank, and I'd seen her hand cups of tea and cocoa over the fence to his office window more than once, and sometimes they yarned for a while.

"She said: 'Good morning, Mr Mitchell.'

"I said: 'Good morning, Miss.'

"There's some girls I can't talk to like I'd talk to other girls. She asked me if I'd caught any fish, and I said: 'No, Miss.' She asked me if it wasn't me down there fishing with Mr Drew the other evening, and I said: 'Yes—it was me.' Then presently she asked me straight if he was fishing down the creek that afternoon. I guessed they'd been down fishing for each other before. I said: 'No, I thought he was out of town.' I knew he was pretty bad at the Royal. I asked her if she'd like to have a try with my line, but she said No, thanks, she must be going; and she went off up the creek. I reckoned Jack Drew had got a bite and landed her. I felt a bit sorry for her, too.

"The next Saturday evening after the rainy Monday at the Doctor's, I went down to fish for tailers—and Lizzie. I went down under the banks to where there was a big she-oak stump half in the water, going quietly, with an idea of not frightening the fish. I was just unwinding the line from my rod when I noticed the end of another rod sticking out from the other side of the stump; and while I watched it was dropped into the water. Then I heard a murmur, and craned my neck round the back of the stump to see who it was. I saw the back view of Jack Drew and Miss Wilson; he had his arm round her waist, and her head was on his shoulder. She said: 'I *will* trust you Jack—I know you'll give up the drink for my sake. And I'll help you, and we'll be so happy!' or words in that direction. A thunderstorm was coming on. The sky had darkened up with a great blue-black storm-cloud rushing over, and they hadn't noticed it. I didn't mind, and the fish bit best in a storm. But just as she said 'happy' came a blinding flash and a crash that shook the ridges, and the first drops came peltering down. They jumped up and climbed the bank, while I perched on the she-oak roots over the water to be out of sight as they

passed. Half-way to the town I saw them standing in the shelter
of an old stone chimney that stood alone. He had his overcoat
round her and was sheltering her from the wind. . . .

"Smoke-oh, Joe. The tea's stewing."

Mitchell got up, stretched himself, and brought the billy and
pint-pots to the head of my camp. The moon had grown misty.
The plain horizon had closed in. A couple of boughs, hanging
from the gnarled and blasted timber over the billabong, were the
perfect shapes of two men hanging side by side. Mitchell scratched
the back of his neck and looked down at the pup curled like a
glob of mud on the sand in the moonlight, and an idea struck him.
He got a big old felt hat he had, lifted his pup, nose to tail, fitted
it in the hat, shook it down, holding the hat by the brim, and
stood the hat near the head of his doss, out of the moonlight.
"He might get moonstruck," said Mitchell, "and I don't want
that pup to be a genius." The pup seemed perfectly satisfied with
this new arrangement.

"Have a smoke," said Mitchell. "You see," he added, with a
sly grin, "I've got to make up the yarn as I go along, and it's
hard work. It seems to begin to remind me of yarns your grandmother or aunt tells of things that happened when she was a girl—
but those yarns are true. You won't have to listen long now; I'm
well on into the second volume.

"After the storm I hurried home to the tent—I was batching
with a carpenter. I changed my clothes, made a fire in the fire-
bucket with shavings and ends of soft wood, boiled the billy, and
had a cup of coffee. It was Saturday night. My mate was at the
Royal; it was cold and dismal in the tent, and there was nothing
to read, so I reckoned I might as well go up to the Royal, too,
and put in the time.

"I had to pass the bank on the way. It was the usual weatherboard box with a galvanized-iron top—four rooms and a passage,
with a detached kitchen and wash-house at the back. The front
room to the right was the office, behind that was the family bedroom; the front room to the left was Miss Wilson's bedroom, and
behind that was the living-room. The *Advertiser* office was next
door. Jack Drew camped in a skillion room behind his printing-
office, and had his meals at the Royal. I noticed the storm had
taken a sheet of iron off the skillion, and supposed he'd sleep at
the Royal that night. Next to the *Advertiser* office was the police-
station and the court-house. Next was the Imperial Hotel where
the scrub-aristocrats went. There was a vacant allotment on the
other side of the bank, and I took a short cut across this to the
Royal.

"They'd forgotten to pull down the blind of the dining-room window, and I happened to glance through and saw she had Jack Drew in there and was giving him a cup of tea. He had a bad cold, I remember, and I suppose his health had got precious to her, poor girl. As I glanced, she stepped to the window and pulled down the blind, which put me out of face a bit—though, of course, she hadn't seen me. I was rather surprised at her having Jack in there, till I heard that the banker, the postmaster, the constable, and some others were making a night of it at the Imperial, as they'd been doing pretty often lately—and went on doing till there was a blow-up about it, and the constable got transferred out back. I used to drink my share then. We smoked and played cards and yarned and filled 'em up again at the Royal till after one in the morning. Then I started home.

"I'd finished giving the bank a couple of coats of stone-colour that week, and was cutting in in dark colour round the spouting, doors, and window-frames that Saturday. My head was pretty clear going home, and as I passed the place it struck me that I'd left out the only varnish brush I had. I'd been using it to give the sashes a coat of varnish colour, and remembered that I'd left it on one of the window-sills—the sill of her bedroom window, as it happened. I knew I'd sleep in next day, Sunday, and guessed it would be hot, and I didn't want the varnish tool to get spoiled; so I reckoned I'd slip in through the side gate, get it, and take it home to camp and put it in oil. The window sash was jammed, I remember, and I hadn't been able to get it up more than a couple of inches to paint the runs of the sash. The grass grew up close under the window, and I slipped in quietly. I noticed the sash was still up a couple of inches. Just as I grabbed the brush I heard low voices inside—Ruth Wilson's and Jack Drew's—in her room.

"The surprise sent about a pint of beer up into my throat in a lump. I tiptoed away out of there. Just as I got clear of the gate I saw the banker being helped home by a couple of cronies.

"I went home to the camp and turned in, but I couldn't sleep. I lay think—think—thinking, till I thought all the drink out of my head. I'd brought a bottle of ale home to last over Sunday, and I drank that. It only made matters worse. I didn't know how I felt—I—well, I felt as if I was as good a man as Jack Drew— I—you see, Joe—you might think it soft—but I loved that girl, not as I've been gone on other girls, but in the old-fashioned, soft, honest, hopeless, far-away sort of way; and now, to tell the straight truth, I thought I might have had her. You lose a thing through being too straight or sentimental, or not having enough cheek; and another man comes along with more brass in his blood and less sentimental rot, and takes it up—and the world respects him, and you feel in your heart that you're a weaker man than he is. Why, part of the time I must have felt like a man does when a better man runs away with his wife. But I'd drunk a lot, and was upset and lonely-feeling that night.

"Oh, but Redclay had a tremendous sensation next day! Jack Drew, of all the men in the world, had been caught in the act of robbing the bank. According to Browne's account in court and in the newspapers, he returned home that night at about twelve o'clock (which I knew was a lie, for I saw him being helped home nearer two), and immediately retired to rest (on top of the quilt, boots and all, I suppose). Some time before daybreak he was roused by a fancied noise (I suppose it was his head swelling); he rose, turned up a night lamp (he hadn't lit it, I'll swear), and went through the dining-room passage and office to investigate (for whisky and water). He saw that the doors and windows were secure, returned to bed, and fell asleep again.

"There is something in a deaf person's being roused easily. I know the case of a deaf chap who'd start up at a step or movement in the house when no one else could hear or feel it; keen sense of vibration, I reckon. Well, just at daybreak (to shorten the yarn) the banker woke suddenly, he said, and heard a crack like a shot in the house. There was a loose flooring-board in the passage that went off like a pistol-shot sometimes when you trod on it; and I guess Jack Drew trod on it, sneaking out, and he weighed nearly twelve stone. If the truth were known, he probably heard Browne poking round, tried the window, found the sash jammed, and was slipping through the passage to the back door. Browne got his revolver, opened his door suddenly, and caught Drew standing between the girl's door (which was shut) and the office door, with his coat on his arm and his boots in his hands. Browne covered him with his revolver, swore he'd shoot if he moved, and yelled for help. Drew stood a moment like a man stunned; then he rushed Browne, and in the struggle the revolver went off, and Drew got hit in the arm. Two of the mounted troopers —who'd been up looking to the horses for an early start somewhere—rushed in then and took Drew. He had nothing to say. What could he say? He couldn't say he was a blackguard who'd taken advantage of a poor unprotected girl because she loved him. They found the back door unlocked, by the way, which was put down to the burglar; of course Browne couldn't explain that he came home too muddled to lock doors after him.

"And the girl? She shrieked and fell when the row started, and they found her like a log on the floor of her room after it was over.

"They found in Jack's overcoat pocket a parcel containing a cold chisel, small screw-wrench, file, and one or two other things that he'd bought that evening to tinker up the old printing-press. I knew that, because I'd lent him a hand a few nights before, and he told me he'd have to get the tools. They found some scratches round the key-hole and knob of the office door that I'd made myself, scraping old splashes of paint off the brass and hand-plate, so as to make a clean finish. Oh, it taught me the value of circumstantial evidence! If I was judge, I wouldn't give a man till the 'risin' av the coort' on it, any more than I would on the bare word of the noblest woman breathing.

"At the preliminary examination Jack Drew said he was guilty. But it seemed that, according to law, he couldn't be guilty until after he was committed. So he was committed for trial at the next Quarter Sessions. The excitement and gabble were worse than the Dean case, or Federation, and sickened me, for they were all on the wrong track. You lose a lot of life through being behind the scenes. But they cooled down presently to wait for the trial.

"They thought it best to take the girl away from the place where she'd got the shock; so the Doctor took her to his house, where he had an old housekeeper who was as deaf as a post—a first-class recommendation for a housekeeper anywhere. He got a nurse from Sydney to attend on Ruth Wilson, and no one except he and the nurse were allowed to go near her. She lay like dead, they said, except when she had to be held down raving; brain fever, they said, brought on by the shock of the attempted burglary and pistol-shot. Dr Lebinski had another doctor up from Sydney at his own expense, but nothing could save her—and perhaps it was as well. She might have finished her life in a lunatic asylum. They were going to send her to Sydney, to a brain hospital; but she died a week before the Sessions. She was right-headed for an hour, they said, and asking all the time for Jack. The Doctor told her he was all right and was coming—and, waiting and listening for him, she died.

"The case was black enough against Drew now. I knew he wouldn't have the pluck to tell the truth now, even if he was that sort of a man. I didn't know what to do, so I spoke to the Doctor straight. I caught him coming out of the Royal, and walked along the road with him a bit. I suppose he thought I was going to show cause why his doors ought to have another coat of varnish.

" 'Hallo, Mitchell!' he said, 'how's painting?'

" 'Doctor!' I said, 'what am I going to do about this business?'

" 'What business?'

" 'Jack Drew's.'

"He looked at me sideways—the swift haunted look. Then he walked on without a word, for half-a-dozen yards, hands behind, and studying the dust. Then he asked, quite quietly:

" 'Do you know the truth?'

" 'Yes.'

"About a dozen yards this time, then he said:

" 'I'll see him in the morning, and see you afterwards,' and he shook hands and went on home.

"Next day he came to me where I was doing a job on a step ladder. He leaned his elbow against the steps for a moment, and rubbed his hand over his forehead as if it ached and he was tired.

" 'I've seen him, Mitchell,' he said.

" 'Yes.'

" 'You were mates with him once out back?'

" 'I was.'

" 'You know Drew's handwriting?'

" 'I should think so.'

"He laid a leaf from a pocket-book on top of the steps. I read the message written in pencil:

"*To Jack Mitchell.—We were mates on the track. If you know anything of my affair, don't give it away.—J.D.*

"I tore the leaf and dropped the bits into the paint-pot.

" 'That's all right,' Doctor,' I said; 'but is there no way?'

" 'None.'

"He turned away, wearily. He'd knocked about so much over the world that he was past bothering about explaining things or being surprised at anything. But he seemed to get a new idea about me; he came back to the steps again, and watched my brush for a while, as if he was thinking, in a broody sort of way, of throwing up his practice and going in for house-painting. Then he said, slowly and deliberately:

" 'If she—the girl—had lived, we might have tried to fix it up quietly. That's what I was hoping for. I don't see how we can help him now, even if he'd let us. He would never have spoken, anyway. We must let it go on, and after the trial I'll go to Sydney and see what I can do at headquarters. It's too late now. You understand, Mitchell?'

" 'Yes. I've thought it out.'

"Then he went away towards the Royal.

"And what could Jack Drew or we do? Study it out whatever way you like. There was only one possible chance to help him, and that was to go to the judge; and the judge that happened to be on that circuit was a man who—even if he did listen to the true story and believe it—would have felt inclined to give Jack all the more for what he was charged with. Browne was out of the question. The day before the trial I went for a long walk in the bush, but couldn't hit on anything that the Doctor might have missed.

"I was in the court—I couldn't keep away. The Doctor was there too. There wasn't so much of a change in Jack as I expected; only he had the jail white in his face already. He stood fingering the rail, as if it was the edge of a table on a platform and he was a tired and bored and sleepy chairman waiting to propose a vote of thanks."

The only well-known man in Australia who reminds me of Mitchell is Bland Holt, the comedian. Mitchell was about as good-hearted as Bland Holt, too, under it all; but he was bigger and roughened by the bush. But he seemed to be taking a heavy part to-night, for, towards the end of his yarn, he got up and walked up and down the length of my bed, dropping the sentences as he turned towards me. He'd folded his arms high and tight, and his face in the moonlight was—well, it was very different from his careless tone of voice. He was like—like an actor acting tragedy and talking comedy. Mitchell went on, speaking quickly—his voice seeming to harden:

"The charge was read out—I forget how it went—it sounded like a long hymn being given out. Jack pleaded guilty. Then he straightened up for the first time and looked round the court, with a calm, disinterested look—as if we were all strangers, and he was noting the size of the meeting. And—it's a funny world, ain't it?—every one of us shifted or dropped his eyes, just as if we were the felons and Jack the judge. Everyone except the Doctor; he looked at Jack and Jack looked at him. Then the Doctor smiled—I can't describe it—and Drew smiled back. It struck me afterwards that I should have been in that smile. Then the Doctor did what looked like a strange thing—stood like a soldier with his hands to attention. I'd noticed that, whenever he'd made up his mind to do a thing, he dropped his hands to his sides: it was a sign that he couldn't be moved. Now he slowly lifted his hand to his forehead, palm out, saluted the prisoner, turned on his heel, and marched from the court-room. 'He's boozin' again,' someone whispered. 'He's got a touch of 'em.' 'My oath, he's ratty!' said someone else. One of the traps said:

" 'Arder in the car-rt!'

"The judge gave it to Drew red-hot on account of the burglary being the cause of the girl's death and the sorrow in a respectable family; then he gave him five years' hard.

"It gave me a lot of confidence in myself to see the law of the land barking up the wrong tree, while only I and the Doctor and the prisoner knew it. But I've found out since then that the law is often the only one that knows it's barking up the wrong tree."

.   .   .

Mitchell prepared to turn in.

"And what about Drew?" I asked.

"Oh, he did his time, or most of it. The Doctor went to head-quarters, but either a drunken doctor from a geebung town wasn't of much account, or they weren't taking any romance just then at headquarters. So the Doctor came back, drank heavily, and one frosty morning they found him on his back on the bank of the creek, with his face like note-paper where the blood hadn't dried on it, and an old pistol in his hand—that he'd used, they said, to shoot Cossacks from horseback when he was a young dude fighting in the bush in Poland."

Mitchell lay silent a good while; then he yawned.

"Ah, well! It's a lonely track the Lachlan's tramping to-night; but I s'pose he's got his ghosts with him."

I'd been puzzling for the last half-hour to think where I'd met or heard of Jack Drew; now it flashed on me that I'd been told that Jack Drew was the Lachlan's real name.

I lay awake thinking a long time, and wished Mitchell had kept his yarn for daytime. I felt—well, I felt as if the Lachlan's story should have been played in the biggest theatre in the world, by the greatest actors, with music for the intervals and situations—deep, strong music, such as thrills and lifts a man from his boot soles. And when I got to sleep I hadn't slept a moment, it seemed to me, when I started wide awake to see those infernal hanging boughs with a sort of nightmare idea that the Lachlan hadn't gone, or had come back, and he and Mitchell had hanged themselves sociably—Mitchell for sympathy and the sake of mateship.

But Mitchell was sleeping peacefully, in spite of a path of moonlight across his face—and so was the pup.

[1896-9   revised 1900]

THE BOOZERS' HOME

"A DIPSOMANIAC," said Mitchell, "needs sympathy and common-sense treatment. (Sympathy's a grand and glorious thing, taking it all round and looking at it any way you will: a little of it makes a man think that the world's a good world after all, and there's room and hope for sinners, and that life's worth living; enough of it makes him sure of it: and an overdose of sympathy makes a man *feel* weak and ashamed of himself, and so moves him to stop whining—and wining—and buck up.)

"Now, I'm not taking the case of a workman who goes on the spree on pay night and sweats the drink out of himself at work next day, nor a slum-bred brute who guzzles for the love of it; but a man with brains, who drinks to drown his intellect or his memory. He's generally a man under it all, and a sensitive, generous, gentle man with finer feelings as often as not. The best and cleverest and whitest men in the world seem to take to drink mostly. It's an awful pity. Perhaps it's because they're straight and the world's crooked and they can see things too plain. And I suppose in the Bush the loneliness and the thoughts of the girl-world they left behind help to sink 'em.

"Now a drunkard seldom reforms at home, because he's always surrounded by the signs of the ruin and misery he has brought on the home; and the sight and thought of it sets him off again before he's had time to recover from the last spree. Then, again, the noblest wife in the world mostly goes the wrong way to work with a drunken husband—nearly everything she does is calculated to irritate him. If, for instance, he brings a bottle home from the pub, it shows that he wants to stay at home and not go back to the pub any more; but the first thing the wife does is to get hold of the bottle and plant it, or smash it before his eyes, and that maddens him in the state he is in then.

"No. A dipsomaniac needs to be taken away from home for a while. I knew a man that got so bad that the way he acted at home one night frightened him, and next morning he went into an inebriate home of his own accord—to a place where his friends had been trying to get him for a year past. For the first day or two he was nearly dead with remorse and shame—mostly shame; and he didn't know what they were going to do to him next—he only wanted them to kill him quick and be done with it. He reckons he felt as bad as if he was in jail. But there were ten other patients there, and one or two were worse than he was, and that comforted him a lot. They compared notes and sympathized and helped each other. They discovered that all their wives were noble women. He struck one or two surprises too—one of the patients was a doctor who'd attended him one time, and another was an old boss of his, and they got very chummy. And there was a man there who was standing for Parliament—he was supposed to be having a rest down the coast. . . . Yes, my old mate felt very bad for the first day or two; it was all Yes, Nurse, and Thank you, Nurse, and Yes, Doctor, and No, Doctor, and Thank you, Doctor. But, inside a week, he was calling the doctor 'Ol' Pill-Box' behind his back, and making love to one of the nurses.

"But he said it was pitiful when women relatives came to visit patients the first morning. It shook the patients up a lot, but I reckon it did 'em good. There were well-bred old lady mothers in black, and hard-working, haggard wives and loving daughters— and the expressions of sympathy and faith and hope in those women's faces! My old mate said it was enough in itself to make a man swear off drink forever. . . . Ah, God—what a world it is!

"Reminds me how I once went with the wife of another old mate of mine to see him. He was in a lunatic asylum. It was about the worst hour I ever had in my life, and I've had some bad ones. The way she tried to coax him back to his old self. She thought she could do it when all the doctors had failed. But I'll tell you about him some other time.

"The old mate said that the principal part of the treatment was supposed to be injection of bi-chloride of gold or something, and it was supposed to be a secret. It might have been water and sugar for all he knew, and he thought it was. You see, when patients got better they were allowed out, two by two, on their honour—one to watch the other—and it worked. But it was necessary to have an extra hold on them; so they were told that if they were a minute late for 'treatment', or missed one injection, all the good would be undone. This was dinged into their ears all the time. Same as many things are done in the Catholic religion— to hold the people. My old mate said that, as far as the medical treatment was concerned, he could do all that was necessary himself. But it was the sympathy that counted, especially the sympathy between the patients themselves. They always got hold of a new patient and talked to him and cheered him up; he nearly always came in thinking he was the most miserable wretch in this world. And it comforts a man and strengthens him and makes him happier to meet another man who's worse off or sicker, or has been worse swindled than he has been. That's human nature. . . . And a man will take draughts from a nurse and eat for her when he wouldn't do it for his own wife—not even though she had been a trained nurse herself. And if a patient took a bad turn in the night at the Boozers' Home and got up to hunt the snakes out of his room, he wouldn't be sworn at, or laughed at, or held down; no, they'd help him shoo the snakes out and comfort him. My old mate said that, when he got better, one of the new patients reckoned that he licked St Pathrick at managing snakes. And when he came out he didn't feel a bit ashamed of his experience. The institution didn't profess to cure anyone of drink, only to mend up shattered nerves and build up wrecked constitutions; give them back some will power if they weren't too far gone. And they set my old mate on his feet all right. When he went in his life seemed lost, he had the horror of being sober, he couldn't start the day without a drink or do any business without it. He couldn't live for more than two hours without a drink; but when he came out he didn't feel as if he wanted it. He reckoned that those six weeks in the institution were the happiest he'd ever spent in his life, and he wished the time had been longer; he says he'd never met with so much sympathy and genius, and humour and human nature, under one roof before. And he said it was nice and novel to be looked after and watched and physicked and bossed by a pretty nurse in uniform—but I don't suppose he told his wife that. And when he came out he never took the trouble to hide the fact that he'd been in. If any of his friends had a drunkard in the family, he'd recommend the institution and do his best to get him into it. But when he came out he firmly believed that if he took one drink he'd be a lost man. He made a mania of that. One curious effect was that, for some time after he left the institution, he'd sometimes feel suddenly in high spirits—with nothing to account for it—something like he used to feel when he had half a dozen whiskies in him; then suddenly he'd feel depressed and sort of hopeless—with nothing to account for that either—just as if he was suffering a recovery. But those moods never lasted long and he soon grew out of them altogether. He didn't flee temptation. He'd knock round the pubs on Saturday nights with his old mates, but never drank anything but soft stuff—he was always careful to smell his glass for fear of an accident or a trick. He drank gallons of ginger-beer, milk-and-soda and lemonade; and he got very fond of sweets, too—he'd never liked them before. He said he enjoyed the novelty of the whole thing and his mates amused him at first; but he found he had to leave them early in the evening, and, after a while, he dropped them altogether. They seemed such fools when they were drunk (they'd never seemed fools to him before). And, besides, as they got full, they'd get suspicious of him, and then mad at him, because he couldn't see things as they could. That reminds me that it nearly breaks a man's heart when his old drinking chum turns teetotaller—it's worse than if he got married or died. When two mates meet and one is drunk and the other sober there is only one of two things for them to do if they want to hit it together—either the drunken mate must get sober or the sober mate drunk. And that reminds me: Take the case of two old mates who've been together all their lives, say they always had their regular sprees together and went through the same stages of drunkenness together, and suffered their recoveries and sobered up together, and each could stand about the same quantity of drink and one never got drunker than the other. Each, when he's boozing, reckons his mate the cleverest man and the hardest case in the world—second to himself. But one day it happens, by a most extraordinary combination of circumstances, that Bill, being sober, meets Jim very drunk, and pretty soon Bill is the most disgusted man in this world. He never would have dreamed that his old mate could make such a fool and such a public spectacle of himself. And Bill's disgust intensifies all the time he is helping Jim home, and Jim arguing with him and wanting to fight him, and slobbering over him and wanting to love him by turns, until Bill swears he'll give Jim a hammering as soon as ever he's able to stand steady on his feet."

.   .   .

"I suppose your old boozing mate's wife was very happy when he reformed," I said to Mitchell.

"Well, no," said Mitchell, rubbing his head rather ruefully. "I suppose it was an exceptional case. But I knew her well, and the fact is that she got more discontented and thinner, and complained and nagged him worse than she'd ever done in his drinking days. And she'd never been afraid of him. Perhaps it was this way: She loved and married a careless, good-natured, drinking scamp, and when he reformed and became a careful, hard-working man, and an honest and respected fellow-townsman, she was disappointed in him. He wasn't the man that won her heart when she was a girl. Or maybe he was only company for her when he was half drunk. Or maybe lots of things. Perhaps he'd killed the love in her before he reformed—and reformed too late. I wonder how a man feels when he finds out for the first time that his wife doesn't love him any longer? But my old mate wasn't the nature to find out that sort of thing. Ah, well! If a woman caused all our trouble, my God! women have suffered for it since—and they suffer like martyrs mostly and with the patience of working bullocks. Anyway it goes, if I'm the last man in the world, and the last woman is the worst, and there's only room for one more in Heaven, I'll step down at once and take my chance in Blazes."

[1899   revised 1901]

4

THE IRON-BARK CHIP

DAVE REGAN and party—bush fencers, tank-sinkers, rough carpenters, etc.—were finishing the third and last culvert of their contract on the last section of the new railway line, and had already sent in their vouchers for the completed contract, so that there might be no excuse for extra delay in connection with the cheque.

Now it had been expressly stipulated in the plans and specifications that the timber for certain beams and girders was to be iron-bark and no other, and Government inspectors were authorized to order the removal from the ground of any timber or material they might deem inferior, or not in accordance with the stipulations. The railway contractor's foreman and inspector of sub-contractors was a practical man and a bushman, but he had been a timber-getter himself; his sympathies were bushy, and he was on winking terms with Dave Regan. Besides, extended time was expiring, and the contractors were in a hurry to complete the line. But the Government inspector was a reserved man who poked round on his independent own and appeared in lonely spots at unexpected times—with apparently no definite object in life— like a grey kangaroo bothered by a new wire fence, but unsuspicious of the presence of humans. He wore a grey suit, rode, or mostly led, an ashen-grey horse; the grass was long and grey, so he was seldom spotted until he was well within the horizon and bearing leisurely down on a party of sub-contractors, leading his horse.

Now iron-bark was scarce and distant on those ridges, and another timber, similar in appearance but much inferior in grain and "standing" quality, was plentiful and close at hand. Dave and party were "about full of" the job and place, and wanted to get their cheque and be gone to another "spec" they had in view. So they came to reckon they'd get the last girder from a handy tree, and have it squared, in place, and carefully and conscientiously tarred before the inspector happened along, if he did. But they didn't. They got it squared, and ready to be lifted into its place; the kindly darkness of tar was ready to cover a fraud that took four strong men with crow-bars and levers to shift; and now (such is the regular cussedness of things) as the fraudulent piece of timber lay its last hour on the ground, looking and smelling to their guilty imaginations like anything but iron-bark, they were aware of the Government inspector drifting down upon them obliquely, with something of the atmosphere of a casual Bill or Jim who had dropped out of his easy-going track to see how they were getting on, and borrow a match. They had more than half hoped that, as he had visited them pretty frequently during the progress of the work, and knew how near it was to completion, he wouldn't bother coming any more. But it's the way with the Government. You might move heaven and earth in vain endeavour to get the "Govermunt" to flutter an eyelash over something of the most momentous importance to yourself and mates and the district —even to the country; but just when you are leaving authority severely alone, and have strong reasons for not wanting to worry or interrupt it, and not desiring it to worry about you, it will take a fancy into its head to come along and bother.

"It's always the way!" muttered Dave to his mates. "I knew the beggar would turn up! . . . And the only cronk log we've had, too!" he added, in an injured tone. "If this had 'a' been the only blessed iron-bark in the whole contract, it would have been all right. . . . Good-day, sir!" (to the inspector). "It's hot?"

The inspector nodded. He was not of an impulsive nature. He got down from his horse and looked at the girder in an abstracted way; and presently there came into his eyes a dreamy, far-away, sad sort of expression, as if there had been a very sad and painful occurrence in his family, way back in the past, and that piece of timber in some way reminded him of it and brought the old sorrow home to him. He blinked three times, and asked, in a subdued tone:

"Is that iron-bark?"

Jack Bently, the fluent liar of the party, caught his breath with a jerk and coughed, to cover the gasp and gain time. "I—iron-bark? Of course it is! I thought you would know iron-bark, mister." (Mister was silent.) "What else d'yer think it is?"

The dreamy, abstracted expression was back. The inspector, by-the-way, didn't know much about timber, but he had a great deal of instinct, and went by it when in doubt.

"L—look here, mister!" put in Dave Regan, in a tone of innocent puzzlement and with a blank bucolic face. "B—but don't the plans and specifications say iron-bark? Ours does, anyway. I—I'll git the papers from the tent and show yer, if yer like."

It was not necessary. The inspector admitted the fact slowly.

He stooped and with an absent air picked up a chip. He looked at it abstractedly for a moment, blinked his threefold blink; then, seeming to recollect an appointment, he woke up suddenly and asked briskly:

"Did this chip come off that girder?"

Blank silence. The inspector blinked six times, divided in threes, rapidly, mounted his horse, said "Day", and rode off.

Regan and party stared at each other.

"Wha—what did he do that for?" asked Andy Page, the third in the party.

"Do what for, you fool?" inquired Dave.

"Ta—take that chip for?"

"He's taking it to the office!" snarled Jack Bently.

"What—what for? What does he want to do that for?"

"To get it blanky well analysed! You ass! Now are yer satisfied?" And Jack sat down hard on the timber, jerked out his pipe, and said to Dave, in a sharp, toothache tone:

"Gimmiamatch!"

"We—well! what are we to do now?" inquired Andy, who was the hardest grafter, but altogether helpless, hopeless, and useless in a crisis like this.

"Grain and varnish the bloomin' culvert!" snapped Bently.

But Dave's eyes, that had been ruefully following the inspector, suddenly dilated. The inspector had ridden a short distance along the line, dismounted, thrown the bridle over a post, laid the chip (which was too big to go in his pocket) on top of it, got through the fence, and was now walking back at an angle across the line in the direction of the fencing party, who had worked up on the other side, a little more than opposite the culvert.

Dave took in the lay of the country at a glance and thought rapidly.

"Gimme an iron-bark chip!" he said suddenly.

Bently, who was quick-witted when the track was shown him, as is a kangaroo dog (Jack ran by sight, not scent), glanced in the line of Dave's eyes, jumped up, and got a chip about the same size as that which the inspector had taken.

Now the "lay of the country" sloped generally to the line from both sides, and the angle between the inspector's horse, the fencing party, and the culvert was well within a clear concave space; but a couple of hundred yards back from the line and parallel to it (on the side on which Dave's party worked their timber) a fringe of scrub ran to within a few yards of a point which would be about in line with a single tree on the cleared slope, the horse, and the fencing party.

Dave took the iron-bark chip, ran along the bed of the water-course into the scrub, raced up the siding behind the bushes, got safely though without breathing across the exposed space, and brought the tree into line between him and the inspector, who was talking to the fencers. Then he began to work quickly down the slope towards the tree (which was a thin one), keeping it in line, his arms close to his sides, and working, as it were, down the trunk of the tree, as if the fencing party were kangaroos and Dave was trying to get a shot at them. The inspector, by-the-by, had a habit of glancing now and then in the direction of his horse, as though under the impression that it was flighty and restless and inclined to bolt on opportunity. It was an anxious moment for all parties concerned—except the inspector. They didn't want *him* to be perturbed. And, just as Dave reached the foot of the tree, the inspector finished what he had to say to the fencers, turned, and started to walk briskly back to his horse. There was a thunderstorm coming. Now was the critical moment—there were certain pre-arranged signals between Dave's party and the fencers which might have interested the inspector, but none to meet a case like this.

Jack Bently gasped and started forward with an idea of intercepting the inspector and holding him for a few minutes in bogus conversation. Inspirations come to one at a critical moment, and it flashed on Jack's mind to send Andy instead. Andy looked as innocent and guileless as he was, but was uncomfortable in the vicinity of "funny business", and must have an honest excuse. "Not that that mattered," commented Jack afterwards; "it would have taken the inspector ten minutes to get at what Andy was driving at, whatever it was."

"Run, Andy! Tell him there's a heavy thunderstorm coming and he'd better stay in our humpy till it's over. Run! Don't stand staring like a blanky fool. He'll be gone!"

Andy started. But just then, as luck would have it, one of the fencers started after the inspector, hailing him as "Hi, mister!" He wanted to be set right about the survey or something—or to pretend to want to be set right—from motives of policy which I haven't time to explain here.

That fencer explained afterwards to Dave's party that he "seen what you coves was up to", and that's why he called the inspector back. But he told them that after they had told their yarn—which was a mistake.

"Come back, Andy!" cried Jack Bently.

Dave Regan slipped round the tree, down on his hands and knees, and made quick time through the grass which, luckily, grew pretty tall on the thirty or forty yards of slope between the tree and the horse. Close to the horse, a thought struck Dave that pulled him up, and sent a shiver along his spine and a hungry feeling under it. The horse would break away and bolt! But the case was desperate. Dave ventured an interrogatory "Cope, cope, cope?" The horse turned its head wearily and regarded him with a mild eye, as if he'd expected him to come, and come on all fours, and wondered what had kept him so long; then he went on thinking. Dave reached the foot of the post, the horse obligingly leaning over on the other leg. Dave reared head and shoulders cautiously behind the post, like a snake; his hand went up twice, swiftly—the first time he grabbed the inspector's chip, and the second time he put the iron-bark one in its place. He drew down and back, and scuttled off for the tree like a gigantic tailless goanna.

A few minutes later he walked up to the culvert from along the creek, smoking hard to settle his nerves.

The sky seemed to darken suddenly; the first great drops of the thunderstorm came pelting down. The inspector hurried to his horse, and cantered off along the line in the direction of the fettlers' camp.

He had forgotten all about the chip, and left it on top of the post!

Dave Regan sat down on the beam in the rain and swore comprehensively.

.   .   .

But when the rain held they went to work with easy consciences —as comfortable as if the inspector *had* taken the chip.

[*1898-9*]

THE LOADED DOG

DAVE REGAN, Jim Bently, and Andy Page were sinking a shaft at Stony Creek in search of a rich gold quartz reef which was supposed to exist in the vicinity. There is always a rich reef supposed to exist in the vicinity; the only questions are whether it is ten feet or hundreds beneath the surface, and in which direction. They had struck some pretty solid rock, also water which kept them baling. They used the old-fashioned blasting-powder and time-fuse. They'd make a sausage or cartridge of blasting-powder in a skin of strong calico or canvas, the mouth sewn and bound round the end of the fuse; they'd dip the cartridge in melted tallow to make it water-tight, get the drill-hole as dry as possible, drop in the cartridge with some dry dust, and wad and ram with stiff clay and broken brick. Then they'd light the fuse and get out of the hole and wait. The result was usually an ugly pot-hole in the bottom of the shaft and half a barrow-load of broken rock.

There was plenty of fish in the creek, fresh-water bream, cod, cat-fish, and tailers. The party were fond of fish, and Andy and Dave of fishing. Andy would fish for three hours at a stretch if encouraged by a "nibble" or a "bite" now and then—say once in twenty minutes. The butcher was always willing to give meat in exchange for fish when they caught more than they could eat; but now it was winter, and these fish wouldn't bite. However, the creek was low, just a chain of muddy water-holes, from the hole with a few bucketfuls in it to the sizable pool with an average depth of six or seven feet, and they could get fish by baling out the smaller holes or muddying up the water in the larger ones till the fish rose to the surface. There was the cat-fish, with spikes growing out of the sides of its head, and if you got pricked you'd know it, as Dave said. Andy took off his boots, tucked up his trousers, and went into a hole one day to stir up the mud with his feet, and he knew it. Dave scooped one out with his hand and got pricked, and he knew it too; his arm swelled, and the pain throbbed up into his shoulder, and down into his stomach too, he said, like a toothache he had once, and kept him awake for two nights—only the toothache pain had a "burred edge", Dave said.

Dave got an idea.

"Why not blow the fish up in the big water-hole with a cartridge?" he said. "I'll try it."

He thought the thing out and Andy Page worked it out. Andy usually put Dave's theories into practice if they were practicable, or bore the blame for the failure and the chaffing of his mates if they weren't.

He made a cartridge about three times the size of those they used in the rock. Jim Bently said it was big enough to blow the bottom out of the river. The inner skin was of stout calico; Andy stuck the end of a six-foot piece of fuse well down in the powder and bound the mouth of the bag firmly to it with whipcord. The idea was to sink the cartridge in the water with the open end of the fuse attached to a float on the surface, ready for lighting. Andy

dipped the cartridge in melted bees'-wax to make it water-tight.
"We'll have to leave it some time before we light it," said Dave,
"to give the fish time to get over their scare when we put it in,
and come nosing round again; so we'll want it well water-tight."

Round the cartridge Andy, at Dave's suggestion, bound a strip
of sail canvas—that they used for making water-bags—to increase
the force of the explosion, and round that he pasted layers of
stiff brown paper—on the plan of the sort of fireworks we called
"gun-crackers". He let the paper dry in the sun, then he sewed
a covering of two thicknesses of canvas over it, and bound the
thing from end to end with stout fishing-line. Dave's schemes were
elaborate, and he often worked his inventions out to nothing.
The cartridge was rigid and solid enough now—a formidable
bomb; but Andy and Dave wanted to be sure. Andy sewed on
another layer of canvas, dipped the cartridge in melted tallow,
twisted a length of fencing-wire round it as an afterthought, dipped
it in tallow again, and stood it carefully against a tent-peg, where
he'd know where to find it, and wound the fuse loosely round it.
Then he went to the camp-fire to try some potatoes which were
boiling in their jackets in a billy, and to see about frying some
chops for dinner. Dave and Jim were at work in the claim that
morning.

They had a big black young retriever dog—or rather an over-
grown pup, a big, foolish, four-footed mate who was always slobbering round them and lashing their legs with his heavy tail that
swung round like a stock-whip. Most of his head was usually a
red, idiotic, slobbering grin of appreciation of his own silliness.
He seemed to take life, the world, his two-legged mates, and his
own instinct as a huge joke. He'd retrieve anything: he carted
back most of the camp rubbish that Andy threw away. They had
a cat that died in hot weather, and Andy threw it a good distance
away in the scrub; and early one morning the dog found the cat,
after it had been dead a week or so, and carried it back to camp,
and laid it just inside the tent-flaps, where it could best make its
presence known when the mates should rise and begin to sniff
suspiciously in the sickly smothering atmosphere of the summer
sunrise. He used to retrieve them when they went in swimming;
he'd jump in after them, and take their hands in his mouth, and
try to swim out with them, and scratch their naked bodies with his
paws. They loved him for his good-heartedness and his foolishness,
but when they wished to enjoy a swim they had to tie him up
in camp.

He watched Andy with great interest all the morning making
the cartridge, and hindered him considerably, trying to help; but

about noon he went off to the claim to see how Dave and Jim were getting on, and to come home to dinner with them. Andy saw them coming, and put a panful of mutton-chops on the fire. Andy was cook to-day; Dave and Jim stood with their backs to the fire, as Bushmen do in all weathers, waiting till dinner should be ready. The retriever went nosing round after something he seemed to have missed.

Andy's brain still worked on the cartridge; his eye was caught by the glare of an empty kerosene-tin lying in the bushes, and it struck him that it wouldn't be a bad idea to sink the cartridge packed with clay, sand, or stones in the tin, to increase the force of the explosion. He may have been all out, from a scientific point of view, but the notion looked all right to him. Jim Bently, by the way, wasn't interested in their "damned silliness". Andy noticed an empty treacle-tin—the sort with the little tin neck or spout soldered on to the top for the convenience of pouring out the treacle—and it struck him that this would have made the best kind of cartridge-case; he would only have had to pour in the powder, stick the fuse in through the neck, and cork and seal it with bees'-wax. He was turning to suggest this to Dave, when Dave glanced over his shoulder to see how the chops were doing— and bolted. He explained afterwards that he thought he heard the pan spluttering extra, and looked to see if the chops were burning. Jim Bently looked behind and bolted after Dave. Andy stood stock-still, staring after them.

"Run, Andy! run!" they shouted back at him. "Run!!! Look behind you, you fool!" Andy turned slowly and looked, and there, close behind him, was the retriever with the cartridge in his mouth —wedged into his broadest and silliest grin. And that wasn't all. The dog had come round the fire to Andy, and the loose end of the fuse had trailed and waggled over the burning sticks into the blaze; Andy had slit and nicked the firing end of the fuse well, and now it was hissing and spitting properly.

Andy's legs started with a jolt; his legs started before his brain did, and he made after Dave and Jim. And the dog followed Andy.

Dave and Jim were good runners—Jim the best—for a short distance; Andy was slow and heavy, but he had the strength and the wind and could last. The dog leapt and capered round him, delighted as a dog could be to find his mates, as he thought, on for a frolic. Dave and Jim kept shouting back: "Don't foller us! don't foller us, you coloured fool!" but Andy kept on, no matter how they dodged. They could never explain, any more than the dog, why they followed each other, but so they ran, Dave keeping in Jim's track in all its turnings, Andy after Dave, and the dog circling round Andy—the live fuse swishing in all directions and hissing and spluttering and stinking. Jim yelling to Dave not to follow him, Dave shouting to Andy to go in another direction—to "spread out"—and Andy roaring at the dog to go home. Then Andy's brain began to work, stimulated by the crisis; he tried to get a running kick at the dog, but the dog dodged; he snatched up sticks and stones and threw them at the dog and ran on again. The retriever saw that he'd made a mistake about Andy, and left him and bounded after Dave. Dave, who had the presence of mind to think that the fuse's time wasn't up yet, made a dive and a grab for the dog, caught him by the tail, and as he swung round snatched the cartridge out of his mouth and flung it as far as he could: the dog immediately bounded after it and retrieved it. Dave roared and cursed at the dog, who, seeing that Dave was offended, left him and went after Jim, who was well ahead. Jim swung to a sapling and went up it like a native bear; it was a young sapling, and Jim couldn't safely get more than ten or twelve feet from the ground. The dog laid the cartridge, as carefully as if it was a kitten, at the foot of the sapling, and capered and leaped and whooped joyously round under Jim. The big pup reckoned that this was part of the lark—he was all right now—it was Jim who was out for a spree. The fuse sounded as if it were going a mile a minute. Jim tried to climb higher and the sapling bent and cracked. Jim fell on his feet and ran. The dog swooped on the cartridge and followed. It all took but a very few moments. Jim ran to a digger's hole, about ten feet deep, and dropped down into it—landing on soft mud—and was safe. The dog grinned sardonically down on him, over the edge, for a moment, as if he thought it would be a good lark to drop the cartridge down on Jim.

"Go away, Tommy," said Jim feebly, "go away."

The dog bounded off after Dave, who was the only one in sight now; Andy had dropped behind a log, where he lay flat on his face, having suddenly remembered a picture of the Russo-Turkish war with a circle of Turks lying flat on their faces (as if they were ashamed) round a newly arrived shell.

There was a small hotel or shanty on the creek, on the main road, not far from the claim. Dave was desperate, the time flew much faster in his stimulated imagination than it did in reality, so he made for the shanty. There were several casual Bushmen on the verandah and in the bar; Dave rushed into the bar, banging the door to behind him. "My dog!" he gasped, in reply to the astonished stare of the publican, "the blanky retriever—he's got a live cartridge in his mouth——"

The retriever, finding the front door shut against him, had

bounded round and in by the back way, and now stood smiling in the doorway leading from the passage, the cartridge still in his mouth and the fuse spluttering. They burst out of that bar. Tommy bounded first after one and then after another, for, being a young dog, he tried to make friends with everybody.

The Bushmen ran round corners, and some shut themselves in the stable. There was a new weatherboard and corrugated-iron kitchen and wash-house on piles in the back-yard, with some women washing clothes inside. Dave and the publican bundled in there and shut the door—the publican cursing Dave and calling him a crimson fool, in hurried tones, and wanting to know what the hell he came here for.

The retriever went in under the kitchen, amongst the piles, but, luckily for those inside, there was a vicious yellow mongrel cattle-dog sulking and nursing his nastiness under there—a sneaking, fighting, thieving canine, whom neighbours had tried for years to shoot or poison. Tommy saw his danger—he'd had experience from this dog—and started out and across the yard, still sticking to the cartridge. Half-way across the yard the yellow dog caught him and nipped him. Tommy dropped the cartridge, gave one terrified yell, and took to the Bush. The yellow dog followed him to the fence and then ran back to see what he had dropped.

Nearly a dozen other dogs came from round all the corners and under the buildings—spidery, thievish, cold-blooded kangaroo-dogs, mongrel sheep- and cattle-dogs, vicious black and yellow dogs—that slip after you in the dark, nip your heels, and vanish without explaining—and yapping, yelping small fry. They kept at a respectable distance round the nasty yellow dog, for it was dangerous to go near him when he thought he had found some-thing which might be good for a dog to eat. He sniffed at the cartridge twice, and was just taking a third cautious sniff when——

It was a very good blasting-powder—a new brand that Dave had recently got up from Sydney; and the cartridge had been excellently well made. Andy was very patient and painstaking in all he did, and nearly as handy as the average sailor with needles, twine, canvas, and rope.

Bushmen say that that kitchen jumped off its piles and on again. When the smoke and dust cleared away, the remains of the nasty yellow dog were lying against the paling fence of the yard looking as if he had been kicked into a fire by a horse and afterwards rolled in the dust under a barrow, and finally thrown against the fence from a distance. Several saddle-horses, which had been "hanging-up" round the verandah, were galloping wildly down the road in clouds of dust, with broken bridle-reins flying;

and from a circle round the outskirts, from every point of the
compass in the scrub, came the yelping of dogs. Two of them
went home, to the place where they were born, thirty miles away,
and reached it the same night and stayed there; it was not till
towards evening that the rest came back cautiously to make
inquiries. One was trying to walk on two legs, and most of 'em
looked more or less singed; and a little, singed, stumpy-tailed dog,
who had been in the habit of hopping the back half of him along
on one leg, had reason to be glad that he'd saved up the other
leg all those years, for he needed it now. There was one old
one-eyed cattle-dog round that shanty for years afterwards who
couldn't stand the smell of a gun being cleaned. He it was who
had taken an interest, only second to that of the yellow dog, in
the cartridge. Bushmen said that it was amusing to slip up on his
blind side and stick a dirty ramrod under his nose: he wouldn't
wait to bring his solitary eye to bear—he'd take to the Bush and
stay out all night.

For half an hour or so after the explosion there were several
Bushmen round behind the stable who crouched, doubled up,
against the wall, or rolled gently on the dust, trying to laugh without shrieking. There were two white women in hysterics at the
house, and a half-caste rushing aimlessly round with a dipper of
cold water. The publican was holding his wife tight and begging
her between her squawks, to "hold up for my sake, Mary, or I'll
lam the life out of ye".

Dave decided to apologize later on, "when things had settled
a bit", and went back to camp. And the dog that had done it all,
"Tommy", the great, idiotic mongrel retriever, came slobbering
round Dave and lashing his legs with his tail, and trotted home
after him, smiling his broadest, longest, and reddest smile of
amiability, and apparently satisfied for one afternoon with the fun
he'd had.

Andy chained the dog up securely, and cooked some more
chops, while Dave went to help Jim out of the hole.

And most of this is why, for years afterwards, lanky, easy-going
Bushmen, riding lazily past Dave's camp, would cry, in a lazy
drawl and with just a hint of the nasal twang:

"'El-lo, Da-a-ve! How's the fishin' getting on, Da-a-ve?"

[1899?]

GETTIN' BACK ON DAVE REGAN

A RATHER FISHY YARN FROM THE BUSH

(As told by James Nowlett, Bullock-driver)

You might work this yarn up. I've often thought of doin' it meself, but I ain't got the words. I knowed a lot of funny an' rum yarns about the Bush, an' I often wished I had the gift o' writin'. I could tell a lot better yarns than the rot they put in books sometimes, but I never had no eddication. But you might be able to work this yarn up—as yer call it.

There useter be a teamsters' camp six or seven miles out of Mudgee, at a place called th' Old Pipeclay, in the days before the railroad went round to Dubbo, an' most of us bullickies useter camp there for the night. There was always good water in the crick, an' sometimes we'd turn the bullicks up in the ridges an' gullies behind for grass, an' camp there for a few days, and do our washin' an' mendin', an' make new yokes perhaps, an' tinker up the waggons.

There was a woman livin' on a farm there named Mrs Hardwick —an' she *was* a hard wick. Her husban', Jimmy Hardwick, was throwed from his horse agenst a stump one day when he was sober, an' he was killed—an' she was a widder. She had a tidy bit o' land, an' a nice bit of a orchard an' vineyard, an' some cattle, an' they say she had a tidy bit o' money in the bank. She had the worst tongue in the district, no one's character was safe with her; but she wasn't old, an' she wasn't bad-lookin'—only hard— so there was some fellers hangin' round arter her. An' Dave Regan's horse was hangin' up outside her place as often as anybody else's. Dave was a native an' a Bushy, an' a drover an' a digger, an' he was a bit soft in them days—he got hard enough arterwards.

Mrs Hardwick hated bullick-drivers—she had a awful down on bullickies—I dunno why. We never interfered with her fowls, an' as for swearin'! why, she could swear herself. Jimmy Hardwick was a bullick-driver when she married him, an' p'r'aps that helped to account for it. She wouldn't let us boil our billies at her kitchen fire, same as any other Bushwoman, an' if one of our bullicks put his nose under her fence for a mouthful of grass, she'd set her dogs onter him. An' one of her dogs got something what disagreed with him one day, an' she accused us of layin' poisoned baits. An' arter that, she 'pounded some of our bullicks that got

105

into her lucerne paddick one night when we was on the spree in Mudgee, an' put heavy damages on 'em. She'd left the slip-rails down on purpose, I believe. She talked of puttin' the police onter us, jest as if we was a sly grog shop. (If *she'd* kept a sly grog shop she'd have had a different opinion about bullick-drivers.) An' all the bullick-drivers hated her because she hated bullickies.

Well, one wet season half a dozen of us chaps was camped there for a fortnight, because the roads was too boggy to travel, an' one night they got up a darnse at Peter Anderson's shanty acrost the ridges, an' a lot of gals an' fellers turned up from all round about in spite of the pourin' rain. Someone had kidded Dave Regan that Mother Hardwick was comin', an' he turned up, of course, in spite of a ragin' toothache he had. He was always ridin' the high horse over us bullickies. It was a very cold night, enough to cut the face an' hands off yer, so we had a roarin' fire in the big bark-an'-slab kitchen where the darnsin' was. It was one of them big, old-fashioned, clay-lined fireplaces that goes right acrost the end of the room, with a twenty-five foot slab-an'-tin chimbly outside.

Dave Regan was pretty wild about being had, an' we copped all the gals for darnsin'; he couldn't get one that night, an' when he wasn't proddin' out his tooth with a red-hot wire someone was chaffin' him about Mrs Hardwick. So at last he got disgusted an' left; but before he went he got a wet three-bushel flour bag an' climbed up very quietly onter the roof by the battens an' log weights an' riders, an' laid the wet bag very carefully acrost the top of the chimbly flue.

An' we was a mortal hour tryin' to find out what was the matter with that infernal chimbly, and tackin' bits o' tin an' baggin' acrost the top of the fireplace under the mantelshelf to try an' stop it from smokin', an' all the while the gals set there with the water runnin' out of their eyes. We took the green back-log out an' fetched in a dry one, but that chimbly smoked worse than ever, an' we had to put the fire out altogether, an' the gals set there shiverin' till the rain held up a bit an' the sky cleared, an' then someone goes out an' looks up an' sings out: "Why, there's somethin' acrost the top of the blazin' chimbly!" an' someone else climbs up an' fetches down the bag. But the darnse was spoilt, an' the gals was so disgusted that they went off with their fellers while the weather held up. They reckoned some of us bullickies did it for a lark.

An' arter that Dave'd come ridin' past, an' sing out to know if we knew of a good cure for a smokin' chimbly, an' them sorter things. But he always got away before we could pull him off of his horse. Three of us chased him on horseback one day, but we didn't ketch him.

So we made up our minds to git back on Dave some way or other, an' it come about this way.

About six months arter the smoked-out darnse, four or five of us same fellers was campin' on th' Pipeclay agen, an' it was a dry season. It was dryer an' hotter than it was cold 'n' wet the larst time. Dave was still hangin' round Mrs Hardwick's an' doin' odd jobs for her. Well, one very hot day we seen Dave ridin' past into Mudgee, an' we knowed he'd have a spree in town that night, an' call at Mrs Hardwick's for sympathy comin' out next day; an' arter he'd been gone an hour or two, Tom Tarrant comes drivin' past on his mail-coach, an' drops some letters an' papers an' a bag o' groceries at our camp.

Tom was a hard case. I remember wonst I was drivin' along a lonely bit o' track, an' it was a grand mornin', an' I felt great, an' I got singin' an' practisin' a recitation that I allers meant to give at a Bush dance some night. (I never sung or spouted poetry unless I was sure I was miles away from anyone.) An' I got worked up, an' was wavin' me arms about an' throwin' it off of me chest, when Tom's coach comes up behind, round a bend in the road, an' took me by surprise. An' Tom looked at me very hard an' he says: "What are yer shoutin' an' swearin' an' darnsin' an' goin' on at the bullicks like that for, Jimmy? They seem to be workin' all right." It took me back, I can tell yer. The coach was full of grinnin' passengers, an' the worst of it was that I didn't know how long Tom had been drivin' slow behind me an' takin' me out of windin'. There's nothin' upsets a cove as can't sing so much as to be caught singin' or spoutin' poetry when he thinks he's privit'.

An' another time I remember Tom's coach broke down on the track, an' he had to ride inter town with the mails on horseback; an' he left a couple of greenhides, for Skinner the tanner at Mudgee, for me to take on in the waggon, an' a bag of potatoes for Murphy the storekeeper at Home Rule, an' a note that said: "Render unto Murphy the things which is murphies, and unto Skinner them things which is skins." Tom was a hard case.

Well, this day, when Tom handed down the tucker an' letters, he got down to stretch his legs and give the horses a breathe. The coach was full of passengers, an' I noticed they all looked extra glum an' sulky, but I reckoned it was the heat an' dust. Tom looked extra solemn, too, an' no one was talkin'. Then I suddenly began to notice something in the atmosphere, as if there was a dead beast not far away, an' my mates started sniffin' too.

An' that reminds me, it's funny why some people allers sniff hard instead of keepin' their noses shut when there's a stink; the more it stinks the more they sniff. Tom spit in the dust an' thought a while; then he took a parcel out of the boot an' put it on the corner post of the fence. "There," he said, "there's some fresh fish that come up from Sydney by train an' Cobb & Co.'s coach larst night. They're meant for White the publican at Gulgong, but they won't keep this weather till I git out there. Pity to waste them! you chaps might as well have a feed of 'em. I'll tell White they went bad an' I had to throw them out," says Tom. Then he got on to the coach agen an' drove off in a cloud o' dust. We undone the brown paper, an' the fish was in a small deal box, with a lid fastened by a catch. We nicked back the catch an' the lid flew open, an' then we knowed where the smell comed from all right. There wasn't any doubt about that! We didn't have to put our noses in the box to see if the fish was bad. They was packed in salt, but that made no difference.

You know how a smell will start sudden in the Bush on a hot, still day, an' then seem to take a spell, an' then get to work agen stronger than ever. You might be clost alongside of a horse that has been dead a fortnight an' smell nothin' particular till you start to walk away, an' the further you go the worse it stinks. It seems to smell most round in a circle of a hundred yards or so. But these fish smelt from the centre right out. Tom Tarrant told us arter-wards that them fish started to smell as soon as he left Mudgee. At first they reckoned it was a dead horse by the road; but arter a while the passengers commenced squintin' at each other sus-picious like, an' the conversation petered out, an' Tom thought he felt all their eyes on his back, an' it was very uncomfortable; an' he sat tight an' tried to make out where the smell come from; an' it got worse every hundred yards—like as if the track was lined with dead horses, an' everyone dead longer than the last—till it was like drivin' a funeral. An' Tom never thought of the fish till he got down to stretch his legs and fetched his nose on a level with the boot.

Well, we shut down the lid of that box quick an' took it an' throwed it in the bushes a good way away from the camp, but next mornin', while we was havin' breakfast, Billy Grimshaw got a idea, an' arter breakfast he wetted a canvas bag he had an' lit up his pipe, an' went an' got that there box o' fish, an' put it in the wet bag, an' wrapped it tight round it an' tied it up tight with string. Billy had a nipper of a nephew with him, about fourteen, named Tommy, an' he was a sharp kid if ever there was one. So Billy says: "Look here, Tommy, you take this fish up to Mrs

Hardwick's an' tell her that Dave Regan sent 'em with his compliments, an' he hopes she'll enjoy 'em. Tell her that Dave fetched 'em from Mudgee, but he's gone back to look for a pound note that he dropped out of a hole in his pocket somewheers along the road, an' he asked you to take the fish up." So Tommy takes the fish an' goes up to the house with 'em. When he come back he says that Mrs Hardwick smiled like a parson an' give him a shillin'—an' he didn't wait. We watched the house, an' about half-an-hour arterwards we seen her run out of the kitchen with the open box in her hand, an' run a good way away from the house an' throw the fish inter the bushes, an' then go back quick, holdin' her nose.

An' jest then, as luck would have it, we seen Dave Regan ridin' up from the creek towards the house. He got down an' went into the kitchen, an' then come backin' out agen in a hurry with her in front of him. We could hear her voice from where we was, but we couldn't hear what she said. But we could see her arms wavin' as if she was drivin' fowls, an' Dave backed all the way to his horse and gets on an' comes ridin' away quick, she screamin' arter him all the time. When he got down opposite the camp we sung out to know what was the matter. "What have you been doin' to Mrs Hardwick, Dave?" we says. "We heerd her goin' for yer proper jest now." "Damned if I know," says Dave. "I ain't done nothin' to her that I knows of. She's called me everything she can lay her tongue to, an' she's ravin' about my stinkin' fish, or somethin'. I can't make it out at all. I believe she's gone ratty."

"But you *must* have been doin' somethin' to the woman," we says, "or else she wouldn't have gone on at yer like that."

But Dave swore he hadn't, an' we talked it over for a while an' couldn't make head nor tail of it, an' we come to the conclusion that it was only a touch o' the sun.

"Never mind, Dave," we says. "Go up agen in a day or two, when she's cooled down, an' find out what the matter is. Or write to her. It might only have been someone makin' mischief. That's what it is."

But Dave only sat an' rubbed his head, an' presently he started home to wherever he was hangin' out. He wanted a quiet week to think.

"Her chimbly might have been smokin', Dave," we shouted arter him, but he was too dazed like to ketch on.

Well, in a month or two we was campin' there agen, an' we found she'd fenced in a lane to the crick she had no right to, an' we had to take the bullicks a couple o' miles round to grass an' water. Well, the first mornin' we seen her down in the corner of her paddick near the camp drivin' some heifers, an' Billy Grimshaw went up to the fence an' spoke to her. Billy was the only one of us that dared face her, and he was the only one she was ever civil to—p'r'aps because Billy had a squint an' a wall eye and that put her out of countenance.

Billy took off his hat very respectful an' sings out: "Mrs Hardwick" (It was Billy's bullicks she'd "pounded", by the way.)

"What is it?" she says.

"I want to speak to you, Mrs Hardwick," says Billy.

"Well, speak," she says. "I've got no time to waste talkin' to bullick-drivers."

"Well, the fact is, Mrs Hardwick," says Billy, "that I want to explain somethin', an' apologise for that young scamp of a nephew o' mine, young Tommy. He ain't here or I'd make him beg your pardon hisself, or I'd cut him to pieces with the bullick-whip. I heard all about Dave Regan sendin' you that stinkin' fish, an' I think it was a damned mean, dirty thing to do—to send stinkin' fish to a woman, an' especially to a widder an' an unprotected woman like you, Mrs Hardwick. I've had mothers an' sisters of me own. An' I want to tell yer that I'm sorry a relation o' mine ever had anythin' to do with it. As soon as I heerd of it I give young Tommy a lambastin' he won't forgit in a hurry."

"Did Tommy know the fish was bad?" she says.

"It doesn't matter a rap," says Billy; "he had no right to go takin' messages from nobody to nobody."

Mrs Hardwick thought a while. Then she says: "P'r'aps arter all Dave Regan didn't know the fish was bad. I've often thought I might have been in too much of a hurry. Things go bad so quick out here in this weather. An' Dave was always very friendly. I can't understand why he'd do a dirty thing on me like that. I never done anything to Dave."

Now I forgot to tell you that Billy had a notion that Dave helped drive his bullicks to pound that time, though I didn't believe it. So Billy says:

"Don't you believe that for a minute, Mrs Hardwick. Dave knew what he was a-doin' of all right; an' if I ketch him *I'll* give him a beltin' for it if no one else is man enough to stand up for a woman!" says Billy.

"How d'yer know Dave knew?" says Mrs Hardwick.

"Know!" says Billy. "Why, he talked about it all over the district."

"What!" she screamed out, an' I moved away from that there fence, for she had a stick to drive them heifers with. But Billy stood his ground. "Is that the truth, Billy Grimshaw?" she screams.

"Yes," he says. "I'll take me oath on it. He blowed about it all over the district, as if it was very funny, an' he says—" An' Billy stopped.

"What did he say?" she shouted.

"Well, the fact is," says Billy, "that I hardly like to tell it to a lady. I wouldn't like to tell yer, Mrs Hardwick."

"But you'll have to tell me, Billy Grimshaw," she screams. "I have a right to know. If you don't tell me I'll pull him next week an' have it dragged out of you in the witness-box!" she says, "an' I'll have satisfaction out of him in the felon's dock of a court of law!" she says. "What did the villain say?" she screams.

"Well," says Billy, "if yer must have it—an' anyway, I'm hanged if I'm goin' to stand by an' see a woman scandalized behind her back—if yer must have it I'll tell yer. Dave said that the fish didn't smell no worse than your place anyway."

We got away from there then. She cut up too rough altogether. I can't tell you what she said—I ain't got the words. She went up to the house, an' we seen the farm-hand harnassin' up the horse, an' we reckoned she was goin' to drive into town straight away an' take out a summons agenst Dave Regan. An' jest then Dave hisself comes ridin' past—jest when he was most wanted, as usual. He always rode fast past Mrs Hardwick's nowadays, an' never stopped there, but Billy shouted after him:

"Hullo, Dave! I want to speak to yer," shouts Billy. An' Dave yanks his horse round.

"What is it, Billy?" he says.

"Look here, Dave," says Billy. "You had your little joke about the chimbly, an' we had our little joke about the fish an' Mrs Hardwick, so now we'll call it quits. A joke's a joke, but it can go too far, an' this one's gettin' too red hot altogether. So we've fixed it up with Mrs Hardwick."

"What fish an' what joke?" says Dave, rubbin' his head. "An' what have yer fixed up with Mrs Hardwick? Whatever are yer talkin' about, Billy?"

So Billy told him all about us sendin' the stinkin' fish to Mrs Hardwick by Tommy, an' sayin' Dave sent 'em—Dave rubbin' the back of his neck an' starin' at Billy all the time. "An' now," says Billy, "I won't say anything about them bullicks; but I went up an' seen Mrs Hardwick this mornin', an' told her the whole truth about them fish, an' how you knowed nothin' about it, an' I apologised an' told her we was very sorry; an' she says she was very sorry too on your account, an' wanted to see yer. I promised to tell yer as soon as I seen yer. It ought to be fixed up. You

ought to go right up to the house an' see her now. She's awfully
cut up about it."

"All right," says Dave, brightenin' up. "It was a dirty, mean
trick anyway to play on a cove; but I'll go up an' see her." An' he
went there 'n' then.

An' about fifteen minutes arterwards he comes boltin' back
from the house one way an' his horse the other. The horse acted
as if it had a big scare, an' so did Dave. Billy went an' ketched
Dave's horse for him, an' I got Dave a towel to wipe the dirty
dish-water off of his face an' out of his hair an' collar, an' I give
him a piece of soap to rub on the places where he'd been scalded.

"Why, the woman must be ravin' mad," I says. "Whatever did
yer say to her this time, Dave? Yer allers gettin' inter hot water
with her."

"I didn't say nothin'," says Dave. "I jest went up laughin' like,
an' says, 'How are yer, Mrs Hardwick?' an' she ups an' lets me
have a dish of dirty wash-up water, an' then on top of that she
let fly with a dipper of scaldin'-hot, greasy water outer the boiler.
She's gone clean ravin' mad, I think."

"She's as mad as a hatter, right enough, Dave," says Billy
Grimshaw. "Don't you go there no more, Dave, it ain't safe."
An' we lent Dave a hat an' a clean shirt, an' he went on inter
town. "You ought to have humoured her," says Billy, as Dave
rode away. "You ought to have told her to put a wet bag over
her chimbly an' hang the fish inside to smoke." But Dave was too
stunned to ketch on. He went on inter the town an' got on a
howlin' spree. An' while he was soberin' up the thing began to
dawn on him. An' the nex' time he met Billy they had a fight.
An' Dave got another woman to speak to Mrs Hardwick, an' Mrs
Hardwick ketched young Tommy goin' past her place one day an'
bailed him up an' scared the truth out of him.

"Look here!" she says to him, "I want the truth, the whole
truth, an' nothin' but the truth about them fish, an' if I don't get
it outer you I'll wring yer young neck for tryin' to poison me,
an' save yer from the gallust!" she says to Tommy.

So he told her the whole truth, swelp him, an' got away; an' he
respected Mrs Hardwick arter that.

An' next time we come past with the teams we seen Dave's
horse hangin' up outside Mrs Hardwick's, an' we went some miles
further along the road an' camped in a new place where we'd be
more comfortable. An' ever arter that we used to always whip up
an' drive past her place as if we didn't know her.

[1898-1901]

5

NO PLACE FOR A WOMAN

HE had a selection on a long box-scrub siding of the ridges, about half a mile back and up from the coach road. There were no neighbours that I ever heard of, and the nearest "town" was thirty miles away. He grew wheat among the stumps of his clearing, sold the crop standing to a cockie who lived ten miles away and had some surplus sons; or, some seasons, he reaped it by hand, had it thrashed by travelling "steamer" (portable steam engine and machine), and carried the grain into the mill, a few bags at a time, on his rickety dray.

He had lived alone for upwards of fifteen years, and was known to those who knew him as "Ratty Howlett".

Trav'lers and strangers failed to see anything uncommonly ratty about him. It was known, or, at least, it was believed without question, that while at work he kept his horse saddled and bridled, and hung up to the fence, or grazing about, with the saddle on—or, anyway, close handy for a moment's notice—and whenever he caught sight, over the scrub and through the quarter-mile break in it, of a traveller on the road, he would jump on his horse and make after him. If it was a horseman he usually pulled him up inside of a mile. Stories were told of unsuccessful chases, misunderstandings, and complications arising out of Howlett's mania for running down and bailing up travellers. Sometimes he caught one every day for a week, sometimes not one for weeks—it was a lonely track.

The explanation was simple, sufficient, and perfectly natural—from a bushman's point of view. Ratty only wanted to have a yarn. He and the traveller would camp in the shade for half-an-hour or so, and yarn and smoke. The old man would find out where the traveller came from, and how long he'd been there, and where he was making for, and how long he reckoned he'd be away; and ask if there had been any rain along the traveller's back track, and how the country looked after the drought; and he'd get the traveller's ideas on abstract questions—if he had any. If it was a footman (swagman) and he was short of tobacco, old Howlett always had half a stick ready for him. Sometimes, but very rarely, he'd invite the swagman back to the hut for a pint of tea, or a bit of meat, flour, tea, or sugar to carry him along the track.

And, after the yarn by the road, they said, the old man would ride back, refreshed, to his lonely selection, and work on into the night as long as he could see his solitary old plough-horse or the scoop of his long-handled shovel.

And so it was that I came to make his acquaintance—or, rather, that he made mine. I was cantering easily along the track—I was making for the north-west with a pack-horse—when about a mile beyond the track to the selection I heard "Hi, Mister!" and saw a dust cloud following me. I had heard of "Old Ratty Howlett" casually, and so was prepared for him.

A tall, gaunt man on a little horse. He was clean-shaven, except for a frill beard round under his chin, and his long, wavy, dark hair was turning grey: a square, strong-faced man, and reminded me of one full-faced portrait of Gladstone more than any other face I had seen. He had large, reddish-brown eyes, deep set under heavy eyebrows, and with something of the blackfellow in them —the sort of eyes that will peer at something on the horizon that no one else can see. He had a way of talking to the horizon, too —more than to his companion; and he had a deep vertical wrinkle in his forehead that no smile could lessen.

I got down and got out my pipe, and we sat on a log and yarned awhile on bush subjects; and then, after a pause, he shifted uneasily, it seemed to me, and asked rather abruptly, and in an altered tone, if I was married. A queer question to ask a traveller; more especially in my case, as I was little more than a boy then.

He talked on again of old things and places where we had both been, and asked after men he knew, or had known—drovers and others—and whether they were living yet. Most of his inquiries went back before my time; but some of the drovers, one or two overlanders with whom he had been mates in his time, had grown old into mine, and I knew them. I notice now, though I didn't then—and if I had it would not have seemed strange from a bush point of view—that he didn't ask for news, nor seem interested in it.

Then after another uneasy pause, during which he scratched crosses in the dust with a stick, he asked me, in the same queer tone and without looking at me or looking up, if I happened to know anything about doctoring—if I'd ever studied it.

I asked him if anyone was sick at his place. He hesitated, and said "No". Then I wanted to know why he had asked me that question, and he was so long about answering that I began to think he was hard of hearing, when, at last, he muttered something about my face reminding him of a young fellow he knew of who'd gone to Sydney to "study for a doctor". That might have been, and looked natural enough; but why didn't he ask me straight out if I was the chap he "knowed of"? Travellers do not like beating about the bush in conversation.

He sat in silence for a good while, with his arms folded, and looking absently away over the dead level of the great scrubs that spread from the foot of the ridge we were on, to where a blue peak or two of a distant range showed above the bush on the horizon.

I stood up and put my pipe away and stretched. Then he seemed to wake up. "Better come back to the hut and have a bit of dinner," he said. "The missus will about have it ready, and I'll spare you a handful of hay for the horses."

The hay decided it. It was a dry season. I was surprised to hear of a wife, for I thought he was a hatter—I had always heard so; but perhaps I had been mistaken, and he had married lately; or had got a housekeeper. The farm was an irregularly shaped clearing in the scrub, with a good many stumps in it, with a broken-down two-rail fence along the frontage, and logs and "dog-leg" the rest. It was about as lonely-looking a place as I had seen, and I had seen some out-of-the-way, God-forgotten holes where men lived alone. The hut was in the top corner, a two-roomed slab hut, with a shingle roof, which must have been uncommon round there in the days when that hut was built. I was used to bush carpentering, and saw that the place had been put up by a man who had plenty of life and hope in front of him, and for someone else beside himself. But there were two unfinished skillion rooms built on to the back of the hut; the posts, sleepers, and wall-plates had been well put up and fitted, and the slab walls were up, but the roof had never been put on. There was nothing but burrs and nettles inside those walls, and an old wooden bullock plough and a couple of yokes were dry-rotting across the back doorway. The remains of a straw-stack, some hay under a bark humpy, a small iron plough, and an old stiff coffin-headed grey draught-horse were all that I saw about the place.

But there was a bit of a surprise for me inside, in the shape of a clean white tablecloth on the rough slab table which stood on stakes driven into the ground. The cloth was coarse, but it was a tablecloth—not a spare sheet put on in honour of unexpected visitors—and perfectly clean. The tin plates, pannikins, and jam tins that served as sugar-bowls and salt-cellars were polished brightly. The walls and fireplace were whitewashed, the clay floor swept, and clean sheets of newspaper laid on the slab mantelshelf under the row of biscuit tins that held the groceries. I thought that his wife, or housekeeper, or whatever she was, was a clean and tidy woman about a house. I saw no woman; but on the sofa—a light, wooden, batten one, with runged arms at the ends—lay a woman's dress on a lot of sheets of old stained and faded newspapers. He looked at it in a puzzled way, knitting his forehead, then took it up absently and folded it. I saw then that it was a riding skirt and jacket. He bundled them into the newspapers and took them into the bedroom.

"The wife was going on a visit down the creek this afternoon," he said rapidly, and without looking at me, but stooping as if to have another look through the door at those distant peaks. "I suppose she got tired o' waitin', and went and took the daughter with her. But, never mind, the grub is ready." There was a camp-oven with a leg of mutton and potatoes sizzling in it on the hearth, and billies hanging over the fire. I noticed the billies had been scraped, and the lids polished.

There seemed to be something queer about the whole business, but then he and his wife might have had a "breeze" during the morning. I thought so during the meal, when the subject of women came up, and he said one never knew how to take a woman, etc.; but there was nothing in what he said that need necessarily have referred to his wife or to any woman in particular. For the rest he talked of old bush things, droving, digging, and old bushranging—but never about live things and living men, unless any of the old mates he talked about happened to be alive by accident. He was very restless in the house, and never took his hat off.

There was a dress and a woman's old hat hanging on the wall near the door, but they looked as if they might have been hanging there for a lifetime. There seemed something queer about the whole place—something wanting; but then all out-of-the-way bush homes are haunted by that something wanting, or, more likely, by the spirits of the things that should have been there, but never had been.

As I rode down the track to the road I looked back and saw old Howlett hard at work in a hole round a big stump with his long-handled shovel.

I'd noticed that he moved and walked with a slight list to port, and put his hand once or twice to the small of his back, and I set it down to lumbago, or something of that sort.

Up in the Never Never I heard from a drover who had known

Howlett that his wife had died in the first year, and so this mysterious woman, if she was his wife, was, of course, his second wife. The drover seemed surprised and rather amused at the thought of old Howlett going in for matrimony again.

.   .   .

I rode back that way five years later, from the Never Never. It was early in the morning—I had ridden since midnight. I didn't think the old man would be up and about; and, besides, I wanted to get on home, and have a look at the old folk and the mates I'd left behind—and the girl. But I hadn't got far past the point where Howlett's track joined the road, when I happened to look back and saw him on horseback, stumbling down the track. I waited till he came up.

He was riding the old grey draught-horse this time, and it looked very much broken down. I thought it would have come down every step, and fallen like an old rotten humpy in a gust of wind. And the old man was not much better off. I saw at once that he was a very sick man. His face was drawn, and he bent forward as if he was hurt. He got down stiffly and awkwardly, like a hurt man, and as soon as his feet touched the ground he grabbed my arm, or he would have gone down like a man who steps off a train in motion. He hung towards the bank of the road, feeling blindly, as it were, for the ground, with his free hand, as I eased him down. I got my blanket and calico from the pack saddle to make him comfortable.

"Help me with my back agen the tree," he said. "I must sit up —it's no use lyin' me down."

He sat with his hand gripping his side, and breathed painfully.

"Shall I run up to the hut and get the wife?" I asked.

"No." He spoke painfully. "No!" Then, as if the words were jerked out of him by a spasm: "She ain't there."

I took it that she had left him.

"How long have you been bad? How long has this been coming on?"

He took no notice of the question. I thought it was a touch of rheumatic fever, or something of that sort. "It's gone into my back and sides now—the pain's worse in me back," he said presently.

I had once been mates with a man who died suddenly of heart disease while at work. He was washing a dish of dirt in the creek near a claim we were working; he let the dish slip into the water, fell back, crying: "Oh, my back!" and was gone. And now I felt by instinct that it was poor old Howlett's heart that was wrong.

A man's heart is in his back as well as in his arms and hands.

The old man had turned pale with the pallor of a man who turns faint in a heat wave, and his arms fell loosely, and his hands rocked helplessly with the knuckles in the dust. I felt myself turning white, too, and the sick, cold, empty feeling in my stomach, for I knew the signs. Bushmen stand in awe of sickness and death.

But after I'd fixed him comfortably and given him a drink from the water-bag the greyness left his face, and he pulled himself together a bit; he drew up his arms and folded them across his chest. He let his head rest back against the tree—his slouch hat had fallen off, revealing a broad, white brow, much higher than I expected. He seemed to gaze on the azure fin of the range showing above the dark blue-green bush on the horizon.

Then he commenced to speak—taking no notice of me when I asked him if he felt better now—to talk in that strange, absent, far-away tone that awes one. He told his story mechanically, monotonously—in set words, as I believe now, as he had often told it before; if not to others, then to the loneliness of the bush. And he used the names of people and places that I had never heard of—just as if I knew them as well as he did.

"I didn't want to bring her up the first year. It was no place for a woman. I wanted her to stay with her people and wait till I'd got the place a little more ship-shape. The Phippses took a selection down the creek. I wanted her to wait and come up with them so's she'd have some company—a woman to talk to. They came afterwards, but they didn't stop. It was no place for a woman.

"But Mary would come. She wouldn't stop with her people down country. She wanted to be with me, and look after me, and work and help me."

He repeated himself a great deal—said the same thing over and over again sometimes. He was only mad on one track. He'd tail off and sit silent for a while; then he'd become aware of me in a hurried, half-scared way, and apologize for putting me to all that trouble, and thank me. "I'll be all right d'reckly. Best take the horses up to the hut and have some breakfast; you'll find it by the fire. I'll foller you, d'reckly. The wife'll be waitin' an'———" He would drop off, and be going again presently on the old track:

"Her mother was coming up to stay a while at the end of the year, but the old man hurt his leg. Then her married sister was coming, but one of the youngsters got sick and there was trouble at home. I saw the doctor in the town—thirty miles from here—and fixed it up with him. He was a boozer—I'd 'a' shot him afterwards. I fixed up with a woman in the town to come and stay. I thought Mary was wrong in her time. She must have been a

month or six weeks out. But I listened to her. . . . Don't argue
with a woman. Don't listen to a woman. Do the right thing. We
should have had a mother woman to talk to us. But it was no
place for a woman!"

He rocked his head, as if from some old agony of mind, against
the tree-trunk.

"She was took bad suddenly one night, but it passed off. False
alarm. I was going to ride somewhere, but she said to wait till
daylight. Someone was sure to pass. She was a brave and sensible
girl, but she had a terror of being left alone. It was no place for
a woman!

"There was a black shepherd three or four miles away. I rode
over while Mary was asleep, and started the black boy into town.
I'd 'a' shot him afterwards if I'd 'a' caught him. The old black
gin was dead the week before, or Mary would 'a' bin all right.
She was tied up in a bunch with strips of blanket and greenhide,
and put in a hole. So there wasn't even a gin near the place. It
was no place for a woman!

"I was watchin' the road at daylight, and I was watchin' the
road at dusk. I went down in the hollow and stooped down to get
the gap agen the sky, so's I could see if anyone was comin' over.
. . . I'd get on the horse and gallop along towards the town for
five miles, but something would drag me back, and then I'd race
for fear she'd die before I got to the hut. I expected the doctor
every five minutes.

"It come on about daylight next morning. I ran back'ards and
for'ards between the hut and the road like a madman. And no one
come. I was running amongst the logs and stumps, and fallin'
over them, when I saw a cloud of dust agen sunrise. It was her
mother an' sister in the spring-cart, an' just catchin' up to them
was the doctor in his buggy with the woman I'd arranged with in
town. The mother and sister was staying at the town for the night,
when they heard of the black boy. It took him a day to ride there.
I'd 'a' shot him if I'd 'a' caught him ever after. The doctor'd been
on the drunk. If I'd had the gun and known she was gone I'd
have shot him in the buggy. They said she was dead. And the
child was dead, too.

"They blamed me, but I didn't want her to come; it was no
place for a woman. I never saw them again after the funeral.
I didn't want to see them any more."

He moved his head wearily against the tree, and presently
drifted on again in a softer tone—his eyes and voice were growing
more absent and dreamy and far away.

"About a month after—or a year, I lost count of the time long ago—she came back to me. At first she'd come in the night, then sometimes when I was at work—and she had the baby—it was a girl—in her arms. And by-and-by she came to stay altogether. . . . I didn't blame her for going away that time—it was no place for a woman. . . . She was a good wife to me. She was a jolly girl when I married her. The little girl grew up like her. I was going to send her down country to be educated—it was no place for a girl.

"But a month, or a year ago, Mary left me and took the daughter, and never came back till last night—this morning, I think it was. I thought at first it was the girl with her hair done up, and her mother's skirt on, to surprise her old dad. But it was Mary, my wife—as she was when I married her. She said she couldn't stay, but she'd wait for me on the road; on—the road. . . ."

His arms fell, and his face went white. I got the water-bag. "Another turn like that and you'll be gone," I thought, as he came to again. Then I suddenly thought of a shanty that had been started, when I came that way last, ten or twelve miles along the road towards the town. There was nothing for it but to leave him and ride on for help, and a cart of some kind.

"You wait here till I come back," I said. "I'm going for the doctor."

He roused himself a little. "Best come up to the hut and get some grub. The wife'll be waiting. . . ." He was off the track again.

"Will you wait while I take the horse down to the creek?"

"Yes—I'll wait by the road."

"Look!" I said, "I'll leave the water-bag handy. Don't move till I come back."

"I won't move—I'll wait by the road," he said.

I took the pack-horse, which was the freshest and best, threw the pack-saddle and bags into a bush, left the other horse to take care of itself, and started for the shanty, leaving the old man with his back to the tree, his arms folded, and his eyes on the horizon.

One of the chaps at the shanty rode on for the doctor at once, while the other came back with me in a spring-cart. He told me that old Howlett's wife had died in child-birth the first year on the selection—"she was a fine girl he'd heered!" He told me the story as the old man had told it, and in pretty well the same words, even to giving it as his opinion that it was no place for a woman. "And he 'hatted' and brooded over it till he went ratty."

I knew the rest. He not only thought that his wife, or the ghost of his wife, had been with him all those years, but that the child had lived and grown up, and that the wife did the housework; which, of course, he must have done himself.

When we reached him his knotted hands had fallen for the last time, and they were at rest. I only took one quick look at his face, but could have sworn that he was gazing at the blue fin of the range on the horizon of the bush.

Up at the hut the table was set as on the first day I saw it, and breakfast in the camp-oven by the fire.

[1899? revised 1899]

JOE WILSON'S COURTSHIP

THERE are many times in this world when a healthy boy is happy. When he is put into knickerbockers, for instance, and "comes a man to-day", as my little Jim used to say. When they're cooking something at home that he likes. When the "sandy-blight" or measles breaks out amongst the children, or the teacher or his wife falls dangerously ill—or dies, it doesn't matter which—"and there ain't no school". When a boy is naked and in his natural state for a warm climate like Australia, with three or four of his schoolmates, under the shade of the creek-oaks in the bend where there's a good clear pool with a sandy bottom. When his father buys him a gun, and he starts out after kangaroos or 'possums. When he gets a horse, saddle, and bridle of his own. When he has his arm in splints or a stitch in his head—he's proud then, the proudest boy in the district.

I wasn't a healthy-minded, average boy: I reckon I was born for a poet by mistake, and grew up to be a Bushman, and didn't know what was the matter with me—or the world—but that's got nothing to do with it.

There are times when a man is happy. When he finds out that the girl loves him. When he's just married. When he's a lawful father for the first time, and everything is going on all right: some men make fools of themselves then—I know I did. I'm happy to-night because I'm out of debt and can see clear ahead, and because I haven't been easy for a long time.

But I think that the happiest time in a man's life is when he's courting a girl and finds out for sure that she loves him and hasn't a thought for anyone else. Make the most of your courting days, you young chaps, and keep them clean, for they're about the only days when there's a chance of poetry and beauty coming into this life. Make the best of them and you'll never regret it the longest day you live. They're the days that the wife will look back to, anyway, in the brightest of times as well as in the blackest, and there shouldn't be anything in those days that might hurt her when she looks back. Make the most of your courting days, you young chaps, for they will never come again.

A married man knows all about it—after a while: he sees the woman world through the eyes of his wife; he knows what an extra moment's pressure of the hand means, and, if he has had a hard life, and is inclined to be cynical, the knowledge does him no good. It leads him into awful messes sometimes, for a married man, if he's inclined that way, has three times the chance with a woman that a single man has—because the married man knows. He is privileged; he can guess pretty closely what a woman means when she says something else; he knows just how far he can go; he can go farther in five minutes towards coming to the point with a woman than an innocent young man dares go in three weeks. Above all, the married man is more decided with women; he takes them and things for granted. In short he is—well, he is a married man. And, when he knows all this, how much better or happier is he for it? Mark Twain says that he lost all the beauty of the river when he saw it with a pilot's eye—and there you have it.

But it's all new to a young chap, provided he hasn't been a young blackguard. It's all wonderful, new, and strange to him. He's a different man. He finds that he never knew anything about women. He sees none of woman's little ways and tricks in his girl. He is in heaven one day and down near the other place the next; and that's the sort of thing that makes life interesting. He takes his new world for granted. And, when she says she'll be his wife——!

Make the most of your courting days, you young chaps, for they've got a lot of influence on your married life afterwards—a lot more than you'd think. Make the best of them, for they'll never come any more, unless we do our courting over again in another world. If we do, I'll make the most of mine.

But, looking back, I didn't do so badly after all. I never told you about the days I courted Mary. The more I look back the more I come to think that I made the most of them, and if I had no more to regret in married life than I have in my courting days, I wouldn't walk to and fro in the room, or up and down the yard in the dark sometimes, or lie awake some nights thinking. . . . Ah, well!

I was between twenty-one and thirty then: birthdays had never been any use to me, and I'd left off counting them. You don't take much stock in birthdays in the Bush. I'd knocked about the country for a few years, shearing and fencing and droving a little, and wasting my life without getting anything for it. I drank now and then, and made a fool of myself. I was reckoned "wild"; but I only drank because I felt less sensitive, and the world seemed a lot saner and better and kinder when I had a few drinks: I loved my fellow-man then and felt nearer to him. It's better to be thought "wild" than to be considered eccentric or ratty. Now, my old mate, Jack Barnes, drank—as far as I could see—first because he'd inherited the gambling habit from his father along with his father's luck: he'd the habit of being cheated and losing very bad, and when he lost he drank. Till drink got a hold on him. Jack was sentimental too, but in a different way. I was sentimental about other people—more fool I!—whereas Jack was sentimental about himself. Before he was married, and when he was recovering from a spree, he'd write rhymes about "Only a boy, drunk by the roadside", and that sort of thing; and he'd call 'em poetry, and talk about signing them and sending them to the *Town and Country Journal*. But he generally tore them up when he got better. The Bush is breeding a race of poets, and I don't know what the country will come to in the end.

Well. It was after Jack and I had been out shearing at Beenaway shed in the Big Scrubs. Jack was living in the little farming town of Solong, and I was hanging round. Black, the squatter, wanted some fencing done and a new stable built, or buggy and harness-house, at his place at Haviland, a few miles out of Solong. Jack and I were good Bush carpenters, so we took the job to keep us going till something else turned up. "Better than doing nothing," said Jack.

"There's a nice little girl in service at Black's," he said. "She's more like an adopted daughter, in fact, than a servant. She's a real good little girl, and good-looking into the bargain. I hear that young Black is sweet on her, but they say she won't have anything to do with him. I know a lot of chaps that have tried for her, but they've never had any luck. She's a regular little dumpling, and I like dumplings. They call her 'Possum. You ought to try a bear up in that direction, Joe."

I was always shy with women—except perhaps some that I should have fought shy of; but Jack wasn't—he was afraid of no woman, good, bad, or indifferent. I haven't time to explain why, but somehow, whenever a girl took any notice of me I took it for granted that she was only playing with me, and felt nasty about it. I made one or two mistakes, but—ah well!

"My wife knows little 'Possum," said Jack. "I'll get her to ask her out to our place and let you know."

I reckoned that he wouldn't get me there then, and made a note to be on the watch for tricks. I had a hopeless little love-story behind me, of course. I suppose most married men can look back to their lost love; few marry the first flame. Many a married man looks back and thinks it was damned lucky that he didn't get the girl he couldn't have. Jack had been my successful rival, only he didn't know it—I don't think his wife knew it either. I used to think her the prettiest and sweetest little girl in the district.

But Jack was mighty keen on fixing me up with the little girl at Haviland. He seemed to take it for granted that I was going to fall in love with her at first sight. He took too many things for granted as far as I was concerned, and got me into awful tangles sometimes.

"You let me alone, and I'll fix you up, Joe," he said, as we rode up to the station. "I'll make it all right with the girl. You're rather a good-looking chap. You've got the sort of eyes that take with girls, only you don't know it; you haven't got the go. If I had your eyes along with my other attractions, I'd be in trouble on account of a woman about once a week."

"For God's sake shut up, Jack," I said.

Do you remember the first glimpse you got of your wife? Perhaps not in England, where so many couples grow up together from childhood; but it's different in Australia, where you may hail from two thousand miles away from where your wife was born, and yet she may be a countrywoman of yours, and a country-woman in ideas and politics too. I remember the first glimpse I got of Mary.

It was a two-storey brick house with wide balconies and veran-dahs all round, and a double row of pines down to the front gate. Parallel at the back was an old slab-and-shingle place, one room deep and about eight rooms long, with a row of skillions at the back: the place was used for kitchen, laundry, servants' rooms, etc. This was the old homestead before the new house was built. There was a wide, old-fashioned, brick-floored verandah in front, with an open end; there was ivy climbing up the verandah post on one side and a baby-rose on the other, and a grape-vine near the chimney. We rode up to the end of the verandah, and Jack called to see if there was anyone at home, and Mary came trotting out; so it was in the frame of vines that I first saw her.

More than once since then I've had a fancy to wonder whether the rose-bush killed the grape-vine or the ivy smothered 'em both in the end. I used to have a vague idea of riding that way some day to see. You do get strange fancies at odd times.

Jack asked her if the boss was in. He did all the talking. I saw a little girl, rather plump, with a complexion like a New England or Blue Mountain girl, or a girl from Tasmania or from Gippsland in Victoria. Red and white girls were very scarce in the Solong district. She had the biggest and brightest eyes I'd seen round there, dark hazel eyes, as I found out afterwards, and bright as a 'possum's. No wonder they called her 'Possum. I forgot at once that Mrs Jack Barnes was the prettiest girl in the district. I felt a sort of comfortable satisfaction in the fact that I was on horse-back: most Bushmen look better on horseback. It was a black filly, a fresh young thing, and she seemed as shy of girls as I was myself. I noticed Mary glanced in my direction once or twice to see if she knew me; but, when she looked, the filly took all my attention. Mary trotted in to tell old Black he was wanted, and after Jack had seen him, and arranged to start work next day, we started back to Solong.

I expected Jack to ask me what I thought of Mary—but he didn't. He squinted at me sideways once or twice and didn't say anything for a long time, and then he started talking of other things. I began to feel wild at him. He seemed so damnably satisfied with the way things were going. He seemed to reckon that I was a gone case now; but, as he didn't say so, I had no way of getting at him. I felt sure he'd go home and tell his wife that Joe Wilson was properly gone on little 'Possum at Haviland. That was all Jack's way.

Next morning we started to work. We were to build the buggy-house at the back near the end of the old house, but first we had to take down a rotten old place that might have been the original hut in the Bush before the old house was built. There was a window in it, opposite the laundry window in the old place, and the first thing I did was to take out the sash. I'd noticed Jack yarning with 'Possum before he started work. While I was at work at the window he called me round to the other end of the hut to help him lift a grindstone out of the way; and when we'd done it, he took the tips of my ear between his fingers and thumb and stretched it and whispered into it:

"Don't hurry with that window, Joe; the strips are hardwood and hard to get off—you'll have to take the sash out very carefully so as not to break the glass." Then he stretched my ear a little more and put his mouth closer.

"Make a looking-glass of that window, Joe," he said.

I was used to Jack, and when I went back to the window I started to puzzle out what he meant, and presently I saw it by chance.

That window reflected the laundry window: the room was dark inside and there was a good clear reflection; and presently I saw Mary come to the laundry window and stand with her hands behind her back, thoughtfully watching me. The laundry window had an old-fashioned hinged sash, and I like that sort of window—there's more romance about it, I think. There was thick dark-green ivy all round the window, and Mary looked prettier than a picture. I squared up my shoulders and put my heels together and put as much style as I could into the work. I couldn't have turned round to save my life.

Presently Jack came round, and Mary disappeared.

"Well?" he whispered.

"You're a fool, Jack," I said. "She's only interested in the old house being pulled down."

"That's all right," he said. "I've been keeping an eye on the business round the corner, and she ain't interested when *I'm* round this end."

"You seem mighty interested in the business," I said.

"Yes," said Jack. "This sort of thing just suits a man of my rank in times of peace."

"What made you think of the window?" I asked.

"Oh, that's as simple as striking matches. I'm up to all those dodges. Why, where there wasn't a window, I've fixed up a piece of looking-glass to·see if a girl was taking any notice of me when she thought I wasn't looking."

He went away, and presently Mary was at the window again, and this time she had a tray with cups of tea and a plate of cake and bread-and-butter. I was prising off the strips that held the sash, very carefully, and my heart suddenly commenced to gallop, without any reference to me. I'd never felt like that before, except once or twice. It was just as if I'd swallowed some clockwork arrangement, unconsciously, and it had started to go without warning. I reckon it was all on account of that blarsted Jack working me up. He had a quiet way of working you up to a thing that made you want to hit him sometimes—after you'd made an ass of yourself.

I didn't hear Mary at first. I hoped Jack would come round and help me out of the fix, but he didn't.

"Mr—Mr Wilson!" said Mary. She had a sweet voice.

I turned round.

"I thought you and Mr Barnes might like a cup of tea."

"Oh, thank you!" I said, and I made a dive for the window, as if hurry would help it. I trod on an old cask-hoop; it sprang up and dinted my shin and I stumbled—and that didn't help matters much.

"Oh! did you hurt yourself, Mr Wilson?" cried Mary.

"Hurt myself! Oh no, not at all, thank you," I blurted out. "It takes more than that to hurt me."

I was about the reddest, shy, lanky fool of a Bushman that was ever taken at a disadvantage on foot, and when I took the tray my hands shook so that a lot of the tea was spilt into the saucers. I embarrassed her too, like the damned fool I was, till she must have been as red as I was, and it's a wonder we didn't spill the whole lot between us. I got away from the window in as much of a hurry as if Jack had cut his leg with a chisel and fainted, and I was running with whisky for him. I blundered round to where he was, feeling like a man feels when he's just made an ass of himself in public. The memory of that sort of thing hurts you worse and makes you jerk your head more impatiently than the thought of a past crime would, I think.

I pulled myself together when I got to where Jack was.

"Here, Jack!" I said. "I've struck something all right; here's some tea and brownie—we'll hang out here all right."

Jack took a cup of tea and a piece of cake and sat down to enjoy it, just as if he'd paid for it and ordered it to be sent out about that time.

He was silent for a while, with the sort of silence that always made me wild at him. Presently he said, as if he'd just thought of it:

"That's a very pretty little girl, 'Possum, isn't she, Joe? Do you notice how she dresses?—always fresh and trim. But she's got on her best bib-and-tucker to-day, and a pinafore with frills to it. And it's ironing-day, too. It can't be on your account. If it was Saturday or Sunday afternoon, or some holiday, I could understand it. But perhaps one of her admirers is going to take her to the church bazaar in Solong to-night. That's what it is."

He gave me time to think over that.

"But yet she seems interested in you, Joe," he said. "Why didn't you offer to take her to the bazaar instead of letting another chap get in ahead of you? You miss all your chances, Joe."

Then a thought struck me. I ought to have known Jack well enough to have thought of it before.

"Look here, Jack," I said. "What have you been saying to that girl about me?"

"Oh, not much," said Jack. "There isn't much to say about you."

"What did you tell her?"

"Oh, nothing in particular. She'd heard all about you before."

"She hadn't heard much good, I suppose," I said.

"Well, that's true, as far as I could make out. But you've only got yourself to blame. I didn't have the breeding and rearing of you. I smoothed over matters with her as much as I could."

"What did you tell her?" I said. "That's what I want to know."

"Well, to tell the truth, I didn't tell her anything much. I only answered questions."

"And what questions did she ask?"

"Well, in the first place, she asked if your name wasn't Joe Wilson; and I said it was, as far as I knew. Then she said she heard that you wrote poetry, and I had to admit that that was true."

"Look here, Jack," I said, "I've two minds to punch your head."

"And she asked me if it was true that you were wild," said Jack, "and I said you was, a bit. She said it seemed a pity. She asked me if it was true that you drank, and I drew a long face and said that I was sorry to say it was true. She asked me if you had any friends, and I said none that I knew of, except me. I said that you'd lost all your friends; they stuck to you as long as they could, but they had to give you best, one after the other."

"What next?"

"She asked me if you were delicate, and I said no, you were as tough as fencing-wire. She said you looked rather pale and thin, and asked me if you'd had an illness lately. And I said no—it was all on account of the wild, dissipated life you'd led. She said it was a pity you hadn't a mother or a sister to look after you— it was a pity that something couldn't be done for you, and I said it was, but I was afraid that nothing could be done. I told her that I was doing all I could to keep you straight."

I knew enough of Jack to know that most of this was true. And so she only pitied me after all. I felt as if I'd been courting her for six months and she'd thrown me over—but I didn't know anything about women yet.

"Did you tell her I was in jail?" I growled.

"No, by Gum! I forgot that. But never mind. I'll fix that up all right. I'll tell her that you got two years' hard for horse-stealing. That ought to make her interested in you, if she isn't already."

We smoked a while.

"And was that all she said?" I asked.

"Who?—Oh! 'Possum," said Jack, rousing himself. "Well—no; let me think——We got chatting of other things—you know a married man's privileged, and can say a lot more to a girl than a single man can. I got talking nonsense about sweethearts, and one thing led to another till at last she said, 'I suppose Mr Wilson's got a sweetheart, Mr Barnes?' "

"And what did you say?" I growled.

"Oh, I told her that you were a holy terror amongst the girls," said Jack. "You'd better take back that tray, Joe, and let us get to work."

I wouldn't take back the tray—but that didn't mend matters, for Jack took it back himself.

I didn't see Mary's reflection in the window again, so I took the window out. I reckoned that she was just a big-hearted, impulsive little thing, as many Australians girls are, and I reckoned that I was a fool for thinking for a moment that she might give me a second thought, except by way of kindness. Why! young Black and half a dozen better men than me were sweet on her, and young Black was to get his father's station and the money—or rather his mother's money, for she held the stuff (she kept it close too, by all accounts). Young Black was away at the time, and his mother was dead against him about Mary, but that didn't make any difference, as far as I could see. I reckoned that it was only just going to be a hopeless, heart-breaking, stand-far-off-and-worship affair as far as I was concerned—like my first love affair, that I haven't told you about yet. I was tired of being pitied by good girls. You see, I didn't know women then. If I had known, I think I might have made more than one mess of my life.

Jack rode home to Solong every night. I was staying at a pub some distance out of town, between Solong and Haviland. There were three or four wet days, and we didn't get on with the work. I fought shy of Mary till one day she was hanging out clothes and the line broke. It was the old-style sixpenny clothes-line. The clothes were all down, but it was clean grass, so it didn't matter much. I looked at Jack.

"Go and help her, you capital Idiot!" he said, and I made the plunge.

"Oh, thank you, Mr Wilson!" said Mary, when I came to help. She had the broken end of the line and was trying to hold some of the clothes off the ground, as if she could pull it an inch with the heavy wet sheets and tablecloths and things on it, or as if it would do any good if she did. But that's the way with women—especially little women—some of 'em would try to pull a store bullock if they got the end of the rope on the right side of the fence. I took the line from Mary, and accidentally touched her soft, plump little hand as I did so: it sent a thrill right through me. She seemed a lot cooler than I was.

Now, in cases like this, especially if you lose your head a bit, you get hold of the loose end of the rope that's hanging from the post with one hand, and the end of the line with the clothes on with the other, and try to pull 'em far enough together to make a knot. And that's about all you do for the present, except look like a fool. Then I took off the post end, spliced the line, took it over the fork, and pulled, while Mary helped me with the prop. I thought Jack might have come and taken the prop from her, but he didn't; he just went on with his work as if nothing was happening inside the horizon.

She'd got the line about two-thirds full of clothes; it was a bit short now, so she had to jump and catch it with one hand and hold it down while she pegged a sheet she'd thrown over. I'd made the plunge now, so I volunteered to help her. I held down the line while she threw the things over and pegged out. As we got near the post and higher I straightened out some ends and pegged myself. Bushmen are handy at most things. We laughed, and now and again Mary would say: "No, that's not the way, Mr Wilson; that's not right; the sheet isn't far enough over; wait till I fix it," etc. I'd a reckless idea once of holding her up while she pegged, and I was glad afterwards that I hadn't made such a fool of myself.

"There's only a few more things in the basket, Miss Brand," I said. "You can't reach—I'll fix 'em up."

She seemed to give a little gasp.

"Oh, those things are not ready yet," she said, "they're not rinsed," and she grabbed the basket and held it away from me. The things looked the same to me as the rest on the line; they looked rinsed enough and blued too. I reckoned that she didn't want me to take the trouble, or thought that I mightn't like to be seen hanging out clothes, and was only doing it out of kindness.

"Oh, it's no trouble," I said; "let me hang 'em out. I like it. I've hung out clothes at home on a windy day," and I made a reach into the basket. But she flushed red, with temper I thought, and snatched the basket away.

"Excuse me, Mr Wilson," she said, "but those things are not ready yet!" and she marched into the wash-house.

"Ah well! you've got a little temper of your own," I thought to myself.

When I told Jack, he said that I'd made another fool of myself. He said I'd both disappointed and offended her. He said that my line was to stand off a bit and be serious and melancholy in the background.

That evening when we'd started home, we stopped some time yarning with a chap we met at the gate; and I happened to look back, and saw Mary hanging out the rest of the things—she thought that we were out of sight. Then I understood why those things weren't ready while we were round.

For the next day or two Mary didn't take the slightest notice of me, and I kept out of her way. Jack said I'd disillusioned her—and hurt her dignity—which was a thousand times worse. He said I'd spoilt the thing altogether. He said that she'd got an idea that I was shy and poetic, and I'd only shown myself the usual sort of Bush-whacker.

I noticed her talking and chatting with other fellows once or twice, and it made me miserable. I got drunk two evenings running, and then, as it appeared afterwards, Mary consulted Jack, and at last she said to him, when we were together:

"Do you play draughts, Mr Barnes?"

"No," said Jack.

"Do you, Mr Wilson?" she asked, suddenly turning her big, bright eyes on me, and speaking to me for the first time since last washing-day.

"Yes," I said, "I do a little." Then there was a silence, and I had to say something else.

"Do you play draughts, Miss Brand?" I asked.

"Yes," she said, "but I can't get anyone to play with me here of an evening, the men are generally playing cards or reading." Then she said: "It's very dull these long winter evenings when you've got nothing to do. Young Mr Black used to play draughts, but he's away."

I saw Jack winking at me urgently.

"I'll play a game with you, if you like," I said, "but I ain't much of a player."

"Oh, thank you, Mr Wilson! When shall you have an evening to spare?"

We fixed it for that same evening. We got chummy over the draughts. I had a suspicion even then that it was a put-up job to keep me away from the pub.

Perhaps she found a way of giving a hint to old Black without committing herself. Women have ways—or perhaps Jack did it. Anyway, next day the Boss came round and said to me:

"Look here, Joe, you've got no occasion to stay at the pub. Bring along your blankets and camp in one of the spare rooms of the old house. You can have your tucker here."

He was a good sort, was Black the squatter: a squatter of the old school, who'd shared the early hardships with his men, and couldn't see why he should not shake hands and have a smoke and a yarn over old times with any of his old station hands that happened to come along. But he'd married an Englishwoman after the hardships were over, and she'd never got any Australian notions.

Next day I found one of the skillion rooms scrubbed out and a bed fixed up for me. I'm not sure to this day who did it, but I supposed that good-natured old Black had given one of the women a hint. After tea I had a yarn with Mary, sitting on a log of the wood-heap. I don't remember exactly how we both came to be there, or who sat down first. There was about two feet between us. We got very chummy and confidential. She told me about her childhood and her father.

He'd been an old mate of Black's, a younger son of a well-to-do English family (with blue blood in it, I believe), and sent out to Australia with a thousand pounds to make his way, as many younger sons are, with more or less. They think they're hard done by; they blue their thousand pounds in Melbourne or Sydney, and they don't make any more nowadays, for the roarin' days have been dead these thirty years. I wish I'd had a thousand pounds to start on!

Mary's mother was the daughter of a German immigrant who selected up there in the old days. She had a will of her own as far as I could understand, and bossed the home till the day of her death. Mary's father made money, and lost it, and drank—and died. Mary remembered him sitting on the verandah one evening with his hand on her head, and singing a German song (the "Lorelei", I think it was) softly, as if to himself. Next day he stayed in bed, and the children were kept out of the room; and, when he died, the children were adopted round (there was a little money coming from England).

Mary told me all about her girlhood. She went first to live with a sort of cousin in town, in a house where they took in cards on a tray, and then she came to live with Mrs Black, who took a fancy to her at first. I'd had no boyhood to speak of, so I gave her some of my ideas of what the world ought to be, and she seemed interested.

Next day there were sheets on my bed, and I felt pretty cocky until I remembered that I'd told her I had no one to care for me; then I suspected pity again.

But next evening we remembered that both our fathers and mothers were dead, and discovered that we had no friends except

Jack and old Black, and things went on very satisfactorily.

And next day there was a little table in my room with a crocheted cover and a looking-glass.

I noticed the other girls began to act mysterious and giggle when I was round, but Mary didn't seem aware of it.

We got very chummy. Mary wasn't comfortable at Haviland. Old Black was very fond of her and always took her part, but she wanted to be independent. She had a great idea of going to Sydney and getting into the hospital as a nurse. She had friends in Sydney, but she had no money. There was a little money coming to her when she was twenty-one—a few pounds—and she was going to try and get it before that time.

"Look here, Miss Brand," I said, after we'd watched the moon rise. "I'll lend you the money. I've got plenty—more than I know what to do with."

But I saw I'd hurt her. She sat up very straight for a while, looking before her; then she said it was time to go in, and said: "Good-night, Mr Wilson."

I reckoned I'd done it that time; but Mary told me afterwards that she was only hurt because it struck her that what she said about money might have been taken for a hint. She didn't understand me yet, and I didn't know human nature. I didn't say anything to Jack—in fact, about this time I left off telling him about things. He didn't seem hurt; he worked hard and seemed happy.

I really meant what I said to Mary about the money. It was pure good nature. I'd be a happier man now, I think, and richer man perhaps, if I'd never grown any more selfish than I was that night on the wood-heap with Mary. I felt a great sympathy for her—but I got to love her. I went through all the ups and downs of it. One day I was having tea in the kitchen, and Mary and another girl, named Sarah, reached me a clean plate at the same time: I took Sarah's plate because she was first, and Mary seemed very nasty about it, and that gave me great hopes. But all next evening she played draughts with a drover that she'd chummed up with. I pretended to be interested in Sarah's talk, but it didn't seem to work.

A few days later a Sydney jackeroo visited the station. He had a good pea-rifle, and one afternoon he started to teach Mary to shoot at a target. They seemed to get very chummy. I had a nice time for three or four days, I can tell you. I was worse than a wall-eyed bullock with the pleuro. The other chaps had a shot out of the rifle. Mary called "Mr Wilson" to have a shot, and I made a worse fool of myself by sulking. If it hadn't been a blooming jackeroo I wouldn't have minded so much.

Next evening the jackeroo and one or two other chaps and the girls went out 'possum-shooting. Mary went. I could have gone, but I didn't. I mooched round all the evening like an orphan bandicoot on a burnt ridge, and then I went up to the pub and filled myself with beer, and damned the world, and came home and went to bed. I think that evening was the only time I ever wrote poetry down on a piece of paper. I got so miserable that I enjoyed it.

I felt better next morning, and reckoned I was cured. I ran against Mary accidentally and had to say something.

"How did you enjoy yourself yesterday evening, Miss Brand?" I asked.

"Oh, very well, thank you, Mr Wilson," she said. Then she asked, "How did you enjoy yourself, Mr Wilson?"

I puzzled over that afterwards, but couldn't make anything out of it. Perhaps she only said it for the sake of saying something. But about this time my handkerchiefs and collars disappeared from the room and turned up washed and ironed and laid tidily on my table. I used to keep an eye out, but could never catch anybody near my room. I straightened up, and kept my room a bit tidy, and when my handkerchief got too dirty and I was ashamed of letting it go to the wash, I'd slip down to the river after dark and wash it out, and dry it next day, and rub it up to look as if it hadn't been washed, and leave it on my table. I felt so full of hope and joy that I worked twice as hard as Jack, till one morning he remarked casually:

"I see you've made a new mash, Joe. I saw the half-caste cook tidying up your room this morning and taking your collars and things to the wash-house."

I felt very much off colour all the rest of the day, and I had such a bad night of it that I made up my mind next morning to look the hopelessness square in the face and live the thing down.

.   .   .

It was the evening before Anniversary Day. Jack and I had put in a good day's work to get the job finished, and Jack was having a smoke and a yarn with the chaps before he started home. We sat on an old log along by the fence at the back of the house. There was Jimmy Nowlett the bullock-driver, and long Dave Regan the drover, and big Jim Bullock the fencer, and one or two others. Mary and the station girls and one or two visitors were sitting under the old verandah. The jackeroo was there too, so I felt happy. It was the girls who used to bring the chaps hanging round. They were getting up a dance party for Anni-

versary night. Along in the evening another chap came riding up
to the station: he was a big shearer, a dark, handsome fellow who
looked like a gipsy: it was reckoned that there was foreign blood
in him. He went by the name of Romany. He was supposed to
be shook after Mary too. He had the nastiest temper and the best
violin in the district, and the chaps put up with him a lot because
they wanted him to play at Bush dances. The moon had risen
over Pine Ridge, but it was dusky where we were. We saw
Romany loom up, riding in from the gate; he rode round the end
of the coach-house and across towards where we were—I suppose
he was going to tie up his horse at the fence; but about half-way
across the grass he disappeared. It struck me that there was something peculiar about the way he got down, and I heard a sound
like a horse stumbling.

"What the hell's Romany trying to do?" said Jimmy Nowlett.
"He couldn't have fell off his horse—or else he's drunk."

A couple of chaps got up and went to see. Then there was that
waiting, mysterious silence that comes when something happens
in the dark and nobody knows what it is. I went over, and the
thing dawned on me. I'd stretched a wire clothes-line across there
during the day, and had forgotten all about it for the moment.
Romany had no idea of the line, and, as he rode up, it caught
him on a level with his elbows and scraped him off his horse. He
was sitting on the grass, swearing in a surprised voice, and the
horse looked surprised too. Romany wasn't hurt, but the sudden
shock had spoilt his temper. He wanted to know who'd put up
that bloody line. He came over and sat on the log. The chaps
smoked a while.

"What did you git down so sudden for, Romany?" asked Jim
Bullock presently. "Did you hurt yerself on the pommel?"

"Why didn't you ask the horse to go round?" asked Dave Regan.

"I'd only like to know who put up that bleeding wire!" growled
Romany.

"Well," said Jimmy Nowlett, "if we'd put up a sign to beware
of the line you couldn't have seen it in the dark."

"Unless it was a transparency with a candle behind it," said
Dave Regan. "But why didn't you get down on one end, Romany,
instead of all along? It wouldn't have jolted yer so much."

All this with the Bush drawl, and between the puffs of their
pipes. But I didn't take any interest in it. I was brooding over
Mary and the jackeroo.

"I've heard of men getting down over their horse's head," said
Dave presently, in a reflective sort of way; "in fact I've done it

myself—but I never saw a man get off backwards over his horse's rump."

But they saw that Romany was getting nasty, and they wanted him to play the fiddle next night, so they dropped it.

Mary was singing an old song. I always thought she had a sweet voice, and I'd have enjoyed it if that damned jackeroo hadn't been listening too. We listened in silence until she'd finished.

"That gal's got a nice voice," said Jimmy Nowlett.

"Nice voice!" snarled Romany, who'd been waiting for a chance to be nasty. "Why, I've heard a tom-cat sing better."

I moved, and Jack—he was sitting next to me—nudged me to keep quiet. The chaps didn't like Romany's talk about 'Possum at all. They were all fond of her: she wasn't a pet or a tomboy, for she wasn't built that way, but they were fond of her in such a way that they didn't like to hear anything said about her. They said nothing for a while, but it meant a lot. Perhaps the single men didn't care to speak for fear that it would be said that they were gone on Mary. But presently Jimmy Nowlett gave a big puff at his pipe and spoke:

"I suppose you got bit too in that quarter, Romany?"

"Oh, she tried it on, but it didn't go," said Romany. "I've met her sort before. She's setting her cap at that jackeroo now. Some girls will run after anything with trousers on," and he stood up.

Jack Barnes must have felt what was coming, for he grabbed my arm and whispered: "Sit still, Joe, damn you! He's too good for you!" but I was on my feet and facing Romany as if a giant hand had reached down and wrenched me off the log and set me there.

"You're a damned crawler, Romany!" I said.

Little Jimmy Nowlett was between us and the other fellows round us before a blow got home. "Hold on, you damned fools!" they said. "Keep quiet till we get away from the house!" There was a little clear flat down by the river and plenty of light there, so we decided to go down there and have it out.

Now I never was a fighting man; I'd never learnt to use my hands. I scarcely knew how to put them up. Jack often wanted to teach me, but I wouldn't bother about it. He'd say: "You'll get into a fight some day, Joe, or out of one, and shame me;" but I hadn't the patience to learn. He'd wanted me to take lessons at the station after work, but he used to get excited, and I didn't want Mary to see him knocking me about. Before he was married Jack was always getting into fights—he generally tackled a better man and got a hiding; but he didn't seem to care so long as he made a good show—though he used to explain the thing away from a scientific point of view for weeks after. To tell the truth, I had a horror of fighting; I had a horror of being marked about the face; I think I'd sooner stand off and fight a man with revolvers than fight him with fists; and then I think I would say, last thing: "Don't shoot me in the face!" Then again I hated the idea of hitting a man. It seemed brutal to me. I was too sensitive and sentimental, and that was what the matter was. Jack seemed very serious on it as we walked down to the river, and he couldn't help hanging out blue lights.

"Why didn't you let me teach you to use your hands?" he said. "The only chance now is that Romany can't fight after all. If you'd waited a minute I'd have been at him." We were a bit behind the rest, and Jack started giving me points about lefts and rights, and "half-arms", and that sort of thing. "He's left-handed, and that's the worst of it," said Jack. "You must only make as good a show as you can, and one of us will take him on afterwards."

But I just heard him and that was all. It was to be my first fight since I was a boy, but, somehow, I felt cool about it—sort of dulled. If the chaps had known all they would have set me down as a cur. I thought of that, but it didn't make any difference with me then; I knew it was a thing they couldn't understand. I knew I was reckoned pretty soft. But I knew one thing that they didn't know. I knew that it was going to be a fight to a finish, one way or the other. I had more brains and imagination than the rest put together, and I suppose that that was the real cause of most of my trouble. I kept saying to myself, "You'll have to go through with it now, Joe, old man! It's the turning-point of your life." If I won the fight, I'd set to work and win Mary; if I lost, I'd leave the district for ever. A man thinks a lot in a flash sometimes; I used to get excited over little things, because of the very paltriness of them, but I was mostly cool in a crisis—Jack was the reverse. I looked ahead: I wouldn't be able to marry a girl who could look back and remember when her husband was beaten by another man—no matter what sort of brute the other man was.

I never in my life felt so cool about a thing. Jack kept whispering instructions, and showing with his hands, up to the last moment, but it was all lost on me.

Looking back, I think there was a bit of romance about it: Mary singing under the vines to amuse a jackeroo dude, and a coward going down to the river in the moonlight to fight for her.

It was very quiet in the little moonlit flat by the river. We took off our coats and were ready. There was no swearing or barracking. It seemed an understood thing with the men that if I went out

first round Jack would fight Romany; and if Jack knocked him
out somebody else would fight Jack to square matters. Jim Bullock
wouldn't mind obliging for one; he was a mate of Jack's, but he
didn't mind who he fought so long as it was for the sake of
fair play—or "peace and quietness", as he said. Jim was very
good-natured. He backed Romany, and of course Jack backed me.

As far as I could see, all Romany knew about fighting was to
jerk one arm up in front of his face and duck his head by way
of a feint, and then rush and lunge out. But he had the weight
and strength and length of reach, and my first lesson was a very
short one. I went down early in the round. But it did me good;
the blow and the look I'd seen in Romany's eyes knocked all the
sentiment out of me. Jack said nothing—he seemed to regard it
as a hopeless job from the first. Next round I tried to remember
some things Jack had told me, and made a better show, but I
went down in the end.

I felt Jack breathing quick and trembling as he lifted me up.

"How are you, Joe?" he whispered.

"I'm all right," I said.

"It's all right," whispered Jack in a voice as if I was going
to be hanged, but it would soon be all over. "He can't use his
hands much more than you can—take your time, Joe—try to
remember something I told you, for God's sake!"

When two men fight who don't know how to use their hands,
they stand a show of knocking each other about a lot. I got
some awful thumps, but mostly on the body. Jimmy Nowlett began
to get excited and jump round—he was an excitable little fellow.

"Fight! you ————!" he yelled. "Why don't you fight? That
ain't fightin'. Fight, and don't try to murder each other. Use your
crimson hands or, by God, I'll chip you! Fight, or I'll blanky well
bullock-whip the pair of you;" then his language got awful. They
said we went like windmills, and that nearly every one of the
blows we made was enough to kill a bullock if it had got home.
Jimmy stopped us once, but they held him back.

Presently I went down pretty flat, but the blow was well up on
the head and didn't matter much—I had a good thick skull. And
I had one good eye yet.

"For God's sake, hit him!" whispered Jack—he was trembling
like a leaf. "Don't mind what I told you. I wish I was fighting
him myself! Get a blow home, for God's sake! Make a good show
this round and I'll stop the fight."

That showed how little even Jack, my old mate, understood me.

I had the Bushman up in me now, and wasn't going to be
beaten while I could think. I was wonderfully cool, and learning

to fight. There's nothing like a fight to teach a man. I was thinking fast, and learning more in three seconds than Jack's sparring could have taught me in three weeks. People think that blows hurt in a fight, but they don't—not till afterwards. I fancy that a fighting man, if he isn't altogether an animal, suffers more mentally than he does physically.

While I was getting my wind I could hear through the moonlight and still air the sound of Mary's voice singing up at the house. I thought hard into the future, even as I fought. The fight only seemed something that was passing.

I was on my feet again and at it, and presently I lunged out and felt such a jar in my arm that I thought it was telescoped. I thought I'd put out my wrist and elbow. And Romany was lying on the broad of his back.

I heard Jack draw three breaths of relief in one. He said nothing as he straightened me up, but I could feel his heart beating. He said afterwards that he didn't speak because he thought a word might spoil it.

I went down again, but Jack told me afterwards that he *felt* I was all right when he lifted me.

Then Romany went down, then we fell together, and the chaps separated us. I got another knock-down blow in, and was beginning to enjoy the novelty of it, when Romany staggered and limped.

"I've done," he said. "I've twisted my ankle." He'd caught his heel against a tuft of grass.

"Shake hands," yelled Jimmy Nowlett.

I stepped forward, but Romany took his coat and limped to his horse.

"If yer don't shake hands with Wilson, I'll lamb yer!" howled Jimmy; but Jack told him to let the man alone, and Romany got on his horse somehow and rode off.

I saw Jim Bullock stoop and pick up something from the grass, and heard him swear in surprise. There was some whispering, and presently Jim said:

"If I thought that, I'd kill him."

"What is it?" asked Jack.

Jim held up a butcher's knife. It was common for a man to carry a butcher's knife in a sheath fastened to his belt.

"Why did you let your man fight with a butcher's knife in his belt?" asked Jimmy Nowlett.

But the knife could easily have fallen out when Romany fell, and we decided it that way.

"Anyway," said Jimmy Nowlett, "if he'd stuck Joe in hot blood before us all it wouldn't be so bad as if he sneaked up and stuck him in the back in the dark. But you'd best keep an eye over yer shoulder for a year or two, Joe. That chap's got Eye-talian blood in him somewhere. And now the best thing you chaps can do is to keep your mouth shut and keep all this dark from the gals."

Jack hurried me on ahead. He seemed to act queer, and when I glanced at him I could have sworn that there was water in his eyes. I said that Jack had no sentiment except for himself, but I forgot, and I'm sorry I said it.

"What's up, Jack?" I asked.

"Nothing," said Jack.

"What's up, you old fool?" I said.

"Nothing," said Jack, "except that I'm damned proud of you, Joe, you old ass!" and he put his arm round my shoulders and gave me a shake. "I didn't know it was in you, Joe—I wouldn't have said it before, or listened to any other man say it, but I didn't think you had the pluck—God's truth, I didn't. Come along and get your face fixed up."

We got into my room quietly, and Jack got a dish of water, and told one of the chaps to sneak a piece of fresh beef from somewhere.

Jack was as proud as a dog with a tin tail as he fussed round me. He fixed up my face in the best style he knew, and he knew a good many—he'd been mended himself so often.

While he was at work we heard a sudden hush and a scraping of feet amongst the chaps that Jack had kicked out of the room, and a girl's voice whispered: "Is he hurt? Tell me. I want to know; I might be able to help."

It made my heart jump, I can tell you. Jack went out at once, and there was some whispering. When he came back he seemed wild.

"What is it, Jack?" I asked.

"Oh, nothing," he said, "only that damned slut of a half-caste cook overheard some of those blanky fools arguing as to how Romany's knife got out of the sheath, and she's put a nice yarn round amongst the girls. There's a regular bobbery, but it's all right now. Jimmy Nowlett's telling 'em lies at a great rate."

Presently there was another hush outside, and a saucer with vinegar and brown paper was handed in.

One of the chaps brought some beer and whisky from the pub, and we had a quiet little time in my room. Jack wanted to stay all night, but I reminded him that his little wife was waiting for

him in Solong, so he said he'd be round early in the morning, and
went home.

I felt the reaction pretty bad. I didn't feel proud of the affair
at all. I thought it was a low, brutal business all round. Romany
was a quiet chap after all, and the chaps had no right to chyack
him. Perhaps he'd had a hard life, and carried a big swag of
trouble that we didn't know anything about. He seemed a lonely
man. I'd gone through enough myself to teach me not to judge
men. I made up my mind to tell him how I felt about the matter
next time we met. Perhaps I made my usual mistake of bothering
about "feelings" in another party that hadn't any feelings at all—
perhaps I didn't; but it's generally best to chance it on the kind
side in a case like this. Altogether I felt as if I'd made another
fool of myself and been a weak coward. I drank the rest of the
beer and went to sleep.

About daylight I woke and heard Jack's horse on the gravel.
He came round the back of the buggy-shed and up to my door,
and then, suddenly, a girl screamed out. I pulled on my trousers
and 'lastic-side boots and hurried out. It was Mary herself, dressed,
and sitting on an old stone step at the back of the kitchen with
her face in her hands, and Jack was off his horse and stooping
by her side with his hand on her shoulder. She kept saying: "I
thought you were———! I thought you were———!" I didn't
catch the name. An old single-barrel, muzzle-loader shot-gun was
lying in the grass at her feet. It was the gun they used to keep
loaded and hanging in straps in a room off the kitchen ready for
a shot at a cunning old hawk that they called "'Tarnal Death",
and that used to be always after the chickens.

When Mary lifted her face it was as white as note-paper, and
her eyes seemed to grow wilder when she caught sight of me.

"Oh, you did frighten me, Mr Barnes," she gasped. Then she
gave a little ghost of a laugh and stood up, and some colour
came back.

"Oh, I'm a little fool!" she said quickly. "I thought I heard
old 'Tarnal Death at the chickens, and I thought it would be a
great thing if I got the gun and brought him down; so I got up
and dressed quietly so as not to wake Sarah. And then you came
round the corner and frightened me. I don't know what you must
think of me, Mr Barnes."

"Never mind," said Jack. "You go and have a sleep, or you
won't be able to dance to-night. Never mind the gun—I'll put
that away." And he steered her round to the door of her room
off the brick verandah where she slept with one of her other girls.

"Well, that's a rum start!" I said.

"Yes, it is," said Jack; "it's very funny. Well, how's your face this morning, Joe?"

He seemed a lot more serious than usual.

We were hard at work all the morning cleaning out the big wool-shed and getting it ready for the dance, hanging hoops for the candles, making seats, etc. I kept out of sight of the girls as much as I could. One side of my face was a sight and the other wasn't too classical. I felt as if I had been stung by a swarm of bees.

"You're a fresh, sweet-scented beauty now, and no mistake, Joe," said Jimmy Nowlett—he was going to play the accordion that night. "You ought to fetch the girls now, Joe. But never mind, your face'll go down in about three weeks."

My lower jaw is crooked yet; but that fight straightened my nose that had been knocked crooked when I was a boy—so I didn't lose much beauty by it.

When we'd done in the shed, Jack took me aside and said:

"Look here, Joe! If you won't come to the dance to-night—and I can't say you'd ornament it—I tell you what you'll do. You get little Mary away on the quiet and take her out for a stroll—and act like a man. The job's finished now, and you won't get another chance like this."

"But how am I to get her out?" I said.

"Never you mind. You be mooching round down by the big peppermint-tree near the river-gate, say about half-past ten."

"What good'll that do?"

"Never you mind. You just do as you're told, that's all you've got to do," said Jack, and he went home to get dressed and bring his wife.

After the dancing started that night I had a peep in once or twice. The first time I saw Mary dancing with Jack, and looking serious; and the second time she was dancing with the blarsted jackeroo dude, and looking excited and happy. I noticed that some of the girls, that I could see sitting on a stool along the opposite wall, whispered, and gave Mary black looks as the jackeroo swung her past. It struck me pretty forcibly that I should have taken fighting lessons from him instead of from poor Romany. I went away and walked about four miles down the river road, getting out of the way into the Bush whenever I saw any chap riding along. I thought of poor Romany and wondered where he was, and thought that there wasn't much to choose between us as far as happiness was concerned. Perhaps he was walking by himself in the Bush, and feeling like I did. I wished I could shake hands with him.

But somehow, about half-past ten, I drifted back to the river slip-rails and leant over them, in the shadow of the peppermint-tree, looking at the rows of river-willows in the moonlight. I didn't expect anything, in spite of what Jack said.

I didn't like the idea of hanging myself: I'd been with a party who found a man hanging in the Bush, and it was no place for a woman round where he was. And I'd helped drag two bodies out of the Cudgegong river in a flood, and they weren't sleeping beauties. I thought it was a pity that a chap couldn't lie down on a grassy bank in a graceful position in the moonlight and die just by thinking of it—and die with his eyes and mouth shut. But then I remembered that I wouldn't make a beautiful corpse, anyway it went, with the face I had on me.

I was just getting comfortably miserable when I heard a step behind me, and my heart gave a jump. And I gave a start too.

"Oh, is that you, Mr Wilson?" said a timid little voice.

"Yes," I said. "Is that you, Mary?"

And she said yes. It was the first time I called her Mary, but she did not seem to notice it.

"Did I frighten you?" I asked.

"No—yes—just a little," she said. "I didn't know there was anyone———" then she stopped.

"Why aren't you dancing?" I asked her.

"Oh, I'm tired," she said. "It was too hot in the wool-shed. I thought I'd like to come out and get my head cool and be quiet a little while."

"Yes," I said, "it must be hot in the wool-shed."

She stood looking out over the willows. Presently she said: "It must be very dull for you, Mr Wilson—you must feel lonely. Mr Barnes said———" Then she gave a little gasp and stopped —as if she was just going to put her foot in it.

"How beautiful the moonlight looks on the willows!" she said.

"Yes," I said, "doesn't it? Supposing we have a stroll by the river."

"Oh, thank you, Mr Wilson. I'd like it very much."

I didn't notice it then, but, now I come to think of it, it was a beautiful scene: there was a horse-shoe of high blue hills round behind the house, with the river running round under the slopes, and in front was a rounded hill covered with pines, and pine ridges, and a soft blue peak away over the ridges ever so far in the distance.

I had a handkerchief over the worst of my face, and kept the best side turned to her. We walked down by the river, and didn't say anything for a good while. I was thinking hard. We came to a white smooth log in a quiet place out of sight of the house.

"Suppose we sit down for a while, Mary," I said.

"If you like, Mr Wilson," she said.

There was about a foot of log between us.

"What a beautiful night!" she said.

"Yes," I said, "isn't it?"

Presently she said: "I suppose you know I'm going away next month, Mr Wilson?"

I felt suddenly empty. "No," I said, "I didn't know that."

"Yes," she said, "I thought you knew. I'm going to try and get into the hospital to be trained for a nurse, and if that doesn't come off I'll get a place as assistant public-school teacher."

We didn't say anything for a good while.

"I suppose you won't be sorry to go, Miss Brand?" I said.

"I—I don't know," she said. "Everybody's been so kind to me here."

She sat looking straight before her, and I fancied her eyes glistened. I put my arm round her shoulders, but she didn't seem to notice it. In fact, I scarcely noticed it myself at the time.

"So you think you'll be sorry to go away?" I said.

"Yes, Mr Wilson. I suppose I'll fret for a while. It's been my home, you know."

I pressed my hand on her shoulder, just a little, so as she couldn't pretend not to know it was there. But she didn't seem to notice.

"Ah, well," I said, "I suppose I'll be on the wallaby again next week."

"Will you, Mr Wilson?" she said. Her voice seemed very soft.

I slipped my arm round her waist, under her arm. My heart was going like clockwork now.

Presently she said:

"Don't you think it's time to go back now, Mr Wilson?"

"Oh, there's plenty of time!" I said. I shifted up, and put my arm farther round, and held her closer. She sat straight up, looking right in front of her, but she began to breathe hard.

"Mary," I said.

"Yes," she said.

"Call me Joe," I said.

"I—I don't like to," she said. "I don't think it would be right."

So I just turned her face round and kissed her. She clung to me and cried.

"What is it, Mary?" I asked.

She only held me tighter and cried.

"What is it, Mary?" I said. "Ain't you well? Ain't you happy?"

"Yes, Joe," she said, "I'm very happy." Then she said: "Oh, your poor face! Can't I do anything for it?"

"No," I said. "That's all right. My face doesn't hurt me a bit now."

But she didn't seem right.

"What is it, Mary?" I said. "Are you tired? You didn't sleep last night————" Then I got an inspiration.

"Mary," I said, "what were you doing out with the gun this morning?"

And after some coaxing it all came out, a bit hysterical.

"I couldn't sleep—I was frightened. Oh! I had such a terrible dream about you, Joe! I thought Romany came back and got into your room and stabbed you with his knife. I got up and dressed, and about daybreak I heard a horse at the gate; then I got the gun down from the wall—and—and Mr Barnes came round the corner and frightened me. He's something like Romany, you know."

Then I got as much of her as I could into my arms,

And, oh, but wasn't I happy walking home with Mary that night! She was too little for me to put my arm round her waist, so I put it round her shoulder, and that felt just as good. I remember I asked her who'd cleaned up my room and washed my things, but she wouldn't tell.

She wouldn't go back to the dance yet; she said she'd go into her room and rest a while. There was no one near the old verandah; and when she stood on the end of the floor she was just on a level with my shoulder.

"Mary," I whispered, "put your arms round my neck and kiss me."

She put her arms round my neck, but she didn't kiss me; she only hid her face.

"Kiss me, Mary!" I said.

"I—I don't like to," she whispered.

"Why not, Mary?"

Then I felt her crying or laughing, or half crying and half laughing. I'm not sure to this day which it was.

"Why won't you kiss me, Mary? Don't you love me?"

"Because," she said, "because—because I—I don't—I don't think it's right for—for a girl to—to kiss a man unless she's going to be his wife."

Then it dawned on me! I'd forgot all about proposing.

"Mary," I said, "would you marry a chap like me?"

And that was all right.

.   .   .

Next morning Mary cleared out my room and sorted out my things, and didn't take the slightest notice of the other girls' astonishment.

But she made me promise to speak to old Black, and I did the same evening. I found him sitting on the log by the fence, having a yarn on the quiet with an old Bushman; and when the old Bushman got up and went away, I sat down.

"Well, Joe," said Black, "I see somebody's been spoiling your face for the dance." And after a bit he said: "Well, Joe, what is it? Do you want another job? If you do, you'll have to ask Mrs Black, or Bob" (Bob was his eldest son); "they're managing the station for me now, you know." He could be bitter sometimes in his quiet way.

"No," I said; "it's not that, Boss."

"Well, what is it, Joe?"

"I—well, the fact is, I want little Mary."

He puffed at his pipe for a long time, then I thought he spoke.

"What did you say, Boss?" I said.

"Nothing, Joe," he said. "I was going to say a lot, but it wouldn't be any use. My father used to say a lot to me before I was married."

I waited a good while for him to speak.

"Well, Boss," I said, "what about Mary?"

"Oh! I suppose that's all right, Joe," he said. "I—I beg your pardon. I got thinking of the days when I was courting Mrs Black."

[*1900?*]

BRIGHTEN'S SISTER-IN-LAW

JIM was born on Gulgong, New South Wales. We used to say "on" Gulgong—and old diggers still talked of being "on th' Gulgong"—though the gold-field there had been worked out for years, and the place was only a dusty little pastoral town in the scrubs. Gulgong was about the last of the great alluvial rushes of the roaring days—and dreary and dismal enough it looked when I was there. The expression "on" came from being on the "diggings" or gold-field—the workings or the gold-field was all underneath, of course, so we lived (or starved) *on* them—not in nor at 'em.

Mary and I had been married about two years when Jim came. His name wasn't "Jim", by the way, it was "John Henry", after an uncle godfather; but we called him Jim from the first—(and before it)—because Jim was a popular Bush name, and most of my old mates were Jims. The Bush is full of good-hearted scamps called Jim.

We lived in an old weatherboard shanty that had been a sly grog shop, and the Lord knows what else! in the palmy days of Gulgong; and I did a bit of digging ("fossicking", rather), a bit of shearing, a bit of fencing, a bit of Bush carpentering, tank-sinking—anything, just to keep the billy boiling.

We had a lot of trouble with Jim with his teeth. He was bad with every one of them, and we had most of them lanced—couldn't pull him through without. I remember we got one lanced and the gum healed over before the tooth came through, and we had to get it cut again. He was a plucky little chap, and after the first time he never whimpered when the doctor was lancing his gum: he used to say "tar" afterwards, and want to bring the lance home with him.

The first turn we got with Jim was the worst. I had had the wife and Jim out camping with me in a tent at a dam I was making at Cattle Creek; I had two men working for me, and a boy to drive one of the tip-drays, and I took Mary out to cook for us. And it was lucky for us that the contract was finished and we got back to Gulgong, and within reach of a doctor, the day we did. We were just camping in the house, with our goods and chattels anyhow, for the night; and we were hardly back home an hour when Jim took convulsions for the first time.

Did you ever see a child in convulsions? You wouldn't want to see it again: it plays the devil with a man's nerves. I'd got the beds fixed up on the floor, and the billies on the fire—I was going to make some tea, and put a piece of corned beef on to boil overnight—when Jim (he'd been queer all day, and his mother was trying to hush him to sleep)—Jim, he screamed out twice. He'd been crying a good deal, and I was dog-tired and worried (over some money a man owed me) or I'd have noticed at once that there was something unusual in the way the child cried out: as it was I didn't turn round till Mary screamed: "Joe! Joe!" You know how a woman cries out when her child is in danger or dying—short, and sharp, and terrible. "Joe! Look! look! Oh, my God! our child! Get the bath, quick! quick! it's convulsions!"

Jim was bent back like a bow, stiff as a bullock-yoke, in his mother's arms, and his eyeballs were turned up and fixed—a thing I saw twice afterwards, and don't want ever to see again.

I was falling over things getting the tub and the hot water, when the woman who lived next door rushed in. She called to her husband to run for the doctor, and before the doctor came she and Mary had got Jim into a hot bath and pulled him through.

The neighbour woman made me up a shake-down in another room, and stayed with Mary that night; but it was a long while before I got Jim and Mary's screams out of my head and fell asleep.

You may depend I kept the fire in, and a bucket of water hot over it, for a good many nights after that; but (it always happens like this) there came a night, when the fright had worn off, when I was too tired to bother about the fire, and that night Jim took us by surprise. Our wood-heap was done, and I broke up a new chair to get a fire, and had to run a quarter of a mile for water; but this turn wasn't so bad as the first, and we pulled him through.

You never saw a child in convulsions? Well, you don't want to. It must be only a matter of seconds, but it seems long minutes; and half an hour afterwards the child might be laughing and playing with you, or stretched out dead. It shook me up a lot. I was always pretty high-strung and sensitive. After Jim took the first fit, every time he cried, or turned over, or stretched out in the night, I'd jump: I was always feeling his forehead in the dark to see if he was feverish, or feeling his limbs to see if he was "limp" yet. Mary and I often laughed about it—afterwards. I tried sleeping in another room, but for nights after Jim's first attack I'd be just dozing off into a sound sleep when I'd hear him scream, as plain as could be, and I'd hear Mary cry: "Joe!—Joe!"— short, sharp, and terrible—and I'd be up and into their room like a shot, only to find them sleeping peacefully. Then I'd feel Jim's head and his breathing for signs of convulsions, see to the fire and water, and go back to bed and try to sleep. For the first few nights I was like that all night, and I'd feel relieved when daylight came. I'd be in first thing to see if they were all right; then I'd sleep till dinner-time if it was Sunday or I had no work. But then I was run down about that time: I was worried about some money for a wool-shed I put up and never got paid for; and, besides, I'd been pretty wild before I met Mary.

I was fighting hard then—struggling for something better. Both Mary and I were born to better things, and that's what made the life so hard for us.

Jim got on all right for a while: we used to watch him well, and have his teeth lanced in time.

It used to hurt and worry me to see how—just as he was getting fat and rosy and like a natural happy child, and I'd feel proud to take him out—a tooth would come along, and he'd get thin and white and pale and bigger-eyed and old-fashioned. We'd say: "He'll be safe when he gets his eye-teeth": but he didn't get them till he was two; then: "He'll be safe when he gets his two-year-old teeth": they didn't come till he was going on for three.

He was a wonderful little chap—yes, I know all about parents thinking that their child is the best in the world. If your boy is small for his age, friends will say that small children make big men; that he's a very bright, intelligent child, and that it's better to have a bright, intelligent child than a big, sleepy lump of fat. And if your boy is dull and sleepy, they say that the dullest boys make the cleverest men—and all the rest of it. I never took any notice of that sort of clatter—took it for what it was worth; but, all the same, I don't think I ever saw such a child as Jim was when he turned two. He was everybody's favourite. They spoilt him rather. I had my own ideas about bringing up a child. I reckoned Mary was too soft with Jim. She'd say: "Put that" (whatever it was) "out of Jim's reach, will you, Joe?" and I'd say: "No! leave it there, and make him understand he's not to have it. Make him have his meals without any nonsense, and go to bed at a regular hour," I'd say. Mary and I had many a breeze over Jim. She'd say that I forgot he was only a baby: but I held that a baby could be trained from the first week; and I believe I was right.

But, after all, what are you to do? You'll see a boy that was brought up strict turn out a scamp; and another that was dragged up anyhow (by the hair of the head, as the saying is) turn out well. Then, again, when a child is delicate—and you might lose him any day—you don't like to spank him, though he might be turning out a little fiend, as delicate children often do. Suppose you gave a child a hammering, and the same night he took convulsions, or something, and died—how'd you feel about it? You never know what a child is going to take, any more than you can tell what some women are going to say or do.

I was very fond of Jim, and we were great chums. Sometimes I'd sit and wonder what the deuce he was thinking about, and often, the way he talked, he'd make me uneasy. When he was two he wanted a pipe above all things, and I'd get him a clean new clay and he'd sit by my side, on the edge of the verandah, or on a log of the wood-heap, in the cool of the evening, and suck away at his pipe, and try to spit when he saw me do it. He seemed to understand that a cold empty pipe wasn't quite the thing, yet to have the sense to know that he couldn't smoke tobacco yet: he made the best he could of things. And if he broke a clay pipe he wouldn't have a new one, and there'd be a row; the old one had to be mended up, somehow, with string or wire. If I got my hair cut, he'd want his cut too; and it always troubled him to see me shave—as if he thought there must be something wrong somewhere, else he ought to have to be shaved too. I lathered him one day, and pretended to shave him: he sat through it as solemn as an owl, but didn't seem to appreciate it—perhaps he had sense enough to know that it couldn't possibly be the real thing. He felt his face, looked very hard at the lather I scraped off, and whimpered: "No blood, daddy!"

I used to cut myself a good deal: I was always impatient over shaving.

Then he went in to interview his mother about it. She understood his lingo better than I did.

But I wasn't always at ease with him. Sometimes he'd sit looking into the fire, with his head on one side, and I'd watch him and wonder what he was thinking about (I might as well have wondered what a Chinaman was thinking about) till he seemed at least twenty years older than me: sometimes, when I moved or spoke, he'd glance round just as if to see what that old fool of a dadda of his was doing now.

I used to have a fancy that there was something Eastern or Asiatic—something older than our civilization or religion—about old-fashioned children. Once I started to explain my idea to a woman I thought would understand—and as it happened she had an old-fashioned child, with very slant eyes—a little tartar he was too. I suppose it was the sight of him that unconsciously reminded me of my infernal theory, and set me off on it, without warning me. Anyhow, it got me mixed up in an awful row with the woman and her husband—and all their tribe. It wasn't an easy thing to explain myself out of it, and the row hasn't been fixed up yet. There were some Chinamen in the district.

I took a good-size fencing contract, the frontage of a ten-mile paddock, near Gulgong, and did well out of it. The railway had got as far as the Cudgegong river—some twenty miles from Gulgong and two hundred from the coast—and "carrying" was good then. I had a couple of draught-horses that I worked in the tip-drays when I was tank-sinking, and one or two others running in the Bush. I bought a broken-down waggon cheap, tinkered it up myself—christened it "The Same Old Thing"—and started carrying from the railway terminus through Gulgong and along the Bush roads and tracks that branch out fanlike through the scrubs to the one-pub towns and sheep and cattle stations out there in the howling wilderness. It wasn't much of a team. There were the two heavy horses for "shafters"; a stunted colt that I'd bought out of the pound for thirty shillings; a light, spring-cart horse; an old grey mare, with points like a big red-and-white Australian store bullock, and with the grit of an old washerwoman to work; and a horse that had spanked along in Cobb & Co.'s mail-coach in his time. I had a couple there that didn't belong to me: I worked them for the feeding of them in the dry weather. And I had all sorts of harness that I mended and fixed up myself. It was a mixed team, but I took light stuff, got through pretty quick, and freight rates were high. So I got along.

Before this, whenever I made a few pounds I'd sink a shaft somewhere, prospecting for gold; but Mary never let me rest till she talked me out of that.

I made up my mind to take on a small selection farm—that an old mate of mine had fenced in and cleared, and afterwards chucked up—about thirty miles out west of Gulgong, at a place called Lahey's Creek. (The places were all called Lahey's Creek, or Spicer's Flat, or Murphy's Flat, or Ryan's Crossing, or some such name—round there.) I reckoned I'd have a run for the horses and be able to grow a bit of feed. I always had a dread of taking Mary and the children too far away from a doctor—or a good woman neighbour; but there were some people came to live on Lahey's Creek, and besides, there was a young brother of Mary's—a young scamp (his name was Jim, too, and we called him "Jimmy" at first to make room for our Jim—he hated the name "Jimmy" or James). He came to live with us—without asking—and I thought he'd find enough work at Lahey's Creek to keep him out of mischief. He wasn't to be depended on much—he thought nothing of riding off, five hundred miles or so, "to have a look at the country"—but he was fond of Mary, and he'd stay by her till I got someone else to keep her company while I was on the road. He would be a protection against "sundowners" or any shearers who happened to wander that way in the "D.T.'s" after a spree. Mary had a married sister come to live at Gulgong just before we left, and nothing would suit her and her husband but we must leave little Jim with them for a month or so—till we got settled down at Lahey's Creek. They were newly married.

Mary was to have driven into Gulgong, in the spring-cart, at the end of the month and taken Jim home; but when the time came she wasn't too well—and, besides, the tyres of the cart were loose, and I hadn't time to get them cut, so we let Jim's time run on a week or so longer, till I happened to come out through Gulgong from the river with a small load of flour for Lahey's Creek way. The roads were good, the weather grand—no chance of it raining, and I had a spare tarpaulin if it did—I would only camp out one night; so I decided to take Jim home with me.

Jim was turning three then, and he was a cure. He was so old-fashioned that he used to frighten me sometimes—I'd almost think that there was something supernatural about him; though, of course, I never took any notice of that rot about some children being too old-fashioned to live. There's always the ghoulish old hag (and some not so old nor haggish either) who'll come round and shake up young parents with such croaks as "You'll never rear that child—he's too bright for his age." To the devil with them! I say.

But I really thought that Jim was too intelligent for his age, and I often told Mary that he ought to be kept back, and not let talk too much to old diggers and long lanky jokers of Bushmen who rode in and hung their horses outside my place on Sunday afternoons.

I don't believe in parents talking about their own children ever-lastingly—you get sick of hearing them; and their kids are generally little devils, and turn out larrikins as likely as not.

But, for all that, I really think that Jim, when he was three years old, was the most wonderful little chap, in every way, that I ever saw.

For the first hour or so along the road he was telling me all about his adventures at his auntie's.

"But they spoilt me too much dad," he said, as solemn as a native bear. "An' besides, a boy ought to stick to his parrans!"

I was taking out a cattle-pup for a drover I knew, and the pup took up a good deal of Jim's time.

Sometimes he'd jolt me, the way he talked; and other times

I'd have to turn my head away and cough, or shout at the horses, to keep from laughing outright. And once, when I was taken that way, he said:

"What are you jerking your shoulders and coughing, and grunting, and going on that way for, dad? Why don't you tell me something?"

"Tell you what, Jim?"

"Tell me some talk."

So I told him all the talk I could think of. And I had to brighten up, I can tell you, and not draw too much on my imagination— for Jim was a terror at cross-examination when the fit took him; and he didn't think twice about telling you when he thought you were talking nonsense. Once he said:

"I'm glad you took me home with you, dad. You'll get to know Jim."

"What!" I said.

"You'll get to know Jim."

"But don't I know you already?"

"No, you don't. You never has time to know Jim at home."

And, looking back, I saw that it was cruel true. I had known in my heart all along that this was the truth; but it came to me like a blow from Jim. You see, it had been a hard struggle for the last year or so; and when I was home for a day or two I was generally too busy, or too tired and worried, or full of schemes for the future, to take much notice of Jim. Mary used to speak to me about it sometimes. "You never take notice of the child," she'd say. "You could surely find a few minutes of an evening. What's the use of always worrying and brooding? Your brain will go with a snap some day, and, if you get over it, it will teach you a lesson. You'll be an old man, and Jim a young one, before you realize that you had a child once. Then it will be too late."

This sort of talk from Mary always bored me and made me impatient with her, because I knew it all too well. I never worried for myself—only for Mary and the children. And often, as the days went by, I said to myself: "I'll take more notice of Jim and give Mary more of my time, just as soon as I can see things clear ahead a bit." And the hard days went on, and the weeks, and the months, and the years———— Ah, well!

Mary used to say, when things would get worse: "Why don't you talk to me, Joe? Why don't you tell me your thoughts, instead of shutting yourself up in yourself and brooding—eating your heart out? It's hard for me: I get to think you're tired of me, and selfish. I might be cross and speak sharp to you when you are in trouble. How am I to know, if you don't tell me?"

But I didn't think she'd understand.

And so, getting acquainted, and chumming and dozing, with the gums closing over our heads here and there, and the ragged patches of sunlight and shade passing up, over the horses, over us, on the front of the load, over the load, and down on to the white, dusty road again——Jim and I got along the lonely Bush road and over the ridges, some fifteen miles before sunset, and camped at Ryan's Crossing on Sandy Creek for the night. I got the horses out and took the harness off. Jim wanted badly to help me, but I made him stay on the load; for one of the horses—a vicious, red-eyed chestnut—was a kicker: he'd broken a man's leg. I got the feed-bags stretched across the shafts, and the chaff-and-corn into them; and there stood the horses all round with their rumps north, south, and west, and their heads between the shafts, munching and switching their tails. We use double shafts, you know, for horse-teams—two pairs side by side—and prop them up, and stretch bags between them, letting the bags sag to serve as feed-boxes. I threw the spare tarpaulin over the wheels on one side, letting about half of it lie on the ground in case of damp, and so making a floor and a break-wind. I threw down bags and the blankets and 'possum rug against the wheel to make a camp for Jim and the cattle-pup, and got a gin-case we used for a tucker-box, the frying-pan and billy down, and made a good fire at a log close handy, and soon everything was comfortable. Ryan's Crossing was a grand camp. I stood with my pipe in my mouth, my hands behind my back, and my back to the fire, and took the country in.

Reedy Creek came down along a western spur of the range: the banks here were deep and green, and the water ran clear over the granite bars, boulders, and gravel. Behind us was a dreary flat covered with those gnarled, grey-barked, dry-rotted "native apple-trees" (about as much like apple-trees as the native bear is like any other), and a nasty bit of sand-dusty road that I was always glad to get over in wet weather. To the left on our side of the creek were reedy marshes, with frogs croaking, and across the creek the dark box-scrub-covered ridges ended in steep sidings coming down to the creek-bank, and to the main road that skirted them, running on west up over a saddle in the ridges and on towards Dubbo. The road by Lahey's Creek to a place called Cobborah branched off, through dreary apple-tree and stringy-bark flats, to the left, just beyond the crossing: all these fanlike branch tracks from the Cudgegong were inside a big horse-shoe in the Great Western Line, and so they gave small carriers a chance, now that Cobb & Co.'s coaches and the big teams and vans had shifted out of the main western terminus. There were tall she-oaks all along the creek, and a clump of big ones over a deep water-hole just above the crossing. The creek-oaks have rough-barked trunks, like English elms, but are much taller, and higher to the branches—and the leaves are reedy; Kendall, the Australian poet, calls them the "she-oak harps Æolian". Those trees are always sigh-sigh-sighing—more of a sigh than a sough or the "whoosh" of gum-trees in the wind. You always hear them sighing, even when you can't feel any wind. It's the same with telegraph wires: put your head against a telegraph-post on a dead, still day, and you'll hear and feel the far-away roar of the wires. But then the oaks are not connected with the distance, where there might be wind; and they don't *roar* in a gale, only sigh louder and softer according to the wind, and never seem to go above or below a certain pitch —like a big harp with all the strings the same. I used to have a theory that those creek-oaks got the wind's voice telephoned to them, so to speak, through the ground.

I happened to look down, and there was Jim (I thought he was on the tarpaulin, playing with the pup): he was standing close beside me with his legs wide apart, his hands behind his back, and his back to the fire.

He held his head a little on one side, and there was such an old, old, wise expression in his big brown eyes—just as if he'd been a child for a hundred years or so, or as though he were listening to those oaks and understanding them in a fatherly sort of way.

"Dad!" he said presently. "Dad! do you think I'll ever grow up to be a man?"

"Wh—why, Jim?" I gasped.

"Because I don't want to."

I couldn't think of anything against this. It made me uneasy. But I remembered *I* used to have a childish dread of growing up to be a man.

"Jim," I said, to break the silence, "do you hear what the she-oaks say?"

"No, I don't. Is they talking?"

"Yes," I said, without thinking.

"What is they saying?" he asked.

I took the bucket and went down to the creek for some water for tea. I thought Jim would follow with a little tin billy he had, but he didn't: when I got back to the fire he was again on the 'possum rug, comforting the pup. I fried some bacon and eggs that I'd brought out with me. Jim sang out from the waggon:

"Don't cook too much, dad—I mightn't be hungry."

I got the tin plates and pint-pots and things out on a clean new

flour-bag, in honour of Jim, and dished up. He was leaning back
on the rug looking at the pup in a listless sort of way. I reckoned
he was tired out, and pulled the gin-case up close to him for a
table and put his plate on it. But he only tried a mouthful or two,
and then he said:

"I ain't hungry, dad! You'll have to eat it all."

It made me uneasy—I never liked to see a child of mine turn
from his food. They had given him some tinned salmon in Gulgong, and I was afraid that that was upsetting him. I was always
against tinned muck.

"Sick, Jim?" I asked.

"No, dad, I ain't sick; I don't know what's the matter with me."

"Have some tea, sonny?"

"Yes, dad."

I gave him some tea, with some milk in it that I'd brought in
a bottle from his aunt's for him. He took a sip or two and then
put the pint-pot on the gin-case.

"Jim's tired, dad," he said.

I made him lie down while I fixed up a camp for the night.
It had turned a bit chilly, so I let the big tarpaulin down all round
—it was made to cover a high load, the flour in the waggon didn't
come above the rail, so the tarpaulin came down well on to the
ground. I fixed Jim up a comfortable bed under the tail-end of
the waggon: when I went to lift him in he was lying back, looking
up at the stars in a half-dreamy, half-fascinated way that I didn't
like. Whenever Jim was extra old-fashioned, or affectionate, there
was danger.

"How do you feel now, sonny?"

It seemed a minute before he heard me and turned from the
stars.

"Jim's better, dad." Then he said something like: "The stars
are looking at me." I thought he was half asleep. I took off his
jacket and boots, and carried him in under the waggon and made
him comfortable for the night.

"Kiss me 'night-night, daddy," he said.

I'd rather he hadn't asked me—it was a bad sign. As I was
going to the fire he called me back.

"What is it, Jim?"

"Get me my things and the cattle-pup, please, daddy."

I was scared now. His things were some toys and rubbish he'd
brought from Gulgong, and I remembered the last time he had
convulsions he took all his toys and a kitten to bed with him.
And "'night-night" and "daddy" were two-year-old language to

Jim. I'd thought he'd forgotten those words—he seemed to be going back.

"Are you quite warm enough, Jim?"

"Yes, dad."

I started to walk up and down—I always did this when I was extra worried.

I was frightened now about Jim, though I tried to hide the fact from myself. Presently he called me again.

"What is it, Jim?"

"Take the blankets off me, fahver—Jim's sick!" (They'd been teaching him to say father.)

I was scared now. I remembered a neighbour of ours had a little girl die (she swallowed a pin), and when she was going she said:

"Take the blankets off me, muvver—I'm dying."

And I couldn't get that out of my head.

I threw back a fold of the 'possum rug and felt Jim's head—he seemed cool enough.

"Where do you feel bad, sonny?"

No answer for a while; then he said suddenly, but in a voice as if he were talking in his sleep:

"Put my boots on, please, daddy. I want to go home to muvver!"

I held his hand, and comforted him for a while; then he slept—in a restless, feverish sort of way.

I got the bucket I used for water for the horses and stood it over the fire; I ran to the creek with the big kerosene-tin bucket and got it full of cold water and stood it handy. I got the spade (we always carried one to dig wheels out of bogs in wet weather) and turned a corner of the tarpaulin back, dug a hole, and trod the tarpaulin down into the hole, to serve for a bath in case of the worst. I had a tin of mustard, and meant to fight a good round for Jim if death came along.

I stooped in under the tail-board of the waggon and felt Jim. His head was burning hot, and his skin parched and dry as a bone.

Then I lost nerve and started blundering backward and forward between the waggon and the fire, and repeating what I'd heard Mary say the last time we fought for Jim: "God! don't take my child! God! don't take my boy!" I'd never had much faith in doctors, but, my God! I wanted one then. The nearest was fifteen miles away.

I threw back my head and stared up at the branches in desperation; and——Well, I don't ask you to take much stock in this, though most old Bushmen will believe anything of the Bush by night; and——Now, it might have been that I was all unstrung, or it might have been a patch of sky outlined in the gently moving branches, or the blue smoke rising up. But I saw the figure of a woman, all white, come down, down, nearly to the limbs of the trees, point on up the main road, and then float up and up and up and vanish, still pointing. I thought Mary was dead! Then it flashed on me———

Four or five miles up the road, over the saddle, was an old shanty that had been a half-way inn before the Great Western Line got round as far as Dubbo and took the coach traffic off those old Bush roads. A man named Brighten lived there. He was a selector; did a little farming, and as much sly grog selling as he could. He was married—but it wasn't that: I'd thought of them, but she was a childish, worn-out, spiritless woman, and both were pretty "ratty" from hardship and loneliness—they weren't likely to be of any use to me. But it was this: I'd heard talk, among some women in Gulgong, of a sister of Brighten's wife who'd gone out to live with them lately: she'd been a hospital matron in the city, they said; and there were yarns about her. Some said she got the sack for exposing the doctors—or carrying on with them—I didn't remember which. The fact of a city woman going out to live in such a place, with such people, was enough to make talk among women in a town twenty miles away, but then there must have been something extra about her, else Bushmen wouldn't have talked and carried her name so far; and I wanted a woman out of the ordinary now. I even reasoned this way, thinking like lightning, as I knelt over Jim between the big back wheels of the waggon.

I had an old racing mare that I used as a riding hack, following the team. In a minute I had her saddled and bridled; I tied the end of a half-full chaff-bag, shook the chaff into each end and dumped it on to the pommel as a cushion or buffer for Jim; I wrapped him in a blanket, and scrambled into the saddle with him.

The next minute were were stumbling down the steep bank, clattering and splashing over the crossing, and struggling up the opposite bank to the level. The mare, as I told you, was an old racer, but broken-winded—she must have run without wind after the first half-mile. She had the old racing instinct in her strong, and whenever I rode in company I'd have to pull her hard else she'd race the other horse or burst. She ran low fore and aft, and was the easiest horse I ever rode. She ran like wheels on rails, with a bit of a tremble now and then—like a railway carriage— when she settled down to it.

The chaff-bag had slipped off, in the creek I suppose, and I let the bridle-rein go and held Jim up to me like a baby the whole way. Let the strongest man, who isn't used to it, hold a baby in one position for five minutes—and Jim was fairly heavy. But I never felt the ache in my arms that night—it must have gone before I was in a fit state of mind to feel it. And at home I'd often growled about being asked to hold the baby for a few minutes. I could never brood comfortably and nurse a baby at the same time. It was a ghostly moonlight night. There's no timber in the world so ghostly as the Australian Bush in moonlight—or just about daybreak. The all-shaped patches of moonlight falling between ragged, twisted boughs; the ghostly blue-white bark of the "white-box" trees; a dead naked white ring-barked tree or dead white stump starting out here and there, and the ragged patches of shade and light on the road that made anything, from the shape of a spotted bullock to a naked corpse laid out, stark. Roads and tracks through the Bush made by moonlight—every one seeming straighter and clearer than the real one: you have to trust to your horse then. Sometimes the naked white trunk of a red stringy-bark tree, where a sheet of bark had been taken off, would start out like a ghost from the dark Bush. And dew or frost glistening on these things, according to the season. Now and again a great grey kangaroo, that had been feeding on a green patch down by the road, would start with a "thump-thump", and away up the siding.

The Bush seemed full of ghosts that night—all going my way—and being left behind by the mare. Once I stopped to look at Jim: I just sat back and the mare "propped"—she'd been a stock-horse and was used to "cutting-out". I felt Jim's hands and forehead; he was in a burning fever. I bent forward, and the old mare settled down to it again. I kept saying out loud—and Mary and me often laughed about it (afterwards): "He's limp yet!—Jim's limp yet!" (the words seemed jerked out of me by sheer fright)—"He's limp yet!" till the mare's feet took it up. Then, just when I thought she was doing her best and racing her hardest, she suddenly started forward, like a cable tram gliding along on its own and the grip put on suddenly. It was just what she'd do when I'd be riding alone and a strange horse drew up from behind —the old racing instinct. I *felt* the thing too! I felt as if a strange horse *was* there! And then—the words just jerked out of me by sheer funk—I started saying: "Death is riding to-night! . . . Death is racing to-night! . . . Death is riding to-night!" till the hoofs took that up. And I believe the old mare felt the black horse at her side and was going to beat him or break her heart.

I was mad with anxiety and fright; I remember I kept saying: "I'll be kinder to Mary after this! I'll take more notice of Jim!" and the rest of it.

I don't know how the old mare got up the last "pinch". She

must have slackened pace, but I never noticed it: I just held Jim
up to me and gripped the saddle with my knees—I remember the
saddle jerked from the desperate jumps of her till I thought the
girth would go. We topped the gap and were going down into a
gully they called Dead Man's Hollow, and there, at the back of
a ghostly clearing that opened from the road where there were
some black-soil springs, was a long, low, oblong weatherboard-
and-shingle building, with blind, broken windows in the gable-ends,
and a wide steep verandah roof slanting down almost to the level
of the window-sills—there was something sinister about it, I
thought—like the hat of a jail-bird slouched over his eyes. The
place looked both deserted and haunted. I saw no light, but that
was because of the moonlight outside. The mare turned in at the
corner of the clearing to take a short cut to the shanty, and, as
she struggled across some marshy ground, my heart kept jerking
out the words: "It's deserted! They've gone away! It's deserted!"
The mare went round to the back and pulled up between the back
door and a big bark-and-slab kitchen. Someone shouted from
inside:

"Who's there?"

"It's me. Joe Wilson. I want your sister-in-law—I've got the
boy—he's sick and dying!"

Brighten came out, pulling up his moleskins. "What boy?" he
asked.

"Here, take him," I shouted, "and let me get down."

"What's the matter with him?" asked Brighten, and he seemed
to hang back. And just as I made to get my leg over the saddle,
Jim's head went back over my arm, he stiffened, and I saw his
eyeballs turned up and glistening in the moonlight.

I felt cold all over then and sick in the stomach—but *clear-
headed* in a way: strange, wasn't it? I don't know why I didn't
get down and rush into the kitchen to get a bath ready. I only felt
as if the worst had come, and I wished it were over and gone.
I even thought of Mary and the funeral.

Then a woman ran out of the house—a big, hard-looking
woman. She had on a wrapper of some sort, and her feet were
bare. She laid her hand on Jim, looked at his face, and then
snatched him from me and ran into the kitchen—and me down
and after her. As great good luck would have it, they had some
dirty clothes on to boil in a kerosene-tin—dish-cloths or something.

Brighten's sister-in-law dragged a tub out from under the table,
wrenched the bucket off the hook, and dumped in the water, dish-
cloths and all, snatched a can of cold water from a corner, dashed
that in, and felt the water with her hand—holding Jim up to her

hip all the time—and I won't say how he looked. She stood him in the tub and started dashing water over him, tearing off his clothes between the splashes.

"Here, that tin of mustard—there on the shelf!" she shouted to me.

She knocked the lid off the tin on the edge of the tub, and went on splashing and spanking Jim.

It seemed an eternity. And I? Why, I never thought clearer in my life. I felt cold-blooded—I felt as if I'd like an excuse to go outside till it was all over. I thought of Mary and the funeral—and wished that that was past. All this in a flash, as it were. I felt that it would be a great relief, and only wished the funeral was months past. I felt—well, altogether selfish. I only thought for myself.

Brighten's sister-in-law splashed and spanked him hard—hard enough to break his back I thought, and—after about half an hour it seemed—the end came: Jim's limbs relaxed, he slipped down into the tub, and the pupils of his eyes came down. They seemed dull and expressionless, like the eyes of a new baby, but he was back for the world again.

I dropped on the stool by the table.

"It's all right," she said. "It's all over now. I wasn't going to let him die." I was only thinking: "Well, it's over now, but it will come on again. I wish it was over for good. I'm tired of it."

She called to her sister, Mrs Brighten, a washed-out, helpless little fool of a woman, who'd been running in and out and whimpering all the time:

"Here, Jessie! bring the new white blanket off my bed. And you, Brighten, take some of that wood off the fire, and stuff something in that hole there to stop the draught."

Brighten—he was a nuggety little hairy man with no expression to be seen for whiskers—had been running in with sticks and back logs from the wood-heap. He took the wood out, stuffed up the crack, and went inside and brought out a black bottle—got a cup from the shelf, and put both down near my elbow.

Mrs Brighten started to get some supper or breakfast, or whatever it was, ready. She had a clean cloth, and set the table tidily. I noticed that all the tins were polished bright (old coffee- and mustard-tins and the like that they used instead of sugar-basins and tea-caddies and salt-cellars), and the kitchen was kept as clean as possible. She was all right at little things. I knew a haggard, worked-out Bushwoman who put her whole soul—or all she'd got left—into polishing old tins till they dazzled your eyes.

I didn't feel inclined for corned beef and damper, and post-

and-rail tea. So I sat and squinted, when I thought she wasn't looking, at Brighten's sister-in-law. She was a big woman, her hands and feet were big, but well-shaped and all in proportion—they fitted her. She was a handsome woman—about forty, I should think. She had a square chin and a straight thin-lipped mouth—straight save for a hint of a turn down at the corners, which I fancied (and I have strange fancies) had been a sign of weakness in the days before she grew hard. There was no sign of weakness now. She had hard grey eyes and blue-black hair. She hadn't spoken yet. She didn't ask me how the boy took ill or I got there, or who or what I was—at least not until the next evening at tea-time.

She sat upright with Jim wrapped in the blanket and laid across her knees, with one hand under his neck and the other laid lightly on him, and she just rocked him gently.

She sat looking hard and straight before her, just as I've seen a tired needlewoman sit with her work in her lap and look away back into the past. And Jim might have been the work in her lap, for all she seemed to think of him. Now and then she knitted her forehead and blinked.

Suddenly she glanced round and said—in a tone as if I was her husband and she didn't think much of me:

"Why don't you eat something?"

"Beg pardon?"

"Eat something!"

I drank some tea, and sneaked another look at her. I was beginning to feel more natural, and wanted Jim again, now that the colour was coming back into his face and he didn't look like an unnaturally stiff and staring corpse. I felt a lump rising, and wanted to thank her. I sneaked another look at her.

She was staring straight before her—I never saw a woman's face change so suddenly—I never saw a woman's eyes so haggard and hopeless. Then her great chest heaved twice, I heard her draw a long shuddering breath, like a knocked-out horse, and two great tears dropped from her wide-open eyes down her cheeks like rain-drops on a face of stone. And in the firelight they seemed tinged with blood.

I looked away quick, feeling full up myself. And presently (I hadn't seen her look round) she said:

"Go to bed."

"Beg pardon?" (Her face was the same as before the tears.)

"Go to bed. There's a bed made for you inside on the sofa."

"But—the team—I must———"

"What?"

"The team. I left it at the camp. I must look to it."

"Oh! Well, Brighten will ride down and bring it up in the morning—or send the half-caste. Now you go to bed, and get a good rest. The boy will be all right. I'll see to that."

I went out—it was a relief to get out—and looked to the mare. Brighten had got her some corn and chaff in a candle-box, but she couldn't eat yet. She just stood or hung resting one hind leg and then the other, with her nose over the box—and she sobbed. I put my arms round her neck and my face down on her ragged mane, and cried for the second time since I was a boy.

As I started to go in I heard Brighten's sister-in-law say, suddenly and sharply:

"Take *that* away, Jessie."

And presently I saw Mrs Brighten go into the house with the black bottle.

The moon had gone behind the range. I stood for a minute between the house and the kitchen and peeped in through the kitchen window.

She had moved away from the fire and sat near the table. She bent over Jim and held him up close to her and rocked herself to and fro.

I went to bed and slept till the next afternoon. I woke just in time to hear the tail-end of a conversation between Jim and Brighten's sister-in-law. He was asking her out to our place and she promising to come.

"And now," says Jim, "I want to go home to 'muffer' in 'The Same Ol' Fling'."

"What?"

Jim repeated.

"Oh! 'The Same Old Thing'—the waggon."

The rest of the afternoon I poked round the gullies with old Brighten, looking at some "indications" (of the existence of gold) he had found. It was no use trying to "pump" him concerning his sister-in-law; Brighten was an "old hand", and had learned in the old bushranging and cattle-stealing days to know nothing about other people's business. And, by the way, I noticed then that the more you talk and listen to a bad character, the more you lose your dislike for him.

I never saw such a change in a woman as in Brighten's sister-in-law that evening. She was bright and jolly, and seemed at least ten years younger. She bustled round and helped her sister to get tea ready. She rooted out some old china that Mrs Brighten had stowed away somewhere, and set the table as I seldom saw it set out there. She propped Jim up with pillows, and laughed and played with him like a great girl. She described Sydney and Sydney life as I'd never heard it described before; and she knew as much about the Bush and old digging days as I did. She kept old Brighten and me listening and laughing till nearly midnight. And she seemed quick to understand everything when I talked. If she wanted to explain anything that we hadn't seen, she wouldn't say that it was "like a—like a—" and hesitate (you know what I mean); she'd hit the right thing on the head at once. A squatter with a very round, flaming red face and a white cork hat had gone by in the afternoon: she said it was "like a mushroom on the rising moon". She gave me a lot of good hints about children.

But she was quiet again next morning. I harnessed up, and she dressed Jim and gave him his breakfast, and made a comfortable place for him on the load with the 'possum rug and a spare pillow. She got up on the wheel to do it herself. Then was the awkward time. I'd half start to speak to her, and then turn away and go fixing up round the horses, and then make another false start to say good-bye. At last she took Jim up in her arms and kissed him, and lifted him on the wheel; but he put his arms tight round her neck and kissed her—a thing Jim seldom did with anybody, except his mother, for he wasn't what you'd call an affectionate child—he'd never more than offer his cheek to me, in his old-fashioned way. I'd got up the other side of the load to take him from her.

"Here, take him," she said.

I saw his mouth twitching as I lifted him. Jim seldom cried nowadays—no matter how much he was hurt. I gained some time fixing Jim comfortable.

"You'd better make a start," she said. "You want to get home early with that boy."

I got down and went round to where she stood. I held out my hand and tried to speak, but my voice went like an ungreased waggon wheel, and I gave it up and only squeezed her hand.

"That's all right," she said; then tears came into her eyes, and she suddenly put her hand on my shoulder and kissed me on the cheek. "You be off—you're only a boy yourself. Take care of that boy; be kind to your wife, and take care of yourself."

"Will you come to see us?"

"Some day," she said.

I started the horses, and looked round once more. She was looking up at Jim, who was waving his hand to her from the top of the load. And I saw that haggard, hungry, hopeless look come into her eye in spite of the tears.

.   .   .

I smoothed over that story and shortened it a lot when I told it to Mary—I didn't want to upset her. But, some time after I brought Jim home from Gulgong, and while I was at home with the team for a few days, nothing would suit Mary but she must go over to Brighten's shanty and see Brighten's sister-in-law. So James drove her over one morning in the spring-cart: it was a long way, and they stayed at Brighten's overnight and didn't get back till late the next afternoon. I'd got the place in a pig-muck, as Mary said, "doing for" myself, and I was having a snooze on the sofa when they got back. The first thing I remember was someone stroking my head and kissing me, and I heard Mary saying: "My poor boy! My poor old boy!"

I sat up with a jerk. I thought that Jim had gone off again. But it seems that Mary was only referring to me. Then she started to pull grey hairs out of my head and put 'em in an empty match-box—to see how many she'd get. She used to do this when she felt a bit soft. I don't know what she said to Brighten's sister-in-law or what Brighten's sister-in-law said to her, but Mary was extra gentle for the next few days.

[1898 (verse 1889)   revised 1900]

"WATER THEM GERANIUMS"

I

A LONELY TRACK

THE time Mary and I shifted out into the Bush from Gulgong to "settle on the land" at Lahey's Creek.

I'd sold the two tip-drays that I used for tank-sinking and dam-making, and I took the traps out in the waggon on top of a small load of rations and horse-feed that I was taking to a sheep-station out that way. Mary drove out in the spring-cart. You remember we left little Jim with his aunt in Gulgong till we got settled down. I'd sent James (Mary's brother) out the day before, on horseback, with two or three cows and some heifers and steers and calves we had, and I'd told him to clean up a bit, and make the hut as bright and cheerful as possible before Mary came.

We hadn't much in the way of furniture. There was the four-poster cedar bedstead that I bought before we were married, and Mary was rather proud of it: it had turned posts and joints that bolted together. There was a plain hardwood table, that Mary called her "ironing-table", upside down on top of the load, with the bedding and blankets between the legs; there were four of those common black kitchen-chairs—with apples painted on the hard board backs—that we used for the parlour; there was a cheap batten sofa with arms at the ends and turned rails between the uprights of the arms (we were a little proud of the turned rails); and there was the camp-oven, and the three-legged pot, and pans and buckets, stuck about the load and hanging under the tail-board of the waggon.

There was the little Wilcox & Gibb's sewing-machine—my present to Mary when we were married (and what a present, looking back to it!). There was a cheap little rocking-chair, and a looking-glass and some pictures that were presents from Mary's friends and sister. She had her mantelshelf ornaments and crockery and nick-nacks packed away, in the linen and old clothes, in a big tub made of half a cask, and a box that had been Jim's cradle. The live stock was a cat in one box, and in another an old rooster, and three hens that formed cliques, two against one, turn about, as three of the same sex will do all over the world. I had my old cattle-dog, and of course a pup on the load—I always had a pup that I gave away, or sold and didn't get paid for, or had "touched" (stolen) as soon as it was old enough. James had his three spidery, sneaking, thieving, cold-blooded kangaroo-dogs with him. I was taking out three months' provisions in the way of ration-sugar, tea, flour, and potatoes, etc.

I started early, and Mary caught me up at Ryan's Crossing on Sandy Creek, where we boiled the billy and had some dinner.

Mary bustled about the camp and admired the scenery and talked too much, for her, and was extra cheerful, and kept her face turned from me as much as possible. I soon saw what was the matter. She'd been crying to herself coming along the road. I thought it was all on account of leaving little Jim behind for the first time. She told me that she couldn't make up her mind till the last moment to leave him, and that, a mile or two along the road, she'd have turned back for him, only that she knew her sister would laugh at her. She was always terribly anxious about the children.

We cheered each other up, and Mary drove with me the rest of the way to the creek, along the lonely branch track, across native apple-tree flats. It was a dreary, hopeless track. There was no horizon, nothing but the rough ashen trunks of the gnarled and stunted trees in all directions, little or no undergrowth, and the ground, save for the coarse, brownish tufts of dead grass, as bare as the road, for it was a dry season: there had been no rain for months, and I wondered what I should do with the cattle if there wasn't more grass on the creek.

In this sort of country a stranger might travel for miles without seeming to have moved, for all the difference there is in the scenery. The new tracks were "blazed"—that is, slices of bark cut off from both sides of trees, within sight of each other, in a line, to mark the track until the horses and wheel-marks made it plain. A smart Bushman, with a sharp tomahawk, can blaze a track as he rides. But a Bushman a little used to the country soon picks out differences amongst the trees, half unconsciously as it were, and so finds his way about.

Mary and I didn't talk much along this track—we couldn't have heard each other very well, anyway, for the "clock-clock" of the waggon and the rattle of the cart over the hard lumpy ground. And I suppose we both began to feel pretty dismal as the shadows lengthened. I'd noticed lately that Mary and I had got out of the habit of talking to each other—noticed it in a vague sort of way that irritated me (as vague things will irritate one) when I thought of it. But then I thought: "It won't last long—I'll make life brighter for her by-and-by."

As we went along—and the track seemed endless—I got brooding, of course, back into the past. And I feel now, when it's too late, that Mary must have been thinking that way too. I thought of my early boyhood, of the hard life of "grubbin'" and "milkin'" and "fencin'" and "ploughin'" and "ring-barkin'", etc., and all for nothing. The few months at the little bark-school, with a teacher who couldn't spell. The cursed ambition or craving that tortured my soul as a boy—ambition or craving for—I didn't know what for! For something better and brighter, anyhow. And I made the life harder by reading at night.

It all passed before me as I followed on in the waggon, behind Mary in the spring-cart. I thought of these old things more than I thought of her. She had tried to help me to better things. And I tried too—I had the energy of half-a-dozen men when I saw a road clear before me, but shied at the first check. Then I brooded, or dreamed of making a home—that one might call a home—for Mary—some day. Ah, well!———

And what was Mary thinking about, along the lonely, changeless miles? I never thought of that. Of her kind, careless, gentleman father, perhaps. Of her girlhood. Of her homes—not the huts and camps she lived in with me. Of our future?—she used to plan a lot, and talk a good deal of our future—but not lately. These things didn't strike me at the time—I was so deep in my own brooding. Did she think now—did she begin to feel now that she had made a great mistake and thrown away her life, but must make the best of it? This might have roused me, had I thought of it. But whenever I thought Mary was getting indifferent towards me, I'd think: "I'll soon win her back. We'll be sweethearts again —when things brighten up a bit."

It's an awful thing to me, now I look back to it, to think how far apart we had grown, what strangers we were to each other. It seems, now, as though we had been sweethearts long years before, and had parted, and had never really met since.

The sun was going down when Mary called out: "There's our place, Joe!"

She hadn't seen it before, and somehow it came new and with a shock to me, who had been out here several times. Ahead, through the trees to the right, was a dark green clump of she-oaks standing out of the creek, darker for the dead grey grass and blue-grey bush on the barren ridge in the background. Across the creek (it was only a deep, narrow gutter—a water-course with a chain of water-holes after rain), across on the other bank, stood the hut, on a narrow flat between the spur and the creek, and a little higher than this side. The land was much better than on our old selection, and there was good soil along the creek on both sides: I expected a rush of selectors out here soon. A few acres round the hut was cleared and fenced in by a light two-rail fence of timber split from logs and saplings. The man who took up this selection left it because his wife died here.

It was a small oblong hut built of split slabs, and he had roofed it with shingles which he split in spare times. There was no verandah, but I built one later on. At the end of the house was a big slab-and-bark shed, bigger than the hut itself, with a kitchen, a skillion for tools, harness, and horse-feed, and a spare bedroom partitioned off with sheets of bark and old chaff-bags. The house itself was floored roughly, with cracks between the boards; there were cracks between the slabs all round—though he'd nailed strips of tin, from old kerosene-tins, over some of them; the partitioned-off bedroom was lined with old chaff-bags with news-papers pasted over them for wall-paper. There was no ceiling, calico or otherwise, and we could see the round pine rafters and battens, and the under ends of the shingles. But ceilings make a hut hot and harbour insects and reptiles—snakes sometimes. There was one small glass window in the "dining-room" with three panes and a sheet of greased paper, and the rest were rough wooden shutters. There was a pretty good cow-yard and calf-pen, and—that was about all. There was no dam or tank (I made one later on); there was a water-cask, with the hoops falling off and the staves gaping, at the corner of the house, and spouting, made of lengths of bent tin, ran round under the eaves. Water from a new shingle roof is wine-red for a year or two, and water from a stringy-bark roof is like tan-water for years. In dry weather the selector had got his house water from a cask sunk in the gravel at the bottom of the deepest water-hole in the creek. And the longer the drought lasted, the farther he had to go down the creek for his water, with a cask on a cart, and take his cows to drink, if he had any. Four, five, six, or seven miles—even ten miles to water is nothing in some places.

. . .

James hadn't found himself called upon to do more than milk old "Spot" (the grandmother cow of our mob), pen the calf at night, make a fire in the kitchen, and sweep out the house with a bough. He helped me unharness and water and feed the horses, and then started to get the furniture off the waggon and into the house. James wasn't lazy—so long as one thing didn't last too long; but he was too uncomfortably practical and matter-of-fact for me. Mary and I had some tea in the kitchen. The kitchen was permanently furnished with a table of split slabs, adzed smooth on top, and supported by four stakes driven into the ground, a three-legged stool and a block of wood, and two long stools made of half-round slabs (sapling trunks split in halves) with auger-holes bored in the round side and sticks stuck into them for legs. The floor was of clay; the chimney of slabs and tin; the fireplace was about eight feet wide, lined with clay, and with a blackened pole across, with sooty chains and wire hooks on it for the pots.

Mary didn't seem able to eat. She sat on the three-legged stool near the fire, though it was warm weather, and kept her face turned from me. Mary was still pretty, but not the little dumpling she had been: she was thinner now. She had big dark hazel eyes that shone a little too much when she was pleased or excited. I thought at times that there was something very German about her expression; also something aristocratic about the turn of her nose, which nipped in at the nostrils when she spoke. There was nothing aristocratic about me. Mary was German in figure and walk. I used sometimes to call her "Little Duchy" and "Pigeon Toes". She had a will of her own, as shown sometimes by the obstinate knit in her forehead between the eyes.

Mary sat still by the fire, and presently I saw her chin tremble.

"What is it, Mary?"

She turned her face farther from me. I felt tired, disappointed, and irritated—suffering from a reaction.

"Now, what is it, Mary?" I asked; "I'm sick of this sort of thing. Haven't you got everything you wanted? You've had your own way. What's the matter with you now?"

"You know very well, Joe."

"But I *don't* know," I said. I knew too well.

She said nothing.

"Look here, Mary," I said, putting my hand on her shoulder, "don't go on like that; tell me what's the matter."

"It's only this," she said suddenly, "I can't stand this life here; it will kill me!"

I had a pannikin of tea in my hand, and I banged it down on the table.

"This is more than a man can stand!" I shouted. "You know very well that it was you that dragged me out here. You run me on to this! Why weren't you content to stay in Gulgong?"

"And what sort of a place was Gulgong, Joe?" asked Mary quietly.

(I thought even then in a flash what sort of a place Gulgong was. A wretched remnant of a town on an abandoned gold-field. One street, each side of the dusty main road; three or four one-storey square brick cottages with hip roofs of galvanized iron that glared in the heat—four rooms and a passage—the police-station, bank manager and schoolmaster's cottages, etc. Half-a-dozen tumble-down weatherboard shanties—the three pubs, the two stores, and the post-office. The town tailing off into weatherboard boxes with tin tops, and old bark huts—relics of the digging days —propped up by many rotting poles. The men, when at home, mostly asleep or droning over their pipes or hanging about the verandah posts of the pubs, saying, "'Ullo, Bill!" or "'Ullo, Jim!" —or sometimes drunk. The women, mostly hags, who blackened each other's and girls' characters with their tongues, and criticized the aristocracy's washing hung out on the line: "And the colour of the clothes! Does that woman wash her clothes at all? or only soak 'em and hang 'em out?"—that was Gulgong.)

"Well, why didn't you come to Sydney, as I wanted you to?" I asked Mary.

"You know very well, Joe," said Mary quietly.

(I knew very well, but the knowledge only maddened me. I had had an idea of getting a billet in one of the big wool-stores— I was a fair wool expert—but Mary was afraid of the drink. I could keep well away from it so long as I worked hard in the Bush.

I had gone to Sydney twice since I met Mary, once before we were married, and she forgave me when I came back; and once afterwards. I got a billet there then, and was going to send for her in a month. After eight weeks she raised the money somehow and came to Sydney and brought me home. I got pretty low down that time.)

"But, Mary," I said, "it would have been different this time. You would have been with me. I can take a glass now or leave it alone."

"As long as you take a glass there is danger," she said.

"Well, what did you want to advise me to come out here for, if you can't stand it? Why didn't you stay where you were?" I asked.

"Well," she said, "why weren't you more decided?"

I'd sat down, but I jumped to my feet then.

"Good God!" I shouted, "this is more than any man can stand. I'll chuck it all up! I'm damned well sick and tired of the whole thing."

"So am I, Joe," said Mary wearily.

We quarrelled badly then—that first hour in our new home. I know now whose fault it was.

I got my hat and went out and started to walk down the creek. I didn't feel bitter against Mary—I had spoken too cruelly to her to feel that way. Looking back, I could see plainly that if I had taken her advice all through, instead of now and again, things would have been all right with me. I had come away and left her crying in the hut, and James telling her, in a brotherly way, that it was all her fault. The trouble was that I never liked to "give in" or go half-way to make it up—not half-way—it was all the way or nothing with our natures.

"If I don't make a stand now," I'd say, "I'll never be master. I gave up the reins when I got married, and I'll have to get them back again."

What women some men are! But the time came, and not many years after, when I stood by the bed where Mary lay, white and still; and, amongst other things, I kept saying: "I'll give in, Mary —I'll give in," and then I'd laugh. They thought that I was raving mad, and took me from the room. But that time was to come.

As I walked down the creek track in the moonlight the question rang in my ears again, as it had done when I first caught sight of the house that evening:

"Why did I bring her here?"

I was not fit to "go on the land". The place was only fit for some stolid German, or Scotsman, or even Englishman and his wife, who had no ambition but to bullock and make a farm of the place. I had only drifted here through carelessness, brooding, and discontent.

I walked on and on till I was more than half-way to the only neighbours—a wretched selector's family, about four miles down the creek—and I thought I'd go on to the house and see if they had any fresh meat.

A mile or two farther on I saw the loom of the bark hut they lived in, on a patchy clearing in the scrub, and heard the voice of the selector's wife—I had seen her several times: she was a gaunt, haggard Bushwoman, and, I supposed, the reason why she hadn't gone mad through hardship and loneliness was that she hadn't either the brains or the memory to go farther than she could see through the trunks of the "apple-trees".

"You, An-nay!" (Annie.)

"Ye-es" (from somewhere in the gloom).

"Didn't I tell yer to water them geraniums!"

"Well, didn't I?"

"Don't tell lies or I'll break yer young back!"

"I did, I tell yer—the water won't soak inter the ashes."

Geraniums were the only flowers I saw grow in the drought out there. I remembered this woman had a few dirty grey-green leaves behind some sticks against the bark wall near the door; and in spite of the sticks the fowls used to get in and scratch beds under the geraniums, and scratch dust over them, and ashes were thrown there—with an idea of helping the flower, I suppose; and greasy dish-water, when fresh water was scarce—till you might as well try to water a dish of fat.

Then the woman's voice again:

"You, Tom-may!" (Tommy.)

Silence, save for an echo on the ridge.

"Y-o-u, T-o-m-*may*!"

"Ye-e-s!" shrill shriek from across the creek.

"Didn't I tell you to ride up to them new people and see if they want any meat or anythink?" in one long screech.

"Well—I karnt find the horse."

"Well-find-it-first-think-in-the-morning-and —— And-don't-for-git-to-tell-Mrs-Wi'son-that-mother'll-be-up-as-soon-as-she-can."

.   .   .

I didn't feel like going to the woman's house that night. I felt—and the thought came like a whip-stroke on my heart—that this was what Mary would come to if I left her here.

I turned and started to walk home, fast. I'd made up my mind.

I'd take Mary straight back to Gulgong in the morning—I forgot about the load I had to take to the sheep-station. I'd say, "Look here, Girlie" (that's what I used to call her), "we'll leave this wretched life; we'll leave the Bush for ever! We'll go to Sydney, and I'll be a man! and work my way up." And I'd sell waggon, horses, and all, and go.

When I got to the hut it was lighted up. Mary had the only kerosene lamp, a slush lamp, and two tallow candles going. She had got both rooms washed out—to James's disgust, for he had to move the furniture and boxes about. She had a lot of things unpacked on the table; she had laid clean newspapers on the mantelshelf—a slab on two pegs over the fireplace—and put the little wooden clock in the centre and some of the ornaments on each side, and was tacking a strip of vandyked American oil-cloth round the rough edge of the slab.

"How does that look, Joe? We'll soon get things ship-shape."

I kissed her, but she had her mouth full of tacks. I went out in the kitchen, drank a pint of cold tea, and sat down.

Somehow I didn't feel satisfied with the way things had gone.

[1900?]

II

"PAST CARIN' "

NEXT morning things looked a lot brighter. Things always look brighter in the morning—more so in the Australian Bush, I should think, than in most other places. It is when the sun goes down on the dark bed of the lonely Bush, and the sunset flashes like a sea of fire and then fades, and then glows out again, like a bank of coals, and then burns away to ashes—it is then that old things come home to one. And strange, new-old things too, that haunt and depress you terribly, and that you can't understand. I often think how, at sunset, the past must come home to new-chum black sheep, sent out to Australia and drifted into the Bush. I used to think that they couldn't have much brains, or the loneliness would drive them mad.

I'd decided to let James take the team for a trip or two. He could drive all right; he was a better business man, and no doubt would manage better than me—as long as the novelty lasted; and I'd stay at home for a week or so, till Mary got used to the place, or I could get a girl from somewhere to come and stay with her. The first weeks or few months of loneliness are the worst, as a rule, I believe, as they say the first weeks in jail are—I was never there. I know it's so with tramping or hard graft: the first day or two are twice as hard as any of the rest. But, for my part, I could never get used to loneliness and dullness; the last days used to be the worst with me: then I'd have to make a move, or drink. When you've been too much and too long alone in a lonely place, you begin to do queer things and think queer thoughts—provided you have any imagination at all. You'll sometimes sit of an evening and watch the lonely track, by the hour, for a horseman or a cart or someone that's never likely to come that way—someone, or a stranger, that you can't and don't really expect to see. I think that most men who have been alone in the Bush for any length of time —and married couples too—are more or less mad. With married couples it is generally the husband who is painfully shy and awkward when strangers come. The woman seems to stand the loneliness better, and can hold her own with strangers, as a rule. It's only afterwards, and looking back, that you see how queer you got. Shepherds and boundary-riders, who are alone for months, *must* have their periodical spree, at the nearest shanty, else they'd go raving mad. Drink is the only break in the awful monotony, and the yearly or half-yearly spree is the only thing they've got to look forward to: it keeps their minds fixed on something definite ahead.

But Mary kept her head pretty well through the first months of loneliness. *Weeks*, rather, I should say, for it wasn't as bad as it might have been farther up-country: there was generally someone came of a Sunday afternoon—a spring-cart with a couple of women, or maybe a family—or a lanky shy Bush native or two on lanky shy horses. On a quiet Sunday, after I'd brought Jim home, Mary would dress him and herself—just the same as if we were in town—and make me get up on one end and put on a collar and take her and Jim for a walk along the creek. She said she wanted to keep me civilized. She tried to make a gentleman of me for years, but gave it up gradually.

Well. It was the first morning on the creek: I was greasing the waggon-wheels, and James out after the horse, and Mary hanging out clothes, in an old print dress and a big ugly white hood, when I heard her being hailed as "Hi, missus!" from the front slip-rails.

It was a boy on horseback. He was a light-haired, very much freckled boy of fourteen or fifteen, with a small head, but with limbs, especially his bare sun-blotched shanks, that might have belonged to a grown man. He had a good face and frank grey eyes. An old, nearly black cabbage-tree hat rested on the butts of his ears, turning them out at right angles from his head, and rather

irty sprouts they were. He wore a dirty torn Crimean shirt; and
pair of man's moleskin trousers rolled up above the knees, with
he wide waistband gathered under a greenhide belt. I noticed,
ater on, that, even when he wore trousers short enough for him,
ie always rolled 'em up above the knees when on horseback, for
ome reason of his own: to suggest leggings, perhaps, for he had
hem rolled up in all weathers, and he wouldn't have bothered to
ave them from the sweat of the horse, even if that horse ever
weated.

He was seated astride a three-bushel bag thrown across the
idge-pole of a big grey horse with a coffin-shaped head, and built
astern something after the style of a roughly put up hip-roofed
box-bark humpy. His colour was like old box-bark, too, a dirty
bluish-grey; and, one time, when I saw his rump looming out of
he scrub, I really thought it was some old shepherd's hut that
I hadn't noticed there before. When he cantered it was like the
humpy starting off on its corner-posts.

"Are you Mrs Wilson?" asked the boy.

"Yes," said Mary.

"Well, mother told me to ride acrost and see if you wanted
anythink. We killed lars' night, and I've fetched a piece er cow."

"Piece of *what*?" asked Mary.

He grinned, and handed a sugar-bag across the rail with something heavy in the bottom of it that nearly jerked Mary's arm out
when she took it. It was a piece of beef that looked as if it had
been cut off with a wood-axe, but it was fresh and clean.

"Oh, I'm so glad!" cried Mary. She was always impulsive, save
to me sometimes. "I was just wondering where we were going to
get any fresh meat. How kind of your mother! Tell her I'm very
much obliged to her indeed." And she felt behind her for a poor
little purse she had. "And now—how much did your mother say
it would be?"

The boy blinked at her, and scratched his head.

"How much will it be?" he repeated, puzzled. "Oh—how much
does it weigh I-s'pose-yer-mean. Well, it ain't been weighed at all
—we ain't got no scales. A butcher does all that sort of think.
We just kills it, and cooks it, and eats it—and goes by guess.
What won't keep we salts down in the cask. I reckon it weighs
about a ton by the weight of it if yer wanter know. Mother thought
that if she sent any more it would go bad before you could scoff it.
I can't see————"

"Yes, yes," said Mary, getting confused. "But what I want to
know is, how do you manage when you sell it?"

He glared at her, and scratched his head. "Sell it? Why, we

only goes halves in a steer with someone, or sells steers to the butcher—or maybe some meat to a party of fencers or surveyors, or tank-sinkers, or them sorter people————"

"Yes, yes; but what I want to know is, how much am I to send your mother for this?"

"How much what?"

"Money, of course, you stupid boy," said Mary. "You seem a very stupid boy."

Then he saw what she was driving at. He began to fling his heels convulsively against the sides of his horse, jerking his body backward and forward at the same time, as if to wind up and start some clockwork machinery inside the horse that made it go and seemed to need repairing or oiling.

"We ain't that sorter people, missus," he said. "We don't sell meat to new people that come to settle here." Then, jerking his thumb contemptuously towards the ridges: "Go over ter Wall's if yer wanter buy meat; they sell meat ter strangers." (Wall was the big squatter over the ridges.)

"Oh!" said Mary, "I'm *so* sorry. Thank your mother for me. She *is* kind."

"Oh, that's nothink. She said to tell yer she'll be up as soon as she can. She'd have come up yisterday evening—she thought yer'd feel lonely comin' new to a place like this—but she couldn't git up."

The machinery inside the old horse showed signs of starting. You almost heard the wooden joints *creak* as he lurched forward, like an old propped-up humpy when the rotting props give way; but at the sound of Mary's voice he settled back on his foundations again. It must have been a very poor selection that couldn't afford a better spare horse than that.

"Reach me that lump er wood, will yer, missus?" said the boy, and he pointed to one of my "spreads" (for the team-chains) that lay inside the fence. "I'll fling it back agin over the fence when I git this ole cow started."

"But wait a minute—I've forgotten your mother's name," said Mary.

He grabbed at his thatch impatiently. "Me mother—Oh!—the old woman's name's Mrs Spicer. (Git up, karnt yer!)" He twisted himself round, and brought the stretcher down on one of the horse's "points" (and he had many) with a crack that must have jarred his wrist.

"Do you go to school?" asked Mary. There was a three-days-a-week school over the ridges at Wall's station.

"No!" he jerked out, keeping his legs going. "Me—why, I'm

going on fur fifteen. The last teacher at Wall's finished me. I'm going to Queensland next month drovin'." (Queensland border was over three hundred miles away.)

"Finished you? How?" asked Mary.

"Me edgercation, of course! How do yer expect me to start this horse when yer keep talkin'?"

He split the "spread" over the horse's point, threw the pieces over the fence, and was off, his elbows and legs flinging wildly, and the old saw-stool lumbering along the road like an old working bullock trying a canter. That horse wasn't a trotter.

And next month he *did* start for Queensland. He was a younger son and a surplus boy on a wretched, poverty-stricken selection; and as there was "northin' doin'" in the district, his father (in a burst of fatherly kindness, I suppose) made him a present of the old horse and a new pair of Blucher boots, and I gave him an old saddle and a coat, and he started for the Never Never country.

And I'll bet he got there. But I'm doubtful if the old horse did.

Mary gave the boy five shillings, and I don't think he had anything more except a clean shirt and an extra pair of white cotton socks.

. . .

"Spicer's farm" was a big bark humpy on a patchy clearing in the native apple-tree scrub. The clearing was fenced in by a light "dog-legged" fence (a fence of sapling poles resting on forks and X-shaped uprights), and the dusty ground round the house was almost entirely covered with cattle-dung. There was no attempt at cultivation when I came to live on the creek; but there were old furrow-marks amongst the stumps of another shapeless patch in the scrub near the hut. There was a wretched sapling cow-yard and calf-pen, and a cow-bail with one sheet of bark over it for shelter. There was no dairy to be seen, and I suppose the milk was set in one of the two skillion rooms, or lean-to's, behind the hut—the other was "the boys' bedroom". The Spicers kept a few cows and steers, and had thirty or forty sheep. Mrs Spicer used to drive down the creek once a week, in her rickety old spring-cart, to Cobborah, with butter and eggs.

The hut was nearly as bare inside as it was out—just a frame of "round-timber" (sapling poles) covered with bark. The furniture was permanent (unless you rooted it up), like in our kitchen: a rough slab table on stakes driven into the ground, and seats made the same way. Mary told me afterwards that the beds in the bag-and-bark partitioned-off room ("mother's bedroom") were simply poles laid side by side on cross-pieces supported by stakes driven into the ground, with straw mattresses and some worn-out bed-clothes. Mrs Spicer had an old patchwork quilt, in rags, and the remains of a white one, and Mary said it was pitiful to see how these things would be spread over the beds—to hide them as much as possible—when she went down there. A packing-case, with something like an old print skirt draped round it, and a cracked looking-glass (without a frame) on top, was the dressing-table. There were a couple of gin-cases for a wardrobe. The boys' beds were three-bushel bags stretched between poles fastened to uprights. The floor was the original surface, tramped hard, worn uneven with much sweeping, and with puddles in rainy weather where the roof leaked. Mrs Spicer used to stand old tins, dishes, and buckets under as many of the leaks as she could. The sauce-pans, kettles, and boilers were old kerosene-tins and billies. They used kerosene-tins, too, cut longways in halves, for setting the milk in. The plates and cups were of tin; there were two or three cups without saucers, and a crockery plate or two—also two mugs, cracked and without handles, one with "For a Good Boy" and the other with "For a Good Girl" on it; but all these were kept on the mantelshelf for ornament and for company. They were the only ornaments in the house, save a little wooden clock that hadn't gone for years. Mrs Spicer had a superstition that she had "some things packed away from the children".

The pictures were cut from old copies of the *Illustrated Sydney News* and pasted on to the bark. I remember this, because I remembered, long ago, the Spencers, who were our neighbours when I was a boy, had the walls of their bedroom covered with illustrations of the American Civil War, cut from illustrated London papers, and I used to "sneak" into "mother's bedroom" with Fred Spencer whenever we got the chance and gloat over the prints. I gave him a blade of a pocket-knife once, for taking me in there.

I saw very little of Spicer. He was a big, dark, dark-haired and whiskered man. I had an idea that he wasn't a selector at all, only a "dummy" for the squatter of the Cobborah run. You see, selectors were allowed to take up land on runs, or pastoral leases. The squatters kept them off as much as possible, by all manner of dodges and paltry persecution. The squatter would get as much freehold as he could afford, "select" as much land as the law allowed one man to take up, and then employ dummies (dummy selectors) to take up bits of land that he fancied about his run, and hold them for him.

Spicer seemed gloomy and unsociable. He was seldom at home. He was generally supposed to be away shearin' or fencin', or

workin' on somebody's station. It turned out that the last six
months he was away it was on the evidence of a cask of beef and
a hide with the brand cut out, found in his camp on a fencing
contract up-country, and which he and his mates couldn't account
for satisfactorily, while the squatter could. Then the family lived
mostly on bread and honey, or bread and treacle, or bread and
dripping, and tea. Every ounce of butter and every egg was needed
for the market, to keep them in flour, tea, and sugar. Mary found
that out, but couldn't help them much—except by "stuffing" the
children with bread and meat or bread and jam whenever they
came up to our place—for Mrs Spicer was proud with the pride
that lies down in the end and turns its face to the wall and dies.

Once, when Mary asked Annie, the eldest girl at home, if she
was hungry, she denied it—but she looked it. A ragged mite she
had with her explained things. The little fellow said:

"Mother told Annie not to say we was hungry if yer asked;
but if yer give us anythink to eat, we was to take it an' say thenk
yer, Mrs Wilson."

"I wouldn't 'a' told yer a lie; but I thought Jimmy would split
on me, Mrs Wilson," said Annie. "Thenk yer, Mrs Wilson."

She was not a big woman. She was gaunt and flat-chested, and
her face was "burnt to a brick", as they say out there. She had
brown eyes, nearly red, and a little wild-looking at times, and a
sharp face—ground sharp by hardship—the cheeks drawn in.
She had an expression like—well, like a woman who had been
very curious and suspicious at one time, and wanted to know
everybody's business and hear everything, and had lost all her
curiosity, without losing the expression or the quick suspicious
movements of the head. I don't suppose you understand. I can't
explain it any other way. She was not more than forty.

I remember the first morning I saw her. I was going up the
creek to look at the selection for the first time, and called at the
hut to see if she had a bit of fresh mutton, as I had none and was
sick of "corned beef".

"Yes—of—course," she said, in a sharp nasty tone, as if to say,
"Is there anything more you want while the shop's open?" I'd
met just the same sort of woman years before while I was carrying
swag between the shearing-sheds in the awful scrubs out west of
the Darling river, so I didn't turn on my heels and walk away.
I waited for her to speak again.

"Come—inside," she said, "and sit down. I see you've got the
waggon outside. I s'pose your name's Wilson, ain't it? You're
thinkin' about takin' on Harry Marshfield's selection up the creek,
so I heard. Wait till I fry you a chop and boil the billy."

Her voice sounded, more than anything else, like a voice coming out of a phonograph—I heard one in Sydney the other day—and not like a voice coming out of her. But sometimes when she got outside her everyday life on this selection she spoke in a sort of—in a sort of lost groping-in-the-dark kind of voice.

She didn't talk much this time—just spoke in a mechanical way of the drought, and the hard times, "an' butter 'n' eggs bein' down, an' her husban' an' eldest son bein' away, an' tnat makin' it so hard for her".

I don't know how many children she had. I never got a chance to count them, for they were nearly all small, and shy as piccaninnies, and used to run and hide when anybody came. They were mostly nearly as black as piccaninnies too. She must have averaged a baby a year for years—and God only knows how she got over her confinements! Once, they said, she only had a black gin with her. She had an elder boy and girl, but she seldom spoke of them. The girl, "Liza", was "in service in Sydney". I'm afraid I knew what that meant. The elder son was "away". He had been a bit of a favourite round there, it seemed.

Someone might ask her: "How's your son Jack, Mrs Spicer?" or: "Heard of Jack lately? and where is he now?"

"Oh, he's somewheres up country," she'd say in the "groping" voice, or "He's drovin' in Queenslan'," or "Shearin' on the Darlin' the last time I heerd from him. We ain't had a line from him since —les' see—since Chris'mas 'fore last."

And she'd turn her haggard eyes in a helpless, hopeless sort of way towards the west—towards "up-country" and "out back".

The eldest girl at home was nine or ten, with a little old face and lines across her forehead: she had an older expression than her mother. Tommy went to Queensland, as I told you. The eldest son at home, Bill (older than Tommy), was a "bit wild".

I've passed the place in smothering hot mornings in December, when the droppings about the cow-yard had crumpled to dust that rose in the warm, sickly, sunrise wind, and seen that woman at work in the cow-yard, "bailing up" and leg-roping cows, milking, or hauling at a rope round the neck of a half-grown calf that was too strong for her (and she was tough as fencing-wire), or humping great buckets of sour milk to the pigs or the "poddies" (hand-fed calves) in the pen. I'd get off the horse and give her a hand sometimes with a young steer or a cranky old cow that wouldn't "bail-up" and threatened her with her horns. She'd say:

"Thenk yer, Mr Wilson. Do yer think we're ever goin' to have any rain?"

I've ridden past the place on bitter black rainy mornings in

June or July and seen her trudging about the yard—that was ankle-deep in black liquid filth—with an old pair of Blucher boots on, and an old coat of her husband's, or maybe a three-bushel bag over her shoulders. I've seen her climbing on the roof by means of the water-cask at the corner, and trying to stop a leak by shoving a piece of tin in under the bark. And when I'd fixed the leak:

"Thenk yer, Mr Wilson. This drop of rain's a blessin'! Come in and have a dry at the fire and I'll make yer a cup of tea." And, if I was in a hurry: "Come in, man alive! Come in! and dry yerself a bit till the rain holds up. Yer can't go home like this! Yer'll git yer death o' cold."

I've even seen her, in the terrible drought, climbing she-oaks and apple-trees by a makeshift ladder, and awkwardly lopping off boughs to feed the starving cattle.

"Jist tryin' ter keep the milkers alive till the rain comes."

They said that when the pleuro-pneumonia was in the district and amongst her cattle she bled and physicked them herself, and fed those that were down with slices of half-ripe pumpkins (from a crop that had failed).

"An', one day," she told Mary, "there was a big barren heifer (that we called Queen Elizabeth) that was down with the ploorer. She'd been down for four days and hadn't moved, when one mornin' I dumped some wheaten chaff—we had a few bags that Spicer brought home—I dumped it in front of her nose, an'—would yer b'lieve me, Mrs Wilson?—she stumbled onter her feet an' chased me all the way to the house! I had to pick up me skirts an' run! Wasn't it redic'lus?"

They had a sense of the ridiculous, most of those poor sun-dried Bushwomen. I fancy that that helped save them from madness.

"We lost nearly all our milkers," she told Mary. "I remember one day Tommy came running to the house and screamed: 'Marther! [mother] there's another milker down with the ploorer!' Jist as if it was great news. Well, Mrs Wilson, I was dead-beat, an' I giv' in. I jist sat down to have a good cry, and felt for my han'kerchief—it *was* a rag of a han'kerchief, full of holes (all me others was in the wash). Without seein' what I was doin' I put me finger through one hole in the han'kerchief an' me thumb through the other, and poked me fingers into me eyes, instead of wipin' them. Then I had to laugh."

There's a story that once, when the Bush, or rather grass, fires were out all along the creek on Spicer's side, Wall's station hands were up above our place, trying to keep the fire back from the boundary, and towards evening one of the men happened to think of the Spicers: they saw smoke down that way. Spicer was away from home, and they had a small crop of wheat, nearly ripe, on the selection.

"My God! that poor devil of a woman will be burnt out, if she ain't already!" shouted young Billy Wall. "Come along, three or four of you chaps"—(it was shearing time, and there were plenty of men on the station).

They raced down the creek to Spicer's, and were just in time to save the wheat. She had her sleeves tucked up, and was beating out the burning grass with a bough. She'd been at it for an hour, and was as black as a gin, they said. She only said when they'd turned the fire: "Thenk yer! Wait an' I'll make some tea."

. . .

After tea the first Sunday she came to see us, Mary asked:

"Don't you feel lonely, Mrs Spicer, when your husband goes away?"

"Well—no, Mrs Wilson," she said in the groping sort of voice. "I uster, once. I remember, when we lived on the Cudgegong river—we lived in a brick house then—the first time Spicer had to go away from home I nearly fretted my eyes out. And he was only goin' shearin' for a month. I muster bin a fool; but then we were only jist married a little while. He's been away drovin' in Queenslan' as long as eighteen months at a time since then. But" (her voice seemed to grope in the dark more than ever) "I don't mind—I somehow seem to have got past carin'. Besides—besides, Spicer was a very different man then to what he is now. He's got so moody and gloomy at home, he hardly ever speaks."

Mary sat silent for a minute thinking. Then Mrs Spicer roused herself:

"Oh, I don't know what I'm talkin' about! You mustn't take any notice of me, Mrs Wilson—I don't often go on like this. I do believe I'm gittin' a bit ratty at times. It must be the heat and the dulness."

But once or twice afterwards she referred to a time "when Spicer was a different man to what he was now."

I walked home with her a piece along the creek. She said nothing for a long time, and seemed to be thinking in a puzzled way. Then she said suddenly:

"What-did-you-bring-her-here-for? She's only a girl."

"I beg pardon, Mrs Spicer."

"Oh, I don't know what I'm talkin' about! I b'lieve I'm gittin' ratty. You mustn't take any notice of me, Mr Wilson."

She wasn't much company for Mary; and often, when she had

a child with her, she'd start taking notice of the baby while Mary was talking, which used to exasperate Mary. But poor Mrs Spicer couldn't help it, and she seemed to hear all the same.

Her great trouble was that she "couldn't git no reg'lar schoolin' for the children."

"I learns 'em at home as much as I can. But I don't git a minute to call me own; an' I'm ginerally that dead-beat at night that I'm fit for nothink."

Mary had some of the children up now and then later on, and taught them a little. When she first offered to do so, Mrs Spicer laid hold of the handiest youngster and said:

"There—do you hear that? Mrs Wilson is goin' to teach yer, an' it's more than yer deserve!" (the youngster had been "cryin' " over something). "Now, go up an' say 'Thenk yer, Mrs Wilson.' And if yer ain't good, and don't do as she tells yer, I'll break every bone in yer young body!"

The poor little devil stammered something, and escaped.

The children were sent by turns over to Wall's to Sunday-school. When Tommy was at home he had a new pair of elastic-side boots, and there was no end of rows about them in the family— for the mother made him lend them to his sister Annie, to go to Sunday-school in, in her turn. There were only about three pairs of anyway decent boots in the family, and these were saved for great occasions. The children were always as clean and tidy as possible when they came to our place.

And I think the saddest and most pathetic sight on the face of God's earth is the children of very poor people made to appear well: the broken worn-out boots polished or greased, the blackened (inked) pieces of string for laces; the clean patched pinafores over the wretched threadbare frocks. Behind the little row of children hand-in-hand—and no matter where they are—I always see the worn face of the mother.

Towards the end of the first year on the selection our little girl came. I'd sent Mary to Gulgong for four months that time, and when she came back with the baby Mrs Spicer used to come up pretty often. She came up several times when Mary was ill to lend a hand. She wouldn't sit down and condole with Mary, or waste her time asking questions, or talking about the time when she was ill herself. She'd take off her hat—a shapeless little lump of black straw she wore for visiting—give her hair a quick brush back with the palms of her hands, roll up her sleeves, and set to work to "tidy up". She seemed to take most pleasure in sorting out our children's clothes, and dressing them. Perhaps she used to dress her own like that in the days when Spicer was a different man from what he was now. She seemed interested in the fashion-plates of some women's journals we had, and used to study them with an interest that puzzled me, for she was not likely to go in for fashion. She never talked of her early girlhood; but Mary, from some things she noticed, was inclined to think that Mrs Spicer had been fairly well brought up. For instance, Dr Balan-fantie, from Cudgegong, came out to see Wall's wife, and drove up the creek to our place on his way back to see how Mary and the baby were getting on. Mary got out some crockery and some table-napkins that she had packed away for occasions like this; and she said that the way Mrs Spicer handled the things, and helped set the table (though she did it in a mechanical sort of way), convinced her that she had been used to table-napkins at one time in her life.

Sometimes, after a long pause in the conversation, Mrs Spicer would say suddenly:

"Oh, I don't think I'll come up next week, Mrs Wilson."

"Why, Mrs Spicer?"

"Because the visits doesn't do me any good. I git the dismals afterwards."

"Why, Mrs Spicer? What on earth do you mean?"

"Oh,-I-don't-know-what-I'm-talkin'-about. You mustn't take any notice of me." And she'd put on her hat, kiss the children—and Mary too, sometimes, as if she mistook her for a child—and go.

Mary thought her a little mad at times. But I seemed to understand.

Once, when Mrs Spicer was sick, Mary went down to her, and down again next day. As she was coming away the second time, Mrs Spicer said:

"I wish you wouldn't come down any more till I'm on me feet, Mrs Wilson. The children can do for me."

"Why, Mrs Spicer?"

"Well, the place is in such a muck, and it hurts me."

We were the aristocrats of Lahey's Creek. Whenever we drove down on Sunday afternoon to see Mrs Spicer, and as soon as we got near enough for them to hear the rattle of the cart, we'd see the children running to the house as fast as they could split, and hear them screaming:

"Oh, marther! Here comes Mr and Mrs Wilson in their spring-cart."

And we'd see her bustle around, and two or three fowls fly out the front door, and she'd lay hold of a broom (made of a bound bunch of "broom-stuff"—coarse reedy grass or bush from the ridges—with a stick stuck in it) and flick out the floor, with a flick or two round in front of the door perhaps. The floor nearly always needed at least one flick of the broom on account of the fowls. Or she'd catch a youngster and scrub his face with a wet end of a cloudy towel, or twist the towel round her finger and dig out his ears—as if she was anxious to have him hear every word that was going to be said.

No matter what state the house would be in she'd always say: "I was jist expectin' yer, Mrs Wilson." And she was original in that, anyway.

She had an old patched and darned white table-cloth that she used to spread on the table when we were there, as a matter of course ("The others is in the wash, so you must excuse this, Mrs Wilson"), but I saw by the eyes of the children that the cloth was rather a wonderful thing to them. "I must really git some more knives an' forks next time I'm in Cobborah," she'd say. "The children break an' lose 'em till I'm ashamed to ask Christians ter sit down ter the table."

She had many Bush yarns, some of them very funny, some of them rather ghastly, but all interesting, and with a grim sort of humour about them. But the effect was often spoilt by her screaming at the children to "Drive out them fowls, karnt yer," or "Take yer maulies [hands] outer the sugar," or "Don't touch Mrs Wilson's baby with them dirty maulies," or "Don't stand starin' at Mrs Wilson with yer mouth an 'ears in that vulgar way."

Poor woman! she seemed everlastingly nagging at the children. It was a habit, but they didn't seem to mind. Most Bushwomen get the nagging habit. I remember one, who had the prettiest, dearest, sweetest, most willing, and affectionate little girl I think I ever saw, and she nagged that child from daylight till dark—and after it. Taking it all round, I think that the nagging habit in a mother is often worse on ordinary children, and more deadly on sensitive youngsters, than the drinking habit in a father.

One of the yarns Mrs Spicer told us was about a squatter she knew who used to go wrong in his head every now and again, and try to commit suicide. Once, when the station-hand, who was watching him, had his eye off him for a minute, he hanged himself to a beam in the stable. The men ran in and found him hanging and kicking. "They let him hang for a while," said Mrs Spicer, "till he went black in the face and stopped kicking. Then they cut him down and threw a bucket of water over him."

"Why! what on earth did they let the man hang for?" asked Mary.

"To give him a good bellyful of it: they thought it would cure him of tryin' to hang himself again."

"Well, that's the coolest thing I ever heard of," said Mary.

"That's jist what the magistrate said, Mrs Wilson," said Mrs Spicer.

"One morning," said Mrs Spicer, "Spicer had gone off on his horse somewhere, and I was alone with the children, when a man came to the door and said:

"'For God's sake, woman, give me a drink!'

"Lord only knows where he came from! He was dressed like a new-chum—his clothes was good, but he looked as if he'd been sleepin' in them in the Bush for a month. He was very shaky. I had some coffee that mornin', so I gave him some in a pint pot; he drank it, and then he stood on his head till he tumbled over, and then he stood up on his feet and said: 'Thenk yer, mum.'

"I was so surprised that I didn't know what to say, so I jist said: 'Would you like some more coffee?'

"'Yes, thenk yer,' he said; 'about two quarts.'

"I nearly filled the pint pot, and he drank it and stood on his head as long as he could, and when he got right end up he said: 'Thenk yer, mum—it's a fine day,' and then he walked off. He had two saddle-straps in his hands."

"Why, what did he stand on his head for?" asked Mary.

"To wash it up and down, I suppose, to get twice as much taste of the coffee. He had no hat. I sent Tommy across to Wall's to tell them that there was a man wanderin' about the Bush in the horrors of drink, and to get someone to ride for the police. But they was too late, for he hanged himself that night."

"Oh Lord!" cried Mary.

"Yes, right close to here, jist down the creek where the track to Wall's branches off. Tommy found him while he was out after the cows. Hangin' to the branch of a tree with the two saddle-straps."

Mary stared at her, speechless.

"Tommy came home yellin' with fright. I sent him over to Wall's at once. After breakfast, the minute my eyes was off them, the children slipped away and went down there. They came back screamin' at the tops of their voices. I did give it to them. I reckon they won't want ter see a dead body again in a hurry. Every time I'd mention it they'd huddle together, or ketch hold of me skirts and howl.

"'Yer'll go agen when I tell yer not to,' I'd say.

"'Oh no, mother,' they'd howl.

"'Yer wanted ter see a man hangin',' I said.

"'Oh, don't, mother! Don't talk about it.'

" 'Yer wouldn't be satisfied till yer see it,' I'd say; 'yer had to see it or burst. Yer satisfied now, ain't yer?'

" 'Oh, don't, mother!'

" 'Yer run all the way there, I s'pose?'

" 'Don't, mother!'

" 'But yer run faster back, didn't yer?'

" 'Oh, don't, mother.'

"But," said Mrs Spicer in conclusion, "I'd been down to see it myself before they was up."

"And ain't you afraid to live alone here, after all these horrible things?" asked Mary.

"Well, no; I don't mind. I seem to have got past carin' for anythink now. I felt it a little when Tommy went away—the first time I felt anythink for years. But I'm over that now."

"Haven't you got any friends in the district, Mrs Spicer?"

"Oh yes. There's me married sister near Cobborah, and a married brother near Dubbo; he's got a station. They wanted to take me an' the children between them, or take some of the younger children. But I couldn't bring my mind to break up the home. I want to keep the children together as much as possible. There's enough of them gone, God knows. But it's a comfort to know that there's someone to see to them if anythink happens to me."

.   .

One day—I was on my way home with the team that day—Annie Spicer came running up the creek in terrible trouble.

"Oh, Mrs Wilson! something terrible's happened at home! A trooper" (mounted policeman—they called them "mounted troopers" out there), "a trooper's come and took Billy!" Billy was the eldest son at home.

"What?"

"It's true, Mrs Wilson."

":What for? What did the policeman say?"

"He—he—he said, 'I—I'm very sorry, Mrs Spicer; but—I—I want William.' "

It turned out that William was wanted on account of a horse missed from Wall's station and sold down-country.

"An' mother took on awful," sobbed Annie; "an' now she'll only sit stock-still an' stare in front of her, and won't take no notice of any of us. Oh! it's awful, Mrs Wilson. The policeman said he'd tell Aunt Emma" (Mrs Spicer's sister at Cobborah) "and send her out. But I had to come to you, an' I've run all the way."

James put the horse to the cart and drove Mary down.

Mary told me all about it when I came home.

"I found her just as Annie said; but she broke down and cried in my arms. Oh, Joe! it was awful! She didn't cry like a woman. I heard a man at Haviland cry at his brother's funeral, and it was just like that. She came round a bit after a while. Her sister's with her now. . . . Oh, Joe! you must take me away from the Bush."

Later on Mary said:

"How the oaks are sighing to-night, Joe!"

          .   .   .

Next morning I rode across to Wall's station and tackled the old man; but he was a hard man, and wouldn't listen to me—in fact, he ordered me off the station. I was a selector, and that was enough for him. But young Billy Wall rode after me.

"Look here, Joe!" he said, "it's a blanky shame. All for the sake of a horse! And as if that poor devil of a woman hasn't got enough to put up with already! I wouldn't do it for twenty horses. *I'll* tackle the boss, and if he won't listen to me, I'll walk off the run for the last time, if I have to carry my swag."

Billy Wall managed it. The charge was withdrawn, and we got young Billy Spicer off up-country.

But poor Mrs Spicer was never the same after that. She seldom came up to our place unless Mary dragged her, so to speak; and then she would talk of nothing but her last trouble, till her visits were painful to look forward to.

"If it only could have been kep' quiet—for the sake of the other children; they are all I think of now. I tried to bring 'em all up decent, but I s'pose it was my fault, somehow. It's the disgrace that's killin' me—I can't bear it."

I was at home one Sunday with Mary and a jolly Bush-girl named Maggie Charlsworth, who rode over sometimes from Wall's station (I must tell you about her some other time; James was "shook after her"), and we got talkin' about Mrs Spicer. Maggie was very warm about old Wall.

"I expected Mrs Spicer up to-day," said Mary. "She seems better lately."

"Why!" cried Maggie Charlsworth, "if that ain't Annie coming running up along the creek. Something's the matter!"

We all jumped up and ran out.

"What is it, Annie?" cried Mary.

"Oh, Mrs Wilson! Mother's asleep, and we can't wake her!"

"What?"

"It's—it's the truth, Mrs Wilson."

"How long has she been asleep?"

"Since lars' night."

"My God!" cried Mary, "*since last night?*"

"No, Mrs Wilson, not all the time; she woke wonst, about daylight this mornin'. She called me and said she didn't feel well, and I'd have to manage the milkin'."

"Was that all she said?"

"No. She said not to go for you; and she said to feed the pigs and calves; and she said to be sure and water them geraniums."

Mary wanted to go, but I wouldn't let her. James and I saddled our horses and rode down the creek.

.   .   .

Mrs Spicer looked very little di.Terent from what she did when I last saw her alive. It was some time before we could believe that she was dead. But she was "past carin' " right enough.

[*1899?   revised 1900-01*]

A DOUBLE BUGGY AT LAHEY'S CREEK

I

SPUDS, AND A WOMAN'S OBSTINACY

EVER since we were married it had been Mary's great ambition to have a buggy. The house or furniture didn't matter so much—out there in the Bush where we were—but, where there were no railways or coaches, and the roads were long, and mostly hot and dusty, a buggy was the great thing. I had a few pounds when we were married, and was going to get one then; but new buggies went high, and another party got hold of a second-hand one that I'd had my eye on, so Mary thought it over and at last she said: "Never mind the buggy, Joe; get a sewing-machine and I'll be satisfied. I'll want the machine more than the buggy, for a while. Wait till we're better off."

After that, whenever I took a contract—to put up a fence or wool-shed, or sink a dam or something—Mary would say: "You ought to knock a buggy out of this job, Joe;" but something always turned up—bad weather or sickness. Once I cut my foot with the adze and was laid up; and, another time, a dam I was making was washed away by a flood before I finished it. Then Mary would say: "Ah, well—never mind, Joe. Wait till we are better off." But she felt it hard the time I built a wool-shed and didn't get paid for it, for we'd as good as settled about another second-hand buggy then.

I always had a fancy for carpentering, and was handy with tools. I made a spring-cart—body and wheels—in spare time, out of colonial hardwood, and got Little the blacksmith to do the ironwork; I painted the cart myself. It wasn't much lighter than one of the tip-drays I had, but it *was* a spring-cart, and Mary pretended to be satisfied with it: anyway, I didn't hear any more of the buggy for a while.

I sold that cart, for fourteen pounds, to a Chinese gardener who wanted a strong cart to carry his vegetables round through the Bush. It was just before our first youngster came: I told Mary that I wanted the money in case of extra expense—and she didn't fret much at losing that cart. But the fact was that I was going to make another try for a buggy, as a present for Mary when the child was born. I thought of getting the turn-out while she was laid up, keeping it dark from her till she was on her feet again, and then showing her the buggy standing in the shed. But she had a bad time, and I had to have the doctor regularly, and get a proper nurse, and a lot of things extra; so the buggy idea was knocked on the head. I was set on it, too: I'd thought of how, when Mary was up and getting strong, I'd say one morning: "Go round and have a look in the shed, Mary; I've got a few fowls for you," or something like that—and follow her round to watch her eyes when she saw the buggy. I never told Mary about that—it wouldn't have done any good.

Later on I got some good timber—mostly scraps that were given to me—and made a light body for a spring-cart. Galletly, the coach-builder at Cudgegong, had got a dozen pairs of American hickory wheels up from Sydney for light spring-carts, and he let me have a pair for cost price and carriage. I got him to iron the cart, and he put it through the paint-shop for nothing. He sent it out, too, at the tail of Tom Tarrant's big van—to increase the surprise. We were swells then for a while; I heard no more of a buggy until after we'd been settled at Lahey's Creek for a couple of years.

I told you how I went into the carrying line, and took up a selection at Lahey's Creek—for a run for the horses and to grow a bit of feed—and shifted Mary and little Jim out there from

Gulgong, with Mary's young scamp of a brother James to keep them company while I was on the road. The first year I did well enough carrying, but I never cared for it—it was too slow; and, besides, I was always anxious when I was away from home. The game was right enough for a single man—or a married one whose wife had got the nagging habit (as many Bushwomen have—God help 'em!), and who wanted peace and quietness sometimes. Besides, other small carriers started (seeing me getting on); and Tom Tarrant, the coach-driver at Cudgegong, had another heavy spring-van built and put it on the roads, and he took a lot of the light stuff.

The second year i made a rise—out of "spuds", of all the things in the world. It was Mary's idea. Down at the lower end of our selection—Mary called it "the run"—was a shallow water-course called Snake's Creek, dry most of the year, except for a muddy water-hole or two; and, just above the junction, where it ran into Lahey's Creek, was a low piece of good black-soil flat, on our side—about three acres. The flat was fairly clear when I came to the selection—save for a few logs that had been washed up there in some big "old man" flood, way back in blackfellows' times; and one day, when I had a spell at home, I got the horses and trace-chains and dragged the logs together—those that wouldn't split for fencing timber—and burnt them off. I had a notion to get the flat ploughed and make a lucerne paddock of it. There was a good water-hole, under a clump of she-oak in the bend, and Mary used to take her stools and tubs and boiler down there in the spring-cart in hot weather and wash the clothes under the shade of the trees—it was cooler, and saved carrying water to the house. And one evening after she'd done the washing she said to me:

"Look here, Joe; the farmers out here never seem to get a new idea: they don't seem to me ever to try and find out beforehand what the market is going to be like—they just go on farming the same old way and putting in the same old crops year after year. They sow wheat, and, if it comes on anything like the thing, they reap and thresh it; if it doesn't, they mow it for hay—and some of 'em don't have the brains to do that in time. Now, I was looking at that bit of flat you cleared, and it struck me that it wouldn't be a half bad idea to get a bag of seed-potatoes, and have the land ploughed—old Corny George would do it cheap—and get them put in at once. Potatoes have been dear all round for the last couple of years."

I told her she was talking nonsense, that the ground was no good for potatoes, and the whole district was too dry. "Everybody

I know has tried it, one time or another, and made nothing of it," I said.

"All the more reason why you should try it, Joe," said Mary. "Just try one crop. It might rain for weeks, and then you'll be sorry you didn't take my advice."

"But I tell you the ground is not potato-ground," I said.

"How do you know? You haven't sown any there yet."

"But I've turned up the surface and looked at it. It's not rich enough, and too dry, I tell you. You need swampy, boggy ground for potatoes. Do you think I don't know land when I see it?"

"But you haven't *tried* to grow potatoes there yet, Joe. How do you know————"

I didn't listen to any more. Mary was obstinate when she got an idea into her head. It was no use arguing with her. All the time I'd be talking she'd just knit her forehead and go on thinking straight ahead, on the track she'd started—just as if I wasn't there —and it used to make me mad. She'd keep driving at me till I took her advice or lost my temper—I did both at the same time, mostly.

I took my pipe and went out to smoke and cool down.

A couple of days after the potato breeze, I started with the team down to Cudgegong for a load of fencing-wire I had to bring out; and after I'd kissed Mary good-bye, she said:

"Look here, Joe, if you bring out a bag of seed-potatoes, James and I will slice them, and old Corny George down the creek would bring his plough up in the dray and plough the ground for very little. We could put the potatoes in ourselves if the ground were only ploughed."

I thought she'd forgotten all about it. There was no time to argue—I'd be sure to lose my temper, and then I'd either have to waste an hour comforting Mary or go off in a "huff", as the women call it, and be miserable for the trip. So I said I'd see about it. She gave me another hug and a kiss. "Don't forget, Joe," she said as I started. "Think it over on the road." I reckon she had the best of it that time.

About five miles along, just as I turned into the main road, I heard someone galloping after me, and I saw young James on his hack. I got a start, for I thought that something had gone wrong at home. I remember, the first day I left Mary on the creek, for the first five or six miles I was half-a-dozen times on the point of turning back—only I thought she'd laugh at me.

"What is it, James?" I shouted, before he came up—but I saw he was grinning.

"Mary says to tell you not to forget to bring a hoe out with you."

"You clear off home!" I said, "or I'll lay the whip about your young hide; and don't come riding after me again as if the run was on fire."

"Well, you needn't get shirty with me!" he said. "*I* don't want to have anything to do with a hoe." And he rode off.

I *did* get thinking about those potatoes, though I hadn't meant to. I knew of an independent man in that district who'd made his money out of a crop of potatoes; but that was away back in the roaring 'fifties—'54—when spuds went up to twenty-eight shillings a hundredweight (in Sydney) on account of the gold rush. We might get good rain now, and, anyway, it wouldn't cost much to put the potatoes in. If they came on well, it would be a few pounds in my pocket; if the crop was a failure, I'd have a better show with Mary next time she was struck by an idea outside housekeeping, and have something to grumble about when I felt grumpy.

I got a couple of bags of potatoes—we could use those that were left over; and I got a small iron plough and a harrow that Little the blacksmith had lying in his yard and let me have cheap —only about a pound more than I told Mary I gave for them. When I took advice, I generally made the mistake of taking more than was offered, or adding notions of my own. It was vanity, I suppose. If the crop came on well I could claim the plough-and-harrow part of the idea, anyway. (It didn't strike me that if the crop failed Mary would have the plough and harrow against me, for old Corny would plough the ground for ten or fifteen shillings.) Anyway, I'd want a plough and harrow later on, and I might as well get it now; it would give James something to do.

I came out by the western road, by Guntawang, and up the creek home; and the first thing I saw was old Corny George ploughing the flat. And Mary was down on the bank super-intending. She'd got James with the trace-chains and the spare horses, and had made him clear off every stick and bush where another furrow might be squeezed in. Old Corny looked pretty grumpy on it—he'd broken all his plough-shares but one in the roots; and James didn't look much brighter. Mary had an old felt hat and a new pair of 'lastic-side boots of mine on, and the boots were covered with clay, for she'd been down hustling James to get a rotten old stump out of the way by the time Corny came round with his next furrow.

"I thought I'd make the boots easy for you, Joe," said Mary.

"It's all right, Mary," I said. "I'm not going to growl." Those boots were a bone of contention between us; but she generally got them off before I got home.

Her face fell a little when she saw the plough and harrow in the waggon, but I said that would be all right—we'd want a plough anyway.

"I thought you wanted old Corny to plough the ground," she said.

"I never said so."

"But when I sent Jim after you about the hoe to put the spuds in, you didn't say you wouldn't bring it," she said.

I had a few days at home, and entered into the spirit of the thing. When Corny was done, James and I cross-ploughed the land, and got a stump or two, a big log, and some scrub out of the way at the upper end and added nearly an acre, and ploughed that. James was all right at most Bush work: he'd bullock so long as the novelty lasted; he liked ploughing or fencing, or any graft he could make a show at. He didn't care for grubbing out stumps, or splitting posts and rails. We sliced the potatoes of an evening— and there was trouble between Mary and James over cutting through the "eyes". There was no time for the hoe—and besides, it wasn't a novelty to James—so I just ran furrows and they dropped the spuds in behind me, and I turned another furrow over them and ran the harrow over the ground. I think I hilled those spuds, too, with furrows—or a crop of Indian corn I put in later on.

It rained heavens-hard for over a week: we had regular showers all through, and it was the finest crop of potatoes ever seen in the district. I believe at first Mary used to slip down at daybreak to see if the potatoes were up; and she'd write to me about them, on the road. I forget how many bags I got; but the few who had grown potatoes in the district sent theirs to Sydney, and spuds went up to twelve and fifteen shillings a hundredweight in that district. I made a few quid out of mine—and saved carriage too, for I could take them out on the waggon. Then Mary began to hear (through James) of a buggy that someone had for sale cheap, or a dogcart that somebody else wanted to get rid of— and let me know about it, in an offhand way.

II

JOE WILSON'S LUCK

THERE was good grass on the selection all the year. I'd picked up a small lot—about twenty head—of half-starved steers for next to nothing, and turned them on the run; they came on wonderfully, and my brother-in-law (Mary's sister's husband), who was running a butchery at Gulgong, gave me a good price for them. His carts ran out twenty or thirty miles, to little bits of gold-rushes that were going on at th' Home Rule, Happy Valley, Guntawang, Tallawang, and Cooyal, and those places round there, and he was doing well.

Mary had heard of a light American waggonette, when the steers went—a tray-body arrangement—and she thought she'd do with that. "It would be better than the buggy, Joe," she said; "there'd be more room for the children, and, besides, I could take butter and eggs to Gulgong, or Cobborah, when we get a few more cows." Then James heard of a small flock of sheep that a selector—who was about starved off his selection out Talbragar way—wanted to get rid of. James reckoned he could get them for less than half-a-crown a head. We'd had a heavy shower of rain that came over the ranges and didn't seem to go beyond our boundaries. Mary said: "It's a pity to see all that grass going to waste, Joe. Better get those sheep and try your luck with them. Leave some money with me, and I'll send James over for them. Never mind about the buggy—we'll get that when we're on our feet."

So James rode across to Talbragar and drove a hard bargain with that unfortunate selector, and brought the sheep home. There were about two hundred, wethers and ewes, and they were young and looked a good breed too, but so poor they could scarcely travel; they soon picked up, though. The drought was blazing all round and out back, and I think that my corner of the ridges was the only place where there was any grass to speak of. We had another shower or two, and the grass held out. Chaps began to talk of "Joe Wilson's luck".

I would have liked to shear those sheep; but I hadn't time to get a shed or anything ready—along towards Christmas there was a bit of a boom in the carrying line. Wethers in wool were going as high as thirteen to fifteen shillings at the Homebush yards at Sydney, so I arranged to truck the sheep down from the river by rail, with another small lot that was going, and I started James off with them. He took the west road, and down Guntawang way a big farmer who saw James with the sheep (and who was speculating, or adding to his stock, or took a fancy to the wool) offered James as much for them as he reckoned I'd get in Sydney, after paying the carriage and the agents and the auctioneer. James put the sheep in a paddock and rode back to me. He was all there where riding was concerned. I told him to let the sheep go. James made a Greener shot-gun, and got his saddle done up, out of that job.

I took up a couple more forty-acre blocks—one in James's name, to encourage him with the fencing. There was a good slice of land in an angle between the range and the creek, farther down, which everybody thought belonged to Wall, the squatter, but Mary got an idea and went to the local land office and found out that it was "unoccupied Crown land", and so I took it up on pastoral lease, and got a few more sheep—I'd saved some of the best-looking ewes from the last lot.

One evening—I was going down next day for a load of fencing-wire for myself—Mary said:

"Joe! do you know that the Matthews have got a new double buggy?"

The Matthews were a big family of cockatoos, along up the main road, and I didn't think much of them. The sons were all "bad-eggs", though the old woman and girls were right enough.

"Well, what of that?" I said. "They're up to their neck in debt, and camping like blackfellows in a big bark humpy. They do well to go flashing round in a double buggy."

"But that isn't what I was going to say," said Mary. "They want to sell their old single buggy, James says. I'm sure you could get it for six or seven pounds; and you could have it done up."

"I wish James to the devil!" I said. "Can't he find anything better to do than ride round after cock-and-bull yarns about buggies?"

"Well," said Mary, "it was James who got the steers and the sheep."

Well, one word led to another, and we said things we didn't mean—but couldn't forget in a hurry. I remember I said something about Mary always dragging me back just when I was getting my head above water and struggling to make a home for her and the children; and that hurt her, and she spoke of the "homes" she'd had since she was married. And that cut me deep.

It was about the worst quarrel we had. When she began to cry I got my hat and went out and walked up and down by the creek. I hated anything that looked like injustice—I was so sensitive about it that it made me unjust sometimes. I tried to think I was right, but I couldn't—it wouldn't have made me feel any better if I could have thought so. I got thinking of Mary's first year on the selection and the life she'd had since we were married.

When I went in she'd cried herself to sleep. I bent over and, "Mary," I whispered.

She seemed to wake up.

"Joe—Joe!" she said.

"What is it, Mary?" I said.

"I'm pretty well sure that old Spot's calf isn't in the pen. Make James go at once!"

Old Spot's last calf was two years old now; so Mary was talking in her sleep, and dreaming she was back in her first year.

We both laughed when I told her about it afterwards; but I didn't feel like laughing just then.

Later on in the night she called out in her sleep:

"Joe—Joe! Put that buggy in the shed, or the sun will blister the varnish!"

I wish I could say that that was the last time I ever spoke unkindly to Mary.

Next morning I got up early and fried the bacon and made the tea, and took Mary's breakfast in to her—like I used to do, sometimes, when we were first married. She didn't say anything—just pulled my head down and kissed me.

When I was ready to start Mary said:

"You'd better take the spring-cart in behind the dray and get the tyres cut and set. They're ready to drop off, and James has been wedging them up till he's tired of it. The last time I was out with the children I had to knock one of them back with a stone: there'll be an accident yet."

So I lashed the shafts of the cart under the tail of the waggon, and mean and ridiculous enough the cart looked, going along that way. It suggested a man stooping along handcuffed, with his arms held out and down in front of him.

It was dull weather, and the scrubs looked extra dreary and endless—and I got thinking of old things. Everything was going all right with me, but that didn't keep me from brooding sometimes—trying to hatch out stones, like an old hen we had at home. I think, taking it all round, I used to be happier when I was mostly hard-up—and more generous. When I had ten pounds I was more likely to listen to a chap who said "Lend me a pound-note, Joe," than when I had fifty; *then* I fought shy of careless chaps—and lost mates that I wanted afterwards—and got the name of being mean. When I got a good cheque I'd be as miserable as a miser over the first ten pounds I spent; but when I got down to the last I'd buy things for the house. And now that I was getting on, I hated to spend a pound on anything. But then, the farther I got away from poverty the greater the fear I had of it—and, besides, there was always before us all the thought of the terrible drought, with blazing runs as bare and dusty as the road, and dead stock rotting every yard all along the barren creeks.

I had a long yarn with Mary's sister and her husband that night in Gulgong, and it brightened me up. I had a fancy that that sort of a brother-in-law made a better mate than a nearer one; Tom Tarrant had one, and he said it was sympathy. But while we were yarning I couldn't help thinking of Mary, out there in the hut on the Creek, with no one to talk to but the children, or James, who was sulky at home, or Black Mary or Black Jimmy (our black boy's father and mother), who weren't over-sentimental. Or maybe a selector's wife (the nearest was five miles away), who could talk only of two or three things—"lambin' " and "shearin' " and "cookin' for the men", and what she said to her old man, and what he said to her—and her own ailments—over and over again. It's a wonder it didn't drive Mary mad!—I know I could never listen to that woman more than an hour. Mary's sister said:

"Now if Mary had a comfortable buggy, she could drive in with the children oftener. Then she wouldn't feel the loneliness so much."

I said "Good-night" then and turned in. There was no getting away from that buggy. Whenever Mary's sister started hinting about a buggy, I reckoned it was a put-up job between them.

III

THE GHOST OF MARY'S SACRIFICE

WHEN I got to Cudgegong I stopped at Galletly's coach-shop to leave the cart. The Galletlys were good fellows: there were two brothers—one was a saddler and harness-maker. Big brown-bearded men—the biggest men in the district, 'twas said.

Their old man had died lately and left them some money; they had men, and only worked in their shops when they felt inclined, or there was a special work to do; they were both first-class trades-men. I went into the painter's shop to have a look at a double buggy that Galletly had built for a man who couldn't pay cash for it when it was finished—and Galletly wouldn't trust him.

looked at me and I looked at him—hard. Then he wheeled off, scowling, and swearing at his horses. I'd given him a hiding, six or seven years before, and he hadn't forgotten it. And I felt then as if I wouldn't mind trying to give someone a hiding.

The goods clerk must have thought that Joe Wilson was pretty grumpy that day. I was thinking of Mary, out there in the lonely hut on a barren creek in the Bush—for it was little better—with no one to speak to except a haggard, worn-out Bushwoman or two that came to see her on Sunday. I thought of the hardships she went through in the first year—that I haven't told you about yet; of the time she was ill, and I away, and no one to understand; of the time she was alone with James and Jim sick; and of the loneliness she fought through out there. I thought of Mary, outside in the blazing heat, with an old print dress and a felt hat, and pair of 'lastic-sides of mine on, doing the work of a station manager as well as that of a housewife and mother. And her cheeks were getting thin, and her colour was going: I thought of the gaunt, brick-brown, saw-file voiced, hopeless and spiritless Bushwomen I knew—and some of them not much older than Mary.

When I went back down into the town I had a drink with Bill Galletly at the Royal, and that settled the buggy; then Bob shouted, and I took the harness. Then I shouted, to wet the bargain. When I was going, Bob said: "Send in that young scamp of a brother of Mary's with the horses: if the collars don't fit I'll fix up a pair of makeshifts, and alter the others." I thought they both gripped my hand harder than usual, but that might have been the beer.

IV

THE BUGGY COMES HOME

I "WHIPPED the cat" a bit, the first twenty miles or so, but then, I thought, what did it matter? What was the use of grinding to save money until we were too old to enjoy it. If we had to go down in the world again, we might as well fall out of a buggy as out of a dray—there'd be some talk about it, anyway, and perhaps a little sympathy. When Mary had the buggy she wouldn't be tied down so much to that wretched hole in the Bush; and the Sydney trips needn't be off either. I could drive down to Wallerawang on the main line, where Mary had some people, and leave the buggy and horses there, and take the train to Sydney; or go right on, by the old coach-road, over the Blue Mountains: it would be a grand drive. I thought best to tell Mary's sister at Gulgong about the buggy; I told her I'd keep it dark from Mary till the buggy came home. She entered into the spirit of the thing, and said she'd give the world to be able to go out with the buggy, if only to see Mary open her eyes when she saw it; but she couldn't go, on account of a new baby she had. I was rather glad she couldn't, for it would spoil the surprise a little, I thought. I wanted that all to myself.

I got home about sunset next day and, after tea, when I'd finished telling Mary all the news, and a few lies as to why I didn't bring the cart back, and one or two other things, I sat with James, out on a log of the wood-heap, where we generally had our smokes and interviews, and told him all about the buggy. He whistled, then he said:

"But what do you want to make it such a bushranging business for? Why can't you tell Mary now? It will cheer her up. She's been pretty miserable since you've been away this trip."

"I want it to be a surprise," I said.

"Well, I've got nothing to say against a surprise, out in a hole like this; but it 'ud take a lot to surprise me. What am I to say to Mary about taking the two horses in? I'll only want one to bring the cart out, and she's sure to ask."

"Tell her you're going to get yours shod."

"But he had a set of slippers only the other day. She knows as much about horses as we do. I don't mind telling a lie so long as a chap has only got to tell a straight lie and be done with it. But Mary asks so many questions."

"Well, drive the other horse up the creek early, and pick him up as you go."

"Yes. And she'll want to know what I want with two bridles. But I'll fix her—you needn't worry."

"And, James," I said, "get a chamois leather and sponge— we'll want 'em anyway—and you might give the buggy a wash down in the creek, coming home. It's sure to be covered with dust."

"Oh!—orlright."

"And if you can, time yourself to get here in the cool of the evening, or just about sunset."

"What for?"

I'd thought it would be better to have the buggy there in the cool of the evening, when Mary would have time to get excited and get over it—better than in the blazing hot morning, when the sun rose as hot as at noon, and we'd have the long broiling day before us.

"What do you want me to come at sunset for?" asked James.

Do you want me to camp out in the scrub and turn up like a looming sundowner?"

"Oh well," I said, "get here at midnight if you like."

We didn't say anything for a while—just sat and puffed at our pipes. Then I said:

"Well, what are you thinking about?"

"I'm thinking it's time you got a new hat, the sun seems to get through your old one too much," and he got out of my reach and went to see about penning the calves. Before we turned in he said:

"Well, what am I to get out of the job, Joe?"

He had his eye on a double-barrel gun that Franca the gunsmith in Cudgegong had—one barrel shot, and the other rifle; so I said:

"How much does Franca want for that gun?"

"Five-ten; but I think he'd take my single barrel off it. Anyway, I can squeeze a couple of quid out of Phil Lambert for the single barrel." (Phil was his bosom chum.)

"All right," I said. "Make the best bargain you can."

He got his own breakfast and made an early start next morning, to get clear of any instructions or messages that Mary might have forgotten to give him overnight. He took his gun with him.

I'd always thought that a man was a fool who couldn't keep a secret from his wife—that there was something womanish about him. I found out. Those three days waiting for the buggy were about the longest I ever spent in my life. It made me scotty with everyone and everything; and poor Mary had to suffer for it. I put in the time patching up the harness and mending the stockyard and the roof, and, the third morning, I rode up the ridges to look for trees for fencing-timber. I remember I hurried home that afternoon because I thought the buggy might get there before me.

At tea-time I got Mary on to the buggy business.

"What's the good of a single buggy to you, Mary?" I asked. "There's only room for two, and what are you going to do with the children when we go out together?"

"We can put them on the floor at our feet, like other people do. I can always fold up a blanket or 'possum rug for them to sit on."

But she didn't take half so much interest in buggy talk as she would have taken at any other time, when I didn't want her to. Women are aggravating that way. But the poor girl was tired and not very well, and both the children were cross. She did look knocked up.

"We'll give the buggy a rest, Joe," she said. (I thought I heard it coming then.) "It seems as far off as ever. I don't know why you want to harp on it to-day. Now, don't look so cross, Joe—I didn't mean to hurt you. We'll wait until we can get a double buggy, since you're so set on it. There'll be plenty of time when we're better off."

After tea, when the youngsters were in bed, and she'd washed up, we sat outside on the edge of the verandah floor, Mary sewing, and I smoking and watching the track up the creek.

"Why don't you talk, Joe?" asked Mary. "You scarcely ever speak to me now: it's like drawing blood out of a stone to get a word from you. What makes you so cross, Joe?"

"Well, I've got nothing to say."

"But you should find something. Think of me—it's very miserable for me. Have you anything on your mind? Is there any new trouble? Better tell me, no matter what it is, and not go worrying and brooding and making both our lives miserable. If you never tell one anything, how can you expect me to understand?"

I said there was nothing the matter.

"But there must be, to make you so unbearable. Have you been drinking, Joe—or gambling?"

I asked her what she'd accuse me of next.

"And another thing I want to speak to you about," she went on. "Now, don't knit up your forehead like that, Joe, and get impatient————"

"Well, what is it?"

"I wish you wouldn't swear in the hearing of the children. Now, little Jim to-day, he was trying to fix his little go-cart and it wouldn't run right, and—and————"

"Well, what did he say?"

"He—he" (she seemed a little hysterical, trying not to laugh)— "he said 'damn it!' "

I had to laugh. Mary tried to keep serious, but it was no use.

"Never mind, old woman," I said, putting an arm round her, for her mouth was trembling, and she was crying more than laughing. "It won't be always like this. Just wait till we're a bit better off."

Just then a black boy we had (I must tell you about him some other time) came sidling along by the wall, as if he were afraid somebody was going to hit him—poor little devil! I never did.

"What is it, Harry?" said Mary.

"Buggy comin', I bin thinkit."

"Where?"

He pointed up the creek.

"Sure it's a buggy?"

"Yes, missus."

"How many horses?"

"One—two."

We knew that he could hear and see things long before we could. Mary went and perched on the wood-heap, and shaded her eyes—though the sun had gone—and peered through between the eternal grey trunks of the stunted trees on the flat across the creek. Presently she jumped down and came running in.

"There's someone coming in a buggy, Joe!" she cried, excitedly. "And both my white table-cloths are rough dry. Harry! put two flat-irons down to the fire, quick, and put on some more wood. It's lucky I kept those new sheets packed away. Get up out of that, Joe! What are you sitting grinning like that for? Go and get on another shirt. Hurry—Why! It's only James—by himself."

She stared at me, and I sat there, grinning like a fool.

"Joe!" she said, "whose buggy is that?"

"Well, I suppose it's yours," I said.

She caught her breath, and stared at the buggy and then at me again. James drove down out of sight into the crossing, and came up close to the house.

"Oh, Joe! what have you done?" cried Mary. "Why, it's a new double buggy!" Then she rushed at me and hugged my head. "Why didn't you tell me, Joe? You poor old boy!—and I've been nagging at you all day!" And she hugged me again.

James got down and started taking the horses out—as if it was an everyday occurrence. I saw the double-barrel gun sticking out from under the seat. He'd stopped to wash the buggy, and I suppose that's what made him grumpy. Mary stood on the veran-dah, with her eyes twice as big as usual and breathing hard—taking the buggy in.

James skimmed the harness off, and the horses shook themselves and went down to the dam for a drink. "You'd better look under the seats," growled James, as he took his gun out with great care.

Mary dived for the buggy. There was a dozen of lemonade and ginger-beer in a candle-box from Galletly—James said that Gal-letly's men had a gallon of beer, and they cheered him, James (I suppose he meant they cheered the buggy), as he drove off; there was a "little bit of a ham" from Pat Murphy, the storekeeper at Home Rule, that he'd "cured himself"—it was the biggest I ever saw; there were three loaves of baker's bread, a cake, and a dozen yards of something "to make up for the children" from Aunt Gertrude at Gulgong; there was a fresh-water cod, that long Dave Regan had caught the night before in the Macquarie river and sent out packed in salt in a box; there was a holland suit for the black boy, with red braid to trim it; and there was a jar of preserved ginger, and some lollies (sweets) ("for the lil' boy"), and a rum-looking Chinese doll and a rattle ("for lil' girl") from Sun Tong Lee, our storekeeper at Gulgong—James was chummy with Sun Tong Lee, and got his powder and shot and caps there on tick when he was short of money. And James said that the people would have loaded the buggy with "rubbish" if he'd waited. They all seemed glad to see Joe Wilson getting on—and these things did me good.

We got the things inside, and I don't think either of us knew what we were saying or doing for the next half-hour. Then James put his head in and said, in a very injured tone:

"What about my tea? I ain't had anything to speak of since I left Cudgegong. I want some grub."

Then Mary pulled herself together.

"You'll have your tea directly," she said. "Pick up that harness at once, and hang it on the pegs in the skillion; and you, Joe, back that buggy under the end of the verandah, the dew will be on it presently—and we'll put wet bags up in front of it to-morrow, to keep the sun off. And James will have to go back to Cudgegong for the cart—we can't have that buggy to knock about in."

"All right," said James—"anything! Only get me some grub."

Mary fried the fish, in case it wouldn't keep till the morning, and rubbed over the table-cloths, now the irons were hot—James growling all the time—and got out some crockery she had packed away that had belonged to her mother, and set the table in a style that made James uncomfortable.

"I want some grub—not a blooming banquet!" he said. And he growled a lot because Mary wanted him to eat his fish without a knife, "and that sort of Tommy-rot". When he'd finished he took his gun, and the black boy, and the dogs, and went out 'possum-shooting.

When we were alone Mary climbed into the buggy to try the seat, and made me get up alongside her. We hadn't had such a comfortable seat for years; but we soon got down, in case anyone came by, for we began to feel like a pair of fools up there.

Then we sat, side by side, on the edge of the verandah, and talked more than we'd done for years—and there was a good deal of "Do you remember?" in it—and I think we got to understand each other better that night.

And at last Mary said: "Do you know, Joe, why I feel to-night just—just like I did the day we were married."

And somehow I had that strange, shy sort of feeling too.

[1899   revised 1900]

THE WRITER WANTS TO SAY A WORD

In writing the first sketch of the Joe Wilson series, which happened to be "Brighten's Sister-in-law", I had an idea of making Joe Wilson a strong character. Whether he is or not, the reader must judge. It seems to me that the man's natural sentimental selfishness, good-nature, "softness", or weakness—call it which you like—developed as I wrote on.

I know Joe Wilson very well. He has been through deep trouble since the day he brought the double buggy to Lahey's Creek. I met him in Sydney the other day. Tall and straight yet—rather straighter than he had been—dressed in a comfortable, serviceable sac suit of "saddle-tweed", and wearing a new sugar-loaf, cabbage-tree hat, he looked over the hurrying street people calmly as though they were sheep of which he was not in charge, and which were not likely to get "boxed" with his. Not the worst way in which to regard the world.

He talked deliberately and quietly in all that roar and rush. He is a young man yet, comparatively speaking, but it would take little Mary a long while now to pick the grey hairs out of his head, and the process would leave him pretty bald.

In two or three short sketches in another book I hope to complete the story of his life.

[*1901*]

6

SEND ROUND THE HAT

"Now this is the creed from the Book of the Bush—
Should be simple and plain to a dunce:
'If a man's in a hole you must pass round the hat—
Were he jail-bird or gentleman once.'"

"Is it any harm to wake yer?"

It was about nine o'clock in the morning, and, though it was Sunday morning, it was no harm to wake me; but the shearer had mistaken me for a deaf jackeroo, who was staying at the shanty and was something like me, and had good-naturedly shouted almost at the top of his voice, and he woke the whole shanty. Anyway he woke three or four others who were sleeping on beds and stretchers, and one on a shake-down on the floor, in the same room. It had been a wet night, and the shanty was full of shearers from Big Billabong Shed which had cut out the day before. My room-mates had been drinking and gambling overnight, and they swore luridly at the intruder for disturbing them.

He was six-foot-three or thereabout. He was loosely built, bony, sandy-complexioned and grey-eyed. He wore a good-humoured grin at most times, as I noticed later on; he was of a type of Bushman that I always liked—the sort that seem to get more good-natured the longer they grow, yet are hard-knuckled and would accommodate a man who wanted to fight, or thrash a bully in a good-natured way. The sort that like to carry somebody's baby round, and cut wood, carry water and do little things for overworked married Bushwomen. He wore a saddle-tweed sac suit two sizes too small for him, and his face, neck, great hands and bony wrists were covered with sun blotches and freckles.

"I hope I ain't disturbing yer," he shouted, as he bent over my bunk, "but there's a cove—"

"You needn't shout!" I interrupted, "I'm not deaf."

"Oh—I beg your pardon!" he shouted. "I didn't know I was yellin'. I thought you was the deaf feller."

"Oh, that's all right," I said. "What's the trouble?"

"Wait till them other chaps is done swearin' and I'll tell yer," he said. He spoke with a quiet, good-natured drawl, with something of the nasal twang, but tone and drawl distinctly Australian —altogether apart from that of the Americans.

"Oh, spit it out for Christ's sake, Long-'un!" yelled One-eyed Bogan, who had been the worst swearer in a rough shed, and he fell back on his bunk as if his previous remarks had exhausted him.

"It's that there sick jackeroo that was pickin'-up at Big Billabong," said the Giraffe. "He had to knock off the first week, an' he's been here ever since. They're sendin' him away to the hospital in Sydney by the speeshall train. They're just goin' to take him up in the waggonette to the railway station, an' I thought I might as well go round with the hat an' get him a few bob. He's got a missus and kids in Sydney."

"Yer always goin' round with yer gory hat!" growled Bogan. "Yer'd blanky well take it round in hell!"

"That's what he's doing, Bogan," muttered "Gentleman Once", on the shake-down, with his face to the wall.

The hat was a genuine "cabbage-tree", one of the sort that "last a lifetime"; it was well coloured, almost black in fact with weather and age, and it had a new strap round the base of the crown. I looked into it and saw a dirty pound note and some silver. I dropped in half a crown, which was more than I could spare, for I had only been a green-hand at Big Billabong.

"Thank yer!" he said. "Now then, you fellers!"

"I wish you'd keep your hat on your head and your money in your pockets and your sympathy somewhere else," growled Jack Moonlight as he raised himself painfully on his elbow and felt under his pillow for two half-crowns. "Here," he said, "here's two half-casers. Chuck 'em in and let me sleep for God's sake!"

Gentleman Once, the gambler, rolled round on his shake-down, bringing his good-looking, dissipated face from the wall. He had turned in in his clothes, and with considerable exertion he shoved his hand down into the pocket of his trousers, which were a tight fit. He brought up a roll of pound notes and could find no silver.

"Here," he said to the Giraffe, "I might as well lay a quid. I'll chance it anyhow. Chuck it in."

"You've got rats this mornin', Gentleman Once," growled the Bogan. "It ain't a blanky horse race."

"P'r'aps I have," said Gentleman Once, and he turned to the wall again with his head on his arm.

"Now, Bogan, yer might as well chuck in somethin'," said the Giraffe.

"What's the matter with the —— jackeroo?" asked the Bogan, tugging his trousers from under the mattress.

Moonlight said something in a low tone.

"The —— he has!" said Bogan. "Well, I pity the ——! Here, I'll chuck in half a —— quid!" and he dropped half a sovereign into the hat.

The fourth man, who was known to his face as "Barcoo-Rot", and behind his back as "the Mean Man", had been drinking all night, and not even Bogan's stump-splitting adjectives could rouse him. So Bogan got out of bed, and calling on us (as blanky female cattle) to witness what he was about to do, he rolled the drunkard over, prospected his pockets till he made up five shillings (or a "caser" in Bush language), and "chucked" them into the hat.

And Barcoo-Rot is probably unconscious to this day that he was ever connected with an act of charity.

The Giraffe struck the deaf jackeroo in the next room. I heard the chaps cursing "Long-'un" for waking them, and "Deaf-'un" for being, as they thought at first, the indirect cause of the disturbance. I heard the Giraffe and his hat being condemned in other rooms and cursed along the verandah where more shearers were sleeping; and after a while I turned out.

The Giraffe was carefully fixing a mattress and pillows on the floor of a waggonette, and presently a man, who looked like a corpse, was carried out and lifted into the trap.

As the waggonette started, the shanty-keeper—a fat, soulless-looking man—put his hand in his pocket and dropped a quid into the hat which was still going round, in the hands of the Giraffe's mate, little Teddy Thompson, who was as far below medium height as the Giraffe was above it.

The Giraffe took the horse's head and led him along on the most level parts of the road towards the railway station, and two or three chaps went along to help get the sick man into the train.

The shearing season was over in that district, but I got a job of house-painting, which was my trade, at the Great Western Hotel (a two-storey brick place), and I stayed in Bourke for a couple of months.

.   .   .

The Giraffe was a Victorian native from Bendigo. He was well known in Bourke and to many shearers who came through the great dry scrubs from hundreds of miles round. He was stakeholder, drunkard's banker, peacemaker where possible, referee or second to oblige the chaps when a fight was on, big brother or uncle to most of the children in town, final court of appeal when the youngsters had a dispute over a footrace at the school picnic, referee at their fights, and he was the stranger's friend.

"The feller as knows can battle around for himself," he'd say. "But I always like to do what I can for a hard-up stranger cove.

I was a green-hand jackeroo once meself, and I know what it is."

"You're always bothering about other people, Giraffe," said Tom Hall, the Shearers' Union Secretary, who was only a couple of inches shorter than the Giraffe. "There's nothing in it, you can take it from me—I ought to know.".

"Well, what's a feller to do?" said the Giraffe. "I'm only hangin' round here till shearin' starts agen, an' a cove might as well be doin' something. Besides, it ain't as if I was like a cove that had old people or a wife an' kids to look after. I ain't got no responsibilities. A feller can't be doin' nothin'. Besides, I like to lend a helpin' hand when I can."

"Well, all I've got to say," said Tom, most of whose screw went in borrowed quids, etc.; "all I've got to say is that you'll get no thanks, and you might blanky well starve in the end."

"There ain't no fear of me starvin' so long as I've got me hands about me; an' I ain't a cove as wants thanks," said the Giraffe.

He was always helping someone or something. Now it was a bit of a "darnce" that we was gettin' up for the girls; again it was Mrs Smith, the woman whose husban' was drowned in the flood in the Bogan River lars' Crismas, or that there poor woman down by the billabong—her husban' cleared out and left her with a lot o' kids. Or Bill Something, the bullocky, who was run over by his own waggon, while he was drunk, and got his leg broke.

Towards the end of his spree One-eyed Bogan broke loose and smashed nearly all the windows of the Carriers' Arms, and next morning he was fined heavily at the police court. About dinner-time I encountered the Giraffe and his hat, with two half-crowns in it for a start.

"I'm sorry to trouble yer," he said, "but One-eyed Bogan carn't pay his fine, an' I thought we might fix it up for him. He ain't half a bad sort of feller when he ain't drinkin'. It's only when he gets too much booze in him."

After shearing, the hat usually started round with the Giraffe's own dirty crumpled pound note in the bottom of it as a send-off, later on it was half a sovereign, and so on down to half a crown and a shilling, as he got short of stuff; till in the end he would borrow a "few bob"—which he always repaid after next shearing —"just to start the thing goin'."

There were several yarns about him and his hat. 'Twas said that the hat had belonged to his father, whom he resembled in every respect, and it had been going round for so many years that the crown was worn as thin as paper by the quids, half-quids, casers, half-casers, bobs and tanners or sprats—to say nothing of the scrums—that had been chucked into it in its time and shaken up.

They say that when a new governor visited Bourke the Giraffe happened to be standing on the platform close to the exit, grinning good-humouredly, and the local toady nudged him urgently and said in an awful whisper: "Take off your hat! Why don't you take off your hat?"

"Why?" drawled the Giraffe, "he ain't hard up, is he?"

And they fondly cherish an anecdote to the effect that, when the One-Man-One-Vote Bill was passed (or Payment of Members, or when the first Labour Party went in—I forget on which occasion they said it was), the Giraffe was carried away by the general enthusiasm, got a few beers in him, "chucked" a quid into his hat, and sent it round. The boys contributed by force of habit, and contributed largely, because of the victory and the beer. And when the hat came back to the Giraffe, he stood holding it in front of him with both hands and stared blankly into it for a while. Then it dawned on him.

"Blowed if I haven't bin an' gone an' took up a bloomin' collection for meself!" he said.

He was almost a teetotaller, but he stood his shout in reason. He mostly drank ginger-beer.

"I ain't a feller that boozes, but I ain't got nothin' agen chaps enjoyin' themselves, so long as they don't go too far."

It was common for a man on the spree to say to him:

"Here! here's five quid. Look after it for me, Giraffe, will yer, till I git off the booze."

His real name was Bob Brothers, and his Bush names "Long-'un", "The Giraffe", "Send-round-the-hat", "Chuck-in-a-bob" and "Ginger-ale".

Some years before, camels and Afghan drivers had been imported to the Bourke district; the camels did very well in the dry country: they went right across country and carried everything from sardines to flooring-boards. And the teamsters loved the Afghans nearly as much as Sydney furniture-makers love the cheap Chinese in the same line. They loved 'em even as union shearers on strike love blacklegs brought up-country to take their places.

Now the Giraffe was a good, straight unionist, but in cases of sickness or trouble he was as apt to forget his unionism, as all Bushmen are at all times (and for all time) to forget their creed. So, one evening, the Giraffe blundered into the Carriers' Arms—of all places in the world—when it was full of teamsters; he had his hat in his hand and some small silver and coppers in it.

"I say, you fellers, there's a poor, sick Afghan in the camp down there along the—"

A big, brawny bullock-driver took him firmly by the shoulders, or, rather, by the elbows, and ran him out before any damage was done. The Giraffe took it as he took most things, good-humouredly; but, about dusk, he was seen slipping down towards the Afghan camp with a billy of soup.

"I believe," remarked Tom Hall, "that when the Giraffe goes to Heaven—and he's the only one of us, as far as I can see, that has a ghost of a show—I believe that when he goes to Heaven, the first thing he'll do will be to take his infernal hat round amongst the angels—getting up a collection for this damned world that he left behind."

"Well, I don't think there's so much to his credit, after all," said Jack Mitchell, shearer. "You see, the Giraffe is ambitious; he likes public life, and that accounts for him shoving himself forward with his collections. As for bothering about people in trouble, that's only common curiosity; he's one of those chaps that are always shoving their noses into other people's troubles. And, as for looking after sick men—why! there's nothing the Giraffe likes better than pottering round a sick man, and watching him and studying him. He's awfully interested in sick men, and they're pretty scarce out here. I tell you there's nothing he likes better—except, maybe, it's pottering round a corpse. I believe he'd ride forty miles to help and sympathize and potter round a funeral. The fact of the matter is that the Giraffe is only enjoying himself with other people's troubles—that's all it is. It's only vulgar curiosity and selfishness. I set it down to his ignorance; the way he was brought up."

A few days after the Afghan incident the Giraffe and his hat had a run of luck. A German, one of a party who were building a new wooden bridge over the Big Billabong, was helping unload some girders from a truck at the railway station, when a big log slipped on the skids and his leg was smashed badly. They carried him to the Carriers' Arms, which was the nearest hotel, and into a bedroom behind the bar, and sent for the doctor. The Giraffe was in evidence as usual.

"It vas not that at all," said German Charlie, when they asked him if he was in much pain. "It vas not that at all. I don't cares a damn for der bain; but dis is der tird year—und I vas going home dis year—after der gontract—und der contract yoost commence!"

That was the burden of his song all through, between his groans.

There were a good few chaps sitting quietly about the bar and verandah when the doctor arrived. The Giraffe was sitting at the end of the counter, on which he had laid his hat while he wiped his face, neck and forehead with a big speckled sweat-rag. It was a very hot day.

The doctor, a good-hearted young Australian, was heard saying something. Then German Charlie, in a voice that rung with pain:

"Make that leg right, doctor—quick! Dis is der tird pluddy year —und I must go home!"

The doctor asked him if he was in great pain.

"Neffer mind der pluddy bain, doctor! Neffer mind der pluddy bain! Dot vas nossing. Make dat leg well quick, doctor. Dis vas der last gontract, and I vas going home dis year." Then the words jerked out of him by physical agony: "Der girl vas vaiting dree year, und—by Got! I must go home."

The publican—Watty Braithwaite, known as "Watty Broad-weight". or, more familiarly, "Watty Bothways"—turned over the Giraffe's hat in a tired, bored sort of way, dropped a quid into it, and nodded resignedly at the Giraffe.

The Giraffe caught up the hint and the hat with alacrity. The hat went all round town, so to speak; and, as soon as his leg was firm enough not to come loose on the road, German Charlie went home.

It was well known that I contributed to the Sydney *Bulletin* and several other papers. The Giraffe's bump of reverence was very large, and swelled especially for sick men and poets. He treated me with much more respect than is due from a Bushman to a man, and with an odd sort of extra gentleness I sometimes fancied. But one day he rather surprised me.

"I'm sorry to trouble yer," he said in a shamefaced way. "I don't know as you go in for sportin', but One-eyed Bogan an' Barcoo-Rot is goin' to have a bit of a scrap down the billybong this evenin', an'—"

"A bit of a what?" I asked.

"A bit of fight to a finish," he said apologetically. "An' the chaps is tryin' to fix up a fiver to put some life into the thing. There's bad blood between One-eyed Bogan and Barcoo-Rot, an' it won't do them any harm to have it out."

It was a great fight, I remember. There must have been a couple of score blood-soaked handkerchiefs (or sweat-rags) buried in a hole on the field of battle, and the Giraffe was busy the rest of the evening helping to patch up the principals. Later on he took up a small collection for the loser, who happened to be Barcoo-Rot in spite of the advantage of an eye.

The Salvation Army lassie, who went round with the *War Cry*, nearly always sold the Giraffe three copies.

A new-chum parson, who wanted a subscription to build or enlarge a chapel, or something, sought the assistance of the Giraffe's influence with his mates.

"Well," said the Giraffe, "I ain't a churchgoer meself. I ain't what you might call a religious cove, but I'll be glad to do what I can to help yer. I don't suppose I can do much. I ain't been to church since I was a kiddy."

The parson was shocked, but later on he learned to appreciate the Giraffe and his mates, and to love Australia for the Bushman's sake, and it was he who told me the above anecdote.

The Giraffe helped fix some stalls for a Catholic church bazaar, and some of the chaps chaffed him about it in the union office.

"You'll be taking up a collection for a joss-house down in the Chinamen's camp next," said Tom Hall in conclusion.

"Well, I ain't got nothin' agen the Roming Carflics," said the Giraffe. "An' Father O'Donovan's a very decent sort of cove. He stuck up for the unions all right in the strike anyway." ("He wouldn't be Irish if he wasn't," someone commented.) "I carried swags once for six months with a feller that was a Carflick, an' he was a very straight feller. And a girl I knowed turned Carflick to marry a chap that had got her into trouble, an' she was always jes' the same to me after as she was before. Besides, I like to help everything that's goin' on."

Tom Hall and one or two others went out hurriedly to have a drink. But we all loved the Giraffe.

He was very innocent and very humorous, especially when he meant to be most serious and philosophical.

"Some of them Bush girls is regular tomboys," he said to me solemnly one day. "Some of them is too cheeky altogether. I remember once I was stoppin' at a place—they was sort of relations o' mine—an' they put me to sleep in a room off the verander, where there was a glass door an' no blinds. An' the first mornin' the girls—they was sort o' cousins o' mine—they come gigglin' and foolin' round outside the door on the verander, an' kep' me in bed till nearly ten o'clock. I had to put me trowsis on under the bedclothes in the end. But I got back on 'em the next night," he reflected.

"How did you do that, Bob?" I asked.

"Why, I went to bed in me trowsis!"

.   .   .

One day I was on a plank, painting the ceiling of the bar of the Great Western Hotel. I was anxious to get the job finished. The work had been kept back most of the day by chaps handing up long beers to me, and drawing my attention to the alleged fact that I was putting on the paint wrong side out. I was slapping it on over the last few boards when:

"I'm very sorry to trouble yer; I always seem to be troublin' yer; but there's that there woman and them girls—"

I looked down—about the first time I had looked down on him —and there was the Giraffe, with his hat brim up on the plank and two half-crowns in it.

"Oh, that's all right, Bob," I said, and I dropped in half a crown.

There were shearers in the bar, and presently there was some barracking. It appeared that that there woman and them girls were strange women, in the local as well as the Biblical sense of the word, who had come from Sydney at the end of the shearing season, and had taken a cottage on the edge of the scrub on the outskirts of the town. There had been trouble this week in connection with a row at their establishment, and they had been fined, warned off by the police, and turned out by their landlord.

"This is a bit too red-hot, Giraffe," said one of the shearers. "Them ——s has made enough out of us coves. They've got plenty of stuff, don't you fret. Let 'em go to ——! I'm blanked if I give a sprat."

"They ain't got their fares to Sydney," said the Giraffe. "An', what's more, the little 'un is sick, an' two of them has kids in Sydney."

"How the —— do you know?"

"Why, one of 'em come to me an' told me all about it."

There was an involuntary guffaw.

"Look here, Bob," said Billy Woods, the Rouseabouts' Secretary, kindly. "Don't you make a fool of yourself. You'll have all the chaps laughing at you. Those girls are only working you for all you're worth. I suppose one of 'em came crying and whining to you. Don't you bother about them. *You* don't know them; they can pump water at a moment's notice. You haven't had any experience with women yet, Bob."

"She didn't come whinin' and cryin' to me," said the Giraffe, dropping his twanging drawl a little. "She looked me straight in the face an' told me all about it."

"I say, Giraffe," said Box-o'-Tricks, "what have you been doin'? You've bin down there on the nod. I'm surprised at yer, Giraffe."

"An' he pretends to be so gory soft an' innocent too," growled the Bogan. "We know all about you, Giraffe."

"Look here, Giraffe," said Mitchell the shearer. "I'd never have thought it of you. We all thought you were the only virgin youth west the river; I always thought you were a moral young man. You mustn't think that because your conscience is pricking you everyone else's is."

"I ain't had anythin' to do with them," said the Giraffe, drawling again. "I ain't a cove that goes in for that sort of thing. But other chaps has, and I think they might as well help 'em out of their fix."

"They're a rotten crowd," said Billy Woods. "You don't know them, Bob. Don't bother about them—they're not worth it. Put your money in your pocket. You'll find a better use for it before next shearing."

"Better shout, Giraffe," said Box-o'-Tricks.

Now in spite of the Giraffe's softness he was the hardest man in Bourke to move when he'd decided on what he thought was "the fair thing to do". Another peculiarity of his was that on occasion, such for instance as "sayin' a few words" at a strike meeting, he would straighten himself, drop the twang, and rope in his drawl, so to speak.

"Well, look here, you chaps," he said now. "I don't know anything about them women. I s'pose they're bad, but I don't suppose they're worse than men has made them. All I know is that there's four women turned out, without any stuff, and every woman in Bourke, an' the police, an' the law agen 'em. An' the fact that they is women is agenst 'em most of all. You don't expect 'em to hump their swags to Sydney! Why, only I ain't got the stuff I wouldn't trouble yer. I'd pay their fares meself. Look," he said, lowering his voice, "there they are now, an' one of the girls is cryin'. Don't let 'em see yer lookin'."

I dropped softly from the plank and peeped out with the rest.

They stood by the fence on the opposite side of the street, a bit up towards the railway station, with their portmanteaus and bundles at their feet. One girl leant with her arms on the fence rail and her face buried in them; another was trying to comfort her. The third girl and the woman stood facing our way. The woman was good-looking; she had a hard face, but it might have been made hard. The third girl seemed half defiant, half inclined to cry. Presently she went to the other side of the girl who was crying on the fence and put her arm round her shoulder. The woman suddenly turned her back on us and stood looking away over the paddocks.

The hat went round. Billy Woods was first, then Box-o'-Tricks, and then Mitchell.

Billy contributed with eloquent silence. "I was only jokin', Giraffe," said Box-o'-Tricks, dredging his pockets for a couple of shillings. It was some time after the shearing, and most of the chaps were hard up.

"Ah, well," sighed Mitchell. "There's no help for it. If the

Giraffe would take up a collection to import some decent girls to this God-forgotten hole there might be some sense in it. . . . It's bad enough for the Giraffe to undermine our religious prejudices, and tempt us to take a morbid interest in sick chows and Afghans, and blacklegs and widows; but when he starts mixing us up with strange women it's time to buck." And he prospected his pockets and contributed two shillings, some odd pennies, and a pinch of tobacco dust.

"I don't mind helping the girls, but I'm damned if I'll give a penny to help the old ———," said Tom Hall.

"Well, she was a girl once herself," drawled the Giraffe.

The Giraffe went round to the other pubs and to the union offices, and when he returned he seemed satisfied with the plate, but troubled about something else.

"I don't know what to do for them for to-night," he said. "None of the pubs or boardin'-houses will hear of them, an' there ain't no empty houses, an' the women is all agen 'em."

"Not all," said Alice, the big, handsome barmaid from Sydney. "Come here, Bob." She gave the Giraffe half a sovereign and a look for which some of us would have paid him ten pounds— had we had the money, and had the look been transferable.

"Wait a minute, Bob," she said, and she went in to speak to the landlord.

"There's an empty bedroom at the end of the store in the yard," she said when she came back. "They can camp there for to-night if they behave themselves. You'd better tell 'em, Bob."

"Thank yer, Alice," said the Giraffe.

Next day, after work, the Giraffe and I drifted together and down by the river in the cool of the evening, and sat on the edge of the steep, drought-parched bank.

"I heard you saw your lady friends off this morning, Bob," I said, and was sorry I said it, even before he answered.

"Oh, they ain't no friends of mine," he said. "Only four poor devils of women. I thought they mightn't like to stand waitin' with the crowd on the platform, so I jest offered to get their tickets an' told 'em to wait round at the back of the station till the bell rung. . . . An' what do yer think they did, Harry?" he went on, with an exasperatingly unintelligent grin. "Why, they wanted to kiss me."

"Did they?"

"Yes. An' they would have done it, too, if I hadn't been so long. . : . Why, I'm blessed if they didn't kiss me hands."

"You don't say so."

"God's truth. Somehow I didn't like to go on the platform with them after that; besides they was cryin', and I can't stand women cryin'. But some of the chaps put them into an empty carriage." He thought a moment. Then:

"There's some terrible good-hearted fellers in the world," he reflected.

I thought so too.

"Bob," I said, "you're a single man. Why don't you get married and settle down?"

"Well," he said, "I ain't got no wife an' kids, that's a fact. But it ain't my fault."

He may have been right about the wife. But I thought of the look that Alice had given him, and—

"Girls seem to like me right enough," he said, "but it don't go no further than that. The trouble is that I'm so long, and I always seem to get shook after little girls. At least there was one little girl in Bendigo that I was properly gone on."

"And wouldn't she have you?"

"Well, it seems not."

"Did you ask her?"

"Oh, yes, I asked her right enough."

"Well, and what did she say?"

"She said it would be redicilus for her to be seen trottin' alongside of a chimbly like me."

"Perhaps she didn't mean that. There are any amount of little women who like tall men."

"I thought of that too—afterwards. P'r'aps she didn't mean it that way. I s'pose the fact of the matter was that she didn't cotton on to me, and wanted to let me down easy. She didn't want to hurt me feelin's, if yer understand—she was a very good-hearted little girl. There's some terrible tall fellers where I come from, and I know two as married little girls."

He seemed a hopeless case.

"Sometimes," he said, "sometimes I wish that I wasn't so blessed long."

"There's that there deaf jackeroo," he reflected presently. "He's something in the same fix about girls as I am. He's too deaf and I'm too long."

"How do you make that out?" I asked. "He's got three girls, to my knowledge, and, as for being deaf, why, he gasses more than any man in the town, and knows more of what's going on than old Mother Brindle the washerwoman."

"Well, look at that now!" said the Giraffe, slowly. "Who'd have thought it? He never told me he had three girls, an' as for hearin' news, I always tell him anything that's goin' on that I think he doesn't catch. He told me his trouble was that whenever he went out with a girl people could hear what they was sayin'—at least they could hear what she was sayin' to him, an' draw their own conclusions, he said. He said he went out one night with a girl, and some of the chaps foxed 'em an' heard her sayin' 'don't' to him, an' put it all round town."

"What did she say 'don't' for?" I asked.

"He didn't tell me that, but I s'pose he was kissin' her or huggin' her or something."

"Bob," I said presently, "didn't you try the little girl in Bendigo a second time?"

"No," he said. "What was the use. She was a good little girl, and I wasn't goin' to go botherin' her. I ain't the sort of cove that goes hangin' round where he isn't wanted. But somehow I couldn't stay about Bendigo after she gave me the hint, so I thought I'd come over an' have a knock round on this side for a year or two."

"And you never wrote to her?"

"No. What was the use of goin' pesterin' her with letters? I know what trouble letters give me when I have to answer one. She'd have only had to tell me the straight truth in a letter an' it wouldn't have done me any good. But I've pretty well got over it by this time."

A few days later I went to Sydney. The Giraffe was the last I shook hands with from the carriage window, and he slipped something in a piece of newspaper into my hand.

"I hope yer won't be offended," he drawled, "but some of the chaps thought you mightn't be too flush of stuff—you've been shoutin' a good deal; so they put a quid or two together. They thought it might help yer to have a bit of a fly round in Sydney."

.   .   .

I was back in Bourke before next shearing. On the evening of my arrival I ran against the Giraffe; he seemed strangely shaken over something, but he kept his hat on his head.

"Would yer mind takin' a stroll as fur as the billerbong?" he said. "I got something I'd like to tell yer."

His big, brown, sun-burnt hands trembled and shook as he took a letter from his pocket and opened it.

"I've just got a letter," he said. "A letter from that little girl at Bendigo. It seems it was all a mistake. I'd like you to read it. Somehow I feel as if I want to talk to a feller, and I'd rather talk to you than any of them other chaps."

It was a good letter, from a big-hearted little girl. She had been breaking her heart for the great ass all these months. It seemed that he had left Bendigo without saying good-bye to her. "Somehow I couldn't bring meself to it," he said, when I taxed him with it. She had never been able to get his address until last week; then she got it from a Bourke man who had gone south. She called him "an awful long fool", which he was, without the slightest doubt, and she implored him to write, and come back to her.

"And will you go back, Bob?" I asked.

"My oath! I'd take the train to-morrer only I ain't got the stuff. But I've got a stand in Big Billerbong Shed an' I'll soon knock a few quid together. I'll go back as soon as ever shearin's over. I'm goin' to write away to her to-night."

The Giraffe was the ringer of Big Billabong Shed that season. His tallies averaged 120 a day. He only sent his hat round once during shearing, and it was noticed that he hesitated at first and only contributed half a crown. But then it was a case of a man being taken from the shed by the police for wife desertion.

"It's always that way," commented Mitchell. "Those soft, good-hearted fellows always end by getting hard and selfish. The world makes 'em so. It's the thought of the soft fools they've been that finds out sooner or later and makes 'em repent. Like as not the Giraffe will be the meanest man out back before he's done."

When Big Billabong cut out, and we got back to Bourke with our dusty swags and dirty cheques, I spoke to Tom Hall.

"Look here, Tom," I said. "That long fool, the Giraffe, has been breaking his heart for a little girl in Bendigo ever since he's been out back, and she's been breaking her heart for him, and the ass didn't know it till he got a letter from her just before Big Billabong started. He's going to-morrow morning."

That evening Tom stole the Giraffe's hat. "I s'pose it'll turn up in the mornin'," said the Giraffe. "I don't mind a lark," he added, "but it does seem a bit red-hot for the chaps to collar a cove's hat and a feller goin' away for good, p'r'aps, in the mornin'."

Mitchell started the thing going with a quid.

"It's worth it," he said, "to get rid of him. We'll have some peace now. There won't be so many accidents or women in trouble when the Giraffe and his blessed hat are gone. Anyway, he's an eyesore in the town, and he's getting on my nerves for one. . . . Come on, you sinners! Chuck 'em in; we're only taking quids and half-quids."

About daylight next morning Tom Hall slipped into the Giraffe's room at the Carriers' Arms. The Giraffe was sleeping peacefully. Tom put the hat on a chair by his side. The collection had been a record one, and, besides the packet of money in the crown of the hat, there was a silver-mounted pipe with case—the best that could be bought in Bourke, a gold brooch, and several trifles— besides an ugly valentine of a long man in his shirt walking the room with a twin on each arm.

Tom was about to shake the Giraffe by the shoulder, when he noticed a great foot, with about half a yard of big-boned ankle and shank, sticking out at the bottom of the bed. The temptation was too great. Tom took up the hair-brush, and, with the back of it, he gave a smart rap on the point of an in-growing toe-nail, and slithered.

We heard the Giraffe swearing good-naturedly for a while, and then there was a pregnant silence. He was staring at the hat we supposed.

We were all up at the station to see him off. It was rather a long wait. The Giraffe edged me up to the other end of the platform.

He seemed overcome.

"There's—there's some terrible good-hearted fellers in this world," he said. "You mustn't forget 'em, Harry, when you make a big name writin'. I'm—well, I'm blessed if I don't feel as if I was jist goin' to blubber!"

I was glad he didn't. The Giraffe blubberin' would have been a spectacle. I steered him back to his friends.

"Ain't you going to kiss me, Bob?" said the Great Western's big, handsome barmaid, as the bell rang.

"Well, I don't mind kissin' you, Alice," he said, wiping his mouth. "But I'm goin' to be married, yer know." And he kissed her fair on the mouth.

"There's nothin' like gettin' into practice," he said, grinning round.

We thought he was improving wonderfully; but at the last moment something troubled him.

"Look here, you chaps," he said hesitatingly, with his hand in his pocket, "I don't know what I'm going to do with all this stuff. There's that there poor washerwoman that scalded her legs liftin' the boiler of clothes off the fire—"

We shoved him into the carriage. He hung—about half of him—out the window, wildly waving his hat, till the train disappeared in the scrub.

.   .   .

And, as I sit here writing by lamplight at mid-day, in the midst of a great city of shallow social sham, of hopeless, squalid poverty, of ignorant selfishness, cultured or brutish, and of noble and heroic endeavour frowned down or callously neglected, I am almost aware of a burst of sunshine in the room, and a long form leaning over my chair, and:

"Excuse me for troublin' yer; I'm always troublin' yer; but there's that there poor woman. . . ."

And I wish I could immortalize him!

[1900-01]

A FRAGMENT OF AUTOBIOGRAPHY

I

THE TENT AND THE TREE

I HAD a dreamy recollection of the place as a hut; some of my people said it was a tent, on a good frame—for Father was a carpenter; but Mother tells me that he built a little bark room in front, lined with "scrim" papered with newspapers, with a white-washed floor with mats, a fireplace in front, by the side of the door, and a glass door!—relic of the rush, I suppose. The tent was the same that I was born in on the Grenfell gold-field some three years before, and had been brought back to Pipeclay. There was a tree in front of the tent—or hut—a bluegum I think, and I know it had a forked trunk; and on the ground between the tree and the hut had stood a big bark public-house, one of seven in the gully in the palmy days of Pipeclay. Some of the postholes were there yet, and I used to fall into them, until Father filled them up. Pipeclay had petered out before my people went with the rush to Grenfell. Pipeclay was a stony, barren ridge, two little gullies full of digger holes caving in, a little brown flat, a few tumble-down haunted huts, an old farm or two on the outskirts, blue-grey scrub, Scotch thistles, prickly pears, Bathurst burrs, lank weeds, goats, and utter dreariness and desolation. But the hills were still blue in the distance. I took screaming fits, they said, and would lie down and roll out of the tent, through the room and across the flat till I was tired: then I'd sleep. But this was before I became conscious of the World.

That tree haunted my early childhood. I had a childish dread that it would fall on the tent. I felt sure it would fall some day. Perhaps I looked up, and the white clouds flying over made the top of the tree seem to move. The tent and the tree are the first things I remember. They stood there back at the beginning of the World, and it was long before I could conceive of either having been removed.

There was Father and Mother and a baby brother, but I *seemed* to come into the world alone—they came into my life later on. Father said that I suggested throwing the baby down a diggers' hole, or drowning him, like a surplus kitten. They say I got a tin of jam one day and obstinately denied it, though my mouth, hands and pinny were covered with jam: which was strange, for I was painfully and unhappily conscientious and truthful for many long years.

When I was about three, or three and a half, I read the paper, they tell me—or at least I thought I did. I'd get it and stare at it hard, and rustle it as I'd heard it rustle when Father turned it. About this time I was butted by a billy-goat—and I carry the scar, and several others, on my head to his day—but I don't remember the goat. It belonged to Granny. Grandfather had bullock-teams and a sawpit. Granny lived in an old weatherboard place, that had been a public-house, about a hundred yards further along in the World. I used to go to Granny's and get coffee. I liked coffee. One day she told me that the blacks had come and drank up all the coffee and I didn't like the blacks after that. I don't remember that the old lady had any special points about her, except her nose and chin, but I was extremely fond of her until the day she died. When I was about four and my brother two we had a song about Aunty—Aunty Phoebe I think it was— that Mother had taught us. It was a song calling Aunty to come. Sometimes Mother would tell us that if we sang that song Aunty would come, and we'd sing it, and sure enough she'd come while we were singing it, and rush in and kiss us. We thought it very wonderful.

Then a tremendous thing happened. Father built a two-roomed slab-and-bark hut over on the flat on the other side of the gully—and on the other side of the World as it was then: and Grandfather came with a load of stringy-bark slabs and stringy-bark poles for a kitchen. And Granny and the rest were going to Mudgee (about five miles away) or to some other place away out of the World. The dining-room had a good pine floor, and there were two dogs, and a church with a double tower, and a sentry on the mantelshelf, and the sofa tick had a holland cover—

I remember this because we weren't allowed to get on to it. About this time I was put into knickerbockers, and "come a man", and began to take an interest in lady visitors. I had two pair of pants, one of tweed and the other of holland I think, and one morning I tore the dark pair on a stump. Then a young lady came—a jolly, stylish girl whom I greatly admired. I was called but didn't show up for some time. I'd washed my face and damped my hair and combed it, but it was too wet and all in furrows. I'd dragged the holland pants on over the tweed ones. I shook hands with the young lady and hoped she'd excuse me for keeping her waiting, but the fact of the matter was, I said, that my trousers were broke in a rather awkward place. I told Mother later in confidence that I didn't think she was very ladylike, or she wouldn't have laughed so. I was very hurt about it.

But we didn't seem to live in the new house any time before a more tremendous thing happened. We were in a cart with bedding and a goat and a cat in a basket and fowls in a box, and there were great trees all along, and teams with loads of bark and rafters, and tables upside down with bedding and things between the legs, and buckets and pots hanging round, and gold cradles, gold dishes, windlass boles and picks and shovels; and there were more drays and carts and children and women and goats—some tied behind the carts; and men on horses and men walking. All the World was shifting as fast as ever it could.

Gulgong, the last of the great alluvial or "poor man's" rushes, had broken out. And it seemed no time, but it must have been months, and may have been a year or so, before a still greater thing than ever happened. Father's party had bottomed on payable gold, and we went with Mother and some aunts on a trip to Sydney. We saw Grandfather at Mudgee—he was up with one of his teams I suppose: it was in a public-house and Grandfather was singing songs; and we saw Granny at Wallerawang, where the railway was, and where she'd gone to live. I remember little of the coach journey down, except that I felt smothered and squeezed once or twice, and it was jolly. I must have slept a lot. We went to sleep on chairs in the waiting-room at the railway station, and when I woke up somebody said it was Sydney, and there was a lot of smoke, and it was raining.

I remembered little of Sydney, except that we stayed at a place in Castlereagh Street and the woman's name was Mrs Kelly. We must have picnicked at Manly Beach or somewhere, for we had a picture at home of a Newfoundland dog with the sea behind him, and that picture meant Sydney to me for a long time afterwards. Mrs Kelly had a swing in her back yard, and one day I was swinging high and told Mrs Kelly's little girl that I was going right up to Heaven, and she said I was a very wicked little boy to say such a thing. I couldn't understand why. Mrs Kelly's little boy taught us to say "Ally-looyer! I hardly knew yer!"

I must have seen and remembered Pinchgut, or else Mrs Kelly's little boy told me about it, for when I returned to Gulgong I informed a lady that I'd found out where babies come from—I was quite sure they came from Pinchgut. I had a new suit of velveteen knickerbockers, but I don't remember what Charlie had. One day we got out in the street and the door shut behind us and we got frightened, and lost, and knocked and hammered at the wrong door, and it opened and we went into the wrong house. It was awful, but they didn't hurt us. The girls took us up in their arms and kissed us and gave us cake, and one of them took us home. I remember that Mrs Kelly was very angry about it, because, she said, it was a bad house: but we couldn't see anything bad about it—they might have kept us there, or killed us, or given us to a policeman; we thought it was a good house.

But a more terrible thing happened. There was a hole in the fence, where some palings had fallen out, at the bottom of Mrs Kelly's yard, and through there there was a coach-builder's or wheelwright's shop, with a big heap of chips and shavings at the bottom of their yard, against our fence. One day Charlie and I got through the hole and started to put shavings and chips back through into Mrs Kelly's yard for her to light her fire with. We thought it would be a pleasant surprise, I suppose. But all of a sudden a man came running down the yard with a saw in his hand, while another man shouted to him from the shop: "Cut their heads off, Bill! Cut both their heads off!" I don't know whether I got through the hole first, or Charlie, but there wasn't much time between us. When they soothed us and got us a little calmer we were both determined that we wanted to go straight back home to Gulgong at once.

I remembered even less of the journey home than I did of the journey down. There was an inn where we stayed for a night, so we must have taken the coach journey by van and not by Cobb & Co's. The landlady knocked at the door and asked if we'd take in another little boy to sleep there for the night, so the place must have been full. There was trouble in the morning about a bottle of smelling salts I broke and something I spilt on my knickerbockers.

Then the hut on Gulgong, and Father had killed a pig. Mother asked us if we knew him again; and I said to him: "Ally-looyer—I hardly knew yer, Father!" And Father seemed surprised.

He was always working, or going somewhere with an axe or a pick and shovel on his shoulder, and coming home late. I remember watching for the glint of his white moles in the dusk, and sometimes following him out again after tea, when it was moonlight, and he went a little way with the axe on his shoulder to split firewood from a log. He worked in a claim in the Happy Valley, and again on the Canadian Lead. I had childish fancies of Happy Valley, because of the name, but I saw it in after years, and a more dismal hole of a gully I'd seldom set eyes on.

Sometimes we'd go for a drive round the fields in a cart with Mother and one or two other diggers' wives, and stop at a claim where one of their husbands worked. And if it was his shift below his mate would sing out, "Below there! Peter!" (or Tom), "here's someone wants to see you!" and he'd be drawn up all covered with yellow mullock. I have an idea that those diggers didn't want to be bothered by their families while they were digging for gold.

Strange to say there were periods during my childhood when I seemed to live alone: when Mother and brothers, but not so often Father, seemed to go completely out of my life. Maybe I dreamed a lot, or perhaps they were away on visits. But I remember a cubby house and a boy they wouldn't let us play with afterwards because they said he was a bad boy. As I grew, the feeling of loneliness and the desire to be alone increased.

I had a fondness for dolls, especially wooden Judy dolls, and later on developed a weakness for cats—which last has clung to me to this day. My aunts always said I should have been a girl.

Aunt Phoebe was living at Gulgong and she had a sewing-machine and a parrot; and there were honeysuckles in front of her house (we called huts houses—or "places" when they had more than one room). I believed the parrot understood people, and I used to talk to him a good deal. I used to be there often, and when I was about six I fell in love with an elderly married lady who kept a lolly shop next door to Aunt Phoebe's. Her husband was away and she seemed lonely. She was forty or fifty and had moles and a moustache. I remember I went into her shop one day, to buy lollies; she was busy sewing, and she was worried, and she said "Oh bother!" and it hurt me so much that I cried. I'd come in the back way, and so I went into the kitchen and dried my eyes on a tea-towel. She seemed greatly affected and comforted me, and gave me a lot of lollies—and she wouldn't take a penny. I didn't go in to Aunt Phoebe's until I felt quite sure my eyes were all right. I kept big things like that locked up tight in my heart, but the lady told Aunt. I was a very sensitive child.

And there were the diggers, grand fellows—Harry Brentnal and

Jack Ratcliffe and the rest of them, and we had money boxes. And there were circuses—and one day we were walking with Aunt and she said, "Look quick! There's Maggie Oliver." And I looked and saw the most beautiful woman I had ever seen. She was fixing up a vine round a verandah. And one night, in a place they called a theatre, I heard another most beautiful woman sing:

> Out in the wide world, out in the street,
> Asking a penny from each one I meet,
> Cheerless I wander about all the day
> Casting my young life in sorrow away!

That infernal song haunted me for years, especially the last line.

There was a pretty woman living in a hut near us who used to sing "Love Amongst the Rowses" and have a black eye. I said I wanted to go and fight her husband—but perhaps she loved him. About this time I used to tell people that I was going on for seven. I seemed to stay going on for seven for a long time, but I began to feel old.

They said that Gulgong was done, and one day Mother and Father packed up all the things. Next morning we were waked early; there was a dray at the door and we heard a great scraping overhead. Suddenly we saw the sky and next moment were nearly blinded by a shower of pungent stringy-bark dust. Father was taking off the roof of the hut—for we carried the house with us in those days.

We were back at Pipeclay again. There was someone living in the new house on the flat, so we camped for a night or so with the Spencers. They had also shifted on to the flat and built a slab house. They used to live in a hut near the tent by the tree, but I didn't remember them then. I wanted to go across the gully with some of the Spencers' children and see the tent we used to live in, but they told me it was gone. Anyway I wanted to see for myself, or see the place, and whether the tree was still standing, but it was getting dusk, and the gully was full of dangerous digger holes, so weren't let go. We'd brought the lining of the Gulgong hut with us—"scrim" or bagging with the newspapers still pasted on it—and our table stood outside, where the dray had dumped it with the rest of the load; so we children pulled a big piece of the lining over the table, and let it hang down all round, to make a cubby house, and we all got under—Spencer had a big family and it was a tight squeeze. And we compared notes and got chummy and told stories. They were the first playmates we had, and we theirs, and we were chums until we were scattered.

The tent and the tree were gone, and Spencer was making a garden there. But the tent and the tree still stand, in a sort of strange, unearthly half light—sadder than any twilight I know of—ever so far away back there at the other end of the past.

II

THE OLD BARK SCHOOL

NOTWITHSTANDING our old trip to Sydney, which we had almost forgotten—and it's strange how boys forget things of their childhood which come back to them as men—notwithstanding our trip to Sydney, the World was encircled by the Mudgee Hills, with Pipeclay as a centre. Mudgee, the town, five miles away, was inside the World: Sydney was somewhere on the edge of the World, or just behind. I used to describe Sydney as a place 170 miles from Pipeclay.

The World could not be flat, because of the hills—we children settled that amongst ourselves. Later on we decided that it couldn't be round, for the same reason. But we took it for granted, what we saw of it. The sky was part of the World, of course, and a dome, just as we saw it, and it ended all round where it touched the hills or flats. The sun—this was my idea—went down behind the ridge across the Cudgegong River, and then all round, behind the Mudgee Mountains, and behind old Mount Buckaroo in the west, and then rose again. It took him all night to go round. These conclusions of ours gave our first schoolmaster a lot of trouble later on. Heaven was up above, where the stars were; God was everywhere; and Satan and the other place were "down there". It was wicked to point at the moon, or swear, or tell lies; it was also wicked to say "devil".

There was the ghost of old Robertson in his deserted slab hut: young Fred Spencer saw him one night through the cracks in the slabs. And there was the ghost of old Joe Swallow in an old stone hut at the foot of Sapling Gully; and the Chinaman's ghost at the Chinaman's grave in Golden Gully; and the Hairy Man in Long Gully. We wouldn't go through any of those gullies after dark. We children used to go out on the flat in the moonlight and sit in a circle, and talk about these spooks till we frightened each other; then one would start to run home and the rest would follow screaming.

Father worked at building and carpentering, round about the

district and in the farming town: Spencer at fencing, clearing, etc., on surrounding runs, and sometimes for wages in a claim. I have described such homes as ours many times in other books: some were better and some were worse. There was a period of tin plates and pint pots and brown ration-sugar, bread-and-treacle and bread-and-dripping. Cows, pigs and fowls came later and there was milk, butter, eggs and bacon. There were times when the Spencers lived on bread and tea and "punkin pie". Perhaps I couldn't realize the sordid hardship and poverty of it now. We couldn't then, because we knew nothing better, and so we didn't feel it.

I hope, in another book, to go deeper into the lives of bush people—there is no room here. There was hardship and poverty, squalor and misery, hatred and uncharitableness, and ignorance; there were many mistakes, but no one was to blame: it was fate—it was fate. The misery and unhappiness that had to be and couldn't be helped. There were lonely foreign fathers, speaking broken English and strangers to their wives and families till the day of their death. A friend, who knows me, writes: "Treated ruthlessly, Rousseaulike, without regard to your own or others' feelings, what a notable book yours would be!" Yes, but what good purpose would it serve, even if I could find a publisher? Looking back, from these, the dark days of my life, to my boyhood and childhood I can find many things that were bright and happy and good and kind and beautiful and heroic—and sad and beautiful too.

I don't want to write a bitter line, if I can help it, except it be against my later self. I want to gather all the best things I can remember and put them in this book; and it will be none the less true. Perhaps it will be the truest I ever wrote. The dead of our family have rested for many long years, the living will rest in good time—and I have grown old in three years.

Shortly after we returned to Pipeclay my brother Peter was born. I spoke of my money box on Gulgong—I had two pounds ten, and I was given to understand that it went to buy Peter. He was bought from a Chinaman—not the vegetable variety, but the sort that used to come round with boxes of drapery and fancy goods slung on their poles. I still stuck to the Pinchgut idea, but a Chinese hawker did call at the house on the morning of the day on which the new baby was sprung on us, and that settled it as far as we children were concerned. I didn't think that Peter was worth two pounds ten as a baby, and couldn't see why I should be called upon to pay for him. I thought it very unjust and brooded over it a bit. My sense of injustice was always very keen. The Spencer children had been found in wombat holes, and they said that that was better than being bought off Chinamen, anyway. But I retorted to the effect that they hadn't been paid for.

There was an old camp for bullock teams on the flat. "Jimmy Nowlett" and "Billy Grimshaw" and others of my earlier characters used to camp there, for quite a spell sometimes in bad weather, or to spell their bullocks, which they'd put in a paddock or back in the ridges. And they'd patch up their waggons and make new yokes, etc. I've seen the great wool teams, with bales packed high, rolling along the rough road like ships in a gale; or bogged to the axle-trees with two or three teams of bullocks yoked to one load and trying in vain to shift. It was cruel for the bullocks. I've seen them go down on their knees and bellow under the blows from heavy handles of the bullock-whips. When Jimmy and his mates were in trouble with their teams we'd be called in and shut up out of hearing. Great flocks of sheep went by in sections, and mobs of bullocks. "Wild cow! Wild cow! Keep yer bloody dogs inside!" "Dave Regan" and others of my drovers used to call with their dusty packhorses. I remember Jimmy Nowlett ground up some charcoal and mixed it with axle grease and rubbed it on my brother Charlie's face: he rubbed it well into his chin and cheeks, with an extra layer under his nose, and assured him that it was the very best whisker seed, the only genuine article, and told him to be careful not to rub it off till the whiskers sprouted. Charlie was a sight, but he screamed and kicked and wouldn't be washed, and had to be put to bed with the whisker seed still on.

Log Paddock had broken out, opposite the old Pipeclay rush, on the old, level, creek and river frontage land grant that had shoved the selections back into the barren stony ridges. I remember the claims being bid for. Down at the far corner of the other end of Log Paddock the old farmers had built a little slab and bark chapel (see "Shall We Gather at the River?": *Children of the Bush*). They got a school teacher to camp there and paid him sixpence or a shilling a head for the children. We went there first, in charge of some older children. I told him that my name was Henery Lawson, and they say he spelled it that way. His was Hanks. I remember little or nothing of that school except great spitting and hard rubbing on slates.

Hanks, they say, used to talk about "improving our moral minds". There was a hedge of roses—a most uncommon thing—round a lucerne paddock on the bank of the creek, on a farm near the school, and one day, in lunch hour, some of us went to the farm and asked permission to pick some roses and were told to take as many as we liked. We came late back to school, each child with a big bunch of the flowers. Hanks was waiting for us, and, as we came up, he took the roses, bunch by bunch, tore them to pieces, and scattered them on the ground; then he marshalled us in: "Mary Cooper, Elizabeth Cooper, Bertha Lambert, Henry Lawson, William Harvey" (etc., etc.). "Stand up! You are guilty of the crime of stealing—stealing flowers from a neighbour!" Then it occurred to little Bertha Lambert to say, in a meek voice: "Please sir, Mrs Southwick said we could take them." "Serve out slates," said Hanks, and he turned to the backboard and started to set [the lesson].

About this time there was an incident which left a very painful impression on my mind for years. We had a quince tree at our place and were strictly forbidden to touch the fruit, which was not ripe at the time. One day my brother Charlie pulled a quince, and persuaded me to have a bite. I was always very fond of quinces. I believe that he gave me the bite out of pure good nature, but the theft was detected—there were few quinces on that tree—and Charlie blurted out in terror that I had taken a bite, anyhow. I was stung by a sense of injustice, and my indignation was roused, for I reckoned that he had only persuaded me to have a bite for fear I might tell on him—or that he wanted me to share the punishment in case of detection. Bursting with indignation, and a perverted sense of injustice, I denied that I had touched the quince at all. Charlie stuck to it, I was believed because I had always been truthful, and he was severely thrashed. He begged me to confess and save him ("Henry, you know you did it! You know you did it!"), but—I don't know what devil possessed me, save that I was horrified that I had told such a lie and in terror lest it should be found out and I branded as a liar—but I stuck to the lie and he to the truth, and he got a second dose and was sent supperless to bed. It was a miserable night and a miserable week for me. I don't think a boy was ever so conscience-stricken or a little soul so self-tortured. He forgave me next morning after breakfast, and might have forgotten all about it in a day or two had I let him. I tried every way to "make it up to him"—he told me not to bother. I said I'd confess—he told me I'd be a fool if I did, and tried his best to persuade me out of it. But, months after, I confessed. They didn't thrash me: better if they had and had done with it.

About this time—or I may have been a little younger—I began to be haunted by the dread of "growing up to be a man". Also I had an idea that I had lived before, and had grown up to be a man and had grown old and died. I confided in Father, and these ideas seemed to trouble him a lot. I slept in a cot beside the bed, and I used to hold his horny hand until I went to sleep. And often I'd say to him: "Father, it'll be a long time before I grow up to be a man, won't it?" and he'd say, "Yes, sonny. Now try and go to sleep." But I grew up to be a man in spite of lying awake worrying about it.

I believe the population of Pipeclay to have been obstinately, mulishly honest whatever else they might have been; but Pipeclay, in common with many worse and some better places, disliked mounted troopers. The men and women were uneasy when one was round, the children were frightened and they hid, and every dog on Pipeclay hated a mounted trooper and would bark himself into convulsions when one appeared on the scene. Perhaps the people disliked the sight of the trooper and were embarrassed by his presence because they *were* honest and poor. Bush children are generally shy of strangers; but I can't account for the dogs— unless it was the uniform. Young Fred Spencer once told my brother and me, in strict confidence, that when he was about ten years old he caught a trooper, tied him to a tree, cut stringy-bark saplings and thrashed him. And when he was tired his father thrashed him. And when his father was tired his uncle thrashed him. And then they let him go. I doubted Fred, but Charlie believed every word. Fred's ambition was to become a jockey: he is now one of the best riders in the west and has ridden many races. Charlie was undecided as to whether he'd join the bush-rangers or the mounted troopers—a state of indecision not uncommon amongst boys before our time, for both troopers and bushrangers came from the same class.

Father and a few others petitioned for a provisional school at Pipeclay—it was Eurunderee now, the black name had been restored. Father built the school. It was of bark. I remembered the dimensions for a long time, but have forgotten them now; anyway it was a mere hut. It was furnished with odds and ends thrown out of the public school in Mudgee, when the public school got new desks, stools and things. Father made blackboards and easels and mended the rickety furniture. The books, slates and things were all second-hand and old.

A selector, an Irishman, named John Tierney, was selected as schoolmaster. He had served in some capacity in the Army in Africa, a paymaster or something. His strong points were penmanship, arithmetic, geography and the brogue; his weak ones were spelling, grammar and singing. He was six feet something and very gaunt. He spent some months "training" in the public school in Mudgee, and had a skillion built on to the school, where he camped. I don't know whether he made his own bed, but his sister-in-law used to send his meals up to the school—one or other of us children used to carry them. I remember carrying a dinner of curried stew and rice, in a cloth between two plates, and a lot of the gravy leaked out. I suppose the dignity of Pipeclay wouldn't have stood his cooking for himself.

The Spencers went a couple of miles over the ridges at the back of Pipeclay to a slab and shingle public school on Old Pipeclay. Maybe their father thought they would get a better education. We went there later on—on account of a difference, I suppose, between our people and Tierney.

There were a good many Germans round; the majority of the farmers were Germans—all the successful ones were. There were a good few Irish, and the yellow and green had not faded yet. So there was fierce sectarian and international bitterness, on top of the usual narrow-minded, senseless, and purposeless little local feuds and quarrels; but there is no room for these things in this book.

The first day, one day in the first week at the Bark School, was a great day in my life, for I was given a copybook and pen and ink for the first time. The master believed in children leaving slate and pencil and commencing with pen and paper as early as possible. While setting me my first copy he told me not to go back and try to "paint" the letters. I am following that rule in this book, with reference to sentences. Better to strike out than paint. We had learnt our A.B.C.—and about a Cat, a Bat, and a Fat Rat—somewhere in the dim past.

It was Robinson Crusoe, by the way, who taught us to read. Mother got a *Robinson Crusoe* and used to read to us of evenings, and when she'd get tired and leave off at a thrilling place we'd get the book and try to spell our way ahead. By the time *Robinson Crusoe* was finished we could go back and read the book through from beginning to end. I wonder if Defoe had any influence on my style? Speaking of books, I was presented, at school break-up, with a copy of a book called *Self-taught Men*, for "general proficiency". My people, for some reason, considered it a very appropriate present. But I wasn't a self-taught man: the world taught me—I wish it had taught me common sense and the business side of my trade.

Then the trouble commenced. The master explained the hemispheres to us on the map, and doubled it back as far as he could to show us how they were intended to come together. We hadn't a globe. I thought the hemispheres should come round the other way; my idea was that the dome of the sky was part of the world and the whole world was shaped like half an orange, with the base for the earth, but I couldn't account for the other half. The master explained that the world was round. I thought it must have something to rest on, but I was willing to let that stand over for a while, and wanted the hill question cleared up. The master got an idia-rubber ball and stuck a pin in it up to the head and told us that the highest mountain in the world would not have the ten thousandth (or somethingth) effect on the roundness of the earth that the head of that pin would on the undness of the ball. That seemed satisfactory. He it was, I think, who tied a string to the neck of a stone ink-bottle and swung it round, to illustrate the power of gravitation and the course of the earth round the sun. And the string broke and the bottle went through a window-pane. But there was no string from the earth to the sun that we could see. Later on I got some vague ideas of astronomy, but could never realize boundless space or infinity. I can't now. That's the main thing that makes me believe in a supreme being. But infinity goes further than the supreme.

A favourite fad of the master's was that the school, being built of old material and standing on an exposed siding, might be blown down at any moment, and he trained the children to dive under the desks at a given signal so that they might have a chance of escaping the falling beams and rafters when the crash came. Most of us, I believe, were privately resolved to dive for the door at the first crack. These things pleased Father when he heard them, for he didn't build things to come down. When the new school was built, the Old Bark School was used by the master as a stable and may be standing still for all I know.

Our school books were published for use in the National Schools of Ireland, and the reading books dealt with Athlone and surrounding places, and little pauper boys and the lady at the great house. The geography said: "The inhabitants of New Holland are amongst the lowest and most degraded to be found on the surface of the earth." Also: "When you go out to play at 1 o'clock the sun will be in the south part of the sky." The master explained this, and we had to take his word for it—but then it was in the book. The geography also stated that in bad seasons the inhabitants of Norway made flour from the inner bark of a kind of tree—which used to make Father wild, for he was a Norwegian. Our name, of course, is Larsen by rights.

There was a Mliss in the school, and a reckless tomboy—a she-devil who chaffed the master and made his life a misery to him—and a bright boy, and a galoot (a hopeless dunce), a joker, and

a sneak, and a sweet gentle affectionate girl, a couple of show
scholars—model pupils the master called 'em—and one who was
always in trouble and mischief and always late, and one who
always wanted to fight, and the rest of them in between. The
children of the Germans were Australians—and children are
children all over the world. There was Cornelius Lyons, who
rolled his r's like a cock dove and had a brogue which made even
the master smile. And there was the obstinate boy, Johnny B——,
who seemed insensible to physical pain. The master called him
out one day: "John B——, stand out!" Johnny stood out. "Hold
out your hand!" Johnny held out his hand, the master struck it,
Johnny placed it behind his back and held out the other, the
master struck that, and Johnny put that hand behind and held out
the first; the master set his teeth, so did Jack—and so on for half
a dozen strokes. Then suddenly the master threw down the cane,
laid his hand on the boy's shoulder and spoke gently to him—and
Jack broke down. Looking back, I don't think it was fair—Jack
could have claimed a foul.

And there was Jim Bullock, whose "eddication was finished"
at the Old Bark School. "Oh yes," he said to me, years later,
while giving me a lift in his dray, "John Tierney finished me
nicely."

Amongst the scholars was a black gohanna. He lived in a dead
hollow tree near the school, and was under the master's immediate
protection. On summer days he'd lay along a beam over the girls'
seats, and improve his mind a little, and doze a lot. The drone
of the school seemed good for his nerves. They say a black
gohanna haunted the tent I was born in, and I remember one in
the house on the flat—I used to see the impression of his toes on
the calico ceiling when he slithered along overhead. It may have
been the same gohanna, and he might have been looking after me,
but I had always a horror of reptiles.

Sometimes, when the master's back was turned for a minute or
so, one of the boys would cry suddenly: "Girls! The gohanna's
fallin'!", and then you'd hear the girls squawk. One form of
alleged punishment in the Old Bark School was to make a bad
boy go and sit with the girls. I was sent there once, by mistake.
I felt the punishment, or the injustice of it, keenly: but I don't
remember that I minded the girls. I grew extremely and most
painfully shy of girls later on, but I've quite grown out of that now.
In fact I rather like sitting with them.

I was slow at arithmetic—it was Father who had the mathemati-
cal head—but I stuck to it. I was, I think, going into compound
fractions when I left school. In '97, when I went to teach a native

school in Maoriland, I could scarcely add a column of figures.
I had to practise nights and fake up sums with answers on the
back of the board, and bluff for all I was worth; for there was a
Maori girl there, about twenty, as big as I am and further advanced
in arithmetic, and she'd watch me like a cat watches a mouse until
she caught me in a mistake. I was required to give the average
attendance to two points of decimals, and I had to study, and
study hard, before I could do it.

My handwriting was always wretched, stiff and cramped and
slow and painful, and it used to worry me a lot. I changed it
many times, and it was only after I went to England, about three
years ago, that I struck a sort of running round-hand which
enabled me to keep within a dozen paragraphs or so of my rate of
composition.

The master used to spell anxiety with a "c", i.e., anxciety—and
many other words to match. I spelled Friday with a "y" for many
years, was always in doubt as to whether the "i" or the "e" came
first in words like receive or believe. I spelled separate with two
"e's", and blare, blair—and so on and so on. Mr Archibald said
I used to be a whale at spelling, and some of my early copy should
be interesting reading. A comp. who used to set my work up on
the *Boomerang* used to complain that my spelling was demoraliz-
ing him. It worried me a great deal; I was very sensitive about it.
I'm not now—not a little bit—I leave it to the comps. Strange
to say my punctuation was good—that must have "come natural"
It's a good idea to get rid of as many stops as you can.

I was fond of grammar, at the Old Bark School, and made rapid
progress in parsing or analysis. I don't bother much about
grammar now—it used to worry and cramp me and keep me back
too much when I started to write. My composition was always
good.

Until I was seventeen and went for a few months to a night
school in Sydney I knew of no monarch of England other than
Queen Victoria—except for a very vague idea of a King William
the Fourth.

I shared the average healthy boy's aversion to school; in fact
it developed into a positive dread, and before I left I had almost
a horror of going to school. Yet I was a "show scholar" or "model
pupil", as the master put it. There were two of us, and I can't
decide now whether we were the makings of noble men or simply
little involuntary and unconscious sneaks, but am rather inclined
to the latter opinion. It seems hard to reconcile the fact that I
hated, or rather dreaded, school with the fact that I was a model
scholar. Perhaps the last fact accounted for the first. I dreaded

school because I was sensitive, conscientious and a model scholar, and had never yet been punished, and it was a strain to keep up the reputation. I was always restless, fond of walking, and I hated confinement. Perhaps that is why, when I started to write, I used to do most of my work after midnight.

The boys went kangarooing and possum hunting, and had their games and superstitions and a contempt for girls, as boys have all over the world. Some played the wag and stole fruit, and told lies and went swimming. I was too conscientious to play truant, and I had a horror of lying or stealing. I might have been happier had it been otherwise. But I couldn't resist the swimming. The water-holes in the creek were full of snags and treacherous, and we were strictly forbidden to bathe there unless one of the elders was with us. After a swim we used to rub our faces, necks and hands with dust lest unwonted cleanliness should betray us.

I was extremely, painfully sensitive, and almost, if not quite, developed religious mania at one time (when I was about fourteen). The Mother was very highly strung and had religious spells. (We went to the other extreme later on in Sydney, during the freethought craze of the eighties, and became freethinkers—or thought we did.) Father always professed to be a freethinker, and he studied the Bible. He was one of the hardest working, kindest hearted men I ever knew. I have known him, after a hard day's work, to sit up all night watching a neighbour's dying child.

I was painfully, unhappily "good", a self-torturer and a nuisance to my playmates. I remember one day the master, with woeful want of tact, gave me a note to take home, informing my people that my brother had played truant from school that day. Charlie was waiting for me outside the school paddock and begged me not to take the note home—to save him and tell the master a fib. He pleaded very hard, but I had to deliver the note. I suffered a great deal more than he did.

I was strong, as proved in school games, and no coward, as was also proved, but I wouldn't fight under any provocation, because I thought it was wrong. Charlie would, on the slightest excuse, and he often wanted to fight for me and gave me a great deal of anxiety on that account. Years after, when we were grown to men, Charlie, who had learned to use his hands, backed me in a fight (girl the indirect cause, of course) and I lost, after spraining my ankle. He was very proud of me on account of my pluck, but he bitterly cursed my lack of science.

I began to be a lonely, unhappy boy and to be considered a little mad, or at least idiotic, by some—my relatives included. My aunts said it was a pity I hadn't been born a girl.

Father built a new sawn-timber hardwood house on the flat with a galvanized-iron roof and a brick chimney, which last was the envy of neighbours who had only slab-and-clay chimneys.

The Mother went to Mudgee for a while, and when she came back she brought a little stranger and-foreigner into the family. We were tall and dark on Mother's side, and generally supposed to have descended from gipsies. We were hot-headed, impulsive, blindly generous, and open-hearted and suspicious by turns. Father was short, nuggety, very fair, with blue eyes; he was domestic, methodical and practical. The little stranger, one of twins, was the first and last creamy-skinned, blue-eyed baby in our family. She only stayed a little while—long enough for us to call her Nettie, short for Henrietta (Granny's name). When the baby fell ill Mother took her to Mudgee, and she died in the room she was born in. (I was born in a tent, Charlie in a bark hut, Peter in a slab house, and Nettie and her sister in a brick one.) When Nettie was dying they sent Mother out of the room, and she sat on a log in the yard—sat very still, they said, staring up at the stars. Father was walking fast along the lonely road to Mudgee, but he was too late. About midnight they called Mother in. The old watchman, passing just then, cried: "Twelve o'clock and all's well!" I have often thought how well it was, for there has ever hung a cloud over our family.

Early in the morning after the funeral, Father took his maul and wedges and cross-cut and went up into the ridge to split rails. I heard the maul and wedges and the song of the saw until dusk. He was trying to work it out of him. After tea he walked to and fro, to and fro in the starlight, with his arms folded and his head down, but now and again he'd put his hands behind him and take a few turns looking up at the stars. I pace the room or the yard a lot nowadays.

When I was nine years old there happened a thing which was to cloud my whole life, to drive me into myself, and to be, perhaps, in a great measure responsible for my writing. I remember we children were playing in the dust one evening, and all that night I had an excruciating ear-ache, and was unspeakably sick on my stomach. Father kept giving me butter and sugar, "to bring it up", which it eventually did. It was the first and last time I had the ear-ache. Next day I was noticeably deaf and remained slightly so till I was fourteen, when I became as deaf as I am now. Before that my eyes were bad but my hearing was always very keen. I remember one night, when I was in bed, Mother was telling a very pathetic story to some visitors, three rooms away,

[and] when she came in to me she found me sobbing. I'd heard every word.

III

THE SELECTION AND A SKETCH OF GRANDFATHER

I DON'T know whether Father took up the selection because he had a liking for farming and believed in the chances, or because the ground was on an old gold-field and he was a digger. He had been a sailor and had passed in navigation; he had also served in a shipbuilding yard and was a good all-round carpenter: he was clever at anything where tools were concerned. I know he had always a fancy for a vegetable garden and a few fruit trees; but our land was about the poorest round there, where selectors were shoved back amongst barren, stony ridges because of old land grants, or because the good land was needed to carry sheep. Our selection, about three hundred acres, lay round a little, rocky, stony, scrubby, useless ridge, fronting the main road; the soil of the narrow sidings, that were not too steep for the plough, was grey and poor, and the gullies were full of waste heaps of clay from the diggers' holes. It was hopeless—only a lifetime of incessant bullocking might have made a farm of the place. I suppose it was the digger's instinct in Father—for a long time he was always putting down a shaft about the place in spare times, or thinking about putting it down. (He had two men on prospecting when he died.)

I'm not going to enter into details of grubbin', clearin', burnin'-off, fencin', ploughin', etc. See "Settling on the Land" and "A Day on a Selection" in *While the Billy Boils*; and for a description of the poorer class selection see "Past Carin'" in *Joe Wilson and His Mates*. In addition to grubbin', etc., we had to reclaim land for ploughing by filling up the diggers' holes. The shafts were driven underneath, of course, so the whole of the waste heaps wouldn't go down. We used to "spread" the lighter dirt—and it didn't improve the poor land; and we carted the hard, lumpy clay away to the boundary in barrows; some of it we used for making a dam. When I left the Old Bark School I used to tail the "cattle" in the gullies and do a bit of ringbarkin'. The "cattle" were a few weedy, stunted cows—one of them barren—and some steers, and were always straying. The elders were mischievous and demoralized the rest; some of them could get through, over or under our scraggy two-rail fence. Ditto the old grey horse—he'd get his forequarters over and slide. Then, when we got new cows one or two of them would be sure to fall down a diggers' hole if we didn't watch sharp. A cow, and sometimes a 'horse, would be cropping the grass round the edge of the shaft, and sometimes, in wet weather, the shaft would fall in, or else the beast, turning round, would miscalculate and slide down. Then the cry of "Cow in a hole!" (it was "Man in a hole!" once or twice), and we'd run in all directions and scare up the male population of Pipeclay; and provided the beast hadn't fallen head first and broken its neck or smothered, they'd rig a Spanish windlass and get it out, little the worse.

It was very scratchy farming as far as I was concerned, but then I was only a child. I had no heart in it—perhaps I realized by instinct that the case was hopeless. But Father stuck to it between building contracts. He used to walk from five to seven miles to work, at first, work twelve hours and walk home again. He'd insult anyone who offered him the loan of a riding horse—I never knew a man so obstinately independent as he was in those days. Then, between jobs, he made a spring-cart, wheels and all—except the iron-work. He could make anything in wood. Then he bought our old grey horse, Prince—used to run in Cobb & Co's. I must tell you about Prince some day, and how he pulled up an hour on the Gulgong road, with a heavy spring-cart load of mails in bad weather, when the coach broke down, but was never the same horse afterwards. Then when Father worked in town he carted home a load of manure every night and spread it on the barren ground. And sometimes at night he'd burn off, and dig in the dam by moonlight. There had been a bullock camp on the level, and several acres where the old road had been were so hard that even a big bullock plough, which father hired for the day, couldn't break up the ground. He broke it later on with charges of blasting-powder! He trenched deep round the house and built frames and planted grape-vines behind, and in front a rose bush and a slip of an ivy plant that had come from England in the early days. The last time I saw the place the house was a mass of vines. The mater talked of christening the farm Arundel, after Father's birthplace in Norway, as soon as we got it ship-shape.

I remember the last questions at night would be: "Are you quite sure all the calves are in the pen?" "Are you quite sure the sliprails are pegged?" And often at daylight the mater would cry, "Get up quick, the cows are getting away!" and one of us boys would turn out and run across the hard baked sods barefoot, or the frosty flats in winter—running hard so that the cold and the burrs wouldn't hurt so much—and head off the cows which had broken through the fence, and were hurrying down the lanes after Spot, their old wall-eyed ringleader, in the direction of a neighbour's wheat or lucerne paddock. Prince got very fat one drought and we couldn't make it out, until one morning a neighbour, getting up earlier than usual, saw Prince's rump sticking out of his haystack, and hit it hard with a paling. Prince was very much surprised, and his condition and the mysterious hole in the stack were accounted for at the same time. I remember often on a bitter cold frosty morning rooting up a camping cow and squatting with my bare, perishing feet on the warm spot where she'd been lying.

After we left the Old Bark School we went for a month or so to the Old Pipeclay school across the ridges. Curtis was the master. His first idea was to unlearn the Old Bark School scholars all that Tierney had taught them. I suppose the mater had fallen out with Tierney, but I used to go to him at night later on and get lessons in arithmetic and grammar. He'd improved in that branch.

At the Old Pipeclay school I worshipped pretty Lucy W——. We were both going into the fourth class when I left, but she used to go home in a different direction. My old sweetheart was Mary B——, the tomboy of the Old Bark School: but one day we quarrelled and she said she wouldn't be my sweetheart any more. I think she made up to Fred Spencer for a while. Fred, by the way, was the Tom Sawyer of our school. Mary's sister Bertha, a prettier girl, began to look kindly on me, but I'd had enough of women.

Childish recollections begin to crowd—recollections of child life and character—but there is no room for them here. It was Curtis, by the way, who first noticed that I was a solitary child. There were days, during play hour, when I liked to get away by myself; and once or twice he tried to draw me out, and asked me whether my schoolmates had been annoying me. But it wasn't that—I couldn't explain what it was. Sometimes I'd run home ahead of the rest, and once or twice Mary came running after me to try to find out what was the matter, but she soon gave it up. It was while at this school that my companions first began to say I was "barmy".

The Mother was ambitious. She used to scribble a lot of poetry and publish some in the local paper. There were nine or ten daughters in her family, most of them big women and all naturally intelligent and refined. Almost any one of them might have made a mark under other conditions. Their lots were cast in the rough early days, in big bark humpies where all things were rough-and-ready and mean and sordid and gipsy-like, and they were brought up surrounded by the roughest of rough crowds on the gold-field; then amongst those left on the abandoned gold-fields, the most unspeakably dreary, narrow and paltry-minded of all communities. (My diggers are idealized, or drawn from a few better class diggers, as my Bushmen are sketched from better class Bushmen.)

The girls used to try to establish little schools, singing classes, etc., and humanize the place, but the horizon was altogether too narrow and hopeless, and, as they grew up, they became embittered. But they had humour, a keen sense of the ridiculous, and that saved them to a great extent.

Grandfather was a big, strong, dark, handsome man, who came from Kent with his family. Wavy black hair, worn long, and profile Roman. His people were supposed to have been gipsies and he was very gipsy-like in his habits. He had sight like a blackfellow and was a first-class Bushman of the old school. He was a humorist of the loud-voiced order. When he was sixty he could handle timber and knock out palings and shingles with any young man. He had the head of an intellectual man, a strong man, a leader of men, and he couldn't read nor write—a fact which he hid successfully from many. He liked to camp by himself in the bush. *He* "never had no eddication", he'd say, and he didn't see what his children wanted with it. He drank. At home he had been known to smash all the crockery and bring home a string of pint pots, and a pile of tin plates, and dump them on the table. He was very mysterious and seldom did things like other men. For instance, he'd go to Mudgee and buy a string of boots for the family, but he wouldn't bring them home. No, not he. He'd roar at one of the girls: "D'yer see that shaller diggers' hole up there on the sidin'?" "Yes, Father." "Then go up there, yer'll find a piece of bark in the bottom—lift it up an' see what yer'll find?" and the girls would find the boots. Again, when they were married and had families he'd visit them in turn, and most unexpectedly of course, once in years. But he wouldn't come up to the door and knock. No. In the morning the daughter or one of the children would look out and see a big man standing at the gate with his back to the house, or, more likely, leaning on a fence across the road. Then, "Why, there's Father!" or "Why, there's Grandfather!" and he'd be brought in. He'd be very clean and have on a full new suit of tweed, with maybe a dandy pair of shoes and a little curl at the bottom of his pants—but his old greasy hat.

"Father, why don't you get another hat?"

"What do I want with another hat? I hain't got two heads, have I?"

He'd leave as unexpectedly as he came.

He nearly always shouted at the top of his voice, and it was a big voice.

"Mr Albury, why do you speak so loud?"

Grandfather, roaring: *"Because I want people to hear me!"*

I've seen a man roll on the ground and shriek at something Grandfather said, and heard him, with a face as solemn as a judge's, tell that man to get up and not be a thundrin' jumpt-up fool.

Save for "thundrin'" or "jumpt-up" I never heard Grandfather swear. There's a legend to the effect that one day, in his young days, he swore so badly at his bullocks that he frightened himself; but I don't believe that.

I worked with him now and again in the mountains in the eighties, humping palings and rails out of gullies. He was taking care of an empty house and camping there. He "had the writin's" (a letter from the owner, authorizing him to act as caretaker). He had great faith in "writin's". (See "Uncle Abe", in "Buckolts' Gate"; *Children of the Bush*.) An ordinary fire wouldn't do Grandfather; he'd pile on logs till he roasted us to the back of the room, and sometimes outside altogether. He was a good cook, and very clean in camp; he'd polish up his tinware till he could shave in it. Saturday afternoon or Sunday morning he'd clean up. The furniture and things would be chucked out with great noise and clatter—the furniture was home-made and strong and could stand it. Then Grandfather would take off his boots, tuck up his trousers and arm himself with a broom and a mop. My business was to run to the tank and back as fast as I could with two buckets. We camped in an outhouse, and when the house was let he was asked to clean it out for the new tenant. It was a great cleaning— I'll never forget it. They say the house was damp all summer, but it was clean. He couldn't do things like an ordinary man. He was fond of dogs, little mongrel dogs, and he'd talk to them, and they seemed to understand. But if a strange dog came sneaking round, Grandfather would lay for him. He wouldn't attack that dog in the ordinary way; he'd heave a chair, or table, or something equally handy. I remember a big hairy thievish dog used to come sneaking round. Grandfather laid for him. He had just finished making a picket gate, and it stood inside the door. It was dark inside and broad moonlight in the yard, and when the dog sneaked into the yard he didn't see us. Suddenly Grandfather jumped up, seized the gate and hove it. It missed the dog by a hair, struck on one corner and smashed to smithereens. I never saw that dog again.

Grandfather was a great man in Mudgee in the early days. He cleared the main street and owned blocks of land in town. He lost them—drink, of course. Amongst other things he was an undertaker. He buried many, and under all sorts of conditions—some in sheets of bark; and he was in great demand at burials. He usually had a coffin cut out roughly and stuck up over the tie-beams of the kitchen to season, and wait. The family hated this sort of thing. They say he generally had an eye on a prospective client, too, and cut his coffin accordingly.

Jones, the legitimate undertaker, made a palisading for a child's grave, gave it a coat of paint and stood it outside his shop to dry. Grandfather, coming along, vaulted in to the palisading, took hold of each side, lifted it and ran, with Jones out and after him. Grandfather ran up a blind lane, dropped the palisading and jumped the fence. Jones took his palisading back in a dray, and nothing would convince him that Grandfather didn't want to steal it.

The old man would suddenly go down on his knees in the middle of the street and stare hard at a stone till the floating population gathered round and put its hand on its knees and stared too. Then he'd get up and go away. And they'd stare harder after him than they had at the stone.

The last time I saw him in Sydney he'd bought some tools and a new carpenter's bag to carry them in. He put the handle of an adze through the loops of the bag and carried it across his back. Out of one side stuck an auger and out of the other the blade of a saw. He walked straight down the middle of George Street, towards Redfern railway station—the tram wasn't there then—and he walked fast. It was Saturday evening and the street was pretty full. Every few yards a passenger, coming in the opposite direction, would catch sight of the point of the saw or auger and duck just in time to save an eye or an ear. Heads were bobbing to right or left all the way. I saw no traces of anger on any of their faces—just mild startled surprise. Just such an expression as a man might wear who has nearly stumbled against a cart coming out of a lane. An uncle and I walked behind the old man all the way and enjoyed the show. One would have thought that he was absolutely unconscious of the mild sensation he was creating, but we knew the old man better than that.

I don't remember ever hearing Grandfather laugh. Little Jimmy Howlett (Nowlett in my books) the bullock-driver could throw some light on the subject. One day he was out looking for a bullock in the scrub just outside Mudgee, and had sat down to rest and smoke on a log on the edge of a little clearing about fifty yards from the road, when he saw Grandfather coming along. The old man seemed rather more mysterious than usual, and Jimmy watched him—he thought perhaps he had come to look for some timber. Grandfather glanced round, very cautiously, like a black-fellow, but he didn't see Jimmy. Then he started to laugh. He laughed till the tears ran down his cheeks. He put his hands on his hips and roared till he doubled up; then, when he recovered, he straightened himself, composed his face and went back whence he'd come. And thereafter it worried Jimmy a good deal at times, for he never could find out what Harry Albury was laughing at that day.

I have moods now, sometimes, when I feel inclined to go out of the world a piece and laugh. But then I am growing old. Father used to work with Grandfather as a young man, and there are many anecdotes. Father got on with him famously, and I never met two characters more opposite in every way. Add to this the fact that Father was a total abstainer. Father used to say that the one thing he liked and admired the old man for, above all else, was that he'd never harp on a string—he'd say a thing and have done with it. Father, you must bear in mind, was married when he used to say this. I never heard the old man say an ill word of anybody. The worst things I remember of him were: 1st, he drank: but I drink too; 2nd, he would seldom sack a man for whom he had no further use—he'd wait for an excuse to have a row with him, and the man would leave bursting with indignation, and burning with a sense of injustice: but that was, in a way, in keeping with the old man's character; 3rd, he got nearly all his stringy-bark palings out of mountain ash: but that was due to (a) the prejudice of his clients (who could never hope to live as long as that timber) in favour of stringy-bark; (b) the extreme scarcity of stringy-bark; (c) the prevalence of mountain ash; 4th, hens used to come round our camp for what they could pick up, and were encouraged, and often picked up more than they came for and left but the head: but then I was fond of poultry too, and the blame, if any, was on our gipsy ancestry. The old man usually had an old horse, bony and angular past description, popularly believed to be as old as himself, and locally known as "Old Albury" too. The old man fed the old horse well, but no power on earth could ever fatten him. (I've noticed that bosses who are extra fond of animals are usually hardest on their men.) I remember seeing the old man throwing out some corn he kept for the horse to a stray fowl. He explained that he was fattening that fowl up for Christmas. I asked if the hen belonged to him, and he said, No, not exactly; but he thought it would about Christmas time. He bought a fowl occasionally, for the sake of appearances and to provide against accidents.

He had, as I said, the sight of a blackfellow, and would bring his heavy eye-brows together and peer at something in the distance, standing and looking for the moment just like a blackfellow and seeing as far.

I got on well with him and was, I think, the only one in the family who could get him to sing. He had a good voice and I used to read old songs to him and he'd get them line by line. Like most illiterate men he remembered nearly all he had ever seen or heard.

Supposed to be without sentiment, I discovered him to be a dumb poet, a poet of the trees, "the timber", and all living things amongst or in them. Supposed to be without affection, I know that in his old age, when the family was scattered and he alone, he made a long and useless journey just to have a look at the ruins of the church he was married in.

Granny was the daughter of an English clergyman; she came out to Australia as an immigrant and went into domestic service Penrith way, where she met Grandfather, who looked like a young god then, and married him for his looks. She went with him over the mountains and went through forty years of a rougher bush life than you could imagine. She was good and well-meaning and old-fashioned—and helpless. The diggers on Pipeclay in its flush days once proposed subscribing to send my mother to England to have her voice trained, but Granny would not hear of it, for she had a horror of any of her children "becoming public".

[1903-04]

COMMENTARY

THESE comments begin in each case with the history of the story concerned. The version which appears to be Lawson's latest authentic text is marked with a star: it serves as the basis for the text as printed in this book. All versions have been compared, and the text given here is free from posthumous emendations.

Abbreviations used are as follows:

C.I.C.F., *The Country I Come From*, 1901
C.O.B., *Children of the Bush*, 1902
J.W.M., *Joe Wilson and His Mates*, 1901
O.S., *Over the Sliprails*, 1900
O.T., *On the Track*, 1900
R.O.S., *The Romance of the Swag*, 1907
S.R.H., *Send Round the Hat*, 1907
S.S.P.V., *Short Stories in Prose and Verse*, 1894
W.B.B., *While the Billy Boils*, 1896

The Bush Undertaker (p. 11)
Antipodean, 1892   *S.S.P.V.*, 1894   M.L., MS. A1867, 1895
W.B.B., 1896   *C.I.C.F.*, 1901*

The Antipodean was an annual published by Chatto and Windus, London, in 1892 and 1893. George Essex Evans and John Tighe Ryan edited the number in which this story appeared. Its original sardonic title was "A Christmas in the Far West; or, The Bush Undertaker". Lawson first used the alternative title for the printing in *Short Stories in Prose and Verse*, thereby concentrating interest on the figure of the hatter.

The original manuscript has disappeared, but we may discern Lawson's developing linguistic skill by reference to the variants between the 1892 and 1894 texts. Most of Lawson's 1894 emendations were restorations of Australian idiom or vocabulary; for example, the genteel "hermit" and the pretentious "solitaire" of 1892 became the earthy "hatter" of 1894. Some of the emendations may have been made by his mother; for example, the Kentish "arternoon" transported with her father to the Australian bush became the standard "afternoon". The London editor of 1892 had felt it necessary to explain, in parenthesis, that a "gohanna" was an "iguana"—a common misconception which Lawson dispelled by preferring "goanna" in 1896, only to find himself obliged to accept the English idea of the reptile in 1901 and revert to "iguana".

Lawson restored a number of bush expressions dropped from the *Antipodean* printing. For example, immediately after Five Bob has swallowed the doughboy with a click of his jaws, we now read: " 'Clean into his liver!' said the old man with a faint smile."

The 1894 version of the story was obviously not a reprint of the *Antipodean* version; it was in all probability set from a revised duplicate of the manuscript used by the English printer. It is instructive to compare some of the constructions in the two versions; indeed, to extend the comparison to the 1895, 1896, and 1900 printings.

Here, for example, are three versions of the sentence telling how the hatter sets out for the grave in the bush:

1892. "This accomplished, he took a pick and shovel and an old bag from under his bunk, and started off over the ridge, followed, of course, by his faithful friend and confidant." (This is not only false to life in the first part; it is false to art in the second.)

1894. Nearer original MS. "This accomplished, he took a pick and shovel, and an old bag from over a stick across the corner of the hut, and started out over the ridge; followed, of course, by his four-legged mate." (Nearer actuality in the first half Rarely were bags thrust under a bunk in the bush, for fear that they would harbour snakes or goannas; but the rail nailed across a corner to carry clothing, bags, and the like was ubiquitous in the bush. Observe the improvement in "four-legged mate", even though in our day it may be considered a cliché.)

1895. Lawson's final version. "This accomplished, he took a pick and shovel and an old sack, and started out over the ridge, followed, of course, by his four-legged mate." (Lawson is trying to be more definite in his imagery, but I doubt that "sack" is any improvement on "bag"—at least for Australians of Lawson's generation, who never called a corn sack anything but a bag.)

It should be noted that the revisions came to make nonsense of part of the text. In the 1892 and 1894 versions the grave was that of a "supposed blackfellow", and the uncertainty as to the occupant's race was maintained to the end. Thus we read of the scene when the hatter has reached the spur running out from the range:

1892. "At the extreme end of this, under some gum-trees, was a little mound of earth barely defined in the grass. This was the supposed blackfellow's grave, about which the old man had some doubts."

1894. "At the extreme end of this, under some gum-trees, was a little mound of earth, barely defined in the grass and indented in the centre as all blackfellow's graves were. This was the supposed blackfellow's grave, about which the old man had some doubts."

Both of these versions lead naturally and logically to the old man's speculation, on digging out the bones and putting them together on the grass, "as to whether they belonged to black or white, male or female" and to his inability to arrive at any conclusion.

For *While the Billy Boils* the 1894 version was retained, minus the sentence, "This was the supposed blackfellow's grave, about which the old man had some doubt." The "supposed" was also removed from the short earlier paragraph following the completion of his cooking, viz., "The last sentence referred to the cooking, the first to a supposed blackfellow's grave about which he was curious." The result of this is that in the 1896 and 1901 versions we are in no doubt that it is a blackfellow's grave. Neither is the old man. Yet he is still made to speculate in 1896 and 1901, as he had justly speculated in 1892-4, whether the bones had "belonged to black or white, male or female".

In this case over-editing has introduced an inconsistency in the representation of the old man's current of thought. It is the sort of inconsistency which escapes an author, who reads into the words the meaning which ought to be there. In such a case it seems plainly necessary to restore "supposed" in the earlier paragraph.

Similarly, the word "lush" in all versions except that of 1892 has puzzled Lawson's posthumous editors, who have gone to prison cant to try to find the explanation for a word which did not become part of Australian English, particularly as a verb. In the 1892 version, when the hatter addressed the corpse, he said, "Yer cud earn mor'n any man in the colony, but yer'd slush it all away in drink." For the 1894 version the phrase "in drink" was omitted, no doubt deliberately; and the verb "slush" appeared as "lush". In my opinion "slush" was a type-setter's error which, although close to an already bizarre original, was never thereafter preferred by Lawson.

Again, it is doubtful whether the progressive comparisons invented for the corpse of Brummy made any improvement on Lawson's homely original. The hatter must "fix" Brummy up for the last time and make him decent (in the grave), "for", as he says to the corpse:

    1892. "'twon't do ter leave yer a-laying here like the fool yer allers was."
    1894. "'twon't do ter leave yer a-lyin' out here like carrion."
    1896. "'twon't do t' leave yer a-lyin' out here like a dead sheep."

It was Lawson himself who rejected "carrion". At first he restored "like the fool yer allers was"—a common expression—but cancelled it and substituted "like a dead sheep".

One typically Lawsonian passage, reminiscent of Bret Harte, does not appear in the *Antipodean* version. It is the hatter's soliloquy immediately after he has made Brummy's last bed, beginning, "'That 'minds me'." This passage is an index to the imaginative character of the story, however realistic the detail may appear.

The conclusion of the story illustrates the artistry of Lawson's method. In 1892 he concluded the story thus: ". . . said with a solemnity that greatly disturbed Five Bob, 'Hashes ter hashes, dus ter dus, Brummy.' Then he sat down and covered his face with his hands./And the sun sank again on the grand Australian bush—the nurse and tutor of eccentric minds, the home of the weird, and much that is different from things in other lands."

This implied that the hatter was emotionally overcome by the religious solemnity of the occasion, and Lawson altered it for *Short Stories in Prose and Verse* to read as it does now, thus deliberately flattening the tone in both paragraphs.

The final paragraph was the subject of debate between Lawson, Arthur Jose, and George Robertson in 1895. Jose marked it all for deletion, which would have ended the story with Brummy walking back to his hut. Lawson marked it all back in again: he wanted to retain the notion of Nature's indifference to human activity, to leave the impression of the bush brooding over the grim episode, and he wanted to put it into a large frame. Robertson thought Lawson's a "better wind-up"; but after Lawson's death someone struck out the final phrase, "and of much that is different from things in other lands", so that in Cecil Mann's edition, 1964, the story closes on a note that is not entirely consistent with the action or with the adjective used the describe the bush, although it may be more striking in isolation: "And the sun sank again on the grand Australian bush—the nurse and tutor of eccentric minds, the home of the weird."

This truncation disturbed the balance of the sentence and in *The Country I Come From* Lawson restored the phrase.

For further comment see Brian Matthews, " 'The Nurse and Tutor of Eccentric Minds' ", in *Australian Literary Studies*, Vol. 4, No. 3, May 1970.

The Drover's Wife (p. 18)

Bulletin, Syd., 23rd July 1892   *S.S.P.V.*, 1894   M.L., MS. A1867, 1895   *W.B.B.*, 1896   *Bulletin Story Book*, 1901   *C.I.C.F.*, 1901*

Since the original manuscript of this story is not available, it is impossible to ascertain the nature and extent of emendations popularly supposed to have been made to it by J. F. Archibald for the first printing. This first version reappeared in *The Bulletin Story Book*, edited by A. G. Stephens, who made only minor emendations. For example, he deleted quotation marks, losing something of Lawson's ironic purpose in the process—as in " 'house' " in the opening paragraph: "The house contains two rooms; is built of round timber, slabs, and stringy bark, and floored with split slabs. A big bark kitchen stands at the end, and is larger than the house itself, verandah included." (*Bulletin Story Book*, p. 75)

Occasionally Stephens rephrased sentences, apparently in the interest of fluency, as in the third and fourth paragraphs, which he rendered: "The drover—an ex-squatter—is away with sheep.

His wife and children are left here alone./The children are playing about the house—four of them, ragged and dried-up looking. Suddenly one yells: 'Snake! Mother, here's a snake!' " (*Ibid.*, p. 75)

There is evidence also that he had in mind a few emendations made for the second printing by the author's mother, Louisa Lawson—in *Short Stories in Prose and Verse*. This collection she printed and published from the office of her monthly magazine, *The Dawn*. Two of these emendations that were carried over into later book printings—in *While the Billy Boils* and *The Country I Come From*—exhibit a tendency to bring Lawson's colloquial idiom, not always to his advantage, into line with nineteenth-century literary practice. For example, a few lines further on Tommy says, not "I'll have him," but "I'll have the ———," and Lawson adds in parenthesis, "he swears like a trooper". In the first printing Tommy does not merely "come reluctantly"; first he issues a natural curse: "The youngster swears beneath his breath, and comes reluctantly, carrying a stick nearly as big as himself. Suddenly he yells, triumphantly:" (*Bulletin*, 23rd July 1892)

In *Short Stories in Prose and Verse* this reads: "The youngster comes reluctantly, carrying a stick bigger than himself. Suddenly he yells, triumphantly:"

It was George Robertson who emended "Suddenly" to "Then" for *While the Billy Boils*—a change which Lawson accepted and preserved when he revised the story in London in 1900 for inclusion in *The Country I Come From*.

As late as 1916 Lawson affirmed—*Henry Lawson: Letters*, Syd., 1970, No. 337—that all the stories carried over from *While the Billy Boils* and *On the Track and Over the Sliprails*, 1900, were in their final form in *The Country I Come From*. He made a few emendations to "The Drover's Wife" which reveal that he had learnt much in the way of self-criticism in the intervening years.

The text which he used to form the revised manuscript for *While the Billy Boils* was that appearing in *Short Stories in Prose and Verse*. After he had worked over it, Arthur W. Jose sub-edited it, and finally George Robertson made a few emendations. Robertson preserved the emended manuscript of *While the Billy Boils* and in 1932 deposited it in two volumes in the Mitchell Library, where it now forms MSS. A1867-8.

These notes cannot run to a complete comparison of the successive texts of the various printings of the stories. That would be an extensive study which, incidentally, would produce valuable evidence for a thesis on the development of Lawson's art as a short story writer. Suffice it to say that a sample selection from "The Drover's Wife" shows that Lawson's emendations added colour and force. The swift brushing in of "King Jimmy" and the additional qualification of the blackfellow, who was also a king, are masterly touches exhibiting an effective impressionistic use of contrast. Jose's emendations for the most part tighten the line. Although it must be admitted that they are inclined to be pedantic, they have two saving virtues: they are not pretentious, and they rarely attempt to add anything. His substitution of "the original curse" for "the curse of Toil" makes effective use of a cultural reference, even though Lawson's original phrase is the more earthy. Robertson's final emendations exhibit a tact for words that may also be observed in his later letters to Lawson. It was he who made Alligator "rush", rather than "dart", after the snake. He has the drover's wife "take up" a handkerchief to wipe her eyes in preference to the over-charged "snatch up" which Lawson had originally used.

One puzzling point in the story is the identity of the baby. Lawson's original text tells us that the woman snatches " 'the baby' from the ground, holds it on her left hip, and reaches for a stick." At this point Tommy is referred to as the "eldest boy"— which argues that there are more than two boys in the family. Tommy is eleven. When she puts the children to bed on the kitchen table the baby has vanished from the story: we learn later that it is a male child, and therefore it cannot be one of the two girls. At this point in the story only four children are present, and the second boy, Jacky, is named. Jacky is old enough to take an intelligent interest in what goes on and to make apposite contributions to the conversation: he talks as if he were at least nine years of age. We conclude that the two girls, who take no part in the action, are younger. "The last two children," we learn, "were born in the bush." The occasion of the bush fire, when the baby was terrified, "was a glorious time for the boys." We must conclude that the "baby" is neither Tommy nor Jacky, and we are left with the unanswered question: Who was the baby, and what happened to him?

This is the only drifting skein in a tightly knit story. In his use of the baby—a stock figure in bush fiction—Lawson creates a fleeting impression which serves the purpose he has in mind. It may be that J. F. Archibald edited the baby out of the original manuscript: we can only regret its disappearance and let it go at that.

A careful reading of the story reveals the germ of several ideas that Lawson was to develop in later stories. For example, the woman's husband had "bought her a buggy" which he had had to sacrifice when ruined by drought: this idea later became "A Double Buggy at Lahey's Creek".

Dame Mary Gilmore has claimed the inspiration for this story. "It was our story," she informed me; "the drover was my father." Lawson himself said that his aunt, Mrs Job Falconer, was the model for the drover's wife. He also wrote of some of the incidents mentioned in the story as having been experienced by his own mother, e.g., the shooting of the mad bullock. At the same time a number of literary and folk influences are discernible, e.g., those of Bret Harte and of the bush yarn. None of these factors detract from the quality of the story as a work of art, based, certainly, on aspects of life in the bush, but existing in the world of Lawson's imagination and coloured by the sense of alienation which the actual bush aroused in him.

First foreign translation: "Das Weib des Viehtreibers", in *Ueber Land und Meer*, Jahrgang 53, Nr 37, Juli 1911.

For further commentary see:

(*a*) Edward Garnett, "An Appreciation" (1902), in Colin Roderick, ed., *Henry Lawson: Criticism*, Syd., A. & R., 1972.

(*b*) Colin Roderick, *Companion to "Henry Lawson: Fifteen Stories"*, Syd., A. & R., 1959;

(*c*) *Ibid.*, *Henry Lawson, Poet and Short Story Writer*, Syd., A. & R., 1966;

(*d*) Brian Matthews, *"The Drover's Wife* Writ Large: One Measure of Lawson's Achievement", in *Meanjin*, No. 112: Vol. 27, No. 1, 1968.

The Union Buries Its Dead (p. 25)

Truth, 16th April 1893   *S.S.P.V.*, 1894   M.L., MS. A1867, 1895 *W.B.B.*, 1896   *C.I.C.F.*, 1901*

Lawson's personal experience of the bush before writing the two stories preceding this one had been limited to life in the Mudgee district and on the Blue Mountains. Outside Mudgee and the Blue Mountains he had lived in Sydney, Brisbane, and Melbourne, and had in fact become an urban man. His construction of characters like the hatter and the drover's wife accordingly drew largely on boyhood impressions, literary experience, and folk tale. In September 1892 he went to Bourke and worked in woolsheds along the Darling River, then tramped to Hungerford and back. He found the experience a searing one, as his letters to his Aunt Emma show (see *Henry Lawson: Letters*, Syd., 1970, Nos. 10, 11). It was redeemed by the warm if sardonic comradeship he found—for the first time—among the officials of the branches of the General Labourers' Union and the Australian Shearers' Union at Bourke. They were a striking group of men, among them being some who went on to make their mark in political and social affairs in New South Wales. From them Lawson caught the idealism that animated the best among them, and this remained for him the touchstone of social perfection. He was later to satirize the betrayal of that idealism: he could never condone political frailty in his democratic commonwealth. The idea of "the union", at the time he wrote this story, was for him the hope of society: it embodied the selfless compassion of man for man that constituted his creed.

The story, accordingly, represents "the union" as the compassionate factor in life. Man is imperfect, and man emerges from the story as selfish and contemptible.

It is to be noted that Lawson was still only 25 when he wrote the story. That he should have been so preoccupied with themes of death and decay at such an early age points to a temperament that desperately needed some explanation of the mystery of life and death.

The title of the story, like the story itself, went through three stages of development—in 1893, 1894, and 1895. The successive changes were small; but they are significant as indexes of Lawson's developing control of words rather than of any development of narrative structure.

In *Truth*, 16th April 1893, the subtitle was "A Bushman's Funeral: A Sketch from Life". In *Short Stories in Prose and Verse*, eighteen months later, it was "A Bushman's Funeral: A Sketch from Life and Death". It was deleted by George Robertson in 1895 without any objection from Lawson.

One flaw in this story is explained by reference to the first printing. It occurs towards the end, at the conclusion of the interment. After the words "when the thump of every sod jolted his heart" there is a rather too sudden leap from the narrator to the author: "I have left out the wattle . . ." As the story now appears, there is a jolt in this, like missing the bottom step on a staircase. In the first two printings Lawson provided a transition with the following sentence: "That's nearly all about the funeral, except that the priest did his work in an unusually callous and business-like way."

Intead of emending this—it offended Jose, who in 1895 marked it "Omit"—Lawson omitted it, thus leaving a gap in the design of the story.

In our own time objection has been taken to the reference to the priest in the story as "the Devil". As the story now appears we hear the voice of the narrator only, even though the epithet is ascribed to one of the characters, and undoubtedly an air of partiality as well as of irreverence emerges. In the 1893 and 1894 printings, however, Lawson entered into the story with an authorial comment: "I looked up and saw a priest standing in the shade of the tree by the cemetery gate. A Church of England parson would have done as well."

This switch from narrator to author in the second sentence was too much for Jose, who queried its meaning. Undoubtedly it had meaning for Lawson, but he was at a loss to explain it and deleted the sentence.

In the first version there was no reference to the dead man's mother, the text reading: "but they found no portraits or love letters or locks of hair, or anything of that kind in his swag— only some papers relating to union matters." It is not unlikely that the reference to the man's mother was inserted by Louisa

Lawson for her printing of the story. At all events Lawson left it in.

The sentiment and construction of the final paragraphs were challenged by Arthur Jose, who wanted it to read: "We did hear, later on, what his real name was, but we have already forgotten it." Lawson sweated over this ending, which conveys the ultimate in indifference. The successive readings of it were:

1893. "I did hear lately what his real name was, but if I do chance to read the real name among the missing friends in some agony column I shall not be aware of it, and therefore not be able to give any information, for I have already forgotten the name." (Clumsy enough, rather remote from the story, and vague.)

1894-1895 proof. "We did hear, later on, what his real name was, but, if we do chance to read it among the missing friends in some agony column, we shall not be aware of it, and therefore not be able to give any information to a 'sorrowing sister' or 'heart-broken mother'—for we have already forgotten his name." (Stronger; related to the participants in the funeral, more concrete, and more definite.)

1896. "We did hear, later on, what his real name was; but if we ever chance to read it in the 'Missing Friends Column', we shall not be able to give any information to heart-broken Mother or Sister or Wife, nor to anyone who could let him hear something, to his advantage—for we have already forgotten the name."

As with the two previous stories, Lawson has not left us this one without a textual conundrum. The funeral took place "exactly at mid-day"; yet on the way to the cemetery it passed three shearers "sitting on the shady side of a fence". Was this a lapse on Lawson's part? Was it in conformity with his impressionist technique? Or was it merely a borrowing of a common bush jest for the purpose of maintaining the ironic tone of the story?

For critical reading on aspects of Lawson's technique raised in the foregoing see the following:

(a) Adele Fuchs, "General Characteristics, Prose Style, and Language", tr. Colin Roderick, in *Henry Lawson: Criticism*, Syd., A. & R., 1972.

(The private student who reads German should refer to Adele Fuchs's book, *Henry Lawson: ein australischer Dichter*, Vienna, 1914, in the Mitchell Library, or procure a photocopy.)

(b) A. A. Phillips, "The Craftsmanship of Lawson", in *Meanjin*, No. 2, 1948; reprinted in Phillips, A. A., *The Australian Tradition*, Melb., Cheshire, 1958, and Semmler, C., ed., *Twentieth Century Australian Literary Criticism*, Melb., O.U.P., 1967;

(c) Moore, T. Inglis, "The Rise and Fall of Henry Lawson", in *Meanjin*, December 1957;

(d) Wilkes, G. A., "Henry Lawson Reconsidered", in *Southerly*, Vol. 25, No. 4, 1965.

"Rats" (p. 29)

Bulletin, 3rd June 1893 *S.S.P.V.*, 1894* M.L., MS. A1867, 1895 *W.B.B.*, 1896

One major textual problem occurs in this story. In this book the text is much the same as when it first appeared in the *Bulletin*, except for the final paragraph, which is absent from the *Bulletin* printing. When preparing the manuscript for *Short Stories in Prose and Verse*, Lawson either restored this paragraph or added it.

Read apart from the rest of Lawson's work, the story may appear to close fittingly with a snap and a laugh at the expense of the old man if one concludes it with Sunlight's observation. This, however, is not Lawson's way. Viewed in the context of Lawson's portrait of the bush, the story undoubtedly loses its sardonic twist by the omission of the final paragraph. Without it the narrator becomes completely involved—and this, too, was not Lawson's manner at this stage of his development.

A careful examination of the MS. in M.L., MS. A1867 suggests that the omission of the final paragraph for the version in *While the Billy Boils* was determined by Arthur W. Jose. It is marked out with lines that may well be Lawson's; but they are faint and half-hearted, and may originally have been made by another reader. Jose has superimposed further scratchings-out with the fine nib he affected. But a definite instruction by Lawson to "omit" or "delete" nowhere appears.

Now it was consistent with Lawson's outlook at this time to turn the joke against the joker. This, I believe, is accepted by all who study Lawson in depth. It was part of his technique to deflate his stories at the conclusion: it was the natural expression of his rejection of sentimentality. The story was not reprinted in *The Country I Come From*, so that we have no way of knowing whether Lawson, if left to himself, would have restored the ending rejected by Jose.

In arriving at a decision whether to restore it or not, we are forced back to a consideration of the sort of people whom Lawson had met in life. Was there among them anyone who, without being certifiably " 'barmy' ", engaged consciously and with malice aforethought in eccentric behaviour that would suggest the conduct of his central character in this story? Reference to Lawson's *Fragment of Autobiography* (see page 243 *ff*.) reveals that there was at least one—his maternal grandfather, Henry Albury, who delighted in mystifying onlookers with illogical and apparently half-witted behaviour. In my view Lawson never intended to leave the reader with the conviction that "Rats" was off his head, even though he, like Brummy, was eccentric. Accordingly, I have preferred Lawson's version to Jose's and have restored the paragraph.

For a review of the range of Lawson's bush characters, see

(*a*) Fred. J. Broomfield, "A Pantheon of Bush Types", in *Henry Lawson: Criticism*, ed. Colin Roderick, Syd., A. & R., 1972.

(*b*) H. M. Green, *A History of Australian Literature*, 2 vols, Syd., A. & R., 1961; Vol. 1, pp. 377-83, 532-51; reprinted in part in *The Stories of Henry Lawson*, Third Series, ed. Cecil Mann, Syd., A. & R., 1964.

Stiffner and Jim (Thirdly Bill) (p. 32)
Pahiatua Herald, 9th March 1894 *Worker*, Syd., 1st September 1894 M.L., MS. A1867, 1895 *W.B.B.*, 1896 *C.I.C.F.*, 1901*

This is the first of Lawson's stories in which the spieler plays a prominent part. It prepares the way for the creation of Steelman, the confidence man.

Stiffner's Hotel, according to the story, is in the South Island of New Zealand; but both it and the people occupying it have their models in New South Wales, even though both the character of Stiffner and the setting for the shanty are clearly imaginative. Lawson had the story published for the first time while he was at Pahiatua, in the North Island; he had not then visited the South Island—that was to come a few weeks later.

Neither action nor atmosphere adhere to a New Zealand setting. A later Stiffner story, "An Incident at Stiffner's" (*Over the Sliprails*, 1901) eschews any attempt to link the shanty with New Zealand; indeed, it is clearly placed in New South Wales. One must conclude that Lawson set the present story in New Zealand merely because he happened to be there at the time and wanted to win over his New Zealand readers. In "An Incident at Stiffner's" the shanty—"an outback pub"—had "a great grey plain stretching away from the door in front, and a mulga scrub from the rear"— a description that fits the scenery across which the spielers flee from Stiffner's wrath in the present story.

Nevertheless, at no time did Lawson vary the setting. In the *Pahiatua Herald* and the *Worker* he had a sardonic postscript: "P.S.—The name of this yarn should have been 'Bill and Stiffner (thirdly Jim)'." This postscript was dropped in his final revision of the story for *The Country I Come From*. He had left it in for *While the Billy Boils*: it was deleted from the final proof by either Arthur Jose or George Robertson.

Lawson's major revisions were made in 1895 for the printing in *While the Billy Boils*. Arthur Jose had only two or three suggestions to make: of them Lawson adopted only one. One of Lawson's emendations was "sheol" for "hell" in Jim's instruction to Bill: "You dump the two swags together and smoke like hell." Jose preferred "hell" to "sheol", but Lawson would have none of it. On the other hand, he did accept Jose's rejection of his emendation of "a nip" for "it" when, following the reunion of the two spielers in the bush, Bill invites Jim to have a drink.

Among Lawson's 1895 additions were the following, the beneficial effect of each of which may be discerned on examining the text:

p. 34. "Stiffner came in. . . .

"Then I hooked carelessly on to the counter with one elbow and looked dreamy-like out across the clearing, and presently I gave a sort of sigh and said:" (Jim's later demeanour, in keeping his hand on Stiffner's repaired boot on the bar counter "in an absent-minded kind of way", demonstrates the significance of this addition.)

"He thought Bill was whipping the cat."

p. 35. " 'How's the slate?' " (Substituted for "How much do we owe you?")

p. 36. "My heart began to beat against the ceiling of my head, and my lungs all choked up in my throat."

p. 37. " 'That's what made him so excited.' " (An adroit touch, calculated to deflate the unsuspecting Jim in one stroke.)

Steelman (p. 38)

Bulletin, 19th January 1895 M.L., MS. A1867, 1895* W.B.B., 1896

This story reveals Lawson's dawning conception of Steelman as a character. The reference to Dunedin beer suggests that he wrote it in 1894, after having become acquainted with the crude model for Steelman in his wanderings about the North Island in the first quarter of that year. The first printed version of the story shows that he had not at that stage conclusively fixed on Steelman as the central character for a series of connected stories on the theme of confidence trickery: it dismissed Steelman with this closing sentence: "That was five years ago, and Steelman is still living with the Browns." Lawson firmly and unequivocally struck this sentence out when revising the story in 1895 for inclusion in *While the Billy Boils*, the reason clearly being that by then the character he had created had assumed more definite form and proportion. His development of the character in the selected stories that follow this one reflects Lawson's growing command over presentation of character in sharply defined portraits, each embodying an aspect of his own artistic constitution.

Steelman's Pupil (p. 40)

Bulletin, 14th December 1895 M.L., MS. A1867, 1895 W.B.B., 1896 C.I.C.F., 1901*

The first story in which Lawson brings Steelman and his foil Smith together, further illustrating Lawson's development of the character as a projection of part of himself. That Lawson was conscious of this is his identification of himself with Smith in a letter of 1916 in which he said, "Smith was my conception of the weaker side of my own nature." (See *Henry Lawson: Letters*, Syd., 1970, No. 312.) The story was bought by Archibald in 1895 and printed quickly so that it could be included in *While the Billy Boils*. The manuscript used by Lawson for revision was the cutting of the *Bulletin* printing in M.L., MS. A1867, illustrated by Minns. In later editions of *While the Billy Boils*, the story ended with "Smith had reformed", the final typically Lawsonian paragraph having been lost in proofs which Lawson did not see. When revising the story in 1900 for inclusion in *The Country I Come From*, he emended this paragraph, thus eschewing the O. Henry type of ending that was alien to his art. I have adopted Lawson's final version for inclusion here.

For further comments on this story see:

(*a*) Colin Roderick, *Companion to "Henry Lawson: Stories for Senior Students"*, Syd., A. & R., 1962.

For references to the Steelman stories as a series, see also

(*b*) A. G. Stephens, "Lawson's Prose", in *Bulletin*, 29th August 1896; reprinted *Henry Lawson: Criticism*, Syd., A. & R., 1971; and notes in

(*c*) *Henry Lawson: Letters*, Syd., A. & R., 1970.

The Geological Spieler (p. 44)
M.L., MS. A1868, 1895*   *W.B.B.*, 1896

One of the few of Lawson's early stories surviving in the original manuscript, this one was written specifically for *While the Billy Boils*. The manuscript was in the handwriting of Lawson's wife, who could have written it out no earlier than November 1895. A few interpolations are in Lawson's hand.

Some bibliographical confusion has arisen through the publication in the *Bulletin* of 24th December 1898 of a different story entitled "The Geological Spielers". This story deals with the same incident, but in a different way: it traverses Steelman's instructions to Smith immediately prior to their meeting the railway gang. This story has never been reprinted: Lawson considered submitting it to Angus and Robertson for inclusion in *On the Track and Over the Sliprails* but rejected it as being too like one already published (M.L., MS. A1892, p. 709). Its similarity, however, is confined to the incident with which both stories deal. Indeed, one of its virtues is to show how Lawson could deal artistically with the same incident in two entirely different ways. Both stories show a further advance in his use of the two figures he has created.

How Steelman Told His Story (p. 51)
Bulletin, 25th February 1899   *O.T.*, 1900   *C.I.C.F.*, 1901*

When Lawson submitted this story for inclusion in *On the Track* he made no change to the text as it had appeared in the *Bulletin*. During the revision of it for *The Country I Come From* he deepened its cynicism by the addition of the following: "If you help relations more than once they'll begin to regard it as a right; and when you're forced to leave off helping them, they'll hate you worse than they'd hate a stranger. No one likes to be deprived of his rights—especially by a relation."

Nowhere in the story does Steelman undertake to do more than give Smith some advice from his own experience; nowhere does he go beyond that. Yet the advice is, in fact, an oblique projectio of his life from birth to marriage. That Smith should have expected something else is a revelation of either innocence or a low intelligence—conveyed in one short sentence. The story itself, Lawson's final portrait of the confidence man, is admirable in its choice of material and superb in its technique: as narrator Lawson keeps himself out of the story, yet he is in every line of it, either as Steelman or as Smith.

Going Blind (p. 55)

Worker, 29th June 1895   M.L., MS. A1867, 1895*   *W.B.B.*, 1896

Lawson moderated the colloquial tone of this story for publication in *While the Billy Boils* by sometimes converting "he'd" to "he had", "we'd" to "we would", "wasn't" to "was not", and so on. He made only minor changes beyond that, adding only two clauses to deepen the significance of existing sentences, e.g., ". . . the butts lasted longer without being charred"; and "his eyes turned to the patch of ceiling as if it were a piece of music and he could read it". One mark of Lawson's linguistic refinement appears in the emended final sentence, which in the *Bulletin* printing had read, "When we parted I felt their grips on my hand for five minutes afterwards."

This story is one of several which Lawson set against the background of cheap lodgings in the city. Another is "Mr Smellingscheck". Both illustrate the restraint which Lawson exercised over sentiment once he had broken free from the technical influence of Dickens and Bret Harte and found his own unemphatic style. Over and above that, this story marks another stage in Lawson's artistic exploitation of his own personality. There is a distinct change in tone in this story that links it with the Mitchell sequence on which he was now engaged. He found himself under the necessity of modulating from the stridency of the Steelman stories before he could move into the quieter and warmer mood of those revolving about the figure of his home-spun philosopher. His use of the first person marks the elementary stage of the establishment of Mitchell as a narrator who will represent this mood and attitude in the author. He had used the names of "Mitchell" and "Jack" in earlier stories; but they were hardly more than names: now he is about to draw together the elements that go to make up the Mitchell exhibited in the sequence that follows. Prior to 1894 Mitchell had been cast in the Steelman mould, as reference to "Mitchell: A Character Sketch" (*Bulletin*, 15th April 1893) reveals.

Our Pipes (p. 59)

Bulletin, 11th May 1895   M.L., MS. A1868, 1895*   *W.B.B.*, 1896

With this story Mitchell reappears, not only as a character, but

also as Lawson's narrator. This is not the first time he has filled
the role—he had told the story in "A Respectable Young Man
with a Portmanteau" (*Worker*, 1st December 1894: Mann, Vol. 3,
p. 133)—but it is the first in which Mitchell as narrator serves as
a philosophical intermediary between Lawson and the reader. It is
instructive to observe how Lawson developed Mitchell as narrator.
Here he serves also as the central character: the narration is
pseudo-autobiographical. By the time Lawson has wrung as much
empirical wisdom out of him as possible, he has returned to the
role of pure narrator, as in "The Blindness of One-eyed Bogan".
He was the means by which Lawson could separate himself from
his tale; the most striking example of this, the most complete,
is "The Boozers' Home", which the untrained reader ignorant of
Lawson's life would not suspect sprang directly out of Lawson's
observation of himself no less than of his companions in Courtenay
Smith's home for inebriates at Willoughby in 1898.

There is a remarkable consistency between the three texts listed
for "Our Pipes", practically the only emendation from the first
printing being the substitution of the third personal pronoun for
"Mitchell" in every case where the text now reads, "He reflected".
I am not at all sure that this improves the casual simplicity of the
technique. At all events, the repetition of "he reflected" does not
jar, it often passes unnoticed, and the reader may not be aware
of it until it is pointed out. In much the same way the innuendo in
giving the comparative length of time between the deaths of the
narrator's mother and father is likely to elude the inattentive
reader.

Bill, the Ventriloquial Rooster (p. 62)

Bulletin, 22nd October 1898   *O.T.*, 1900*

Unlike "Enter Mitchell", which was first published as "That
Swag" (*B.*, 15th December 1894) without involving Mitchell,
this story was ascribed to Mitchell from the outset, even though
—if the date line of "Syd., 1893" in the *Bulletin* of 22nd October
1898, page 32, is to be credited—it was one of Lawson's early
stories and might have been expected to depict Mitchell from
outside the framework of the story. The evolution of Mitchell
from the role of observed character to that of commentator and
narrator is a fascinating study, revealing purposiveness in the
progress of Lawson's art during the years 1893-9.

Lawson made few emendations when revising the story in 1899
for inclusion in *On the Track*. He added the opening clause,
"When we were up country on the selection," to create an easier
approach to the yarn. He struck out one sentence which in the
original followed the sentence, "Bill's a ventriloquist, right enough,"
viz.: "And so he was, and, as it turned out, he was an 'unconscious'
one at that, as the Sydney jackeroo said."

The Blindness of One-eyed Bogan (p. 66)

C.O.B., 1902   *Bulletin*, 4th October 1902   S.R.H., 1907*

This well-composed story was written for book publication. After his return to Sydney in July 1902, Lawson sold the periodical rights in it to the *Bulletin*. A comparison of the two texts reveals how sub-editing, no doubt in the interest of space, had a cramping effect on the impact of the story. In the absence of manuscripts, one cannot but wonder how many of Lawson's earlier stories were inartistically truncated in much the same way. In this instance the *Bulletin* sub-editor deleted the characteristic Lawsonian glide into the story and made it begin: " 'One-eyed Bogan was a hard case, Mitchell,' I said. 'Wasn't he?' "

He also robbed the story of both point and depth by deleting the whole of Mitchell's revelation that Bogan was in fact not completely blind—all of that part of the story beginning: ". . . Then he asked suddenly;/'Did you ever see a blind man cry?' " and ending: "It made me feel like I used to feel sometimes in the days when I felt things . . ."

A third blunder was the deletion of the sentence: " 'Except that his wife made the mistake, Mitchell,' said Tom Hall."

One other example of *Bulletin* editing—by no means the only one—was the substitution of a brother to Jake Boreham named Tom for a sister named Mary.

Robertson followed the structure of the original story when, on purchasing the copyright of *Children of the Bush* from Methuen in 1906, he reprinted it in *Send Round the Hat*, 1907. A minor emendation in the third paragraph, yielding the text as printed in the present book, may well have come from Lawson himself in an attempt at verisimilitude. In the first printing this paragraph reads: "We turned up Hunter Street, out of Pitt Street, where a double line of fast electric tramway was running, and the 'bus companies still holding on, and turned into Warby's Hotel, where . . ."

Robertson made other emendations for the 1923 Platypus edition of *Send Round the Hat*, including the omission of "well hung" in the physical description of Bogan, some of Mitchell's cynical narrator's comments, the dialogue casting doubt on Bogan's paternity of the carroty-headed youngster, and Mitchell's insinuation that Bogan was never totally blind. All of these were restored in later printings, and in Cecil Mann's *The Stories of Henry Lawson*, Second Series, Syd., A. & R., 1964, the text appears in the 1907 form.

If there is any weakness in the story, it lies in the unaccountable ease with which Mitchell and Jake Boreham are able to manage their rickety craft in the turbulent waters of a flash Darling flood. Yet even this may be accepted when it is recalled that it is Mitchell who is telling the story.

It is to be noted that this story introduces us to the spelling of

"Bushman"—capital B—which Lawson insisted on from 1898, evidently to designate the ideal inhabitants of his ideal commonwealth. He also distinguished between the "bush"—the unlovely actual social setting for hardship, poverty, back-biting, incest, and other crimes and misdemeanours large and small—and the "Bush" —the ideal social setting for unselfishness, mateship, nobility, and virtues of all kinds, but also the alien force that vitiated the heroism of these virtues. From 1898 only "Bushwomen" existed, never "bushwomen": they are invariably victims of the Bush. I have respected Lawson's artistic intentions in these stories by reproducing the two spellings as he used them. It will be noted later that Dave Regan and party begin as bushmen but end as Bushmen.

Here, also, is the first reference to the Giraffe's hat—an idea which Lawson was to work up in "Send Round the Hat".

The spelling "Jackeroo", which is to be found in the first original English printing of his stories, arises from his habit of writing capital "J" reduced in size for the traditional lower case "j": the latter never occurs in his manuscripts.

The Hero of Redclay (p. 74)

D.L., MS. 31, 1899 *O.S.*, 1900 *C.I.C.F.*, 1901*

Nothing so effectually proves that Lawson's genius was for the short story as this work. In 1896, as *While the Billy Boils* was going through the press, Robertson urged Lawson to write a novel around the theme of a chivalrous ne'er-do-well's decision to go to jail rather than bring social stigma on a young woman. Lawson agreed to try, and Robertson publicized the forthcoming novel under the title of this story in the publisher's advertisement at the back of the early printings of *While the Billy Boils*. By 1897 Lawson realized that he had no talent for the novel—see *Henry Lawson: Letters*, Syd., 1970, No. 25—and he dropped the idea.

He next endeavoured to give the theme dramatic form in a work that he wrote for Bland Holt in Auckland between November 1897 and February 1898. The play was hopelessly unstageworthy: the manuscript is in the Mitchell Library—in Uncatalogued Manuscripts, Item 184. It is entitled "Pinter's Son Jim". There is reason to believe that Lawson gave it this title in 1899, when he was revising it to offer it to Angus and Robertson for consideration. His wife always referred to it as "Ruth", and it was this title that Lawson gave to a long narrative poem retelling the story for the *Bulletin* of 20th December 1902—see *Henry Lawson: Collected Verse*, Vol. 2, Syd., 1968. The poem is of fair average quality; but for literary quality neither it nor the play comes within reach of the prose tale.

As a reading of the story shows, Lawson was alive to the melodramatic nature of the action. His idea of drama was melodrama, and the story ran the risk of collapsing into melodrama, as the verse rendering of it actually does. What saved it was the technique of story-telling that had by 1899 become second nature to him. There were three factors in this. First, the introduction of the story is effected in a casually naturalistic way. Secondly, Mitchell, as narrator, throws in deflating ironic or sardonic comments on the course of events. And thirdly, the melodramatic elements that remain sit acceptably on the shoulders of the figure of Lebinski, the eccentric cloak-and-dagger Polish ex-revolutionary.

The story nonetheless marks a transition in Lawson's development. Despite his use of the techniques he had developed for the short story during the decade, there is a larger area of human action and reaction touched in this story than in any that preceded it. It may be that Lawson's attempt to write it as a novel was not without benefit. The composition lives as a short story, with its ease, its terseness, its economy; yet it has in it the germ of a novel: if anyone were to refer to it as a condensed novel, objection would be difficult. Viewed as such, "The Hero of Redclay" adumbrates the work which took shape in the stories clustered about the figure of Joe Wilson.

The reference to Tom Drew's death—the manner of it provided an early story, "When the Sun Went Down"—suggests that Lawson's themes were not isolated facets of life but chips of a mosaic that comprised a comprehensive pattern of life. The kaleidoscopic nature of "Pinter's Son Jim", with its montage of scattered scenes, provides further evidence of this. Lawson caught them up from widely distributed points: the only way in which he could bring them together was in clusters or sequences of short stories and sketches.

In the manuscript Lawson first called the township Geebung, emending it to Redclay when he decided, while writing the story, to change the title from "Payable Gold" to "The Hero of Redclay". The MS. reveals that although he altered *Geebung Advertiser* to *Redclay Advertiser*, he overlooked altering *Geebung Chronicle* to *Redclay Chronicle*. It seems to me that adjusting an oversight like this would hardly be called an emendation, and any reader who wished to make the change would be at liberty to do so.

One unaccountable editorial emendation was to spell "billabong" with a capital "B": in every case I have restored "billabong"— which is the invariable spelling in the MS. Similarly throughout with "bank". In the manuscript Lawson wrote of the court scene, "the judge . . . was . . . a man who . . . would have felt inclined to give Jack more for what he had done than for what he was charged with", but this he apparently revised to read, ". . . to give all the more for what he was charged with".

Although Jose may have made most, even all, of the emendations for the printing in *Over the Sliprails*, Lawson very likely saw them all, since two additions to the manuscript are included in the printed story which could have come from no one but him.

They are:

    (a) The paragraph in which Lawson discourses on the resemblance between Mitchell and Bland Holt; and

    (b) The melodramatic sentence: "I felt—well I felt . . . deep, strong music, such as thrills and lifts a man to his boot soles." This sentiment occurs elsewhere in his work.

Undoubtedly it would have been Jose who would have removed the quotation marks from such words as "shoots", "reference", "lots", "spotted", and the like.

It must be borne in mind that "The Hero of Redclay" appeared in *The Country I Come From*, and that in London in 1900 Lawson revised the stories comprising this volume. It is unlikely that the lost proof sheets will ever turn up, so that a comparison of the 1900 and 1901 texts is recommended to the reader interested in the development of Lawson's literary skill.

The Boozers' Home (p. 89)

C.O.B., 1902*   *Australian Star*, Syd., 29th September 1902
S.R.H., 1907

In this story Mitchell appears solely as narrator. He has no part in the action, except as an observer of affairs on visiting an inebriates' asylum. The old mate to whom he refers, it goes without saying, is Lawson himself: the description of his early symptoms of manic depression as well as of other phenomena are proof enough of that. The story is important in its revelation that as yet Lawson had not fallen into an inartistic self-pitying presentation of his vicissitudes. I do not recall any other short story which handles the theme of the alcoholic so delicately. This well-disciplined and gradual unfolding of the mind of the dipsomaniac is a masterly study. Its air of restraint and its conviction are achieved by a technique which alienates author from subject. Lawson achieves the effect of distance by enlisting his *alter ego* as narrator, thus affording himself opportunity to throw in authorial comment without entering into the action in his own person.

The Iron-bark Chip (p. 94)

D.L., MS. 31, 1898-9*   O.T., 1900

"The Iron-bark Chip", written 1898-9, introduces a series of three stories linked with the figure of Dave Regan. Whereas Steelman personified the spieler and Mitchell the bush philosopher, Dave Regan is a focal point for the practical joke. Just as Lawson saw something of himself in Steelman, Smith, and Mitchell, so he entered the persona of Dave Regan in his composition of stories conveying the flavour of bush humour. The stories which Lawson attaches to each of these projections of himself are consistent with his conception of each of the corresponding facets of his own nature.

This story affords further evidence of the integrity of Lawson's art; an idea barely mentioned in one story remains in his mind, to be expanded, sometimes much later, into a complete story. He had already used the notion of passing off one species of timber as another to bring a faint gleam of humour into the pathetic story of Jack Gunther, the blind bushman in the city (see p. 57). As is well known, this fraudulent practice on the part of his maternal grandfather was one of the characteristics that endeared the old man to him (see p. 246).

The circumstances of composition of the story are given in a letter from Lawson to his publisher (see *Henry Lawson: Letters*, Syd., 1970, No. 57).

The manuscript shows subtle textual differences from the printed text, and all of them seem to be truer to Lawson's acquired style of casualness. Unfortunately, since the proofs of *On the Track* have not survived, it is not possible to know whether Lawson or Jose made the emendations in proof. Neither was the story reprinted in *The Country I Come From*, for which Lawson restored the text of the stories included. In view of available evidence, the text printed here may be accepted as Lawson's. I have corrected some obvious errors that occurred in the setting, e.g., the MS. spells the name "Bently" except on one occasion, when "Bentley" is clearly a slip. For this edition I have also restored the final paragraph—the omission of such Lawsonian modulations having been a foible of Jose's; but its retention is a matter of opinion.

The Loaded Dog (p. 98)
J.W.M., 1901*

One of the interesting points of this story is the speed at which it moves: the action takes less time than the reading of the story. The authorial comment at the conclusion lends a touch of convincing naturalism to the composition and reclaims it from classification as a primitive bush yarn. It has in it the possibilities of tragedy, and its suspense is neatly resolved by a modulation that gives it an air of comedy.

No manuscript of this story is available, and there appears to have been no periodical printing.

Gettin' Back on Dave Regan (p. 105)
C.O.B., 1902* *R.O.S.*, 1907

In the two Dave Regan stories preceding this one Lawson made no use of a narrator, and it is significant that neither of them introduces the spirit of malice. This story is much more complex. Not only is there a narrator, but the narrator tells the story as if it were merely the raw material for a literary composition. The effect of this is to give the work an air of familiarity. For the first time we meet Dave Regan not as an innocent bush joker but as a more complex individual to be made the butt of practical jokes. He is a character which Lawson might have exploited more fruitfully had his personality—and his literary control—not begun to disintegrate in 1903. It is not too much to say that Dave Regan died with Lawson's breakdown in December 1902.

No Place for a Woman (p. 113)

Australian Star, 2nd July 1899   M.L., MS. A1891, 1899   *O.T.*, 1900   *C.I.C.F.*, 1901*

The 1900-01 text of this story exhibits several emendations of the 1899 text. These emendations were first made for the version appearing in *On the Track*, but no MS. is available beyond that of the 1899 printing in the Henry Lawson Scrapbook, Vol. 2 (M.L., MS. A1891). This "MS." has only one emendation by Lawson, viz., the restoration of "skillion" for "skilling": the latter is the Standard English form of the word, but it has never been Australian usage. Arthur W. Jose disregarded Lawson's emendation of "skillion" and dutifully substituted "skilling". Another emendation to Lawson's Australian idiom occurs in "clean-shaven", for which Lawson originally wrote "full-shaved". One emendation suggests that Lawson himself revised the story for the first book printing: this was the addition of the revealing sentence, "He was very restless in the house, and never took his hat off."

More important than any of these emendations was the subtle change in Lawson's technique and mood exhibited in this story. Gone is the banter of Steelman, the worldly-wise cynicism of Mitchell, the barrack humour of Dave Regan. In their place is a kindliness towards the unfortunate. It did occur in Lawson's early stories, but it lacked the purity it now achieves. Then it emerged by contrast with cynical or bitter word-play; now it breathes an air of tolerance towards weakness. The story gives the impression that Lawson is now in command of both himself and his art and that he no longer feels himself under any compulsion to be on guard against a lapse into sentimentality.

In several ways, too, this story serves as a bridge. In it the bush is still potent both as "the nurse and tutor of eccentric minds" and as the destructive element in human happiness. In this way the story leads the mind back to Lawson's early work. In addition, it looks forward to the Joe Wilson series. Thematically it anticipates the struggle of a poor, hard-working selector and his wife to carve a living out of the bush. In tone it is pervaded with the quiet homely courage that emerges from the Joe Wilson sequence. In technique it marks a stage in Lawson's recapture of authorial control over theme, tone, and narration. The merging of narrator with author opens the way to the persona of Joe Wilson.

The Joe Wilson Sequence (p. 121)

"Joe Wilson's Courtship" *J.W.M.*, 1901*; "Brighten's Sister-in-Law" *Blackwood's Edinburgh Magazine*, November 1900, *J.W.M.*, 1901*; " 'Water Them Geraniums' ": "I. A Lonely Track"

J.W.M., 1901* and "II. 'Past Carin' '" *Blackwood's*, May 1901, *J.W.M.*, 1901*; "A Double Buggy at Lahey's Creek" *Blackwood's*, February 1901, *J.W.M.*, 1901*

These stories form the most capably constructed of Lawson's narrative sequences. The figure of Joe Wilson is an artistic projection of Lawson himself, and many of the incidents in the series are idealizations of his own experiences. Together these four stories form Lawson's nearest approach to the novel (see Chris Wallace-Crabbe, "Lawson's *Joe Wilson*: A Skeleton Novel", in *Henry Lawson: Criticism*, ed. Colin Roderick, Syd., 1972). Nevertheless, they were not planned as a novel, nor were they composed in the order in which they appeared in *Joe Wilson and His Mates*. They form a sequence rather than a novel, since a great many aspects of Joe Wilson's life and of his relations with his wife are left unresolved: this is the art of the short story, not of the novel. While the major unifying element of the sequence is the character of Joe Wilson, the mood and tone of the stories also contribute to its unity. Lawson wrote three other Joe Wilson stories, "James and Maggie", "Joe Wilson in England", and "Drifting Apart" (see Mann, Vol. 3). None of them is keyed to the mood of the four which he brought together in the order given here to form *Joe Wilson*, Part I of the combined volume entitled *Joe Wilson and His Mates*—not the best order, if the stories were to be considered as chapters of a novel. Lawson—or his editor—was right in leaving the other three out. Nor is there any story resolving the crisis in Joe's life created by Mary's death, as adumbrated in "A Lonely Track" (see p. 171).

The remark by Lawson's wife, in *My Henry Lawson* (Syd., 1944) that he wrote "all of *Joe Wilson and His Mates*" at Mangamaunu in 1897 cannot be accepted: both external and internal evidence are against it.

The first of the stories to be composed, "Brighten's Sister-in-Law" (p. 147), harks back to 1889, when a version appeared in the form of a long narrative poem in the *Town and Country Journal*, 21st December, under the title "Brighten's Sister-in-Law, or The Carrier's Story". Lawson rewrote it as prose in 1898-9 and revised it in London in 1900: it first appeared in *Blackwood's Edinburgh Magazine*, November 1900, and was incorporated into the sequence with very little emendation.

The second story to appear in *Blackwood's* was "A Double Buggy at Lahey's Creek"—February 1901 (p. 189).

This was followed by " 'Past Carin' ' "—May 1901—which in *Joe Wilson* was to become Part II of " 'Water Them Geraniums' " (p. 173). The only difference between the two texts occurs in the first two sentences: in the periodical printing they read: "It was the first morning at our selection on Lahey's Creek. Things looked a lot brighter than they did the night before. Things always . . ." Much of this story consists of episodes previously treated in verse form over many years and now rewritten to support the theme of the gradual weakening of moral fibre by the relentless pressure of the bush. The repetition of an incident in "The Drover's Wife" in which the bushwoman pokes her fingers through the holes in her handkerchief when about to wipe tears from her eyes is ominous evidence that Lawson was by 1900 on the verge either of exhausting his material or of losing control over it—or both.

There is a slight piece of external evidence to suggest that " 'Past Carin' ' " may have been drafted in 1899—before Lawson left Australia—and that it may have been one of the stories that he withheld from consideration by Robertson for inclusion in *On the Track and Over the Sliprails*, 1900. The evidence is tenuous enough; it rests on a letter of 14th January 1899 from Lawson to Robertson about the prose on which he was working for *On the Track*. In the letter to Robertson he speaks of the *Bulletin's* having rejected some of his best pieces, including " 'Past Carin' ' ". (See *Henry Lawson: Letters*, Syd., 1970, No. 54.) Now it was not until May 1899 that Arthur Jose published Lawson's poem by that name, and no story by that name had appeared anywhere. The verso of page 93 of D.L., MS. 31—"The Iron-bark Chip", written 1899—also contains half a page of MS. text of the draft of " 'Past Carin' ' ", and the flow of the narrative shows that this part of " 'Water Them Geraniums' " was composed before "A Double Buggy at Lahey's Creek".

As to Part I—"A Lonely Track" (p. 165)—no evidence of periodical publication before the appearance of *Joe Wilson* is available. One piece of internal evidence points to the conclusion that "A Lonely Track" was written specifically for inclusion in *Joe Wilson* (the book) in order to bridge the gap between "Brighten's Sister-in-Law" and " 'Past Carin' ' ". It is connected with the passage at the end of "A Lonely Track" which recounts Mary's visit to Brighten's hut after Jim's attack of convulsions and her stroking Joe's head and pulling out the grey hairs. This passage formed part of " 'Past Carin' ' " when it appeared in *Blackwood's* in May 1901. Lawson clearly lifted it out afterwards and skilfully dropped it into the new story—where he made it fit well.

William Blackwood may have had the complete manuscript of all the stories available, but other writers were clamouring for inclusion in his quarterly, and time would have prevented complete serial publication. He might perhaps have squeezed one more story into his August number without delaying the setting of the manuscript; in the event, no more of the stories appeared in the magazine. The book came out in December, and six months would have been a short time, even in those days, to produce and publish the book efficiently. The fact that Angus and Robertson also published an edition in 1901 suggests that preparation of the manuscript for typesetting could not have been delayed beyond May of that year.

It would appear then, that to complete the sequence for book publication, Lawson included, not only all of the stories forming Part II of *Joe Wilson and His Mates*—most of them were in existence before 1900; some, indeed, having been written in another form as early as 1894, in New Zealand—but also "Joe Wilson's Courtship", "A Lonely Track", and the epilogue, "The Writer Wants to Say a Word" (p. 207). The epilogue was no doubt calculated to pave the way for the three Joe Wilson stories omitted from the sequence, together with such others as he had it in mind to write. As a means of setting the author apart from his characters, the epilogue fulfils the same function for the sequence as the casual authorial observations that round off so many of Lawson's individual stories.

Readers of Chris Wallace-Crabbe's article should keep in mind that Lawson in 1900 did not refer to the proposed volume as *Joe Wilson*, but as a "series" of connected stories, all of which he listed, and which, in a novelist's hands, might have formed chapters of a novel, but some of which were never written.

Send Round the Hat (p. 208)
C.O.B., 1902* *S.R.H.*, 1907

One of the last of Lawson's stories to be written in London, "Send Round the Hat" is a nostalgic portrait of the sort of life he had known at Bourke ten years earlier. The characters are drawn from that life, but the story is not to be taken as a photographic representation of it. There are invented characters, e.g., Mitchell, as well as characters modelled on such actual persons as Watty Braithwaite, William Woods, and Bob Brothers (the Giraffe). Around the Giraffe—whom he had foreshadowed in "Going Blind"—Lawson draped his idealistic cloak of social humanism, creating a character which supplanted the real man and began a legend. The legend of the Giraffe came to life when half a century later the people of Bendigo accepted it for truth and erected a memorial to him. No evidence for the memorial exists outside Lawson's fiction. Its only warrant is the belief that in the Giraffe Lawson had embodied a social principle which he wrote into the Australian ethos. For it he turned back to the group of men who had first exhibited it to him. In this sense the story becomes a symbol of Lawson's career: in turning back to these men and to their setting he was turning away from Mecca, back to the desert whence, as A. D. Hope puts it in his poem "Australia", "the prophets come".

For further comments on the story and its implications, see

(*a*) H. P. Heseltine, "Saint Henry—Our Apostle of Mateship", in *Quadrant*, No. 1, 1960, reprinted in *Henry Lawson: Criticism*, Syd., A. & R., 1971;

(*b*) Colin Roderick, *Henry Lawson as Poet and Short Story Writer*, Syd., A. & R., 1966.

A Fragment of Autobiography (p. 223)
M.L., MS. A1887-8*, 1903-06

For this excerpt I have gone to the original manuscript, which was not completely printed as Lawson wrote it until 1972. Four successive editors—Bertram Stevens in the *Lone Hand*, June 1908; George Mackaness in *A Selection from the Prose Works of Henry Lawson*, 1928; Marjorie Pizer in *The Men Who Made Australia*, 1957, and Cecil Mann in *The Stories of Henry Lawson*, First Series, 1964—all published edited versions of it, all containing emendations or omissions of one sort or another.

Lawson began the autobiography in November 1903 after receiving an advance of £20 on the £100 agreed upon for a book of 35,000 words. The rest was to be paid at £4 a week. At the end of twenty weeks the MS. was still unfinished. Lawson received another £25 on 18th November 1905, £15 on 3rd April 1906, and a final gift of £19 on handing in some 30,000 words on 10th May 1906. It would be reasonable to conclude that the first three chapters were written in 1903-4.

One of the merits of this so-called autobiography is its revelation that Lawson was from first to last a writer of fiction. The autobiography illuminates the stories as nothing else can. Its mood and tone are those of the Lawson who drew on himself for Steelman, Mitchell, Dave Regan, and Joe Wilson, as well as for aspects of a whole range of characters from Joe Wilson's son "Jim" to Steelman's foil Smith. It echoes phrases and reflects images that occur in the stories. Its representation of Henry Albury removes it from the realm of unadulterated fact to that of the eccentrics who people such of its author's short stories as " 'Rats' " and "The Bush Undertaker". It is typical of Lawson's fiction in its refashioning of incident and character to represent the outlook of the persona which Lawson assumed for the purpose of writing it. With it the wheel comes full circle. Thereafter the Lawson of this book dies, and a second and inferior though still competent artist takes his place.

Additional References

Brereton, J. Le Gay and Lawson, B. L., eds, *Henry Lawson By His Mates*, Syd., A. & R., 1931, new edn 1973

Hadgraft, Cecil, *Australian Literature*, rev. edn, London, Heinemann, 1962

Johnstone, Grahame, ed., *Australian Literary Criticism*, Melb., O.U.P., 1962

Matthews, Brian, *The Receding Wave: Lawson's Prose*, Melb., M.U.P., 1972

Murray-Smith, Stephen, *Henry Lawson*, new edn, Melb., O.U.P., 1962

Prout, Denton, *Henry Lawson: The Grey Dreamer*, Adel., Rigby, 1963